THE END OF THE LINE

THE END OF THE LINE

STEPHEN LEGAULT

TouchWood
Editions

TouchWood Editions
www.touchwoodeditions.com

LIBRARY AND ARCHIVES CANADA CATALOGUING IN PUBLICATION
Legault, Stephen, 1971–
End of the line / Stephen Legault.

Issued also in electronic formats.
ISBN 978-1-926971-04-9

I. Title.

PS8623.E46633E53 2011   C813'.6   C2011-903358-5

Editor: Frances Thorsen
Copyeditor: Lenore Hietkamp
Design and cover illustration: Pete Kohut
Author photo: Dan Anthon

We gratefully acknowledge the financial support for our publishing activities from the Government of Canada through the Canada Book Fund, Canada Council for the Arts, and the province of British Columbia through the British Columbia Arts Council and the Book Publishing Tax Credit.

MIX
Paper from responsible sources
FSC® C016245

The interior pages of this book have been printed on 100% post-consumer recycled paper, processed chlorine free, and printed with vegetable-based inks.

The End of the Line is a work of fiction set in what is known today as Lake Louise, Alberta, but in 1884 was the end of steel for the Canadian Pacific mainline, and was also known as Holt City, The Summit, and later Laggan. While it is based on a real place, and set amid real events in Canada's history, the characters and events portrayed in this novel are products of the author's imagination. Any resemblance to real characters or events is coincidental.

1 2 3 4 5 15 14 13 12 11

PRINTED IN CANADA

To Jenn, Silas, and Rio: my family.
With gratitude to those who helped build this
country by toiling on the CPR, and for whom
this undertaking was the end of the line.

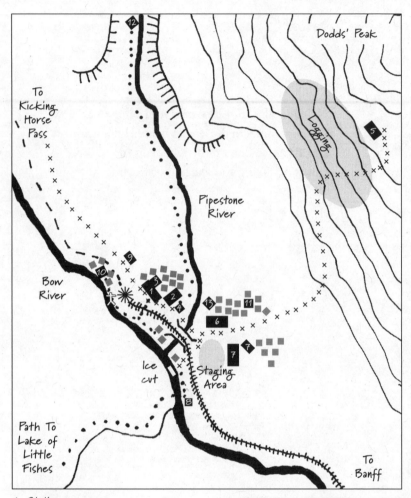

1. Station
2. Holt's Warehouse
3. John Christianson's Cabin
4. Munitions Warehouse
5. Sawmill
6. Mess Hall
7. Barn & Stables
8. Garnet Moberly's Cabin
9. NWMP Barracks
10. Deek Penner's Cabin
11. Frank Dodds' Cabin
12. Frank Dodds' Still
13. Pete & Ralph Mahoney's Cabin

LEGEND

✝   Deek Penner's body found here

xxxx   Tote Road

ⱧⱧⱧⱧⱧ   Rail Road

✳   End of Steel

------   Path of Spring 1884

·····   Trail

ONE

THE END OF TRACK

DEEK PENNER THUMBED THE WORN edges of his hand of cards, his twisted and blackened fingers stiff despite his youth. He was unaware that before the night was over he would be dead, his face pulverized by the ragged edge of a star drill, his body left in a heap by the frozen banks of the Bow River.

He glanced around the table illuminated by two oil lamps hanging from wires affixed to the ceiling of the rough-hewn log cabin. The seven men assembled for their nightly game of cards seemed like ghosts. Faces drawn and gaunt, eyes dark under the shadow of their weary brows, these men were among the five hundred who had come to populate the railway siding of Holt City, just below the crest of the Kicking Horse Pass late in the fall of 1883. It was here that the steel rail had reached on December 8th, the snow already amassing in great heaps along the path of the Canadian Pacific mainline.

Penner regarded the men, and then glanced again at his hand. "One," he finally said, discarding an ace high into the pile of cast offs, drawing a five of clubs, ruining the full house he had put together. He let a faint smile curl the corner of his cracked lips. He had to work with these men; he couldn't afford to win every hand.

As they often did, the men were gathered in the comparatively spacious log cabin of Frank Dodds. Like Penner, Dodds was a foreman on the winter operation. But unlike Penner, Dodds viewed the construction of the Canadian Pacific Railway as his best chance to get rich: Frank Dodds was a moonshiner.

The hand of cards was played and a nervous, slender man in a bowtie surprised himself and everybody else by winning the pot. "Blind luck," slurred Dodds, his disgust with the slight man obvious.

"You played a good hand; take your winnings," said Penner, as the fellow pulled the coins and tattered script towards him, wiping his brow despite the cold.

"Time to get me another cup of *tea*," said Dodds, standing up abruptly and knocking the table so that the paper money and coins the winner was pulling toward himself slid towards the floor. Several of the players' stacks of money were sent flying so that everybody had to scramble for their coins and paper.

"Take it easy, Frank," said Penner in a low voice.

Dodds took an awkward step backwards from the table and seemed to have trouble focusing for a moment. "Shut your yap," he growled at Penner, and then turned towards the tin pot next to the stove in the corner.

Two of Dodds' sawyers picked up their cups and made their way to where he was pouring his elixir. Dodds filled their cups and they each took a satisfying drink. It was obvious from the contented look on the men's faces that Dodds' tea was in fact the moonshine everybody in camp knew he brewed.

Penner shook his head. Whiskey made a man act like a fool, he thought. In the middle of the winter, when all that needed doing was cutting timber for ties and putting away cordwood for fuel, it was bad enough. But in less than two months there would be ten thousand men in this camp, all needing organizing into teams to make the ambitious descent down Kicking Horse Pass. Those men would need their wits, or more than a few of them would be killed. It was to be a dangerous summer even without whiskey. The bottle would make it downright treacherous.

And Deek Penner knew that whiskey wasn't the only thing that would make the summer of 1884 deadly serious for those blasting tunnels down the limestone slopes of the Kicking Horse.

The room was silent. The bowtied clerk looked from one man to the next.

"You should leave it alone," said a man who worked for Penner, looking uncomfortably at his hands.

"What's that?" asked Penner.

"Leave it. Ain't none of your business."

"What ain't none of my business? Its just tea . . ." sneered Penner.

The three men found their seats. The stench of whiskey was palpable in the close cabin.

"Let's play poker," said Dodds, sitting down next to the mousey clerk. "You think you can pull another flush?" he asked, his breath like a heavy fog over the table.

Penner took up the cards, shuffled and cut the deck, and dealt the hand. The betting commenced, and both of Dodds' sawyers and then Penner's man folded. Dodds raised the bet, his eyes glassy in the half light of the lantern. Beneath heavy lids he stared at Penner.

"Let's see your cards," Penner said when the round was done.

"Got me a gunshot straight," Dodds said, showing a seven, nine, ten, and jack of clubs.

"Not so fast," said Penner. He put one card down in front of him. It was the six of hearts. Next the eight of hearts, nine, and jack of hearts. Without even a hint of a smile, he placed the ace of hearts on the table.

"Son of a bitch," said the man who managed the stables, sitting next to Dodds. "He beat you with a flush. Deek beat you with a flush!"

Dodds wheeled on him, his bulk toppling the table, cards, coins, and script sent in a shower to the floor. The three tin cups of whiskey splashed across the table and onto the smooth planks under foot. Dodds' fist connected with the man's nose and a crimson spray of blood erupted from his mangled face. The stable manager was on his feet, backing towards the wall of the log cabin, as Dodds advanced on him, yelling incoherently and throwing punches at the man's face and body.

The rest of the men leapt to their feet, the lantern knocked swinging so that the light in the room swooned.

"Get off him, Frank!" Penner yelled. Dodds' sawyers grabbed at his wildly careening arms, each of them catching elbows in the face and chin as they tried to grapple their foreman as he continued to rain down blows on the smaller man.

Dodds' men finally managed to seize his arms, and Penner shouted "That's enough goddamn it! That's enough!" He wrapped his own huge arms around all three men and pushed them away from the bloodied man, who stood with his face a gory smear, his hands up in front of his mouth. The others rushed in to attend to him as he slouched over and spit a stream of blood onto the floor of the cabin. There were two teeth in the puddle he expelled.

"Get your goddamned hands off me!" Dodds yelled.

"Not till you settle down!" said Penner, his breathing hard but his voice measured.

Dodds struggled, but his sawyers held his arms and Penner held all three of them against the wall of the cabin. On the opposite side of the room, the bloodied stableman slowly stood up, wiping his face with the sleeve of his coat. "You knocked my teeth out." he said matter-of-factly. "And you broke my nose!"

"Lucky that's all I did, you snivelling prick."

"I didn't do nothing to you."

"You're a pansy. You had it coming. You was making fun of my hand. You got what you deserved." Dodds' body was relaxing, his words slurring.

"Frank, you're a disgrace," said Penner, unhanding the man and stepping away from him. "It's really me you want to punch, but instead you pick on a man half your size. You're a goddamned coward."

The sawyers eyed their boss and slowly released his arms. Dodds stood five feet from Penner. It was true that Penner was the biggest man in the room. Even with his heavy coat on, it was easy to see that his girth was massive.

"What's worse," said Penner, turning to face Dodds, "is that you're a drunk and a moonshiner. You're supposed to be a leader for these men, and instead you're making illegal whiskey, robbing them of their hard-earned pay, and turning this camp into a bunch of drunkards." Dodds just grinned. "You're a foreman, Frank. Don't that mean a thing to you?"

"Don't get all high and mighty on me, Penner."

"Well then, do your job!"

"I do my job. Cutting ties. Cutting fuel. Don't tell me how to do my job. I do it just fine."

"With no Red Coats for a hundred miles, our job is more than packing explosives or cutting ties, and you goddamned well know it Frank. Our job is to keep this camp dry. Make sure that when spring comes and this snow melts, we can push the end of the line down the Big Hill and get this job done. Instead, you're making whiskey enough to keep ten thousand men drunk for the summer. Ain't a one of them that will be able to work once you're through with them."

Dodds ran a hand across his face, smearing saliva from the corner of this mouth across his beard. "You are such a high and almighty bastard, Penner. Think you're a big man. Think you're everybody's boss. I got news for you, boy. You ain't *my* boss. You're just a lick-finger of a man. You just keep your nose out of my business, or you're going to be damned sorry."

"You're making this camp drunk, beating on other men. That's my business now, Frank." Penner stood erect before Dodds. "It's my business now."

"What do you aim to do?"

"You won't stop of your own accord; I'm going to shut you down."

"You're a dead man if you try, Penner."

"You threatening me, Frank?"

"I'm telling you to leave well enough alone."

Penner turned to look at the bloodied man again, who was watching him. "Is this letting well enough alone, Frank? What do you think will happen when the first train arrives here come the spring? What do you think is going to happen then? You think those boys will be able to lay track down the Big Hill? What about my men, carrying nitro? What happens then?"

Dodds laughed. "We'll just get us some Chinese to do it. Won't matter then if they blow themselves up!"

"You're an ignorant swine, Frank. You know that?"

"Least I'm no pansy."

"When the spring comes and my men are drunk or fighting when they're supposed to be picking their way down a sheer cliff with a pail of nitro, and they blow themselves up and kill a bunch of good boys trying to earn an honest living, it's you who will have blood on his hands."

Dodds laughed again. "I got blood on my hands now," and he spat on the floor at Penner's boots.

"Tomorrow morning this is going to end. Tomorrow morning I'm going to see Hep and this is going to end."

The room was silent.

"You're a rotten fink, Penner," said Dodds, "and it's going to cost you."

"What are you going to do, Frank? You want to take a swing at me? Here I am. Go ahead. You and I both know what will happen. So go ahead."

"You think Hep Wilcox don't know what's going on? You think he cares a damn?"

"*I* take it to him and he's going to *have* to care. He'll have to do something. We'll call the Red Coats in if we have to. He'll have to care if I take it to him. That's a fact. Come the morning, Frank, I'm shutting you down."

The rest of the room watched as Penner pulled his cap down over his ears, turned up the collar to his coat, opened the door, and stepped out into the darkness.

THE WINTER CAMP was quiet when Penner emerged into the night. He looked up at the stars and calculated that it was midnight. It was very cold, and the stars stood in stark relief against a cloudless sky. Beyond the rim of dark forest the mountains rose in silhouette against the wheel of heaven. With no clouds to hold in the day's faint heat, the evening had become frigid, and Penner guessing it to be minus twenty. His breath formed a dense brume before him.

By starlight he made his way between the ramshackle huts huddled along the banks of the Pipestone River toward his own cabin, a few hundred yards away from the mainline of the Canadian Pacific Railway.

Something would have to be done. It was the end of March,

and though it was nearly impossible to imagine now, in a little over two months as many as ten thousand men would be making their way west, over the prairie from Winnipeg, Brandon, and Regina, for what without a doubt would be the most difficult construction season of the CPR's exhausting journey across Canada. Penner would be in charge of the contract to blast the way down the Big Hill, the thousand-foot plunge on the west side of Kicking Horse Pass, into the valley of the Kicking Horse River. Then, if things went well, come the fall, they would have to do it all over again, blasting their way down the Lower Canyon of the Kicking Horse, an even more treacherous descent than the one they would face in the spring. He needed his men to have their wits about them. If they didn't, many of them would die.

As Penner walked towards his cabin, the snow scrunched under his boots. He'd heard the stories that men, desperate for drink, would hike ten miles through the woods to find a still where they could drink corn whiskey outside the regulated exclusion zone imposed by the CPR. Ten miles for a drink! Some got so drunk that they would wander lost in the woods. Others would fall into one of the region's raging rivers and never be found again. Worse, thought Penner, is that they *would* show up for work a few days later half out of their minds, and imperil the safety of everybody around them. Dropping rail ties on each other's legs; missing their mark when using a sledge hammer and crushing a man's hand; dropping a pail of explosives and blowing themselves, and everybody around them, to pieces.

Penner couldn't stop all that by himself, but he was a foreman, and he had a responsibility to try.

He reached his cabin and stopped. Would telling Hep Wilcox, the winter camp's general manager, make much of a difference? Penner figured Wilcox would have to do something to shut Dodds down, but Penner harboured no illusions that the GM would clean up the entire camp. Not when he had so much *else* at stake.

Penner wondered, given his suspicions about the man, if he could trust the general manager at all. Whiskey was just one thing that threatened the safety of those Penner would be overseeing come the spring. He suspected that there were far worse trials afoot for those working with explosives during the coming season.

He stood at the door to his cabin, regarding the stars and the pale silhouette of the mountains that flanked the valley of the Bow River on either side of him.

"If I wait till morning, it will give Frank time to pull himself together. If I wait till morning I might loose my chance," Penner said aloud to the night sky.

He turned and started back down the path, the snow waist high. Instead of taking the well-worn trail to the general manager's sleeper car parked on the siding, he followed another path, toward the small station building containing the telegraph machine that sat on the banks of the frozen, snow-covered Bow River.

There were no lights on at the distant station as Penner entered a patch of trees spared from Dodds' saw. The forest was close, and the light of the stars grew dim as the trees pressed in overhead. He found his way along the path by feel, unable to stray one way or the other between the six-foot-high snowbanks.

Something would have to be done about the whiskey. And something would have to be done about the explosives contracts, thought Penner. Why did there have to be so much politics around something as simple as blasting a tunnel through the rock?

He was absorbed in that thought when he heard something behind him and stopped. He turned, expecting to see a deer stepping from the woods, but instead was startled to see the shadowy shape of a man not a dozen feet behind him. The bulk of the man's coat, his heavy beaver pelt hat, and the darkness obscured his identity. He closed on Penner fast, and before Penner could move, the figure had raised a metal bar and was swinging it toward his head. Penner called out sharply. The blow struck him across the cheek, crushing his jaw and the bone below his eye, causing his skin to split in two in the frigid cold. He fell sideways into the snow, blood pulsing from the wound.

His assailant stepped close over him. Penner blinked as blood pooled around his eyes. He tried to push himself back in the snow, but was unable to get any purchase in the deep drift next to the path. He felt the life draining from his limbs. His attacker hovered above him like a wraith, hoisting what Penner could now see was a star drill over his head. As he did so, his assailant's face became visible in the faint light of the stars.

Penner managed to mutter a bewildered "*not you?*" through his broken visage before the drill swung down, connecting with his skull again, this time killing him instantly.

TWO

THE RETURN OF DURRANT WALLACE

THE DREAM WAS ALWAYS THE same.

He lay on the frozen earth of Saskatchewan's Cypress Hills, his leg blown apart below the knee, his horse dead beside him. His right hand still clutched his pistol, the six chambers of the revolver empty, its barrel hot from the explosion of the cartridges he had just fired. Where it lay against the ground it melted a small impression in the windblown ice. Snow fell on his face as he blinked into the pale grey sky. He could hear a man laugh, his voice fading into the distance. "Good riddance, Durrant Wallace." Durrant knew that he would bleed to death there on the frozen earth.

Moments before, he had been guiding Mack, his solid twelve-year-old quarter horse, over the windswept hills that marked a high point on Palliser's Triangle. Mack had been his mount since the now famous summer of 1874 when three hundred and fifty men took part in the March West, from Dufferin, Manitoba, to various trading posts scattered across the North West Territories, bringing law and order to the Canadian West. The Cypress Hills were a rugged upland of tangled lodgepole pine and white spruce forests on their summits with bare, rough fescue meadows below. In the summer they bloomed like the fabled Garden of Eden, but now, in the winter of 1881, they were as desolate and unforgiving as the plains of Hades.

Durrant stepped carefully over the stony ground, Mack's reins in his left hand, his Winchester 76 in his right, as he examined the patchy snow and frozen meadow for signs of recent passage. He heard the snap of a frozen branch and dropped onto his right knee. Mack whinnied, the horse's head pitching as he took in an unfamiliar scent. The world around him was gripped in a stony silence. Durrant didn't have time to raise the lever-action Winchester when the woods in front of him exploded with gunfire.

Mack went down heavily beside him, legs thrashing, knocking Durrant to the ground with a violent blow to his chest from the animal's winter-shod hooves. The Winchester was kicked from Durrant's hands, its wooden stock shattering.

Durrant fell on his side, his lungs screaming for air from the blow to the chest as gunfire ricocheted off rocks and into snow all around him. Prone, he reached into his coat and fumbled for his Enfield Mk II revolver, and rising onto his right knee, he aimed into the woods where the gunfire continued. He fired twice left and then twice right, the whir of bullets spinning past his ears. The gunfire created a funnel of sound that seemed to stop time and narrowed his sight into a dark corridor between him and his hidden assailants.

In the passage of a split second, Durrant became aware of his precarious position. He was alone, miles from Fort Walsh, caught in the open, his attackers concealed by the cover of the hilltop's dark forest and undergrowth. He fired the Enfield's final two rounds into the woods, and then worked the pistol's awkward self-extracting cylinder to eject the spent shells.

While he fumbled with the chamber in the frozen air, the fateful bullet found its mark. It might have been his heart if the shot had been a little higher, but instead, the bullet bore into his shin, shattering his tibia two inches below the knee. The force of the blow spun him sideways, his busted leg collapsing, and he fell, face forward, onto the ground. Lying on his side, Durrant fired the two rounds he had managed to load into his pistol towards the woods before the world went dim. He slumped onto his back, his right hand gripping the well-worn handle of the Enfield, his mouth opening and closing as if trying to express the white-hot agony that shot up from his ruined leg.

The gunfire stopped and was replaced by laughter. Good riddance, Durrant Wallace.

The world seemed to disintegrate around him. He would die beside his horse on the barren earth of the Cypress Hills.

THE DREAM WAS always the same. Durrant woke; the Enfield was in his left hand, his face flushed despite the cold, sweat stinging his eyes. He leveled the pistol into the darkness, the hammer back, ready to fire.

Gunfire.

He blinked the sweat from his eyes. The dream was over. He was awake. With his game right hand he wiped the perspiration from his forehead, his left hand still holding the pistol before him. He was in his bunk. This wasn't the Cypress Hills. Not Saskatchewan, but the Alberta Territory. Not 1881, but 1884. Not Fort Walsh: this was Fort Calgary.

He heard more shots. Not an ambush; revellers, drunk on illegal whiskey, bored with the interminable winter of the Alberta foothills.

Durrant lowered the pistol and reached for the lamp beside his bed, his right hand fumbling with the trim wheel while he struck a match with his left. The yellow flame flickered as he adjusted the wick and then a pale glow was cast across the stark room. Bare board walls measuring twelve feet by ten, a rough hewn plank floor, and a single small window shuttered against the unremitting winds and piercing cold; these were the parameters of Durrant Wallace's world.

The table at his bedside held the single lamp, a prized golden locket, and a few well-worn books. On a low bench against the wall adjacent to his bed was his prosthetic leg. He released the hammer and put the Enfield down on the table next to the lamp and reached for the artificial limb. There would be no returning to the temporary sanctuary of a dream-plagued sleep for Durrant this night. The gunfire and the nightmare ensured that he would lay awake until dawn. Come the rising of the sun, his day would begin, almost as bleak as his night.

Durrant used the limb's suction socket to attach it and then reached for his trousers and heavy winter coat. He stood, somewhat awkwardly, and took up his single crutch. He extinguished the lamp, then took the Enfield in his left hand and tramped for the door. Before he reached it, he turned and limped back to his table. He opened the tiny drawer and took a second pistol from it and tucked it into the breast pocket of his coat. Durrant had sworn never to be caught reloading again.

Bracing himself for the cold, Durrant opened the door and felt the icy chill slap him in the face. He stepped from his room into the darkness of the night. It was cloudless above and the stars seemed to rest only a few feet above the Mountie's head, their twinkling undisturbed by campfire, torch or lantern light.

Durrant was neither a commissioned officer nor a mounted horseman; Durrant served the North West Mounted Police in a sort of constabulary purgatory. While some Mounties were pensioned off or put on the dole after being zinged, Durrant had chosen "light duty" instead, and suffered both the insolence of the civilians he tried to police and the unendurable pity of those he served with.

The expanded Fort was only a year old but Durrant knew it well. He'd spent nearly every day of that year confined to its parameters. Durrant's colleagues were gone for weeks at a time riding the rugged foothills, talking with the Blackfoot Nation, or breaking up illegal whiskey and rum operations up and down the Bow and Elbow Rivers. Durrant Wallace, however, veteran of the March West and decorated member of the North West Mounted Police, sorted the mail, sent telegraphs, collected customs from the I.G. Baker Company, and attended to the administrative aspects of the enrolment and discharge of prisoners at the Fort's guard rooms. He hadn't sat a horse since February of 1881: more than three years. What good was a mounted policeman if he couldn't sit a horse, Durrant wondered for the thousandth time, as he made his way through the pallid darkness of the barracks.

Durrant crossed the parade ground, pulling his coat up around his chin. For once the night was still, the temperature a numbing ten degrees below zero Fahrenheit. He slipped the Enfield into his pocket and fitted the regulation seal skin cap on his head, pulling the flaps down over his stinging ears. He stood a moment at the centre of the grounds and contemplated the scene before him.

Fort Calgary was built at the confluence of the Elbow and the Bow Rivers. It had been constructed in 1875 when members of the original NWMP's "F" company had been dispatched under the command of Inspector Brisbois to break up the whiskey trade which had spread malignantly into Blackfoot territory.

During the Fort's early days, the little settlement had grown slowly, and was nothing but a few log buildings chinked with mud that all but disintegrated into the prairie sod during the spring rains. In 1881, when the first cattle were herded along "Stephen Avenue"— then just a dirt track through the centre of mud-splattered tents—the town was still little more than tepees and temporary huts.

During the summer of 1883, construction of the Canadian Pacific Railway steamed west across Alberta and breached the mountains at Bow Gap, and Fort Calgary boomed. That year the original rough-hewn log battlements had been replaced with the Fort's modern buildings. Now a thousand souls called the town home. It boasted more than thirty buildings and hundreds of tents sprawled along the confluence of the two rivers.

Durrant regarded the town beyond the Fort with suspicion. He heard the retort of a long bore rifle to the north, toward the Bow River, and his hand reached into the pocket of his coat for the heavy reassurance of his Enfield.

Durrant had arrived just ahead of the railway, freshly outfitted with a prosthetic leg fashioned at the NWMP Hospital in Regina, where he had spent the better part of two years recovering. When the bloody American Civil War had ended in 1865, more than ten thousand men had needed artificial limbs, and Durrant had benefited from the research that had led to the appendage that he now wore. It had made his time recovering in Regina possible.

Recovering.

The doctors had spoken the word as if it was something that happened *to* you, as if delivered by the Grace of God himself. But Durrant didn't believe in the benediction of an Almighty. Recovery was something that you did *yourself*. Recovery was an act of rebellion against the God who had allowed murderous thugs to shoot your horse and leave you for dead on the hard earth of the Cypress Hills. Durrant was determined to recover. It was his personal rebellion.

Durrant angled north, past the Quartermaster's store, and made measured progress over the icy ruts along the bank of the Bow River. His right hand, twisted and deformed by the frostbite that had overtaken him while he lay clutching the pistol in the frigid Saskatchewan winter, held the polished handle of his crutch awkwardly.

After gaining what mobility he could in the corridor of Regina's small hospital, he taught himself to be a southpaw in the field behind the barracks of the North West Mounted Police in the "Dewdney Section" of the new Territorial capital. There, on the outskirts of the town, Durrant felt like the ten-year-old boy he once had been; hoisting his father's British Bulldog, the small, heavy-gauge pistol made by Webley and Son, and shooting tin cans and his mother's ceramic pots behind the family's weekend farm on the outskirts of Toronto. That had been more than twenty years ago. Now he had to learn again.

At thirty-three, learning to shoot while leaning on a crutch, he grew easily frustrated with his lack of progress. He had plenty of time, though, before he would be steady enough to travel west. He finally left Regina in the spring of 1883. At first, the notion of returning to duty with the NWMP, even if it was light duty, buoyed his flagging spirits. After traveling by wagon over the thawing prairie from Regina to Fort Calgary, while other Red Coats rode proudly out over the plains, Durrant slipped back into melancholia.

Another crack of a rifle brought Durrant back to the present. He passed the lee of the Fort's store, its white washed walls pale in the starlight. Durrant made his way toward a pair of boarding houses surrounded by white tepees and ramshackle cabins, whose occupants were notorious for their revelry.

Durrant muttered a curse into the night air, his words hanging like a frozen mist around his bearded face. The NWMP force was badly outnumbered at Fort Calgary. They faced competing demands: making peace with the mighty Blackfoot Nation that was growing increasingly restless along the Rocky Mountain Front, or quashing the production and trade in whiskey that threatened the speedy completion of the Canadian Pacific Railway. There was often nobody to mind the Fort but Durrant himself. When trouble arose, he was cursed to clomp along on the frozen ground, feeling every bit the fool.

The sound of merrymaking in the distance became clear. Durrant turned the corner of one of the boarding houses and saw the source of the mischief. Behind one of the buildings a group of figures huddled around a fire, the flames casting long shadows across the snowy field that danced on the whitewashed walls of the buildings. The firelight blinded the Mountie to a view of all but those within the lick of the flames. Myopic as his vision was, Durrant could see the bottles of whiskey passed between the estimated two dozen men.

He pushed forward through the snow, his crutch slipping on patches of ice. He crossed to within twenty paces of the men. One man held a rifle above his head and fired it again, then lowered the gun to reload. By its shape, Durrant recognized the rifle as a Sharps Silhouette, a single-shot long-bore rifle used by many ranchers and cattlemen for hunting.

Durrant took the opportunity and raised the Enfield and leveled his aim above the rifleman's head. When the Sharps was raised again, Durrant drew and released a long breath, closed one eye, and fired. The flash from his muzzle and the new gunfire stopped the revelry flat. His shot found its mark, though not dead on, and the rifle leaped from the man's hand to land in the snow behind him.

"Evening, gents," Durrant said in the silence that followed the crack of his pistol. The rifleman stepped from his circle of comrades as if to advance on Durrant. Durrant cocked the Enfield. "Stand your ground, friend," he said.

"I ain't your friend, mister."

"Seems like you fellas have gotten into some whiskey tonight. Care to share?"

"We're just having a little fire is all. No harm done."

"Discharging a rifle inside the town. Drinking whiskey within ten miles of the CPR. This ain't Fort Benton, this is Dominion Territory."

"Harmless fun is all. You could have shot my arm off." The man took another step and Durrant aimed the Enfield high and fired again, the rifleman dropping to a crouch. Several of his friends laughed.

"You think that's funny?" he growled, standing, and turning on his friends. Then he looked back at Durrant. "Why don't you go and sort some post, Red Coat."

"You making a crack?" Durrant took a step forward and re-cocked the Enfield.

"Ain't making no crack about anything. But I'm telling you to leave well enough alone and go back and parley with the red skins or the like," the rifleman said, his voice laced with malice.

"You sure? It sounded to me like maybe you were having a little fun at my expense." Durrant took another step, the crutch catching on a spot of ice, and he slipped forward. Several men winced at the thought of the Mountie falling, the Enfield discharging in their direction as he did.

"Put that goddammed thing away before you take off my head. My rifle's smashed on the ground there," the man said. "There ain't no reason for waving a pistol around."

Durrant held the pistol level. "Who's making the whiskey?" he demanded.

The men were silent, their faces dark, backs to the fire, facing down the lone questioner.

"Pass it forward," Durrant said. "Empty the bottles out and pass them here into the snow. Gently now."

Several men emptied bottles and tossed them into the snow between themselves and Durrant.

"That all of them? Don't make me strip you down to your skivvies."

"That's it," the rifleman said. "That's all we got."

"Who's making it?"

"Who ain't?" said a voice from the circle of dark bodies.

"Yeah, who ain't?" repeated the rifleman. "It's just whiskey."

"It ain't *just* whiskey. It's goin' to be the end of the line for this railroad and that's a fact. Too much whiskey, not enough work from you navvies, and Ottawa is fed up with it."

"It's the middle of the bleeding winter," said a voice from the circle.

"Why don't you get on back to your post, cripple," said another voice.

Durrant raised the Enfield and fired over their heads.

All the men ducked this time. Several cursed him. Durrant took a few steps forward and his face became plain to the men, the light of the fire illuminating it for the first time. Behind the beard, below his eyes and across the bridge of his nose were the scars of his long night on the frozen earth in the Cypress Hills.

Durrant held the Enfield level not ten paces from the nearest man.

"Listen here ..." he started, teeth gritted, his breath coming in heavy clouds in the frozen air.

There was the sound of horses in the night and two Mounties rode into the circle of firelight. The revellers almost looked relieved.

"What's all this shooting about?" the first asked. Durrant saw it was Sub-Inspector Dewalt, Deputy Commander of Fort Calgary.

"This Red Coat's gone mad," the rifleman barked. "Aiming to kill us all over a little harmless fun," he spat as he yelled.

The officer rode around the front of the crowd, the horse pawing the ground. He saw the whiskey bottles and the ruined rifle on the ground. "Doesn't look so harmless to me. Durrant?"

Durrant took a deep breath and blew a thick stream of mist between pursed lips. Already there was frost forming on his beard. "Fellas here thought drinking and shooting up the night was a good way to pass the time. I thought otherwise. The law is the law."

"You're just a goddamned postman here!" shouted a man from the crowd.

Dewalt turned his horse in the snow and bore down on him, "This man's every bit the law in this town as I am. Now put that fire out and head on in to bed or I'll have all you down to the guard room, with Sergeant Wallace here as sentry."

The Mountie turned his horse towards Durrant as the group of men kicked snow onto the flames, which crackled and sizzled. Durrant lowered the Enfield.

Dewalt came up beside him. "You want an arm up?" he asked.

"I'll walk."

"Hold up a minute," said Dewalt. He swung a leg over his mount and dropped down next to Durrant. He was bundled in a greatcoat, its heavy cape reaching to the Sub-Inspector's waist. "Walk with me, Sergeant," he said.

Durrant took a look back over his shoulder at the lone NWMP

constable overseeing the fire being extinguished and then faced his superior officer.

"You aiming to call me on the carpet?"

"Walk with me, Sergeant."

Durrant tucked his pistol into his pocket and started along the frozen ground.

"Things get a little out of hand here tonight?"

"Not as far as I saw it."

"You didn't take things a little too far?"

"I don't think so."

"Durrant, you were shooting over those men's heads."

"I knew what I was doing. They were shooting too."

"Listen, Sergeant, I can't have you picking fights with everybody who fires a rifle or raises a bottle of whiskey to his lips in this town. I just can't have that."

"I thought our job was to put an end to the whiskey trade?"

"It is."

"So I was doing my job."

"Durrant, I don't want to sound like an ass, but it isn't *your* job."

"It's my job long as I wear the serge."

"Well, if you aren't more judicious, you won't be wearing it for long. You're causing more trouble than you solve."

"I'm keeping the peace."

"You're aiming to start a war. This is the Dominion of Canada. We don't ride in, guns blazing. You know that. You *were* one of the best. Time was, you could sit down and make the peace with just about any man, red or white."

"Still can. But I am not going to sit in my bunk while this town gets overrun by whiskey."

"We've got things under control."

Durrant stopped and spat into the snow. "Due respect, sir, things aren't in control. In a couple of months there's going to be ten thousand men heading for the end of track at Holt City, and men like that bunch back there will be getting them drunk on whiskey before they reach Bow Gap. Our job's to stop it."

"Don't try to tell me my job, Sergeant. I know what my work is."

"Well then, do it!"

Dewalt stopped and through the darkness regarded Durrant. The horse moved behind him, and Durrant was aware of the animal's heat. "I've damn near had enough of you, Durrant. If it weren't for Steele himself taking a liking to you, I think I'd have your ass out of my barracks. But the old man seems to have taken a shine to you. Maybe it's because you're both proud, stubborn, hard-headed men. I can't say. But I don't have to put up with you if you are hell-bent to keep the peace with your pistol. You're not to intervene in any more such night-time goings on. Leave that to those of us whose main duty it is, and you keep to the activities of the barracks: the post, the census, and the like. Am I clear, Sergeant?"

Durrant levelled his gaze at him. "So all that back there about me being every bit the law as the next Mountie was just talk . . ."

"Well, there was no need to take your pride. You've given enough."

Durrant felt a wave of humiliation wash over him as if all the snow on the plains that stretched for a thousand miles south and east had suddenly melted and drenched him with an icy tide.

"We clear, Sergeant?" said Dewalt.

"Clear," he finally said, spitting again into the ground.

"Fine then. Now," said Dewalt, fitting a boot into a stirrup, "can I give you an arm up?"

"I'm goin' to take a walk," said Durrant, looking west into the darkness.

"Suit yourself," said the Sub-Inspector, and Durrant thought he heard the man mutter "stubborn son-of-a-bitch" under his breath as he rode off toward the NWMP barracks. He left Durrant to contemplate the cruelty of an Almighty that took a man's leg but left him in a world that expected him to remain unchanged.

Durrant turned his back on the nearly extinguished bonfire and the icy rutted streets of Calgary and walked with his crutch west into the darkness.

He walked until he passed the last of the tents and mud huts and turned west, standing with his face up to the clear night sky, the stars a broad smear across the blackness of space. In the distance he could hear coyotes yelping as they made their way along the banks of the Bow River. Far off, out on the low, rolling foothills, he made out the melancholy howl of a wolf. He knew that far beyond, across the swells of frozen earth, the Rocky Mountains broke against the foothills in nearly impenetrable sheets of limestone. A thin thread of steel snaked its way into the mouth of those mountains, passed the sidings of Padmore and Banff, and wove westward, following the river beside which he stood, until it reached the end of track near the summit of the Kicking Horse Pass, and the tiny tent town of Holt City.

The wolf called again, and this time its howl seemed farther off, as if it was moving away towards the mountains. Much of Durrant's life seemed to feel like that wolf sounded—solitary. Much of his work as a policeman had been just that—alone. Riding for days at a time along the frontier of the Dominion of Canada, intercepting the illegal trade in whiskey and in rum, talking with the great roaming bands of Indians that moved like ephemeral winds across the plains.

There had always been a pack to return to. At Forth Walsh, and latter in Regina, and down at Fort McLeod, there had always been the comfort and companionship of the North West Mounted Police. But now? They had not abandoned him after the incident in the Cypress Hills. But the duties to which he was consigned now seemed far worse than desertion. If he had died that afternoon on the frozen ground at least he would have done so with honour. Durrant was a pony soldier, but now he was treated like a man gone mad at the worst, and at best, like someone who had worn out his usefulness to society.

Durrant stood until his right leg ached where the prosthetic attached to the nub of skin and muscle and bone below his knee. He thought he might wait until the sun broke over the eastern horizon, thought that maybe the dawn of a new day might cast a fresh light on his life and his worth. But at the end of March the sun still rose late over the vast undulating plains, and the cold that bit and the burning ache in his leg that spread to his hips and back told him that the time had come to turn homeward.

Over the icy tracks of the new city, he made his way toward the barracks. The promise of a hot cup of coffee and the woodstove buoyed his spirits enough to urge him through the snow. When he reached the door that led to his hovel, he thought he heard the familiar buzzing from the telegraph machine mounted on a long plank table in the mess of the main barracks. Since being sidelined from active duty, Durrant had taken on such tasks as operating the telegraph wire that had advanced with the railway across the plains. He set aside plans to return to his bunk and instead went into the mess of the main barracks. The hall was a forty-five-by-thirty-foot room that housed the cookstove and main common room for the Fort's constables. At present there were only eight such men residing in rooms that adjoined the mess, but the building could accommodate as many as fifty. The new room already smelled of pipe tobacco and stewed bison meat. The wire machine was in a corner next to the door.

Feeling worn thin, he headed for the stool next to the telegraph table and sat down. He removed his hat and fixed the thick headphones over his head. He took pen and ink and a fresh sheet of paper from the pegboard on the wall and prepared to write. The message was coming from the NWMP headquarters in Regina. He tapped out the ready to receive message and then listened to the Morse code coming over the wire. He decoded the message as it arrived:

> To Sergeant Durrant Wallace.
> From Sam Steele, Commanding.
> News late yesterday. Man found murdered at Holt City, CPR mainline. Forces too thin to send Dewalt's constables. Proceed on next freight to end of track. Uncover identity of assailant and arrest. Report direct to Steele. Confirm.

Durrant felt his pulse quicken in the darkness as he read over the words again. When he was able to slow his breathing and steady his hand, he tapped out a response.

Wallace to Steele. Confirmed. Will proceed at once.

Durrant listened for a further message. It came after a moment.

Welcome back, Durrant. Steele.

Having been shot and left for dead once already in his short life, Durrant wasn't the kind of man who blanched when he faced peril. Even if he had known the difficulty that lay ahead, he would gladly have rushed to face it.

THREE

TRAVELLING COMPANIONS

"CONGRATULATIONS, SERGEANT." RAYMOND DEWALT WAS sitting behind his desk. The pale late-winter light seeped through the small window, its shutters propped open, the pebbled glass frosty and opaque. Despite the biting cold out of doors, he wore the pillbox cap on his head and his formal scarlet surge.

"Thank you, sir," said Durrant, trying to stand straight while leaning on his crutch. He had turned out as neatly as he could that morning, in his full scarlet patrol jacket with the three golden chevrons marking his rank set high up on his arm. He wore his forage cap set rakishly at an angle atop his head. His pistol was secured in its leather holster, custom-made for him in Regina because the force had no such accommodation for a southpaw.

Sub-Inspector Dewalt looked him up and down. Durrant hadn't worn his full patrol uniform since arriving at Fort Calgary. "You look sharp, Sergeant."

"Thank you, sir," said Durrant, his eyes forward.

"Will you be wearing the serge at the end of the line?"

"I thought better of it, sir."

"Yes, indeed," said Dewalt.

"Might not be as practical as civilian attire."

Dewalt nodded. "But you thought to make a show of it?"

Durrant paused a long moment. "Out of respect for the Force, sir."

Again Dewalt nodded. "When do you aim to leave?"

"Tomorrow morning, sir. There's a freight that's heading to Holt City, making some stops along the way in Padmore and in Banff. It will arrive in Holt City tomorrow evening, if there's not too much snow over the tracks."

"It's still pretty wild country."

"Yes, sir."

"What did Steele say?"

"That a man's been killed. He explained that the expeditionary force has higher priorities: keeping tabs on the Blackfoot, watching for unrest with the Cree, intercepting whiskey and rum along the Bow and the Elbow Rivers."

"That makes good sense to me."

"To me as well."

"What else?"

"Sir?"

"What else did Steele say?"

"He said to provision myself for the investigation."

"What will you need?"

"Nothing much, I should think, sir. I may requisition additional warm clothing . . ."

"I expect the Quartermaster will have whatever you need."

"Thank you." Durrant prepared to turn on his crutch and leave the room.

"Sergeant," Dewalt said, standing. He pulled the front of his scarlet tunic down and straightened his heavy leather belt.

"Sir?"

"Holt City is the end of the line. It's March. The snow is ten feet on the ground."

"What's your point, sir?"

"It's going to be hard getting around there."

"You mean hard for *me*?"

"I mean hard for you; hard for anybody."

Durrant gripped his crutch more tightly, his knuckles turning white.

"My point, Sergeant, is why don't you enlist some help? You know: someone who can tote your kit, help you with chores around the bunk." Durrant was silent. "Sergeant, there is no shame in asking for help. You've suffered a terrible loss . . ."

"I can manage."

"Fine!" said Dewalt sharply, then more calmly, "fine, fine. You're a stubborn Scotsman, Wallace. That's fine. You can manage. You go to the end of track and find yourself facing an angry mob of men, or loose your temper because you can't make your way to the pisser in the snow, and you're going to blow your one last chance, Wallace. So get your head out of your arse and think about your future service to the Mounted Police instead of being so goddamned bullish all the time!"

Durrant pivoted on his crutch and made for the door. "Will that be all, sir?"

"Dismissed, Sergeant."

Durrant opened the door and stepped through it. Dewalt blew out a stream of breath through his lips and sat back down. He thought that the end of the line wasn't nearly far enough away for Durrant Wallace to go.

DURRANT LOOKED AT the trunk of his possessions next to the bench that held his prosthetic: his long bison coat, a change of civilian clothes, a thick sealskin hat, and his riding gauntlets. He hadn't sat a horse since that day in the Cypress Hills, but the gloves were still the warmest he owned. His serge, a bedroll, and inside it an oilcloth wrapped around a Winchester Deluxe 73 short-barrelled lever-action repeating rifle. He had adopted and then taught himself to fire that weapon too, shooting left- and single-handed. He inspected the rest of his armament: the Enfield Mk II, cumbersome to reload but accurate and deadly, and of course the snub-nosed British Bulldog, which felt reassuring in his left hand. He put the Bulldog down on his bedstand. It sat next to the golden locket; the same locket that had remained unopened for ten years now but was never far from sight.

He reached for his leg and affixed the suction cup over his stump. He stood and limped to the chest, bent down and grabbed the leather handle and tried to haul the chest to the door, but his leg buckled. Durrant had to catch himself on the wall to keep from falling to the floor. He leaned against the wall, his stomach in a painful knot, his stump aching.

If he was in deep snow at the end of track, with men around

whom he was investigating for murder, a fall in the snow would be humiliating at best, and more than likely the end of his time as a Mountie. Some things a North West Mounted Police officer could survive and some he could not. Weakness would not be tolerated by men who had spent a long, bitter winter struggling in the mountains. If the killer was still in that icy camp and was anything but a half-crazed drunk, he would no doubt seize upon the Mountie's weakness and exploit it to his own advantage. It brought a bitter taste to his mouth to consider it, but he knew Dewalt was right.

THE NORTH WEST Mounted Police stables were divided into two buildings, each measuring ninety-five feet long and thirty feet wide, and were situated on the north side of the main parade ground. The structures, built late in 1883, were so new that their pine boards were still seeping sap when the frozen winter descended on the prairie, so now they were beaded with sticky balls of pine resin. During the summer months the horses were turned out to graze on the broad plains that swept along the banks of the Elbow and Bow Rivers, but during the winter storms and spring gales, they boarded inside.

Durrant made his way across the parade ground, skirting the largest patches of ice and finding better footing where the quarter horses had trampled the ground into frozen ridges and valleys of mud. As hard going as these ice-covered quagmires were to navigate for him, they were easier than the sheets of glass that formed in the broad craters between them.

He reached the stables and steadied himself there a moment. The wind had come up that morning, blowing hard from the west. It was a warming wind, what the Blackfoot called a "snow eater," and the temperature had risen nearly ten degrees in the last hour. By mid-afternoon Durrant expected that the ice he had just navigated would be open water and the frozen mud a thick gumbo that would suck at horse hooves and threaten to detain any wagon or Red River cart that passed through the town's earthen streets.

Durrant made his way along the side of the stables towards the broad double doors. He headed toward the rear of the building where another set of doors opened into a field and where a set of corrals were laid out for finishing the stock. A stout man in shirt-sleeves was circling a quarter horse around the yard, holding in one hand the lead rope, and in the other a long heavy rattle that the Mounties nicknamed an "ukulele" and used to condition a horse to noise.

"She's nearly ready for the likes of you lot," said the man, not looking at Durrant. "Just needs a little more spook trainin' so she won't buck you off at the first sign of trouble."

Durrant stood and watched. Paddy Malloy was ten years Durrant's senior, a compact, red-haired Irishman. He was first assigned to manage the ranch at Pincher Creek, just west of Fort McLeod, which bred horses for the Force. When demand out-stripped the ranch's ability to produce enough stock, the big bellies shut the operation down. Now the Mounties sourced their horses from all over the Territories. It was Paddy's job to finish the stock at Fort Calgary.

"What do you think, Wallace, want to give her a go?"

Durrant looked down at the frozen ground.

"You're going to have to get back on a horse sooner or later."

Durrant spat into the icy earth. "What's her name?" he asked.

"Belle."

"As in Hell's Bell?"

"No," spat the teamster, knowing that Durrant was talking about the hard-driving Major Rogers. "No, just this girl is a real Belle. A real Belle," he said, looking into the horses liquid eyes. "Aren't you, girl?"

Durrant made his way into the half-frozen corral, minding his footing, and stood next to Paddy and Belle.

"So if it's not a mount you want, then what can I do you for?" asked Paddy.

Durrant looked to the far side of the corrals and seemed to notice for the first time a young boy breaking up a bale of hay for two other horses. "I came about the boy. Charlie."

"What about the lad? He in some trouble?" Durrant smiled at Paddy's paternalism.

"Steele asked me to have a look into some difficulty," said Durrant. "Where?"

"End of the line. The Kicking Horse Pass."

BY NOW, THE legend of the Kicking Horse River was well known to people as far east as Winnipeg, and Durrant had certainly heard the tale many times. Captain James Hector was one of Palliser's men assigned the task, in 1858, of exploring the Rocky Mountains to survey the land for the future Dominion of Canada. As he was leading his horse along the treacherous rock falls where a tributary of the now-named river enters the main stem, the beast kicked Hector in the chest. The explorer dropped to the ground, and was presumed stone-cold dead. His men dug a shallow grave along the side of the creek and meant to bury him. But at the last moment, Hector batted an eyelash and the men decided to hold off on the funeral. He was moved to a location near present-day Holt City where a group of Stoney Indians were camping. They pronounced his recovery miraculous. The story was a testament to the isolated and dangerous nature of that perilous country.

"You understand that it may not be the most comfortable of accommodations. This is the end of steel, see. It's nothin' but wilderness. There's no town, no comforts but what we take with us," said Durrant. He was standing in the open door of the barn, facing the yard where the boy named Charlie stood, backlit by the brightening morning. "And I don't really know what we're getting into there. A man has been killed, and it's likely that the murderer is still in the camp. He's not going to want to be found."

The boy made no move. He seemed to recognize that Durrant was speaking as much to himself as to him.

"What I'm trying to say, son, is that if you'd like the opportunity, I'd like you to come along. You're little, but you work real hard. I just need you to know this ain't no spring picnic. You understand?"

Charlie nodded. He stepped into the barn and made for the far corner.

"Paddy tells me you're not too big on talking."

The boy continued toward what Durrant figured was the tack room. He looked back at Durrant and motioned with one hand for the man to follow him. Durrant crossed the floor and stopped next to the boy. He was not five and a half feet tall, and though Paddy said that the youth's age was sixteen, he looked more like fourteen. His skin was smooth and unblemished. His hair was cut short, and stuck like straw from under the wool cap he wore pulled down to his ears. The youth's eyes were startlingly blue, piercing the observer in a way that Durrant almost envied. Eyes of that sort would no doubt unsettle a man if he were held by them too long.

The boy pushed open the door and motioned for Durrant to look. The room was indeed a tack shed, with saddles and halters and bridles arranged on a wall. Lengths of lead ropes were neatly coiled in one long peg. Charlie pointed to the floor. In a small space cleared of tack was a thin bedroll with two woolen blankets over it.

Durrant's eyes met Charlie's. "So what you're telling me is that hard conditions ain't new to you, is that it?" Charlie nodded. He fetched a small black slate from his bag. He pulled a piece of chalk from his pants pocket and tapped on the board. He turned it to Durrant. Durrant read aloud, "When do we go?" The Mountie smiled. "How about now?"

THE INKY SOOT from the locomotive momentarily blotted out the sky as the train rumbled over the new track west of Fort Calgary. Durrant and Charlie sat in the caboose. This ramshackle affair had been built onto a flatbed, and as the train started up the first grade out of the valley of the Bow River, the car pitching precariously from side to side. Durrant gripped the seat of the rough bench.

Durrant and Charlie were not alone. Two brakemen and a line-man rode along with them, their coats and wool caps encrusted in a thick layer of black coal soot. The long, narrow room was stacked with supplies that had been added to the freight train's consignment that morning: crates of canned goods and tobacco products, two heaping piles of woolen blankets that toppled over the moment the train began to lurch out of the Bow River Valley, several bags of mail, and three crates labelled "livestock" that immediately began to cluck as the caboose pitched and rolled. Durrant eyed them suspiciously, as the brakemen and lineman eyed *him* with misgiving. It hadn't taken long for word to pass along the line at the CPR's station at Fort Calgary that a man had been murdered at the end of track, and that the one legged Mountie with the fire-brand temper was being sent there to find the killer.

Durrant pulled the collar of his bison coat up around his ears and closed his eyes as the swaying of the caboose became more rhythmic. Durrant opened his eyes with a start when Charlie pulled on the sleeve of his heavy coat.

"What is it?" he said, his voice gruff. He scanned the caboose for signs of trouble. The lineman and the two brakemen were asleep, propped up on the crates of tinned peaches.

He looked at Charlie and in the dim light could see the boy's eyes were bright. "What is it?" he repeated.

Charlie tugged at Durrant's coat sleeve again. The Mountie pushed himself to standing and bracing himself against the rocking of the railway car, stepped over to where Charlie was kneeling next to a tiny soot stained window. The boy pressed his face against the bevelled, blackened glass for a second, and then turned to look at Durrant, his icy blue eyes shining. He pointed.

The train was passing through a broad, flat prairie with rolling snow-covered foothills on either side; the broad dale of the Bow River was behind them. To the north and to the west the implacable eastern slope of the Rocky Mountains rose. The train was steaming towards the sheer cliffs of the mountains, their east facing crags rising and falling in what Durrant concluded was an endless chain of ramparts. He knew that the steel rail followed the same Bow River that passed through Fort Calgary until it reached Holt City.

He had even found a map in the CPR station and managed to talk the stationmaster into loaning it to him for his official police business. With the train gambolling toward the limestone cliffs, Durrant could understand what a daunting barrier these mountains had posed. Pushing the rail through the Rockies was dangerous and costly, both in terms of human lives, and the treasury, and it was more than a decade behind schedule.

"You've never seen the mountains?" Durrant asked, looking at his travelling companion. The boy shook his head.

"Gonna see lots of those where we're going," Durrant finally said. The boy's eyes remained transfixed on the peaks.

IT WAS NEARLY dark when the train reached Padmore, just inside the mountains. As the train came to a halt, the lineman had taken his lanterns and walked a quarter mile back along the track to set the caution, though no other trains were expected along the new CPR mainline.

"Be about twenty minutes here, Sergeant." The engineer stuck his head into the caboose and addressed Durrant. "You can stretch your legs if you like," he said, and then swallowed hard. "I mean, you can . . ."

"Just leave it," Durrant growled. "I know what you mean." He turned to Charlie. "Have a look around if you like, but mind the whistle."

The boy hopped down from the rear of the train and looked around him. Durrant drew a deep breath. It was cold. He exhaled and his breath froze before him. He buried his hands in his pockets. He could hear men moving crates from one of the box cars onto the siding. Grabbing one of the handles along the railing Durrant peered around the end of the caboose and could see the two brakemen aiding a station master. Charlie was there too, helping one of the men carry a crate nearly as big as he was.

In a few minutes the whistle sounded and Durrant watched Charlie climb the ladder at the car in front of the caboose and he joined the boy inside. The train lurched as they sat back down, side by side in the darkness. When one of the brakemen entered he lit a lantern that cast a warm glow over the tiny space, made more cramped by the presence of its extra cargo.

"You like to work," said Durrant to Charlie, who was looking out the window into the darkness. Charlie nodded.

"He's strong for his age," said one of the brakemen.

Durrant nodded and mumbled, "I'm glad to have you along, lad."

THE WORLD AROUND them was devoid of human life. With every mile they covered on the thin ribbon of steel, they outstripped the reach of civilization and the prospect of aid should it be required.

When they reached Holt City it was close to midnight. Compared to the tiny sidings at Padmore and Banff, Holt City seemed immense. At the end of the construction season there had been nearly ten thousand men working along the mainline where the Bow River veered north, and the rail line would ascend the gentle eastern grade of the Kicking Horse Pass. Now five hundred men remained, but the winter quarters spread out along the confluence of the Bow and Pipestone Rivers for half a mile.

When Durrant stepped off the train the cold hit him in the face like a frozen fist. The sky was now completely clear, and the veil of stars seemed so close that a man on horseback might reach up and scoop up a gloveful to line his pockets.

Charlie stepped off the train behind him, tucking his coat around himself, and dug his hands into his pockets. The soot from the engine and the steam from the brakes swirled along the wooden platform next to the stationhouse. The boardwalk had been scraped clear of snow to facilitate the ease of loading and unloading cargo, but the banks of snow beyond were above Durrant's head. For a moment he saw an image of himself trying to find his way between buildings at the end of the line through icy tunnels of snow.

A lantern's pale light emerged from the darkness and soon it illuminated the man who carried it. He looked the train up and down as he passed the boxcars, and Durrant heard him say a few words to the brakemen. One of them pointed towards Durrant and Charlie.

The lantern bearer was a big man with broad shoulders, and as he came closer Durrant could see his thick moustache and beard. Between his teeth he clenched a pipe that glowed red when he drew on it. His beaverskin hat was pulled down tight against his thick black eyebrows. But he smiled when he saw the two at the end of the train and extended a hand toward Durrant, which the Mountie took. The grip was firm.

"Bob Pen," said the man with a genial smile, the pipe nodding.

"Durrant Wallace."

"Welcome, Sergeant. I'm glad you're here."

"I'd like to say the same, but . . ."

"But a man is dead, and his killer at large, and that's not exactly cause for glad tidings," said Pen.

"No. No, it isn't. I had expected to meet Hep Wilcox, the general manager of this camp," said Durrant.

Pen was examining the train. "Well, Mr. Wilcox asked me to come and meet you. I'm in charge of the labour force for Holt City, and for the camp that's being raised at the Kicking Horse Pass. I meet the trains and make sure the lads coming in find their way to where they are needed. Guess it seemed to make sense that I come and receive you as well."

Durrant nodded.

"You must be tired. Let's get you settled. Who is this?" asked Pen.

"This is my . . . my assistant, Charlie," said Durrant. "He's here to help with my things on account of . . ."

"Yes, yes, on account of your leg. I know the story. No need to explain. Can't see how I could do a lick of good without my two legs. You're a better man than I for continuing to serve your Queen and Country. Good for you, Sergeant."

For a moment Durrant thought to protest, but he just nodded and said to Charlie, "Let's haul our stuff along." Then to Pen, "I understand the NWMP barracks from last summer are still in good effect?"

"I haven't looked in on the cabin, but I assume it is. Let me show you. Come on, boy, you take one end of that trunk and I'll grab the other. It's not far."

Charlie and Pen hauled the trunk along the station platform to where a deep path was beaten into the banks of snow. Once off the platform Durrant's crutch sunk into the snow so that he had to move along hunched over, making an effort to keep upright. The simple covering on the prosthetic's base slipped on the hard-packed snow, and Durrant had to struggle to keep up with Pen and Charlie. After only a few minutes they came to the NWMP cabin that had been built from squared-off timbers the summer before.

Charlie and Pen put the trunk down. "It isn't much to look at. The two lads who was here last summer spent most of the time up and down the line. There's a stove and a couple of bunks and lots of blankets. You should be fine."

"We'll manage," said Durrant. "This isn't a tourist vacation."

"No, it isn't," said Pen, opening the door and pushing it in. There was a thin film of snow on the floor. He held his lantern up and stepped inside. Charlie and Durrant followed. Pen stood next to the wall, the lantern casting its pale light into the coal-black room. On the floor between the two cots, laid out on a burlap tarp, was the body of Deek Penner.

DURRANT WOKE TO A COLD so piercing that he felt as though he was entombed in ice. His face was under the blankets, and even so, it felt as if there was ice hanging from his nose. He drew a breath and the musty scent of old wool permeated his senses. And something else: wood smoke.

He pushed the blankets back with his game right hand. His left cradled the sturdy heft of the British Bulldog. The cold bit at his face. He blinked open his eyes; he felt as though his eyelashes had frozen shut in the numbing cold. He heard the stove door creak open with an audible protest.

He had slept the night with his gloved right hand tucked in his left armpit, but even so, it felt as though it was on fire, burning with the reawakened frostbite that had almost claimed it three years earlier. He pushed himself upright under the heavy weight of the blankets and watched as the lad Charlie dropped a heavy load of lodgepole pine on the floor of the cabin. The tiny square-board shack shook.

"Might not be of the most solid construction," Durrant mumbled.

Charlie shook his head in response, and after wedging the door shut behind him, knelt before the stove and piled thin strips of wood into its belly, blowing on them to ignite the tinder.

"Fire go out in the night?" Durant asked. Charlie nodded. "But you got some embers going?"

Again, the boy nodded, blowing. Durrant could see a glow emerge from the door of the small stove and light up the lad's soft features.

"We're going to need to work shifts," Durrant said from beneath the blankets. "Keep that fire going all the time. If we don't want to end up a frozen slab like Mr. Deek Penner, we're going to need to get into a routine. I can get the wood into the stove alright, so long as it's split. That's going to be your job, Charlie."

Durrant manoeuvred himself onto the side of the bed, finally placing the Bulldog on the small table next beside him where the Enfield service revolver rested. The locket that he prized above all else in the material world rested at the base of the oil lamp. He reached for his prosthetic, buried under the blankets with him to keep it warm, and affixed it, with a grimace, to the stub on this left leg. He sat a moment and contemplated his new surroundings.

The NWMP barracks had been hastily constructed the previous summer as the CPR mainline advanced toward Holt City and Kicking Horse Pass. It measured fifteen feet by twelve, and was made of rough-hewn lodgepole pine logs, chinked with clay. Along one of the narrow walls was a heavy door, bolted now against unwanted visitors, including the biting cold of the Rocky Mountains. On the row of pegs behind the door the two constables who had policed this post would have hung their red serges and riding hats. To the left of the door as one entered was a small desk with a glass lamp atop it where he could do paperwork or prepare a wire for dispatch. Two beds flanked the walls, and between them was the table now supporting Durrant's armament. A tiny window marked the wall above the table, but it was heavily shuttered against the cold. The potbellied stove sat in the corner to the right of the door. It now rattled as it threw off a pleasing heat. The only thing not in the room that had been there the night before was the corpse of Deek Penner.

THE PREVIOUS NIGHT, weary from travel, Durrant had responded to the discovery of Deek Penner's cadaver with indignation. "You didn't have no other place to put him?" he asked as they stood by the open door. The body was wrapped in heavy blankets, but Durrant could see the red stain at the head, and knew that what was beneath the shroud was not for men with weak stomachs.

"Blue Jesus," said Bob Pen. "I didn't know that they put the body in 'ere."

"Well, he can't stay," said Durrant.

Pen considered this. "I reckon we can put him in one of the storerooms at the station."

"Let's get it done," said Durrant. He turned to look at Charlie. "That's you, son."

So the body had been moved. Frozen solid, it was heavy, and Pen had to call on two other men to help with the task. They struggled, side by side, through the deep snow, to manage the two hundred yards from the NWMP barracks to Holt City Station. Charlie's diminutive form seemed unfit to bear such a weight as Deek Penner's frozen remains.

When the cadaver was finally laid to rest in a small storage room at the back of the station, Durrant turned to Charlie. "Can you get back to the barracks and see about building a fire?" The boy nodded and disappeared into the night. Durrant watched him go, his slight frame walking easily now along the snowy trenches.

He turned to Pen. "Did Hep Wilcox say if he'd be in the station in the morning?"

Pen nodded, wiping his gloved hands on some snow as if that might clean away any memory of the stiff corpse he had just helped transport. "I believe Mr. Wilcox is anxious to see this matter put to rest."

Durrant contemplated this choice of words. "As anxious as I am to see the killer brought to justice," he said. Pen just nodded. "I understand there is a doctor who serves this location?"

"That's right. He works the line up and down from Padmore to Holt City and on up the Kicking Horse Pass when there's need. He's a CPR man. Named Armatage."

Durrant looked up and smiled. "Saul Armatage?"

"You know him?"

"You might say that we are acquainted."

"Well, he's in Holt City. I can have him come by to see you if you've need."

"I've no need at present, but in the morning I'll want to do an examination of Mr. Penner."

"I'll see about arranging for him to find you. Breakfast is served for the men at 7:00 AM. You and your boy there are welcome to join in with the meals of course." He tapped out the contents of his pipe on the rough wall of the station. No sooner was it empty than he packed it again with tobacco he found loose in his jacket pocket.

"We appreciate that," said Durrant, and he turned to make his way through the dark tunnel of snow to the barracks.

MORNING FOUND THEM in their cabin, minus the frozen corpse of Deek Penner.

"What's the time?" Durrant asked as he pulled on his coat. Charlie fumbled in his coat and found his pocket watch. He held up seven fingers. "Hungry?" asked Durrant. Charlie nodded. "Alright, son, then let's go see what Holt City has to offer."

Charlie checked the stove and added another wedge of pine, while Durrant made preparations to depart the cabin. He tucked the Bulldog into his left coat pocket and the Webley into the holster Durrant wore over his trousers but concealed beneath the bulk of his greatcoat.

"You know how to shoot?" Durrant asked when he saw Charlie eyeing the revolvers. Charlie nodded. "Your old man teach you?" Charlie shrugged his shoulders. "You got a shooting iron in that little sack of yours?" Charlie looked down and shook his head.

"This not speaking thing is going to get pretty old, soon, son. You and me might want to address that at some point."

Charlie grabbed the slate that he used to write messages on. He drew the chalk from his pocket and wrote in short, staccato strokes. He held it so that Durrant could read it. "We're quite the pair." The Mountie looked at the boy who had returned to preparing to leave the cabin. "We'll see about that," Durrant said. "We'll see."

Charlie pushed open the door with his shoulder and stepped into the morning's cold. He and Durrant walked from the cabin into the new day, just set to dawn.

Durrant looked around. The foreground was dominated by mounds of snow and the ramshackle affair optimistically called Holt City, but beyond that tiny enclave in the wilderness the pale white faces of the mountains loomed. The men faced west as they emerged from their shack, and Charlie pointed to the implacable wall of a sheer mountain above the valley floor, its broad vertical flank plastered with wind-whipped fresh snow. The peak's long, jagged summit was capped with a glacier whose thickness Durrant could scarcely speculate at. The entire range was tipped with light the colour of faded roses, as the sky above slowly progressed from indigo to pink to blue.

"Lord Almighty," Durrant finally said, after they had stood for a full minute absorbing the grandeur of the sight before them. "That is the most beautiful thing I believe I've ever seen." As they stood in the arctic cold, looking west at the Continental Divide, the sun broke over the rounded peaks behind them, and the rose-colored light crept down the face of the peaks high above the valley floor.

With Charlie in the lead the two made their way towards the confluence of the two rivers. The company mess wasn't difficult to find: a long, narrow log building, its boards chinked and cracking in the bitter cold, two chimney's belching thick smoke into the blushing morning air. It sat on the south side of the Pipestone River tucked up against another spread of tumbledown cabins and a massive staging yard where fuel wood was piled thirty feet high and dwarfed by rafts of sleepers, the heavy cross-ties used in railway construction. Stacked in steps that reached up more than fifty feet, the sleepers were each more than eight feet long and weighed as much as one hundred and forty pounds. The cross-ties extended for several hundred yards beyond the barns and stables.

Durrant stepped to the door of the mess hall and pulled it open. The room was dark and warm in contrast to the bright, frigid morning. As the two men stepped inside the clatter of forks on tin plates and the rattle of conversation slowly ebbed, so that when they had closed the door behind them, it was nearly silent.

"Looks like you're not the only one whose tongue the cat got," muttered Durrant to Charlie, whose bright blue eyes smiled as they made their way along the outside wall to the far end of the room where breakfast was served. At a long, low window that separated the mess hall from the kitchen, Charlie took up a plate and filled it with eggs, bacon, and biscuits, and then a mug with steaming dark coffee. The three men working in the kitchen stopped to regard the newcomers. The word that a one-legged Mountie was coming to Holt City to investigate the murder had preceded Durrant's arrival. It seemed that nearly everybody wanted to get a look at this curiosity.

Charlie put a set of utensils in his pocket and pointed his way to a table on the far side of the room that seemed to have space. Durrant followed him, trying to keep the humiliation born from his dependence on the boy at bay, while meeting the gaze of the rough men in the room with his own trail-hardened eyes.

Charlie put Durrant's food on the table. Durrant propped his crutch against the wall-boards of the mess hall behind him while he pivoted into the bench. Charlie went to fetch a plate of food for himself. When he returned, Durrant greeted the man next to him and nodded to those across the table from him. The conversation in the room slowly returned to its normal din. Durrant drank his hot coffee, which warmed him, and ate his breakfast. Charlie sipped at the coffee and took small bites from his plate. Durrant regarded him but said nothing.

"You that Mountie?" the man next to him finally spoke directly to Durrant after a few moments of stoney silence.

"That's right," Durrant said, swallowing a forkful of eggs.

"Here to look into that business with Deek."

"That's right. Don't happen to know who killed the man, do you? Get me back to Fort Calgary that much faster."

The man smelled of wood smoke and sweat. His eyes were barely visible beneath a thick cap pulled tightly over his brow, and his face was masked by a thick black beard that was discolored at the corners of his mouth by tobacco juice. He regarded Durrant coldly. Finally the brown corners of the man's mouth curled a little and he shook his head, seeing the humour in the Mountie's question. "I don't. If I did, though, could I hitch back to Fort Calgary with you? I hear they got running water there now."

"If they do, I ain't never seen it," Durrant said, grinning and shoveling another fork full of breakfast into his mouth.

"Any of you other boys want to talk, you come find me at the Mountie barracks. Young Charlie here'll make sure there's always a pot of coffee on the stove for you, right, Charlie?" Charlie nodded.

A lumbering man passed behind them, plate in hand, heading toward the serving board for another helping. As he did, he tripped over Durrant's crutch, which spanned the distance between the wall-boards and the bench, sending it clattering to the floor. Durrant could smell alcohol on the man, as if he'd bathed in it the night before. Even in the cold of the mess hall, the man seemed to be sweating moonshine.

The men at Durrant's table all stopped eating. The big man behind Durrant just stood there, frozen. Durrant slowly turned to regard him. It felt as though the table drew a deep breath.

"Blue Jesus, pick up the man's crutch, you bloody idiot!" barked the bearded man next to Durrant. The big man balanced his plate and stopped to retrieve the crutch. He righted it against the wall and was rewarded with a sharp slap on the back by the bearded man. He shuffled on to fill his plate with more food.

It came as no surprise that there was whiskey in the camp. He knew that five hundred men laboring through a winter as cold as it was in Holt City would turn to drink for warmth and to alleviate the paralytic ennui brought on with the isolation. There would be time enough to chase down the source of the moonshine; for now, Durrant decided that making peace was more important, so he smiled and the men at the table broke into laughter.

AFTER BREAKFAST DURRANT and Charlie made their way across the Pipestone, Durrant catching himself on the slippery Tote Road that dropped down the bank of the river and climbed back up on the far side. As they approached the station they could see where a few dozen men were already hard at work hefting supplies that the previous evening's freight had delivered. Others would spend their day maintaining the Tote Road that snaked through the valley's deep snow to the summit of the Kicking Horse Pass. Each morning they drew water from the Bow River, accessible through a deep hole in the snow and ice, and filled a massive iron cauldron that was mounted on a buckboard sled. The sled was then driven along the Tote Road to the Kicking Horse Pass, its contents dripping from the cauldron into the ruts of the road. This allowed the buckboards to glide over the tracks despite their heavy loads.

"I'm going to speak with Hep Wilcox," Durrant said to Charlie. "Head back to our bunks and see what you can do to make it feel like a NWMP detachment." Charlie regarded him a moment. "I'll be fine. I can get around fine. Go," he said. Charlie headed back along the path through the snow.

Durrant turned and made his way towards the station where the camp's general manager kept his office. The Mountie hadn't gotten a good look at the building in the darkness when they arrived, but he did now. Like most of the other structures in the town, it had been hastily constructed the previous fall, and Durrant suspected that it, too, wouldn't last out the following summer's construction season. Durrant stepped up from the snowy path onto the broad station platform. The freight that he and Charlie had ridden in from Calgary was still being unloaded. Durrant watched as the men ferried supplies from the boxcars to the landing north of the station.

"That's one train you don't want to mess with," a voice said behind him. Durrant turned to see a well-dressed man standing with his hands buried deep in his pockets by the station's main doors. Durrant turned back to regard the train. "Nitroglycerine," he heard the man say.

The dapper man stepped forward. "You must be Durrant Wallace." He extended a hand sheathed in a black leather glove.

Durrant extended his left. "*Sergeant* Durrant Wallace."

"Sergeant," said the man, taking the Mountie's hand. "I'm Hep Wilcox. I'm the general manager here at the end of steel. I'm glad you've come."

"How much will you put aside by the spring?" Durrant inquired, watching the passage of crates of explosives with suspicion.

"The short answer is as much as we can. The long answer is, well, a little bit more complex."

Wilcox was now beside him, his breath thick in the frigid air. "We have a contract with the Canada Explosives Company out of Mount Saint-Hilaire to manufacture the liquid nitroglycerine for the Upper and Lower Kicking Horse. It's a subcontract, really, through my operation. But the vetting of the bid was done through the Parliament of Canada, as they are paying the bills. I'm not really all that happy with the terms of the deal, but what can you do? We've been having a lot of trouble with quantity. We're yet to see the quality. We'll be running some tests this spring up at the Kicking Horse Pass to assess the power and stability of the mix."

Durrant had lost interest in the troubles of the railroad man, and wanted to turn his attention to the death of Deek Penner. "Can we step inside and talk?" he asked.

"Of course." Wilcox held up a gloved hand to point to the main station door.

The station was the first truly warm space that Durrant had been in since departing Fort Calgary, and it came as a relief. Wilcox led Durrant into the small vestibule, where a broad L-shaped counter separated the entrance way from closed doors beyond. Two small windows flanking the single door to the platform permitted the spectacular light of the day to flood into the room.

"This here is the merchantable counter, where Tom Holt takes care of shipping and receiving for the station," said Wilcox, taking off his glove and tapping the counter top. "Tom manages the stores here, and got the place named after him for his service. Mind, I think he did the naming himself . . ." cracked Wilcox. "Back behind is the telegraph office. John Christianson tends to the wires as well as the store. Through there," pointed Wilcox, "is where we keep the supplies for the men to purchase with their pay." Durrant made note of the heavy lock on the outside of the door.

Wilcox stepped to a third door on the northern wall of the station. "This here is the CPR offices." He pulled a ring of keys from his coat pocket, unlocked the door, and shoved it open. Durrant could see where the door had already cut a groove into the soft, uneven, pine flooring. They stepped into the room. A small stove glowed in the corner and Durrant felt the heat through his heavy clothes. Sweat began to bead on his forehead. "Take your coat off, Sergeant," said Wilcox as he unbuttoned his own. "Would you like coffee? There's a pot there on the stove."

"No, thank you," said Durrant, hanging his coat on a chair while leaning on his crutch.

The office was small and neatly ordered. A compact desk with an oil lamp was pushed against one wall, and there were two chairs arranged near the tiny window that looked out on the rail yard. Durrant could see the men moving about with their crates of raw material to make nitroglycerine through the frosted pane of glass.

He didn't wait for Wilcox to finish pouring coffee for himself before he started. "Do you know who killed Deek Penner, Mr. Wilcox?"

His back to Durrant, Wilcox quickly replied, "If I did, there would be no reason for you to be here, would there Sergeant."

"That may be so, but nevertheless, do you?"

"I do not."

"Do you have any idea who might have wanted Mr. Penner dead?"

"Well, that's another matter altogether." Wilcox sat down next to his desk and put the tin cup with his coffee in it down next to the lamp.

Durrant continued to stand and survey the room as he talked. "So let's make a list, shall we? Who was it that found Mr. Penner's body?"

"That would be John Christianson. John's no killer, I assure you."

"There was a card game that evening. Who was in attendance at that game?" asked Durrant.

"I know that Frank Dodds was there, as it was in his cabin. And John was there, 'cause he told me that he nearly lost his shirt in the game. You'll have to check with one of them to determine who else sat in on the game."

"You didn't ask?"

"Didn't see why. The boys here play cards nearly every night. There's always a dozen games on the go. I don't make it my business to keep track."

"Gambling is illegal."

Wilcox smiled. "I suppose . . ."

"That being said, my concern is not with having a bet now and again. I've been known to play a hand or two of poker myself. It's what nearly always accompanies a game that I'm wondering about. And what happened after this particular game was over is my principal concern."

"Liquor." Wilcox said it in a matter-of-fact tone.

"Is there liquor at any of the games you mention?"

"I imagine there might be a jar here and there."

"This doesn't bother you, Mr. Wilcox?"

"Course it does. Liquor is illegal along the CPR. Selling liquor is prohibited in the camps."

"But you don't know for sure if there's any at Holt City."

Wilcox looked at Durrant as he sipped his coffee. "Sergeant, you and I both know that wherever there are men working, there is whiskey. It's just the way it is. Is it a problem at Holt City? I haven't seen evidence of it. Do I make it my business to meddle with it? So long as it ain't disrupting business, then I got other problems more pressing."

"It's your job, Mr. Wilcox."

The man glared at Durrant.

"As a representative of the CPR, it's your *job* to meddle."

"I don't take kindly to you telling me what my job is, Sergeant Wallace."

"I'm certain you don't, but the fact of the matter is, I've seen more than one man killed 'cause he stuck his nose into a moonshine operation."

"You think that's what happened to Deek?"

"It's possible. Tell me what Deek's responsibilities were."

"He was site foreman for my blasting operations. He was going to be in charge of blasting out the right of way for the Tote Road, for the mainline, and for the tunnels and platforms on the Upper Kicking Horse."

"So he was in a position of authority."

"That's right."

"As a CPR man, he too had a responsibility to meddle in moonshine operations; to report any violations to you, and to the Mounties."

"I guess he did."

"Did he ever report any violations to you?"

"I don't recall ever hearing a word from Deek Penner about moonshine," Wilcox said immediately. Durrant watched him a moment. An awkward silence filled the tiny room.

"You're certain?"

"I don't ever recall."

"That's different than he didn't ever report anything, isn't it?"

"What exactly are you getting at, Sergeant?" said the General Manager, his eyes tightening, his lips thin.

"This morning in the mess I could smell the stench of whiskey on a man who passed me. If it's that obvious to me, then it seems that it must be obvious to just about anybody who cares to look, Deek Penner included. And you as well, sir."

Wilcox drank from his coffee. He's stalling for time, thought Durrant.

"Of course there is whiskey here," Wilcox finally said. "I never said there wasn't. I told you it's in the nature of a camp like Holt City to have a little whiskey from time to time. Probably comes in from Fort Calgary with the mail. Who knows? Did Deek Penner know about it? Likely. Did he care? I can't say. But I know for certain that Deek Penner had his hands full with preparing for the spring push down the Kicking Horse, and unless someone was messing with his explosives, it seems pretty unlikely that he would give a damn about a little booze in the camp."

Durrant nodded. "Well, we'll never know for certain what Deek Penner cared for and didn't." He turned awkwardly in his chair and looked about the tiny window behind him. "Tell me more about Penner's job, sir."

"He was a foreman, as I already said."

"And he was on the CPR roll?"

"He was on my contract. I suppose in a manner of speaking we all are on the CPR roll."

"What exactly was his job?"

"He started as a blaster. He worked the mainline when we did the millage along the Lakehead north of Superior. He was the best blaster I had in my crew, and so when the men I work for won the Kicking Horse contract, I asked him to come on as foreman. He'd have been supervising the crews that will be blasting the line down the Kicking Horse Pass. There'll be two or three hundred men working along that section just on the munitions side of things come the spring."

"It sounds like a big job."

"It is. Out on the prairie it was all about speed, how much track a team could lay down."

"I've heard the stories. Six miles in a day . . ."

"Well, in the mountains it's all about bridges and tunnels. That latter means explosives. We build five hundred yards in a day and it's a good day's work," said Wilcox.

"Did he make enemies among the men he worked with?"

"It's a bit too early to know, really. The team he was putting together never had a cross word for him, and none of the fellas along the Lakehead ever said a bad word. He was a fair man. He worked hard, and expected the same of others. That's why I hired him."

"Any jealousy?"

"You mean someone that might have been passed over for the top job?"

"Yes."

"Not that I know of. You'd have to ask around."

"I will," said Durrant. He reached for his crutch and pushed himself to standing. Wilcox looked relieved that the barrage of questions had come to an end. He made as if ready to stand.

"I have one more question for you, if you don't mind."

"What is it?"

"How well did *you* get on with Mr. Penner?"

Wilcox rose from his chair and put his coffee cup down on his desk. "We got on very well. Deek was like a brother to me, a good man. I chose him because of his honesty and commitment. I asked a lot of him, and he always came through for me."

Durrant regarded Wilcox standing before him. For a man who had just lost a brother he seemed well composed, but then, Durrant knew that the men who worked along the CPR had lost many such comrades to accidents and that they learned to simply move on. He imagined that might well be the case here. "Thank you for your time, sir," Durrant finally said.

"It was no trouble at all."

"Now, I believe its time for me to have a closer look at Mr. Penner himself."

THE TWO MEN stepped outside of the station, Durrant hurrying to pull his gloves on. He followed Wilcox across the station platform.

Durrant observed that Wilcox walked straight and tall, a man of considerable confidence and poise. Durrant had to work hard to keep up with the brisk man. They crossed the yard behind the station and came to the shed where the cadaver of Deek Penner now lay. Durrant paused before the plank door and reached into his trousers for the key to unlock the cast heart lock he had placed on the door late the night before. He swung the door open and a band of light from the bright day fell across the vacant space. The room smelled of split wood and earth, and in the shadows next to the west wall lay the body of Deek Penner. The canvas tarp was pulled up over the man's face and concealed his torso and legs, but the fingers from his left hand hung down below the oilcloth's edge. He turned and said to Wilcox, who hovered close behind, "Would you mind fetching a lantern?"

The general manager snorted in the crisp air as if he was put out by being sent on a common errand, but he wordlessly disappeared in search of the lamp.

Durrant stepped into the shack and crossed the frozen floor to where Deek Penner lay atop a stack of cordwood. He waited a moment for Wilcox to return, leaning his crutch against the split rounds of pine that scented the air with a heady aroma. There was no stench from the body as yet, the temperature having remained well below freezing these past three days. Should the weather turn, however, decomposition would start and the cadaver of Mr. Penner would soon foul the small room.

Without looking he heard Wilcox return, the snow outside the shack crunching beneath his boots.

"Your lantern, Sergeant," the man said behind him. "I'll just hang it here," said Hep, suspending the lamp from a square nail in a crude ceiling joist. It cast a sickly yellow light over the room that made the quarters feel close and stifling despite the cold.

Durrant took hold of the heavy tarp with his left hand and pulled it slowly back from Deek Penner's head. As he did so, he watched from the corner of his eye for any change in expression in the eager Wilcox as the man stepped up to his side. If there was a change, Durrant could not detect it.

Penner's face was caved in so badly that he was likely unrecognizable to any but his closest friends. Congealed, frozen blood had pooled in the sockets of his unseeing eyes and coated his face. Any visible skin was frozen white, and his hair was tipped in a ghostly frost.

Durrant had seen his share of dead men in the decade he had been a North West Mounted Police officer, but he had never seen a man so brutally murdered.

"Is this the first time you've seen the body?" Durrant finally asked Wilcox.

"No," said Wilcox. "When his body was found, I was called to the scene. I dare say, Sergeant, that it was far worse to be the first to come across a man so recently murdered."

"Does this bother you?"

"Of course it does!"

"You don't seem too put out by it."

"Just 'cause I'm not blubbering doesn't mean I don't care about his death."

Durrant continued to consider the corpse before him. The murder of Deek Penner was an act of rage, of ferocity, he thought. He said to Wilcox: "Whoever did this is a monster. This is no simple murder. Whoever killed this man didn't just want him dead. They wanted him mutilated."

"There's no argument about that, Sergeant," said Wilcox looking around him as if the killer might be within earshot.

"There doesn't seem to be any question about how this man died. Blunt force. He's been bludgeoned. Only question is by what . . ."

"There are a hundred things in a camp like this that could be used to kill a man."

Durrant turned back to the corpse and pulled the tarp all the way back. Wilcox stepped forward with the lantern and shone the light into the darkened room. "You go through his pockets?"

"I did not."

"Has anybody?"

"Not that I know of. Maybe the killer did. He ain't been left out for others to pillage, I can assure you. We had him locked up in your barracks before you came last night."

"From this point on, Mr. Wilcox, I am the only one to have access to Mr. Penner's remains. I alone will hold the key to this building."

"As you wish," said Wilcox.

"Now, sir, I will take some time alone with Mr. Penner. Please arrange to have Doctor Armatage join me. We need to conduct a more detailed examination of Mr. Penner's remains before any decomposition takes place."

DURRANT HAD BEGUN to take measurements of the fatal wounds to Deek Penner's face and head when he heard a cough at the door to the shack. His left hand reached for the revolver in his pocket and he turned quickly in the darkness to see the shape of a man darkening the portal.

The man laughed. "What kind of greeting is that for an old friend?" asked the man, stepping from the bright light of day into the gloomy shed.

"Hello, Saul," said Durrant.

"Hello, Durrant." The man stepped up next to the Mountie and, without hesitation, extended his left hand. In his right hand he carried a small black leather satchel. Durrant took the man's hand in his own and grasped it firmly.

"Nice to see a friendly face," Durrant said, regarding the man. He was tall and thin and wore a pencil moustache that curled up at the corners above a narrow beard. The rest of his face was cleanly shaven and dark with a winter tan.

"Likewise, I'm sure." The man smiled broadly and turned to regard the corpse.

"Dewalt didn't tell me it was you who was acting as physician in this God-forsaken wilderness."

"I don't think he knew, to be perfectly honest."

Durrant nodded. "He's as thick as ever."

"Be generous, Durrant. I haven't exactly made my presence known to all our former comrades at arms."

Durrant nodded. "The last I heard you were the attending physician at some eastern facility. York?"

"Kingston. I grew weary with city life. Adventure was what drew me to medicine. And freedom."

"Freedom to freeze your arse off, Saul."

The doctor laughed again. "And you? The last I heard you were stationed at Fort Calgary."

"Still am. Steele has asked me to look into this case because Dewalt is too busy with the Blackfoot and with the bootleggers. Frankly, Saul, I'm happy for the distraction."

"Not enjoying sorting the post and collecting customs?"

Durrant shook his head.

"And how is the leg?"

"It's fine," he said, his mood darkening.

"Well, come by my quarters and we'll have a look."

"I said it's fine."

Armatage laughed again. "Durrant, you can play the tough with everybody else in this camp, but it was me who *sawed* off your leg. And it was me who sewed you back together after your adventure in the Cypress Hills. You can't play the rogue with me. Plus, you must come by. Evelyn will be asking after you, and you must see Oliver. He's four years old. And of course, you've not yet met our little Ben."

Durrant stared at the body before him. He drew a deep breath which slowly seeped between his pursed lips.

"It will be alright, Durrant," said the doctor quietly, laying a hand on Durrant's left arm.

"Now," he said cheerfully, "let's have a better look at Mr. Penner here, or at least what's left of the chap, shall we?"

The two men began their examination of the body. Armatage removed his thick leather gloves and opened his black satchel to withdraw a set of forceps. Durrant noted the strong odour of peroxide that accompanied the opening of the doctor's bag, and was immediately transported back to the Regina hospital where the man had attended to his amputation. It was a most unwelcome sense of déjà vu.

"I don't suppose there's any question about the cause of death?" asked Durrant, forcing himself back to the present.

Armatage was using the forceps to remove something from the cavity on Penner's face. He shook his head. "No, not much question. If I was in Kingston, we could open him up and look at the liver and the stomach and the other organs for signs of poison; it's always possible that he ingested something earlier in the evening that allowed his killer an easier time with his task, but it seems irrelevant to our purpose here."

Durrant nodded. He could hear the sickly sound of the flesh on the dead man's face sticking to the bone where Armatage was picking at the foreign object. "So," said the doctor, holding the forceps before him, a tiny rusty fleck of metal in their grasp. "What we have here is a situation where both the zygomatic bone and the maxilla have been all but pulverised. I'd say the first blow caught him lightly here," said Armatage, pointing to the man's right cheek with his left hand. His fingers were long and thin and looked ghostly in the yellow light. "I say this because of how this fragment of bone," and again he pointed to the maxilla, "is concave, and this one," and here he indicated the frontal bone, "is protruding over the zygomatic bone."

"But he was hit more than once?"

"Oh yes, I'd say at least three or four times, maybe more. It's hard to tell. Too much damage to frontal and temporal bones to be certain, but after he was dead, he was hit at least once or twice. I'd say the first blow stunned him, and the second blow killed him. Can't be certain." The doctor pointed to the cavity where Deek Penner's right eye would have been. "You can see bone shards here. Lots of them. Being frozen like this helps a little because the blood hasn't carried the fragments too far from where they started out."

"What can we tell about the attacker by this?" asked Durrant.

"He would have been strong enough to wield a heavy object. The blunt side of an axe. Maybe a sledge. Could be lots of things around this camp, Durrant."

"Would he need to be exceptionally strong?"

"I don't think so," replied the doctor. "Once our boy Deek was on the ground, it would have been a matter of lifting and letting the weapon fall. Like splitting cordwood."

Durrant breathed heavily. "Not *exactly* like splitting cordwood."

"No, not exactly."

"No indication that this was an axe *blade*?"

"No. The wounds were made with a blunt object. This was a crushing blow, not a cutting blow." Armatage pointed to the rents in the flesh of the man's face. "You can see here the skin has been bruised where it was broken. Nothing here to suggest an axe."

Durrant looked at the doctor. "So just about any man in this camp could be responsible?"

"Based on the nature of these wounds, I'd say yes."

"And what have you got there?" asked Durrant, his eyes fixed on the forceps.

"Well, it looks like a fleck of metal of some kind. Rusted, so that when the weapon connected here," the doctor pointed to the concave shape around Deek Penner's right temple, "it flaked off."

"So now all I have to do is find a sledge, pry bar, or hammer in this camp with a fleck missing from it and I've got my man."

The doctor smiled at him. "Are you suggesting that will be a problem, Sergeant?"

Durrant took the lantern from its peg and held it near the cadaver. He stooped a little to examine the body more closely. "Is this consistent, Saul?" asked Durrant, pointing with his twisted right hand at the flecks of blood on Penner's coat.

Armatage bent and looked closely at the man's heavy winter coat. There was a fine spray of blood around the collar and heavier spots of frozen blood on the chest and shoulders. "You know, Durrant, it's hard for me to say. I've never examined a body this badly mutilated. I've looked at a few poor devils killed when their horses kicked them in the face, but this is something else all together different. And frankly, Durrant, we here in the Dominion are a little behind our cousins to the south when it comes to how we examine a cadaver for this sort of evidence.

"So I'm only surmising when I say this, but I'd guess that this spray of blood is consistent with the man having first been hit while *standing* up. If this man was upright up for the first blow, you'd expect a fair amount of blood to spray across his own shoulders, face, chest, even his arms, wouldn't you? When he was on the ground, there would be some too, as well as across the snow all around him. But my guess is that it would spray out in a different direction."

"The men who recovered the body would have tracked up that snow pretty good in the process," grumbled Durrant. "Not much evidence left on the scene."

"No, not on the scene," said the doctor.

Durrant looked at him. "But the killer?"

"I believe you'll be looking for someone with blood on his coat, Durrant. Maybe on his trousers and boots too, depending on where he stood."

"And from the first blow?"

"I'd say, given the pattern of blood on our boy Deek, that the killer could not have hit him without getting a fair amount of blood on his *own* coat."

Durrant returned his gaze to Deek Penner's corpse. "I guess I'll have to pay a visit to the laundry, won't I?"

Armatage nodded his agreement. "And maybe to Tom Holt's store to see if anybody has replaced a coat in the last few days."

Durrant said, "Give me a hand, will you?" He hung up the lantern again and turned back to the body. "I want to check his pockets. It will be easier for you than me," Durrant said, holding up his twisted right hand to illustrate his point.

Armatage smiled a narrow smile and put down his forceps. He dug his hands into the pockets of Deek Penner's trousers. Durrant watched him. The doctor came out with a handful of blasting caps and fuse wire, and a crumpled up sheet of paper.

"What have you got there?" said Durrant.

Armitage smiled. "Looks like some of Deek's tricks of the trade. Caps and fuse."

"The note?"

Armatage opened it and scanned it. "It's a wire. It's in code."

"Let's have a look," Durrant said, taking it in his left hand and holding it up to the light.

"It's not the NWMP code, that's for certain," said the doctor, "unless you've changed it in the last two years."

"We haven't. I don't recognize it. Penner was just a foreman. What would he be doing with a coded wire?" asked Durrant.

"I'm just a doctor, Durrant. You're the investigator."

Durrant was quiet a moment, holding the folded sheet of paper up before the flickering light. While the message was a mystery, the name at the bottom was clear: the wire was from a man named Kauffman. It was possible, thought not probable, that within the code's secret message was the key to Deek Penner's death.

FIVE
THE WIRE

WHEN DURRANT FINALLY PULLED THE tarp back over the disfigured face of Deek Penner and shouldered the door of the shed shut, it was nearly noon. He had told Armatage that he wanted some time alone with the body, and the doctor had smiled and nodded and left wordlessly. Before Armatage reached the door Durrant said, "Saul, I have to ask . . . Where were you on the night Mr. Penner was murdered?"

Armatage's smile broadened. "Durrant, you haven't changed one bit. I was at Banff Station. Repairing a man's shattered tibia. He had been crushed when the load he was hauling in a push cart shifted and came down on him. I came back on the train the day before you arrived."

Durrant nodded. "I had to ask."

"Of course you did." Armatage's smile remained generous. He turned and left the shack without another word.

Left alone in the cold room, the light of the lamp flickering above his charge, Durrant spent the better part of an hour examining Penner, making sure that nothing had been overlooked. In particular he was looking for something obvious—like a gunshot or stabbing wound—that might lead him in another direction. In the end, there was only one conclusion: Deek Penner's life had ended suddenly and violently, with a crushing blow to the head and face. The man's hands were scratched but not bruised, and there was no blood or skin under his nails, meaning that it was unlikely that the killing blow had come at the end of a long struggle or fight. Penner had been taken by surprise.

Once he had covered up the man, Durrant had looked again at the folded sheet of paper and its unknown code scrawled on it. He knew well enough that there were dozens, if not hundreds, of codes in common use across the telegraph service that now stretched from the Atlantic shores all the way to the end of steel. The NWMP had their own that he was proficient in. The CPR also used a common code that Durrant knew well, having sent and received cables for the last year in Fort Calgary. This one, however, was a mystery to him. He folded the sheet of paper and placed it in his breast pocket for future examination.

During his work in the unheated room, Durrant had grown increasingly cold, and so it was with some relief that he stepped back out into the midday sun, faint as it was. Durrant leaned back against the door of the shed and let his eyes adjust to the blinding glare on the mountains of snow all around.

Durrant could hear men's voices raised somewhere in discussion, and then a staccato burst of laughter. He could hear the sound of wood being chopped and a fiddle being played. The Mountie made his way along the path back to the station, and entering the building, knocked on Wilcox's door.

"Come," he heard the man say.

Durrant opened the door. The heat of the room was quite welcome after nearly two hours in the cold shack.

"Sergeant, you're done?" Wilcox stood up from his desk. Durrant could see a ledger open on the table, and next to it a plate of food left uneaten. Wilcox held a quill in his hand.

"Just getting started, Mr. Wilcox."

"Of course. I meant with the body."

Durrant stepped into the man's office. "I have a couple of things I need from you, Mr. Wilcox. First off, keys. I need a key to the various storerooms and warehouses. I don't want to trouble you or any of the foremen for a key when I want to look around."

"It really won't be any trouble . . ."

"Just the same, I'd like my own keys, sir, and the key for Mr. Penner's bunk. I'll need to look around there, on my own."

"That's no trouble," said Wilcox, his fingers drumming on the table.

"Good. Next, tell me this. If a man or men went missing from the camp, if they didn't show up for work one morning, would you be told?"

"I imagine. The foreman in charge would likely bring it to my attention. After he tried to locate the man, I suppose."

"You mean, check his bunk to see if the man was sleeping off a drunk?"

Wilcox drew a sharp breath. "More likely down with the flu, but yes, after he'd checked his bunk, or the mess ... What are you asking?"

"Has anybody been reported missing since the death of Deek Penner?"

"You're wondering if the killer has left the camp already. I can check with my men. I haven't heard of anybody leaving."

"How often do the trains come and go?"

"Once every day or two, but with all the snow, we've had just a few in the last week. One went as far as Padmore a couple of days ago."

"Doctor Armatage mentioned an injury at Banff Station?"

"Yes, I believe he was on that one. We needed to do a supply run. Stocks were running low. But that train left the day Mr. Penner was killed. Your murderer could not have used it to escape this camp. We were starting to make arrangements to haul provisions in from Banff with horse and sled, but the weather let up and we were able to ..."

Durrant interrupted him. "Could a man leave on foot?"

Wilcox's face betrayed his dislike of being interrogated. "He could. But if your killer did, we wouldn't need to have this discussion. The only road we keep clear is the one to the Kicking Horse Pass, which is getting more and more traffic with the coming of the spring construction season. It would take a hardy soul to set off on foot for Banff Station right now. The mainline would see a man through, but it's a long walk."

"You'll let me know what your foremen say about men gone missing?" Durrant asked. He was looking out the window. "I suppose I should head up to the Kicking Horse Pass in the coming days to talk with anyone who is there now but was *here* on the day and night that Mr. Penner was killed. Will you be able to provide me with a list of such men?

"I don't think there will be many. Deek didn't have much to do with the men up at the Pass as yet. We haven't started to muster any explosives there, but I will prepare a list."

Durrant leaned against the door, looking at Wilcox. "Can you tell me if Deek was into anything else here at Holt City that might have had him cross a man?"

Wilcox looked down in thought. "Let me give that some attention and I shall let you know."

Durrant nodded, then said, "One more thing, Mr. Wilcox . . . I don't want anybody leaving this camp or the Kicking Horse unless I have given my permission. Nobody is to board a train for east of Holt City unless I have spoken with them first."

"Does that include me, sir?"

Durrant looked at him in the pale light from the window. "Yes, sir, it does."

"Very well."

"Now, I'm going to see what your man Christianson has to tell me about finding Mr. Penner with his face bludgeoned."

JOHN CHRISTIANSON SAT behind a desk that housed the telegraph machine. He was tapping out code, his spectacles resting on the tip of his nose. The man was so intent on this task of sending wires that he didn't look up when Durrant entered the main station room from Wilcox's office. Durrant watched the man awhile. He moved with confident ease while at the telegraph machine. He sat erect and composed, though he leaned over from time to time to read the code on some of the cables he had received. It was because of that composure that Durrant was surprised by what happened next.

"Mr. Christianson," Durrant said from behind him. The man jumped, and the sheath of papers he was reading cascaded from the wooden table to the bare plank floor. "I'm sorry," Durrant stepped forward, his crutch making a hollow sound on the floor. "No, no, it's okay, it's okay," John Christianson stammered, dropping to one knee from his stool to sweep up the papers.

"Let me help," Durrant said, putting a hand on the desk to steady himself as he reached for an errant paper.

"It's really okay," Christianson explained. The man sat back down on his stool and tapped the loose papers into a semblance of order. "What can I do for you? Do you need me to dispatch a wire?" Christianson looked up at Durrant, who was still leaning on the table that held the telegraph. It was a smaller version of the model that Durrant had been using in Fort Calgary for the last year, and he regarded it with some interest.

"What model are you using here at Holt City?" Durrant asked.

Christianson straightened his papers again and looked down at the machine as if seeing it for the first time. "It's a Phelps model 1880."

"I'm familiar with the Phelps '76. It's what we've got at Fort Calgary."

"Yes, sir. I know that. I saw that unit when I come through Fort Calgary a year ago. Do you want to send a cable?" asked Christianson again.

Durrant looked over the orderly space. The neat pigeonholes above the desk were filled with the papers and documents that were part and parcel of the telegraph trade. There were spools of telegraph cable script that Christianson would feed into the Phelps and that would be imprinted with the Morse code as it came over the wire. That code would then be translated by hand onto telegraph forms for delivery to their intended recipient. Durrant looked up from his consideration of the telegraph.

"No. I'm sorry. I'm Sergeant Durrant Wallace of the North West Mounted Police. I'm investigating the murder of Deek Penner."

"Everybody at Holt City knows who you are and why you're here," Christianson said sheepishly.

"I understand you found the body of Mr. Penner," asked Durrant

"I did," he said, looking for a pocket to tuck his hands into as he stood up.

"I need to speak to you about that."

"I have these cables to send," said Christianson, turning around and pointing to the stack of papers on the table.

"This is important. Time is of the essence. The killer may have already fled Holt City. If not, he may be the man you sit next to at breakfast tomorrow."

"Goodness," said Christianson, looking down at the floor. He pulled the coat he wore closer around his chest. "Do you want to sit, Mr. Wallace?"

"It's *Sergeant* Wallace," Durrant said. "Tell me how you found Deek Penner."

Christianson blew a stream of air through pursed lips. He closed his eyes and his face twisted into a sour expression. "It was after midnight," he finally said. "We'd been at Frank Dodds' cabin playing cards, as we were apt to do. There ain't nothing to do in Holt City but play cards in the night. Nothing at all. So we'd been to Dodds' cabin, and things broke up, and we all went back to our places. I got a place just here behind the General Store. Tom Holt lets me bunk there. It's pretty good. So I had come back to my place, and before turning in I came in to check the wires. See if there was anything urgent. I usually do. If there is, Mr. Wilcox likes me to deal with it right away, see? And so there was a wire waiting for transcription. I set to receive, and it was in code. It was for Deek. All his wires are in code. I just took it down. When I was done, I went off to find him at this bunk, figuring he'd still be awake."

"Did Mr. Penner receive a lot of wires?"

"Some, he got some."

"How many?"

"Well, I'd have to check the log book, but maybe two or three a week."

"He send a lot?"

"I sent some for him, yes."

"Did he know how to send a wire on his own?"

"I should think so. It ain't that hard once you know the language and the machine."

Durrant wanted to follow this line further, but didn't want to interrupt the man's recollection. "So you went to find Mr. Penner?"

"Yes sir, I did." He seemed to get lost in thought a moment, his eyes momentarily searching the room.

"Did you find him to deliver the cable?"

Christianson seemed to jump at the sound of Durrant's voice.

"He was dead when I come across him."

"Where was this?"

"Between here and his bunk, down along the Bow River." Christianson seemed to shudder and close his eyes again. "Well, sir, I was just coming along the path. I had the cable in my pocket. It was mighty cold, and there was some snow. I was coming along the path, and I had my lamp as a man could get pretty lost in the dark here and freeze to death if he weren't careful. I walked down the path, just where it cuts close to the river there, and I thought I saw someone else walking, but when I shone the lamp, it was someone running away. I called out, 'That you Deek?' I don't know why I did, but I guess 'cause I was looking for him, I had him in mind. The man just kept running. I went on a little ways, and there was blood on the trail. I near stepped in it. I shone the lamp around and saw that someone had gone off the beaten track. You don't do that much, you know. The snow can be near ten feet deep in places. Down by the river the snow isn't quite so deep, and I could see where someone had trampled it all down."

"You followed the tracks?"

"I did, but not far. There was blood, and I got this terrible feeling. I followed just ten feet, that's all I had to, 'cause there he was." Christianson drew a deep breath in and let it out again.

"That's where you found Mr. Penner."

"Yes sir, face down in the snow. I thought maybe he was still alive, you know, like unconscious? So I rolled him over and that's when I knew he was gone."

"What condition was he in?"

"It was horrible, just horrible."

"How did you know it was Mr. Penner?"

"Well, I'd just seen him within the hour. I knew his coat. And there was enough . . ." The man stopped and closed his eyes. "There was enough of his face left to know it was him."

"Can you tell me anything about the man you saw running away?"

"Nothing. Nothing at all," he said quickly.

"Clothing?"

"It was too dark and he was too far away. He must have seen me coming—seen my lamp, and run off."

"Which way was he running?"

"Away from me, off towards Deek's cabin."

"Is there anything else down that way? Besides Deek's place?"

"A few other cabins. There's a trail that crossed the right-of-way there, and circles back to your place, the Mountie place, and then to the Tote Road. A man familiar with the area could run that way and slip on back here without much trouble."

Durrant made note of that. "When you found Mr. Penner, was there any question if he was dead or not?"

"Not once I rolled him over."

Durrant regarded the man. He still had his eyes closed, his hands tucked awkwardly into the pockets of his coat. "Tell me, Mr. Christianson, did you happen to look around in the snow at all?"

"No sir. It must have been minus thirty out. I wasn't about to go digging."

"So you didn't notice if the man who fled had maybe discarded the murder weapon as he did?"

"I didn't see nothing."

"Did you have an impression, sir, when you first saw Mr. Penner, of what might have been used to kill him?"

"Well, it was something heavy. You seen him?"

"I just finished examining the body."

"Then you know."

"I suppose what I'm driving at is, you know the camp, and you know what happens here, what tools these men use. When you saw him, did you think, he's been bludgeoned with a . . ."

Christianson's eyes opened and he looked around the room. "I suppose I thought that someone used a sledge on the man's face."

"RIGHT OVER HERE. This is where I found him," said Christianson. He was walking hurriedly through the cold. "You can see where he was dragged off the path. You can still make out some of the blood through the snow, you see," said Christianson, pointing.

Durrant reached him, breathing plumes of mist into the frigid air. He looked closely and could see a pinkish stain in the snow.

"And this is where I found the body," and Christianson pointed again.

Indeed, a deep depression led from the path toward the flat open area that marked where the Bow River lay sleeping beneath the ice and snow. The mounds of snow that formed deep trenches had been breached by Penner's assailant. It appeared as if the killer had lugged the body into the heavy drifts of snow, as was evidenced by the furrows that stretched several yards in the general direction of the Bow River.

"When you saw this man running from the scene, Mr. Christianson, had he already left the body?"

Christianson seemed to think about this for some time. "I believe so, Sergeant Wallace."

"Did you actually see him in the deep snow?"

Again, the man ruminated on the question. "No, sir. I believe he was on the path when I first saw him."

"You believe?"

"It was night. It was dark. I could only see so much."

"Fine," said Durrant, awkwardly bending down to brush at the fresh ice crystals forming where the frigid air met the dry, cold snow. He pushed snow away with his gloved left hand, his other pressing on his crutch for balance. "Mr. Christianson, would you please point out exactly where you were standing when you first saw the man running."

Christianson nodded and walked back along the path. When he was about fifty feet back, he stopped and turned. "I was about here."

"And," said Durrant, pushing himself upright, "where was the man you saw running when you first laid eyes on him?"

Christianson waved with his arms. "Walk a ways towards that bunk yonder." Durrant did so.

"Keep going. Okay, okay, now stop."

"Right here?"

"Well, like I said, it's hard to tell. Everything looks so different at night, but right around there."

"Some eighty feet. Maybe twenty-five yards."

"I reckon. Thereabouts."

Durrant turned and surveyed the surroundings. It was a desolate stretch of low forest through which the pathway crossed between the main station, and a cluster of squat cabins and shacks built along the banks of the Bow River. The woods were tight except right in the vicinity of where Deek Penner had been killed. There the close forest opened onto the banks of the river itself. Durrant stood there a long minute examining where the body had been recovered. Of course, the scene had been greatly disturbed by the recovery itself, but he wanted to freeze the scene in his mind as he first found it.

"Mr. Christianson," he said, turning back, "would you please walk back towards where you found the corpse, and then show me how far off the trail you had to go in order to discover Mr. Penner's body."

"The snow is mighty deep," the man protested.

"You can return to your quarters afterwards, sir."

"Very well," he sighed, a plume of vapour gathering around his face. He trudged back to the depression in the snow, and then, hesitating, took two or three steps off the path. He sank up to his hips in the snow. "It's deeper than I recall," he said.

"Was Penner buried?"

"No, he was face down. I suppose 'cause he was laid out as he was, he didn't sink into the snow."

Durrant made his way back to where Christianson was chest deep in the banks of snow. "Did you move the body other than to turn it over?"

"No. I couldn't get no grip on him. I tried, but the snow was so deep, it took four of us just to get him moved ten feet."

"Mr. Christianson, once you'd discovered the body, and determined that is was Deek Penner and that he was dead, what did you do?"

"Well, I ran back to see if Mr. Holt was awake, but forgot that he was down at Banff Station securing provisions, so I went to wake up Mr. Wilcox."

"Was he awake when you got to his bunk?"

"No sir, he was asleep."

"How do you know?"

Christianson closed his eyes in thought. "I had to knock pretty loudly on his door. I could hear him snoring."

"And then what happened?"

Christianson seemed to be growing impatient with the questions. "I brought 'im back here. He then sent for some men to recover the body. As the Doc was down in Banff too, we couldn't call on him, though it wouldn't have done any good anyway . . . We got some men together and carried the body yonder to the Mountie's cabin. I suppose where you're staying now with your boy."

"When did you alert the North West Mounted Police?"

"We sent a cable first thing in the morning."

"You waited till then?"

"Well, it was near morning when we finally got old Deek into your cabin. It couldn't have been but a few hours."

"You sent the cable to Regina?"

"Yes sir."

"Who told you to do that?"

"Mr. Wilcox did."

"Did he write the cable?"

"I did. I wrote it. He told me what to tell."

"And what was that?"

"That a man had been killed and that it looked like murder and could the Mounties come and have a look."

Durrant thought about this.

"Why Regina?"

"Well, that's headquarters, ain't it?"

"It is, but Fort Calgary is much closer."

"You'd have to ask Mr. Wilcox. He's the one who told me where to send it."

Durrant looked down again where Christianson was standing in the snow. "You can come out of there now."

Christianson nodded and seemed to swim through the deep drifts until he reached the path. He patted all his clothing to knock the snow off of himself, and then, he looked up at Durrant. "Are you making me out to be a suspect in this killing?" he asked quietly.

Durrant looked at him. The bright sun shining above the rugged peaks to the west, and the intense glare off the snow made his eyes water, the tears pooling and freezing on his skin the moment the air touched them. "It's too early for that."

Christianson exhaled again. "That's good. 'Cause I liked old Deek, and would never have done him harm. That, sir, is a fact." Christianson stood up straight and looked up at the mountains. He seemed to breathe easier after his speech.

"Don't get too comfortable, Mr. Christianson," Durrant said, blinking into the harsh glare of the noonday sun. Its reflection off the bright snow was dazzling. "As far as I'm concerned, there ain't a man in this camp who isn't a suspect right now."

Christianson nodded and pushed more snow from his coat.

"After you found him, Mr. Christianson, did you happen to handle the body?"

"How do you mean like?"

"Did you try to move him?"

"Deek was a big lad. And in this deep snow . . ."

"Is that a no?"

"Well, I tired to be of help to those that carried his body to . . . the Mountie cabin."

"Did you happen to get any of Mr. Penner's blood on you?"

John seemed to shudder and looked down at himself, as if half expecting to see blood there now. "I don't know. I don't believe so."

"Have you been to the laundry since Mr. Penner's death?"

"No. No, I've not been there in a week or so."

"And have you requisitioned any garments from Mr. Holt's store?"

"Not a one."

"There's one more thing, sir," said Durrant, regarding the man brushing more dry snow from his coat. "The wire. This all started with you bringing a wire to Penner. But you never reached him. He was dead. What became of it?"

"Oh my," said Christianson, his eyes searching, "I have no idea. In all the confusion I plain forgot about it!"

"Would it be among your papers at the telegraph office?"

"I don't know. I have to check. I may have stuffed it in my pants pocket," he started patting himself down again, looking for the paper.

"It may be important, Mr. Christianson. Please bring it to me directly when you have located it." said Durrant. "You say that I can return to the NWMP cabin this way?" He pointed towards Penner's cabin. Christianson nodded. "Alright then." Durrant turned and made his way along the new trail towards the barracks.

Christianson stood watching Durrant go until he disappeared from sight, and he continued to stand for some time after.

DURRANT USED THE keys he had obtained from Hep Wilcox to open the door to Penner's cabin. His was set amid a cluster of shacks and tents huddled in a thick stand of trees opposite the CPR right-of-way from the NWMP cabin, and nestled close to the Bow River.

It was a tiny space, with a low narrow cot pressed up against the boards. A small but solid Ransom 1850 stove sat opposite, its stovepipe running up through an opening in the boards of the roof. Bailing wire had been used to secure it, and in places it was patched with tin.

There was a trunk next to the door, its lid closed. There was no lock on it, and Durrant opened it, the aroma of cedar chips, used to stave off garment-eating moths, filling the room. It was of crude construction, and had leather for hinges. Inside were a few pairs of heavy wool trousers, several thick shirts and a jacket worn and frayed at the elbows. A pair of boots sat next to the trunk. There were no papers of any sort to be found there, or anywhere else in the quarters. He opened the stove to inspect the contents. The fire had burned down to almost nothing and he could find no shreds of paper among the pale ashes.

Durrant turned his attention to the bed: it was carefully made, but sparse. The blankets on it were faded and frayed, but not moth-eaten. Next to it was a small oil lamp on an upended crate that had once contained tinned peaches. The lamp was dark and stained with oil. A small tin-type sat in a homemade frame next to the lamp. Durrant picked it up with his left hand. The photograph was of a family; a man and wife, dressed in formal wear, and six children. Durrant assumed that that one of the two strapping lads in the photo was Deek, as the others were school-aged girls. He wondered if they had been notified of his passing.

The Mountie completed his search of the austere quarters. The photograph still in his hands, it struck Durrant that the outcome of his investigation would affect people he had never met, but who would be counting on him to succeed in his undertaking. He put the tin-type back by the lamp and left the tiny cabin to its ghosts.

SIX

SEVEN MEN

"I'M GOING TO WANT TO see the men Deek Penner was playing cards with the night he was killed," Durrant said as he stepped into Wilcox's office. He held in his left hand the script that Wilcox had furnished with the list of men who had participated in the card game the night Deek Penner was killed.

"Good afternoon, Mr. Wallace."

"It's Sergeant Wallace, Mr. Wilcox. I'll need you to arrange for me to see all the men, together, tonight please. In Frank Dodds' cabin."

Wilcox closed the ledger he had been making notes in and twisted in his chair to look at the Mountie. "Okay, well, yes, that can be arranged. I will check with Mr. Dodds."

"This isn't a request, Mr. Wilcox."

Wilcox regarded him a moment. "Frank Dodds doesn't take orders well. He's an independent man."

"I'm certain you will find a way to convince him so that *I* don't have to."

Wilcox drew a slow, laboured breath. "I'll ask the men to gather around eight, after the evening meal."

Durrant opened the door and left without another word.

THREE MEN WERE milling around the counter in the area outside Wilcox's office. Behind the counter that served as the general store, post office, and cable office, Christianson was passing a packet of mail to a man. The four men all turned to look at Durrant as he emerged from Wilcox's office. Their conversation died, and a silence filled the space. Christianson had been leaning on the counter with one elbow, but straightened up as Durrant made his way across the floor to the counter. One of the men made room for him. Durrant could smell the powerful combination of body odour and wood smoke on the men.

"You here to find out who killed Penner?" one of the men asked.

"I am," said Durrant, leaning on the counter, doing his best to appear authoritative, the crutch pushed behind him. "You got something to tell me?"

"I don't," said the man. "But my guess is that Frank Dodds got something he could sure tell."

"Shut up, Ted, you aiming to get your teeth broke?" the man next to him urged.

"Well, everybody in camp knows them two had a hate on for each other," said Ted, looking sharply at his friend. "Don't take no detective to figure that out."

"Why did they hate one another?"

"Penner was always sticking his nose in Frank Dodds' business, accusing him of running moonshine."

"Is he?"

"How should I know? I don't touch the stuff," said Ted, and his two friends burst out laughing and then he joined them.

"Good luck, Red Coat," said Ted.

"Yeah, good luck," said the third man.

"You're going to need it in Holt City," Ted said, moving toward the door.

"And why's that?" Durrant said.

The man called Ted turned and looked at him. His two friends bunched up next to the door, pulling their wool caps down over greasy hair. "This ain't Fort Calgary. You're all alone here. People here liked Deek fine, but there ain't nobody here who is going to say a word against Frank Dodds, even if they seen him crack Deek Penner's skull with their own eyes. That's a fact." Ted pushed open the door and the cold air filled the room as the three men left.

"You think Frank Dodds killed Deek Penner, Mr. Christianson?" said Durrant, still watching the door.

"I don't know, Sergeant Wallace."

"You think it was Dodds you saw running away that night?"

"I can't say . . ."

"Can't, or won't."

"Can't say, sir. Can't say," Christianson was shaking his head, not making eye contact.

"I need to use your telegraph, Mr. Christianson."

"You want for me to send a wire for you, Sergeant?" Christianson looked up at him, smiling weakly.

"No, I'll send it myself. I know the machine. And the North West Mounted Police have their own code."

"Very well," said Christianson, "sit yourself down, Sergeant, make yourself at home." Christianson seemed genuinely happy not to be under the spotlight any longer.

"You need pen and paper, it's all right there."

Durrant watched the man walk to the far side of the L-shaped counter where he had been sorting the mail. Another man entered the room and Christianson greeted him and fetched a package for him. Durrant sat down and thought about his message. He checked the circuit and made the connection with the North West Mounted Police headquarters in Regina. He operated the machine quickly, tapping out the coded cable:

> To Sam Steele, Commanding.
> From Sergeant Durrant Wallace.
> Arrived Holt City. Examined Deek Penner. Cause of death, blow by blunt object. Establishing possible motives. Presence of whiskey with likely connection to the murder. Questioning suspects . . . Will update thereafter.

Durrant sat up straight on the narrow stool as he waited for a reply.

Durrant took Wilcox and others on their word that the corpse was in fact Penner. The weapon used for bludgeoning had not been recovered. It could have been dropped right next to the body and might not be recovered until later in the spring, when the snow finally melted. Durrant made a mental note, however, to search for the weapon in the area around where Penner was found. That would be a good job for Charlie. It occurred to Durrant that the killer might actually be walking the tracks. He could be making his way by shank's pony along the relatively snow-free tracks between Holt City and Banff Station, nearly fifty miles to the east. It was a slim possibility, but still doable. Durrant would wire the stationmaster in Banff and ask that he keep an eye open for a severely frostbitten man arriving from Holt City. It was no surprise that there was whiskey in the camp. Wilcox, as the manager of the camp, should have been doing more to root out this evil. From what he'd learned so far, it sounded like Penner had been poking his nose into at least one moonshiner's business, and it may well have gotten him killed.

His thoughts were interrupted by the buzzing of the telegraph machine. He listened to the coded message and recognized it as the one that the Mounties used. He took a pencil and paper from the pigeonholes above the machine and with his left hand awkwardly scrawled out the incoming note, decoding it as he wrote.

> Confidential Durrant Wallace.
> From Sam Steele, Commanding.
> Determine what can about whiskey. Make investigating murder first priority. Wire with updates daily.

When Durrant had received the note he became aware that Christianson was watching him from behind the counter. He looked up at the man and Christianson smiled and quickly turned back to his own business. Durrant read the note twice, then stood and hopped across the room, opened the door to the stove, and slipped the sheet of paper on top of the hot coals.

THE LAUNDRY WAS located across the confluence of the rivers, close to where a hole had been cut in the ice of the Bow River, from which water was extracted for use around the camp, and for icing the various roads to allow for the smooth passage of buckboards and other wagons. He followed the winding track that lead through a thick grove of trees down to the river. He stepped aside, nearly toppling over into the deep snow, as a sled passed him on the narrow road. It bore the giant tank used to drip water from the Bow River onto the Tote Road that led to the Kicking Horse Pass, up into the woods. Two men sat on the sled's spring-loaded seat, and one of them nodded to the Mountie as the horse team pulled the heavy load up the grade towards the camp. Durrant nodded solemnly in return.

He passed through the trees and could see a small cluster of shacks on the bank of the river, the building serving as the laundry among them. A thick column of grey smoke rose from a heavy chimney, and through the poorly constructed walls tangled threads of steam emerged, so that it appeared as though the entire building was smoking. Durrant opened the door to the shack. He was greeted by a billow of steam reeking of boiled wool. He steeped through the haze and into the dark room.

"Shut the door!" shouted a voice through the mist.

Durrant did as he was told. The room was dense with the pong of filth scrubbed from the camp inhabitants' clothing.

"You need something laundry?" came a voice through the swirling steam. The ceiling was hung with racks of clothes drying in the oppressive heat. Durrant pulled his heavy bison jacket open and with his game hand pulled off his sealskin cap, his hair already damp with sweat.

"No, I came to ask you questions," he said.

A man appeared through the forest of clothing and vapours. "I am Mr. Kim. I do laundry." He was a small man, dressed in a clean grey shirt that had no sleeves and wore a small back watch cap on his head. He was the first man of Chinese descent Durrant had seen since leaving Fort Calgary, where several of Mr. Kim's countrymen served in a similar capacity.

"Mr. Kim, I'm Sergeant Durrant Wallace of the North West Mounted Police."

"I have heard you have come."

"I'm investigating the murder of Deek Penner."

"Mr. Penner was a good man He always leave a good tip."

"Mr. Kim, would it be fair to say that you know most of the men in this camp?"

"Yes, most but not all. Some men never wash. Not once all winter do they wash their clothing," said the man, his face twisting with disgust.

Kim was drying his hand on an apron he wore around his waist. Durrant said, "If I give you the names of some men I am interested in, can you tell me when they were here last?"

"Yes, but Mr. Kim work while you talk. Much work to do . . ." He turned away from the Mountie and found his way back between drying clothing to the central part of the operation. Durrant followed him. The floor of the shack was bare earth and the combination of wool and earth created a pungent odour. Kim stepped between bedsheets and pants and grey work shirts and came to a low cast iron stove that was four feet wide and held a massive boiling cauldron.

"This is Kim Jr.," Mr. Kim said pointing to a boy whose age Durrant could not peg. He could be twelve; he might be Charlie's age. The boy was pulling a coat from the wash with a long stick as opaque water streamed off it. He lifted it out of the boiling vat, dripping water onto the dirt floor, slapped it down on a washboard, and with gloved hands began to scrub it, the excess water running off into a washbasin.

"Mr. Kim, have Frank Dodds or Pete or Ralph Mahoney been in to have any laundry done this week?" Durrant asked, looking at the names on the list Wilcox provided.

Mr. Kim shook his head. "I see Mahoney now and again. But not recent. Frank Dodds, he no come in this week. I tell him no come in. He don't pay? He yell at Kim Jr."

"Why is that?"

"He say we not clean good. He call us names. I tell him to wash own clothes."

Durrant watched the man. "What about Grant McPherson?"

"He work for Mr. Penner. He come in, but not since Mr. Penner die. He come in," the man cocked his head, "two weeks ago. Very dirty clothing. Much dusty. Powder from making dynamite. Very hard to clean."

Durrant nodded. "John Christianson?"

"Yes, he come in often. Very neat, little John. Very tidy."

"When was he last here?"

"Two days ago." Durrant's eyebrow shot up. "Yes, he brought in pants, socks, and waistcoat."

"What about an overcoat."

"No, no overcoat."

"You're sure?"

"Yes, very sure."

"Did you notice anything out of the ordinary about John's wash when he was here last?"

Mr. Kim thought a moment. "Nothing."

"You didn't notice if he had blood on his clothing? He was among the men who handled Mr. Penner's body, is all . . ."

"I sorry, Sergeant, I didn't look close at his clothing. Nothing to notice . . ."

"And Hep Wilcox?"

"Yes, Mr. Wilcox comes in often, but not in the last three days. He don't get dirty like all the other men. You don't get dirty sitting at desk."

Durrant nodded in agreement. "What about Devon Paine?"

"Ah, Mr. Paine."

"He's been in?"

"Yes, smell like horses. Not so bad."

"So he's been in since Mr. Penner was killed."

"He was in to bring laundry yesterday."

"What did he bring in?"

Mr. Kim looked over at his son on the washboard. "That his coat right there!" he said, pointing as the young man scrubbed the heavy riding coat down with his gloved hands.

ONLY DEVON PAINE, who managed the stables and who had been at the card game, had taken a coat to the laundry over the last few days. Durrant aimed to find out who might have a coat with blood on it from the grisly murder. After visiting the laundry, Durrant had collected Charlie to help with the unpleasant task of rummaging through the trash from the camp's four-month stay at the end of steel.

A mound higher than their heads and twenty feet across occupied a clearing in the woods a stone's throw from the Pipestone River, and just south of the mess for the camp.

"It ain't too bad," said Durrant. The boy was using a long stick to dig through the trash. He looked up at the Mountie standing on the periphery of the garbage heap.

"Okay, so from where you're standing maybe it's a little worse." The man and the boy poked through the rubbish. There was a barrel on the edge of the garbage heap and Durrant limped to it, trying not to trip on the irregular ground.

"Come have a look here, lad," he said, one gloved hand resting on the barrel. It was full of ashes. "See if you can't stir up the contents of this here barrel and discover something of use."

Charlie inserted his stick and began to stir. A great plume of ashes rose from the barrel, and Durrant coughed and stepped back. "Blue Jesus, lad . . ."

Charlie continued to stir and then reached in with his bare hand and grabbed something. He held it up. Durrant took it from his hand. It was a blackened buckle from a heavy coat.

IT WAS LATE in the afternoon before he realized how hungry he was. Charlie had long since returned to his bunk, and Durrant had continued searching the trash barrel on his own but found nothing more of the coat. He could not even be certain that it had been a coat, no less one worn by Deek Penner's killer. He would have to search each witness's possessions for a possible garment with blood on it. It was the only way he thought he might find actual physical evidence of the crime.

Durrant made his way from the garbage dump up the icy road and through the tunnels of snow towards the NWMP bunk. When he opened the door to the bunk house, he was greeted by both a blast of warmth and the rich aroma of fresh baking. He stepped in and stood for a moment while his eyes adjusted. Charlie was moving Durant's footlocker to the toe of the Mountie's bed. He stood up when Durrant entered. "What the hell is going on here?"

The boy's pleasant smile faded. He looked around self-consciously. There was a broom near the door. The desk had been adorned with paper and a quill. A bottle of ink sat near the stove where it wouldn't freeze. The beds were neatly made. The oil lamp had been cleaned so its globe was no longer soiled with dark soot. The map that Durrant had borrowed from the stationmaster in Fort Calgary of the CPR's route through the mountains was tacked above the desk.

Durrant stared at the boy, who now simply looked down at his feet. "My God, son, when I said make the quarters passable, I didn't mean for the King himself!" Charlie smiled in relief.

"I need to have a rest before what promises to be a big night. What I have to do, son, is find whatever it was that Deek Penner got his face mashed in with. You saw where they found the body, didn't you? The murder weapon's got to be something big and heavy. Like a sledge or the back of a maul. Christianson says that whoever he seen running from the body that night didn't have anything in his hands. I think maybe the killer saw Christianson coming, and threw the killing tool. It could be out in the snow somewhere. While it's still a little light, have a look around some. If you find anything, leave it and come and fetch me. If anybody bothers you, let me know straight away. I'll handle them."

Charlie was already pulling on his heavy coat. "One more thing, come back and get me up in time for supper, would you? Be careful, son," said Durrant as the boy opened the door. Charlie cast a quick glance back, smiled and was gone.

Durrant sat on the bed awhile, then slowly loosened and slipped off his coat. He checked the pockets and found the sack containing the contents of Penner's pockets. A few currency notes, a set of heavy Yale keys, caps and fuses, and the coded note. Durrant looked at it. The code could be cracked, but he would need a few more examples before he could get to work with it. He would need to question Christianson about further correspondence, and see if he could ascertain the address of the recipient to speed the investigation. Durrant lay back on the bed, pulling some of the neatly folded blankets over him in a haphazard fashion, and fell into a fitful sleep.

IT WAS HALF past eight when Durrant and Wilcox approached the bunk of Frank Dodds. Wilcox carried a lantern. "You know what you're doing?" asked Wilcox as they neared the cabin. In the darkness his tone betrayed both scepticism and a co-conspiratorial notion that the general manager and the Mountie shared the same purpose.

Durrant said nothing and instead knocked on the door. The cabin was of a more solid construction than most in the camp, framed with square timbers with a roof of boards hewn straight and flat; the cabin of a sawyer, of a man who works in the woods, thought Durrant.

"Come!" responded a harsh voice from within, and Durrant pried open the door and stepped inside. Wilcox followed him.

"'Bout goddamned time," barked a large man sitting on the far side of a round table.

Durrant stepped into the room. It was warm and close and he could smell the nervous sweat coming from the six men seated there. The dim cabin bore a fusty odour, as if a rotting burlap sack had been discarded there when the construction season ended and had never been removed. "You're Frank Dodds," said Durrant, moving away from the door so that Wilcox could push it shut behind them.

Dodds didn't rise when the two men entered the room. He didn't offer his hand. He just nodded and said, "I am. And you're the Red Coat here to investigate Deek Penner's murder?"

"I am. My name is Sergeant Durrant Wallace. You may refer to me as Sergeant." Durrant looked around him, imagining these six sitting then, as they were now, but with Penner among them. The card table occupied the centre of the room, with a single bunk pushed against the far wall, and an over-sized stove taking up the corner farthest from the door. The table was crowded with the morose group of men, but there were two empty chairs. Durrant noted Christianson sitting opposite Dodds, his hands folded in front of him, his glasses reflecting the light of the lamp. Durrant stumped to one of the two empty chairs.

"Which one of these was Mr. Penner sitting at?" he asked.

Christianson said helpfully, "He was in this one here."

Durrant leaned his crutch on the table and took off his bison coat. He deftly slipped into the seat, but not before ensuring that every man in the room could see the Enfield pistol strapped to his left side, a belt of cartridges adorning his waist as if he were a law man from south of the Medicine Line.

"If I were a betting man," he said once he was seated, "I'd say that whoever killed Deek Penner is sitting in this room right now."

"Just a goddamned . . ." bawled Dodds.

"Be quiet, Mr. Dodds!" Durrant said evenly but forcefully. Dodds looked as if he had been struck. "You will speak after I ask you a question," Durrant said, "not a goddamned minute before." The men stirred in their seats, and Wilcox, standing near the door, shuffled awkwardly.

"There's always a chance that the killer has left Holt City. He might be frozen in the snow at the Kicking Horse Pass, or along the tracks toward Banff Station. A man in this camp held a grudge against Deek Penner, or owed him money, or Mr. Penner may have known something about some man's business that he shouldn't have, and it got him killed." Durrant rested his left hand on the table, his game right hand on his lap. He slowly looked from one man to the next. "My bet is that one of you men holds the secret to Mr. Penner's untimely demise, and it's my job to find out which one it is. You could save me a lot of time, and yourselves a lot of aggravation, if the killer would simply say so right now."

Durrant looked around the room at the men. Dodds' eyes burned into him, and he held his gaze a moment before he let it drift over the others. Christianson remained with his face downcast. Pete Mahoney had his eyes on Dodds; his older brother Ralph looked at Durrant from beneath a heavy brow. Grant McPherson shifted uncomfortably in his chair. Devon Paine watched the Mountie with expectation.

"I thought not," said Durrant, feigning disappointment.

It was Wilcox who spoke first. "Sergeant Wallace has asked to speak with each of you in turn," he said.

Durrant turned and fixed the man with a stern gaze. "My request extends to you, too, Mr. Wilcox."

He turned back to the table. "The facts of the matter are becoming clear to me already. There is whiskey in this camp. Somebody is making it and distributing it, and come the spring, it stands to disrupt the work of the railway. It may come to pass that Mr. Penner's murder is somehow tied to this. I can't say for certain as yet. But the law is the law, and as a representative of the Dominion Government, I aim to uphold it. Mr. Wilcox has assured me every co-operation, and I expect nothing less of each of you. The fact is, whiskey is being made here. Mr. Wilcox must have his suspicions and has done nothing to act on them, and so is at best negligent in his duties here."

Wilcox drew a deep breath and held it.

"My primary duty will be to discover Mr. Penner's killer, but in the course of that investigation, should I reveal anything about the moonshining going on at Holt City, you can rest assured I will shut it down." He looked around the room again. Dodds glared at Durrant. He could also see that Wilcox bore the expression of a man scorned, and what was worse, in front of a room of his subordinates.

This was exactly where Durrant wanted these men: angry, and off-balance. "Does any man here have anything he wants to say?"

"I take it that's an invitation to speak?" said Dodds in a tone that was low and menacing, like the sound a dog makes when you cross it.

Durrant nodded.

"You come to the wrong place, Sergeant, if you're looking for confessions. Deek Penner must have stuck his nose into somebody's business where it weren't welcome, and it got him killed, but not by anybody sitting in this room."

"How can you be so sure?"

"Deek and I weren't no friends is for sure; maybe I was the only one who was big enough to stand up to him, but I know for a fact I didn't kill him. The rest of these boys ain't got it in 'im. You think little old John there, or that poor boy Paine might have killed a big fellow like Penner? And these boys here," he nodded at the Mahoney brothers, "they work for me."

"And that absolves them?"

"They ain't going to do anything I don't tell them to do."

"This has been very useful commentary, Mr. Dodds. I suppose I shall have to carry out my investigation anyway. I understand there was a card game here the night that Mr. Penner was killed. That correct?" Dodds nodded. "And it was you six, and Mr. Penner playing?" Again, Dodds nodded. "Who was missing from the game?"

"I don't take your meaning." said Dodds.

"Who was missing? There was an empty chair?"

"Nobody was missing."

"Doesn't seem right that a chair should sit unfilled at a game such as the one you hosted."

"Sometimes others will join in. Bob Pen sometimes sits a hand. And my man Griffin will play now and again."

"Mr. Pen I've met. What about this other man?"

"Thompson Griffin," said Frank Dodds. "He's my number two up on the hill. He weren't about that night, must have had other business to attend to."

Durrant made a mental note to track down this man and question him on his whereabouts. "Anything happen that night that might lead one of you to want to kill Mr. Penner?"

"Deek was winning as usual," said Christianson, earning a sharp glance from Dodds.

"He often won?"

"Yes, he was a good player. He'd throw hands to make sure the rest of us didn't get too cross."

"That night, did anybody get cross?"

Christianson looked around the room. His gaze came to rest on Devon Paine, and then Christianson looked down at his hands.

"How'd you get your face all bloodied?" Durrant turned to Paine. Paine looked up. The Mountie held his gaze. "Those bruises and that split lip look to be about three days old to me." Devon looked around the room. Durrant took note that the man wasn't wearing the coat that he had seen in the laundry that afternoon. He had on an old, worn mackinaw that was grey and soiled. "You going to tell me, Mr. Paine?"

"I work with horses," he finally said.

"What of it?"

"I got kicked."

"You crawling across the floor when it happened?"

Christianson snickered, but was silenced by a hard look from Paine. "I was picking ice out from a mare's shoe. She gave me a tap. It's all it takes with those ice shoes the horses wear for the Tote Road."

"When did this occur?"

Paine hesitated; he seemed to be doing a calculation in his head. "Two days now."

"You must have bled a lot," said the Mountie. Paine seemed not to understand the question. "When you got kicked. You must have bled a great deal."

"Some."

"Is that the coat you were wearing when it happened?"

"I can't recall," said Paine, his face perplexed.

Durrant nodded. "So the card game was a peaceful event." The men nodded. "And who left first?"

"I believe it was Deek," said Christianson.

"After that?"

The men were silent.

"It was Paine, weren't it?" asked Dodds.

"Yeah, I believe that's true," said Ralph Mahoney, speaking for the first time.

"Is that right, Mr. Paine?" Durrant asked.

"It must be," he said, looking down.

"But you can't recall?"

"I think that's right."

"Then John, then Grant, I believe," continued Dodds.

"And then Pete and me," said Ralph Mahoney helpfully. His brother nodded.

"Besides Mr. Christianson here, did any of you see Mr. Penner after he left that night?"

The men shook their head.

"And you, Mr. Wilcox?"

"I did not," said the general manager, his arms folded.

Durrant shifted in his chair, easing the pressure on his prosthetic leg. "So none of you had words with Deek Penner that night, and none but John here saw him after he took his leave. Is that correct?" The room was silent. "Well, I don't believe that for a moment." Dodds was about to speak, but Durrant hushed him with a hard look.

"Who else, gentlemen, in this camp might have wanted to see Deek Penner dead?"

"Deek was pretty well liked," acknowledged Christianson quietly.

"That doesn't help your cause Mr. Christianson," said Durrant.

"Blue Jesus, John, would you shut your mouth!" bawled Dodds harshly.

Durrant smiled.

"What about that Grand Trunk man?" asked Dodds.

"That's just a rumour," said Wilcox.

"And what might that rumour be?" questioned Durrant.

Wilcox shrugged. "It's a delicate matter."

Durrant shifted and looked at Wilcox.

"We've suspected a man in the camp has been spying on behalf of the Grand Trunk Railway."

"Deek knew?"

Wilcox looked around the room. "Deek may have found out."

"Do we know this spy's identity?"

"Not as of yet," said Wilcox.

"We shall have to find out," said Durrant. He thought he noted a glimmer of interest in Wilcox's eye. He shifted again and regarded the room full of men watching him.

"Gentlemen, get some rest," he said at long last. "Expect to see me tomorrow." With that, Durrant rose, slipped his bison coat on, and taking his crutch went to the door and vanished out into the frozen night, leaving the rest of the men in silence.

SEVEN

INQUISITION

DURRANT WOKE BELIEVING THAT HE had Frank Dodds exactly where he wanted him: backed into a corner, with nowhere to turn. He lay a moment under the heap of blankets piled high against the cold and went over the confrontation of the night before. Reckless, Sub-Inspector Dewalt would have said; *Diplomacy*, he would recite. Durrant believed that the ragtag complement of men who had been snowbound since December would only respect his authority as the law if he was uncompromising in the execution of it.

"You there, Charlie?" Durrant spoke into the pre-dawn morning. He didn't expect an answer but also heard no sound from the small room. He pushed the blankets off and realized that he was in fact sweating beneath the heavy mound of wool. Durrant affixed his prosthetic and dressed and was about to step to the door when there was a knock. Puzzled, he put one hand on the hilt of his pistol and said, "Come in ..."

Charlie pushed the door open, a dented tin coffee pot in his hand. Durrant smiled at his modesty and relaxed his grip on the Enfield. The boy entered and poured the Sergeant a cup of thick black coffee and then one for himself. Durrant took the mug in his hand and held it appreciatively, absorbing the warmth. He took a sip. "It's warmer out today, ain't it?" asked Durrant.

The boy nodded, and took the writing tablet from the desk and scribbled something on it. Charlie turned it around for Durrant to see. "Cloudy. Maybe chinook on its way," he read. "I see. Well, that would explain it. We're only a few days from the spring equinox," Durrant added, holding the coffee close to his lips. "It's got to warm up in this God-forsaken country sooner or later." Durrant finished his coffee and put the cup down on the desk.

"I'm going to be questioning those men all day today, Charlie.

While I'm at that, I need you to continue your search for the murder weapon. Can you do that, son?"

Charlie smiled and nodded. "Don't catch a cold in the snow, mind you," said Durrant as he pried open the door, and then felt foolish for playing father to the lad.

THE MORNING WAS, in fact, much warmer. Before leaving the cabin Durrant opened his footlocker and found his greatcoat and cape. Exchanging it for the bison robe coat, he rearranged his arsenal and then closed the door behind him. The Mountie made his way to the mess hall along the pathways through the snow, and when he arrived found that breakfast was all but over. He went to the kitchen and was given a plate of eggs, bacon, and biscuits. He found more coffee on the stove and sat down to eat a hasty meal before undertaking the day's inquisition.

Where to start, he wondered? He'd make Dodds wait. He'd catch him off guard at the end of the day. There was a lot to be gained by learning as much as he could *about* Dodds, about his relationship with Penner. Durrant finished and made his way to the stables, drawn by the sound of horses and the ring of the nearby blacksmith plying his trade. Outside, in the yard next to the stables, a few men were fitting a harness onto a team of horses. The doors were open and Durrant stepped to the verge.

"Mr. Paine?" he called into the dim room. These stables, like those in Fort Calgary, were new and still bore the sweet scent of freshly milled pine boards. There were ten stalls along each of the north and south walls of the barn, each separated by a heavy fir joist set deeply in a rough milled post, some of which still had bark clinging to them. Durrant could smell the horses and hear their whinnies as he moved from the flat light of the day into the darkened recess of the barn.

"Paine, you there?" As he called, several of the horses in the barn stamped their feet.

"I'm here. I'm in the tack room. Be right there," called a voice from within the stables. "Come on back, door's open . . ."

Durrant stepped over the threshold and into the barn. Its floor-boards were tracked with snow but were otherwise clean and bare. "Mr. Paine, its Sergeant Wallace. I'd like a word, sir."

From the end of the row of stalls, Paine stuck his head out from the tack room. "Sergeant, please come in. I'm just wrestling with some lead ropes here, and will be free in a moment."

Durrant walked down the centre row of the stables and looked into the tack room. Paine was an average-sized man with a thick crop of black hair and a cleanly shaven face. Durrant noticed that he now wore the heavy canvas coat that he had seen at the laundry the day before. His jeans were tucked into heavy winter riding boots. His eyes were still black and his lip still festering; his nose was set at an awkward angle to his face, and was bruised and had crusted red. As he struggled with the rope, he raised a handkerchief now and again to his nose to dab at a persistent trickle of blood.

Durrant leaned on the door, his face in shadow, his sealskin hat pulled down over his ears. "You're American, Mr. Paine?" He picked up a rope and began to untangle it.

"Born and bred."

"Texas?"

"That's right. Galveston. I ain't been there in near twenty years now. I cut my teeth in the New Mexico Territory, working with a stage company out of Santa Fe."

"You took care of their horses there?"

"Not at first. I rode shotgun for them when I was young and foolish, then drove a stage, and after a couple of years of that took up in the stables. I'm better with horses than I am with people."

"I know that feeling," said Durrant.

"Anyway, that took me north to Montana. I got on with the I.G. Baker Company and that's how I come up to the Dominion Territories," said Paine, sorting out another lead rope and hanging it on a peg on the wall. "I signed on with the CPR when they come across the Saskatchewan River down at Medicine Hat."

"Frank Dodds an American?"

"Half the men working in this camp are." Durrant nodded. "Until the railway, the best way to come up into this country was to take a steamer through the Missouri Country to Fort Benton, then just turn north like. That was the main route for commerce: north south. It's how our man Rogers come up with his crew two years back. It's a hell of a long haul from Fort Calgary to Winnipeg. The I.G. Baker Company still pretty much outfits this whole operation out of Fort Benton, though that's starting to change."

Paine looked up at the Mountie standing in his door way. "Seems pretty clear you don't like Dodds, do you Sergeant Wallace?"

"Ain't much to like, is there? He's a brash man with a short temper, and if I'm not mistaken, he's likely making illegal whiskey inside the Temperance Zone."

Paine started in on another rope. "Won't argue with you about the man's disposition."

"Is Frank Dodds making moonshine?"

"I don't know."

"You don't know or you won't say."

"Sergeant, there's whiskey at Holt City. Hell, there's whiskey anywhere this train has stopped for more than fifteen minutes. Some fellas I know had a still set up in a boxcar on the train last summer. I don't see what the big deal is."

"You drink, Paine."

"I take a drink. But I don't drink that moonshine. That will make a man crazy."

"But you ain't goin' to rat out Frank Dodds . . ."

"What good would that do?"

"Might get me closer to the killer of Deek Penner."

"You think Dodds killed Penner?"

"He could have."

"Lots of people *could* have, Sergeant. Why would Dodds?"

"From what folks are telling me, Penner was a good man. Honest, hard working, a company man. Believed what the CPR is trying to do. He didn't want to see it fall apart because of men getting drunk. Didn't want to see hard-working men like you get blown up with nitro while they were stumbling down a ladder half crazy after a night of binging. I think maybe Penner was onto Dodds' operation, and when Dodds found out, he cracked the man's skull."

Paine continued on with this work. "Maybe," he said nodding. "It's a possibility. Penner was known to have his nose into a lot of business in this camp besides his own."

"How well did you know Penner?"

"Pretty well."

"You think his killer shouldn't be brought to justice?"

"I didn't say that. I just don't have nothing for you on Mr. Dodds."

"What are you afraid of?"

"Who says I'm afraid?"

"You're whole body is saying it, Mr. Paine. People, we're a lot like horses. We get afraid, and it's pretty obvious. We perspire, our eyes shift about, and our hands start to fumble with our work. We tense up. You're scared of Frank Dodds. That much is clear."

"He's my boss, in a manner of speaking. This is a good job. Money's good."

"Dodds ever threaten you?" Paine's brow furrowed and he concentrated on his work. "Mr. Paine?"

"Look, anybody who works for Dodds or around Dodds knows he's got a temper. Ain't a man in this camp except maybe Tom Holt or Hep Wilcox who ain't been threatened by Frank Dodds."

"You still going to maintain that fool story that one of these horses kicked you?" Durrant looked around the tack room. Paine focused on his work. "How'd you get the blood on your coat?"

Paine continued at his knots. "Who says I did?"

"You had it laundered."

"Some law against cleanliness? Bible says it's next to godliness."

Durrant smiled. "Around here it seems next to impossible." Paine smiled too and looked up at the man. Durrant spoke again. "Whose blood was on your coat?"

"It was my own. Got myself tapped by that mare picking ice out of her shoe. I told you."

"You're lying."

"What makes you so certain?"

Durrant regarded the man. "You can't look me in the eye and say it. Oh, now that I point it out you will. Most can, once it's been pointed out to them. But in conversation, you'll look anywhere else. Like down at your hands, as you're doing just now." Paine hung up another lead rope.

"Did Dodds threaten you recently?" Durrant asked. Paine shook his head. He started in on the last rope, working his way through a Gordian knot the size of his fist.

Durrant was no longer looking at the ropes in his own hands. He drew a sharp breath and took a step forward. Paine looked up, startled. "Mr. Paine, a man is dead, and on the night he died, you and those other men were in a cabin with him playing cards. It's a fair bet that you all were the last to see him alive. That makes you all witnesses. It makes at least one of you a prime suspect. *You* recently had your coat laundered, and if I'm not mistaken, it was because there was a mess of blood on it. If it was Deek Penner's blood, then you get to be at the top of my queue. Am I making myself clear?"

Paine looked Durrant in the eye. Paine *was* afraid, but not of him. Paine took a step back from Durrant.

"He threatened me the other night. That night that Deek died." For the first time Paine looked straight at Durrant as he spoke. Durrant reached out with his left hand and grabbed the man by the face.

"Let's have a good look at you," Durrant said hoarsely and pulled the man into the light. "He do this to you?"

"It ain't nothing. I got between a horse and its stall. I told you. My own damned fault."

Durrant held the cowboy's face in his powerful left hand. "That knocked two teeth out?"

"Yeah, I got my face hit pretty good." Paine shook his face and Durrant let go.

"What'd he threaten you about? What did Dodds say?"

"It was just cards."

"When did your horse do this?"

"Next morning."

"Bust up your nose too?"

"Yes, sir. Bled all over myself. A real mess. *Had* to have the coat washed up. Not decent to go around a bloody mess. It ain't right. Now listen, if you don't mind, I need to get back to the tack . . ."

"You listen to me, Paine," said Durrant, his voice a low rumble. "I like you. You seem to like horses, and that makes you a good man in my book. I also think you're lying. If I find out you're covering for Frank Dodds, or are in anyway involved in the death of Deek Penner, what I'm going to do to you will make *this* look like a Sunday picnic. You understand?" Paine nodded and fumbled with the ropes.

IT WAS NEARLY eleven when Durrant left the barn and found his way though the soft snow towards the main station. The chinook wind would raise the temperature another ten degrees by mid-day. Durrant had faced the gale winds of the chinook a dozen times since being posted to Fort Calgary a year before; each time he had noticed that along with the rising temperatures, tempers had flared. The chinook wind made men ill at ease, made their blood boil. Durrant expected to use it to his advantage.

Durrant carefully picked his way along the Tote Road to the munitions warehouse, where he hoped to find Grant McPherson. The large double doors to the warehouse were ajar, but Durrant noticed that they also held a sturdy Yale bolt and a gleaming new cast heart padlock. There were many such locks throughout the camp; the railway used them for securing switches and flatbed cars. Out of inquisitiveness, Durrant dug the set of keys he had taken from Penner's bunk and looked for the match to the heart-shaped lock. He found one stamped with the same brand and tried to insert the key into the lock. It didn't fit. He then tried the remaining half dozen keys, but to his consternation, none would slide into the lock.

He straightened himself. Why would Penner not have a key to his own warehouse? He resolved to find out who *did* have a key. Leaning carefully on his crutch, Durrant swung one of the heavy doors open and the pale morning light fell across the dirt floor of the depot. The room wasn't as dark as he thought it might be, and he noticed that high up on the walls there were wide openings in the boards over which heavy metal wire was tacked. Given the nature of the contents of this building, Durrant understood at once that relying on natural illumination and not kerosene lamps was prudent. There were several men at work in the warehouse, and they looked up and blinked at the backlit Mountie as he entered.

"I'm looking for Grant McPherson," Durrant said to the nearest man. He was cradling a paper-wrapped cylindrical tube the size of a loaf of bread, and Durrant guessed that its contents were best not disturbed.

"He's back yonder," the man said, returning to his task.

He could hear voices from the far end of the warehouse. The building was lined on both walls with large crates and Durrant could clearly discern the warning sign on each: "Caution, explosives."

"Mr. McPherson, it's Sergeant Wallace."

"I'm here," called McPherson, and at the same moment Durrant saw him and two other men gingerly carrying a crate from one side of the room to the other. "Okay, now," said McPherson to the men. "Just there on the floor next to the wall ... That's it." The men carefully lowered the crate to the floor. They stood up straight when it was in place and McPherson said a few words to the men that Durrant could not hear.

"Come on back, Sergeant," he said, as the two men walked toward the door where Durrant stood and brushed past him.

"I suppose you're here to talk about Deek," said McPherson, walking the length of the warehouse, passing in and out of the shadows. He wiped his hands on a worn rag. Durrant noticed that he wasn't wearing an overcoat. When he stopped in front of Durrant, he extended his hand, which Durrant grasped with his left and shook firmly.

"Well, here's as good a place to talk as any," McPherson said. "This *was* Deek's life." He motioned to the stacks of crates all around.

"Is this all nitroglycerine?" Durrant asked.

"Most of it's just the raw ingredients. Some of it's the finished product. We have a few crates of dynamite, but for the most part, we'll be making pure nitro."

For the first time since arriving at Holt City, Durrant felt uncomfortable. "It's pretty unstable stuff," he said, trying to mask his unease.

"You bet, Sergeant," said McPherson, sitting down on a crate. He motioned to a second crate for Durrant to sit. He grinned when he noticed the look on Durrant's face. "Its okay, Sergeant, these ones are just raw silica. We'll be using that to make a little dynamite."

"Why not make dynamite sticks instead of using liquid nitro?" asked Durrant as he sat down and surveyed the room.

"Cost. Dynamite is very expensive, and as you can see, we need a great deal of the stuff. A decision was made to use liquid nitro for most of the work."

Durrant looked at McPherson. "Back up for a moment, please, Mr. McPherson. How does this all work?"

"Nitro?"

"Yes, that, and a decision such as the one to use liquid explosives rather than dynamite."

"Deek was the expert on that. I can tell you how the blasting works, but as for all the decisions, that was Deek and Mr. Wilcox and those above them."

"You were his number two. You must have picked up some insight."

"I just signed on again a month ago. Before that I was up in the woods working for Mr. Dodds. Sure, I heard some things in that time, but not as much as you might expect." McPherson cleaned his hands again on the rag that hung from his pants pocket. Durrant watched him.

"As for how the nitroglycerine works, it's really pretty simple. It's actually a pretty straight forward chemical. As you might know, Mr. Alfred Nobel discovered that if you add a nitrate to glycerol, you can blow things up with it," he laughed.

"Of course, Mr. Nobel discovered the hard way that it's pretty touchy. His own brother blew himself up figuring it out. The liquid looks like thick water; no smell. It's heavy and it's oily," he said, his hands clutching the rag, "and if you drop a bucket of it, they'll be picking up pieces of you for a hundred yards. If what we're trying to do is blast a tunnel through some rock, a crew will work at the site with a star drill and hammers, making a hole big enough that a pail of the explosives could be lowered into it. It's then detonated using a long cable fuse and a blasting cap. It's the most dangerous job on this railway. I know that Wilcox and other contractors have to sometimes bribe the men to take on that task. It's amazing what a few extra pennies will do for a man's motivation."

"How many men have been lost?"

"I don't know that anybody is keeping count."

"It's a fair number?"

"Yes sir. The section of track through the lakehead region above Lake Superior required a great deal of blasting. I wasn't working on that section, but to hear Deek put it, there's a body buried for every mile of track. And that section was easy compared to what we face this spring."

"What about the Chinese?"

"Andrew Onderdonk is the man to talk to about that. He's in charge of the rail coming out of Port Moody. He's making good use of them on his contract. I think there must have been several thousand of them working on the line up the Fraser Canyon from the Port of Vancouver. All we got here are the Irish, Polish, Slovaks, and Italians to do the job."

Durrant was quiet a moment. He flexed his game right hand. "And so you're putting up stores here for use on the mainline down the Kicking Horse?"

"That's right. We're massing the materials here, but soon we'll start shipping stuff on up to the Kicking Horse Pass. It's going to be brewed up once we get the plant in place on the height of land itself. The closer to the operation we can make the stuff, the safer it'll be for everyone. Deek was going to manage the contract to do the blasting down the Kicking Horse Pass; it's what we're all calling the Big Hill. It's a hell of a drop, and to do it we've got to bore right into the side of the mountains in places. Before we can even do that, we need to build the Tote Road along the same course. That's what most of this lot is for, the Tote Road." McPherson motioned to the nitro.

He took a deep breath. "The first tunnel will be about seven miles in, but before that, it's a ramp carved into the side of the mountain all the way down, for miles and miles. This, Sergeant Wallace, is just the first month's worth of explosives.

"I overheard Hep talking with Deek and saying that there was some discussion about which company might supply the remainder of the nitro. And once we get down the Big Hill, we still have to push on down the Lower Canyon of the Kicking Horse, which as I understand is worse still. That's where all the tunnels will be."

"What makes a man want to do this work?" asked Durrant.

McPherson looked thoughtful a moment. "It pays pretty good," he said. "Working with this stuff comes with a premium in pay."

"Not much good if you're scattered to Kingdom Come."

"You ever met a man who was aiming to get himself blown up, Sergeant?"

Durrant shook his head. "What about qualifications?"

McPherson smiled, shook his head, and looked around. "Well, that fella there used some dynamite to blow up a beaver dam on his daddy's place back in Wisconsin a few years back. I think that makes him the most qualified of the lot."

"What about *you*, Mr. McPherson?"

"I come by this honestly. Before the CPR hired me I was working for the Canada Explosives Company. They currently have the contract for the explosives. I was packing this stuff for them out of their Montreal operation."

"Is that where you're from?"

"Do I sound French? No, I'm from Nova Scotia. Cape Breton to be precise, sir. It's been some time. I've mostly had factory jobs in Toronto; did a spell in Buffalo. I was riding along with the last shipments of the year up through the mountains last fall. Deek's number two man had enough, and so I stayed on for the winter. Like I said, I mostly worked for Dodds, but Deek promised me good work come the spring. Now I guess I'll be on for the summer season too."

"How much money is in this room right now, Mr. McPherson?"

McPherson rubbed his hands on his rag and looked around as if totalling up the inventory. "I'd say one hundred thousand dollars' worth."

Durrant stared at the man. "Yes, that's about right," McPherson said nervously.

"You said the Canada Explosives Company currently holds the contract?"

"That's right. They're headquartered in Mount Saint-Hilaire, but they've got operations all over the place."

"You said *current* supplier?"

"There's a lot of competition."

"Is the contract set?"

"I believe for the Big Hill. I don't know about the Lower Canyon."

"Who would know?"

"Deek would have, and the men he worked for, but they are all in Winnipeg. Hep somehow got himself in on that business too, so he likely would be able to say."

"I can have someone speak with them there. The NWMP have a sizeable detachment in that city."

Durrant switched tracks. "Deek Penner was pretty well liked, wasn't he?"

"He was a fair man to work for. Never raised his voice or his hand to a man, despite being one of the biggest fellas in the camp. I'd say he was well liked."

"Did you like him?"

"We were friends. He was my boss, but we was friends, yes."

"His was a plum job, wasn't it?"

"I don't take your meaning."

"His was a good job, well paid."

"We never spoke of it."

"Next to Mr. Wilcox, and maybe Mr. Holt, I'd guess that Mr. Penner was the best paid man in the camp, wouldn't you?"

"I don't rightly know."

"With Mr. Penner dead, who will run the blasting operation down the Big Hill come the spring?"

"I don't know. I suppose the contractor will have to hire a foreman to replace Deek."

"But with less than two months to go before the spring work is to start, and with the logistical preparations already underway, it doesn't leave much time."

"We've just begun to haul material over the sled road up to the Kicking Horse Summit. I understand construction on the munitions plant there will get underway as soon as Bob Pen allocates some labour. The lumber is already cut for the job."

"The Canadian Pacific men and Parliament are putting a great deal of pressure on this operation to complete the railway, and soon."

"I don't know about the politics of things, Sergeant."

"Mr. McPherson, I *think* you *do*. I think you know enough. Enough to know that with Deek Penner dead, the company men will need to fill his position fast, and with someone who knows the operation; someone who can get the job done without an interruption in the construction schedule. One more question," said Durrant. McPherson seemed worn thin. "Where is your coat?"

"Come again, sir?"

"Your coat? Where is it?"

McPherson looked down as if he'd never seen the garment before. "It's back yonder . . ."

"Let's go and fetch it, shall we?"

"What's this got to do with . . ."

Durrant pushed himself to standing. "I get to decide, Mr. McPherson, what's relevant here."

"Fine," McPherson said, standing up. They walked to the back of the warehouse.

"You don't have another one?" McPherson shook his head no. "Have you had this one to the laundry in the last four days?"

Again he looked at it. "No, why?"

Durrant took the coat from him and looked it over carefully. He could find no sign of blood on the coat. He held it to his nose. It smelled *fresh*. "Mr. McPherson, I believe that excepting Frank Dodds, you are the man in Holt City who stands to gain the most with Deek Penner out of the way."

EIGHT

AT WORK IN THE WOODS

DURRANT TOOK HIS NOON MEAL in the mess tent, where it wasn't difficult to find a place to sit with a good deal of elbow room. Word had spread through the camp that the one-legged Mountie was on the warpath, and men were giving him a wider berth than they had just the day before. Nobody, it seemed, wanted to be seen talking with the Red Coat for fear that word would get back to Dodds, or so he imagined.

Durrant ate hash, canned peaches, and hard biscuits. A mangy dog made its way up and down the rows of tables begging for scraps, and Durrant gave it one of his biscuits, which the mutt chewed on for a full five minutes, breaking it into manageable nuggets that he could then swallow. Durrant patted the cur's bony head before it skulked off to the next table. Durrant noticed two men at the next table watching him as he scratched the mutt behind its frostbitten ears. One of the men touched his cap when he stood and nodded at Durrant. He nodded back.

It was early afternoon when Durrant slowly made his way from the small camp that was huddled at the confluence of the Bow and the Pipestone Rivers. The crews were cutting timber on the low flank of a summit capped with a white horn that the navvies called Dodds Peak. Though the distance was just over a mile, the going was slow for the one-legged man. The road that wound through the lodgepole pines up the grade to where the cutting was taking place was well established through heavy use and daily icing. Despite the hard-packed road, Durrant found the walk to the timber operation to be considerable work. He was twenty minutes into his climb when he heard a noise behind him, and putting his hand on the worn grip of his British Bulldog nestled in his coat pocket, turned to see a team of horses pulling a sled used for hauling cordwood slowly approaching from the camp. When the driver saw him he called to his team to stop and the sled came to rest alongside Durrant.

"Ah, it's you, Sergeant," the teamster said by way of greeting.

"It is," replied Durrant curtly.

"Where are you heading?"

"Just out for a walk," Durrant said, his voice clipped.

"You making your way up to the cutting site?"

"I was thinking I might stop in."

The man driving the team looked up the road towards the logging operation. Durrant could read his weathered face, half hidden by a long, grey tattered scarf that bunched up beneath the man's red nose. He's wondering what kind of hell he'll catch from Dodds if he offers me a ride, thought Durrant. The man studied the dark pine forest on either side of the road, calculating.

"Don't suppose you'd care for a lift, would you?"

"You going to get yacked if you give one?"

"Maybe I'll drop you just this side of the site . . ."

Durrant grinned. "Fine then," he said, stepping forward on the road and grabbed the rail of the buck board and hauled his bulk up onto the seat. The two men rode the remainder of the way to the logging operation in silence. True to his word, when the operation came into view, the teamster slowed the horses.

"Hope you don't mind . . ." He said apologetically.

"Don't want there to be any unnecessary trouble," Durrant grinned, easing himself down from the seat, extending his crutch for balance.

The driver seemed to smile beneath his threadbare scarf, for Durrant saw the lines at the corners of the man's eyes tighten. "Little late for that, wouldn't you say, Sergeant?"

Durrant laughed and shook his head, "Well, yes, a little late . . ."

The man said a word to the horses and the team started down the road again, leaving Durrant standing in the sweet-smelling pine forest. Though the trees around him were yet standing, their boughs made heavy with pillows of snow, he could see not far off where the woods had been felled, and the clearings running up the steep slopes of Dodds Peak. The syrupy fragrance of the pines was tempered with the not unpleasant odour of wood smoke from fires built to burn slash and limbs too small to be used as fuel or cross-ties.

Across the clearing Durrant could see that the mill was a simple steam-powered operation that was designed for speed and efficiency at cutting the squared-off timbers for the cross-ties. A group of men used pike poles to angle logs onto the skid of the mill and someone hitched a heavy hook onto the trunk of the timber, which then was set in motion by the mill operator. The outcome of the day's work was laid out next to the mill: hundreds of sleepers neatly stacked along side the steaming building waiting to be transported back down to the staging area next to the railway along the Bow.

Durrant started across the clearing and soon honed in on a place adjacent to the mill where a large fire burned. The smoke from this fire rose up thirty feet and then seemed to flatten out as if it had hit some invisible ceiling that forced it to dissipate like water flowing across a flat rock. He could see a dozen or more men huddled there, warming their hands, smoking pipes or hand rolled tobacco, and drinking from tin cups. When Durrant stepped into the circle of men standing around the fire, their hands stuffed deep into pockets of worn overcoats, the conversation stopped as if a snake had slid amongst a knot of frogs. One man threw the contents of his cup into the fire.

"Good afternoon," Durrant said, making his way carefully around the fire to a place out of the drifting smoke. He could see that none of those he sought was among them.

"Frank Dodds ain't here," said one man.

"Ain't looking for Frank right now," Durrant said. "I'm looking for the Mahoney boys."

The men mumbled among themselves.

"What do you want with them?" asked the same man.

"It's none of your damned business," said Durrant.

The color drained out of the man's face. "Well, I'm the section hand here . . . name's Jameson. I look out for the operation when

Frank or his number two ain't around. Those men are working for me this afternoon."

"Well Mr. Jameson, my name is Sergeant Durrant Wallace of the North West Mounted Police. I'm here investigating a murder, and I can talk to anybody I bloody well please, so if you'd be so good as to point me to where the Mahoney boys is working, I'll be on my way."

"They are working towards the Pipestone," said Jameson, "about five hundred yards that way," he pointed.

"Very well," said Durrant. He turned to set off.

"Sergeant . . ." Durrant turned. "It's rough-going in there . . ." Durrant levelled his gaze at him. "It's just that they are cutting by hand and there haven't been many sleds in and out. It's pretty tough going, well, even for a man with both his legs. The snow's up over your head, you see . . ."

Durrant could feel the heat seeping up his neck like acid. He drew a long slow breath of the cool afternoon air. The men around the fire were silent.

"No disrespect," said Jameson. "Maybe it would be best if I went and collected the boys for you."

Durrant let his breath out between clenched teeth. He knew that he needed to catch the Mahoney brothers off guard in order to question them to the greatest effect, but if he ended up chest deep in the snow and unable to move, he would loose all authority with his witnesses, and with the whole camp for that matter. He calculated the risk.

"Go and fetch those two boys, sir," he finally said, "while I take advantage of the hospitality of this here fire."

By the time Jameson returned, flanked by the Mahoney brothers, Durrant was alone. One by one the loggers and millers had taken their leave of the fire, tossing their coffee and other elixirs into the flames and muttering about getting back to work.

"Sergeant Wallace?" said Jameson, stepped forward.

"Thank you, Mr. Jameson. Would you tell me, please, where I might find Mr. Thompson Griffin today?"

"He'll likely be down at the yard along the tracks right now."

"Very well, Mr. Jameson, that will be all for now."

Jameson looked at the brothers and then turned and retreated into the woods.

"Ralph, would you please wait for me to be finished with your brother over by the sled road," Durrant said without standing.

Ralph looked at his brother Pete, and then with a sideways glace at the Mountie walked a hundred yards distant and sat down on a log waiting to be skidded into the camp. He watched them with interest.

"Not sure what more I can tell you," said Pete Mahoney. "I said all I know the other night."

"You didn't say much of anything," said Durrant.

The man looked into the flames. "Well, I guess all that needed to be said was said . . ."

"By your boss Dodds. You and I both know that's not the truth," said Durrant. Pete looked down at his gnarled hands. "How old are you, Pete?" asked Durrant.

"I'm going to be twenty come June," the man said.

Durrant nodded. He could see that Pete's hands were large and dark from hard work with hammer and saw and likely from a childhood of tough labour. "Your boss isn't here, is he? Where is he?" asked Durrant.

"He's a foreman. He ain't got to tell us where he's at." Durrant looked at the man for a long moment, letting the silence of the woods settle in. "His business takes him all over the slopes of this here mountain cruising timber and laying out plots for us to fell."

"So that's where he's at today?"

"I reckon so."

"Not at his still?"

"I don't know what you're talking about."

"I think you do, Pete."

"I don't. Believe me or don't, but that's the God's honest truth." Mahoney looked down at his hands again. He could see his brother watching him from the corner of his eye.

"You're the younger of the two of you," said Durrant, catching the boy by surprise.

"Yeah, Ralph yonder is three years my senior."

"He look after you?"

"I don't need no looking after."

"I suppose not. But I imagine he sees it different."

"You'd have to ask him."

"I intend to. My point is this, Pete: A man is dead. You and your brother and a handful of others were the last to see him alive. My guess right now is that something happened at that card game that got your boss pretty riled. My guess is that Penner came down on your boss about whiskey. It's just a hunch, but you and I both know that it's only a matter of time before I find out about Dodds' moonshining operation and find evidence that Penner was going to turn him in for making illegal whiskey. Your boss has already told me that you boys work for him and wouldn't do anything without being told to. Now I wonder if that night after the card game broke up, Dodds didn't tell one or the other of you to go and find Penner and bash his skull in."

Pete Mahoney looked up as if he'd been slapped. "We didn't do that!" he shouted.

"You telling me that the card game was all nicey-nicey and that Frank Dodds and Deek Penner didn't have words?"

"Frank and Deek was always at it. Nothing went on that would have led any man to want to kill ol' Deek."

"That's not the way I hear it."

"Well, whoever is telling lies should stop it."

"I hear things got out of hand."

"Well, it didn't."

"You telling me that I've been lied to?"

"Mister, I'm telling you that sure, Deek and Frank got under each other's skin. Hell, we've been shut up here in this frozen hell for four months now. People is getting a little testy. It wasn't nothing out of the ordinary."

"Something happened."

"Nothing happened," said Pete emphatically.

"You're a liar," said Durrant, looking the big man right in the eye. Pete Mahoney's face was still soft; he had tried to grow a beard throughout the winter, but instead he had patches of downy black hair along his jawline and on his chin. Despite the man's childish appearance, Durrant was aware he was dealing with a powerful man, thick in the arms and through the chest. He could see the man's eyes start to darken when he called him a liar.

The corners of Mahoney's mouth pulled back and his eyes widened when he spoke. "You know who is a liar is that snivelling bastard Devon Paine. That's who the liar is. He couldn't keep his goddamned mouth shut about things he's got no right talking about. He got what was coming to him."

Durrant sat silently. The smoke from the fire swirled around his head and drifted through the snow covered pines. After a moment he said quietly, "I never said it was Mr. Paine who told me that something transpired that night, Pete."

The man returned his gaze to his hands. "I got nothing more to say to you."

"I don't suppose you do." Durrant sat a moment looking into the fire. "Where are you from, Mr. Mahoney?"

The man spat on the ground. "My folks got a place just south of Brandon. That's where I was raised," Pete Mahoney said, his voice shaking.

"A farm?"

"Of sorts."

"Not much of a going concern?"

"It's hard country."

"What did you sign on to do for the CPR?"

"We were laying ties."

"That's heavy work." Again, the man nodded. "Why didn't you go home in December? You could have ridden a freight the whole way."

Mahoney shrugged. "Better money working here than freezing through a Manitoba winter."

"Freeze here, freeze there."

Mahoney looked at him. "What are you getting at?"

"Just wondering, is all, why a couple of Manitoba farm boys would want to stay in a camp such as this rather than go home and help with the home place. I think Frank Dodds made you an offer."

"To cut timber. Of course," said Mahoney.

"No, more than that. More than that. I think you signed on to help with his whiskey operation."

Mahoney started to stand up. "I don't . . ."

Durrant put his left hand on the man's leg, and with more strength than the younger man would give him credit for, pushed him back down. Mahoney looked at the Mountie askance. "You can go when I say so, Mr. Mahoney." In his peripheral vision Durrant could see Ralph Mahoney tense. "I think you stayed on in Holt City to make whiskey for Frank Dodds instead of going home to help your mam and your pap with the pigs and cows. Isn't that right?"

Pete just glared at the man.

"And now things have gotten out of hand, which is why your brother over there is wondering just what you're telling me in this long chat we're having here by the fire. I think things got out of hand and your boss Frank Dodds either killed that man Deek Penner or had you boys do it, and now you know that you ain't going back to your family place ever again."

"I got nothing more to say to you."

Durrant took up his crutch in his right hand and pushed himself up from the log on which he was seated. He looked down at Pete Mahoney. "Son," he said so quietly that Mahoney had to look up at him. "In time you're going to see that telling me is a whole lot easier than not telling me what you know. We're stuck here together and I'm not leaving Holt City until I have someone in shackles for the death of Mr. Penner. Am I understood?"

Pete let his gaze slide from the Mountie to his brother who was now standing on the sled road a hundred yards away.

"I'm going to go and talk with your brother now; see if he has any more sense than you do."

Durrant turned to walk away. He took two careful steps, using his crutch to feel along the snow for soft spots that would trip him up and leave him in a heap on the ground when he heard Pete Mahoney clear his throat. "Mr. Wallace."

Durrant turned. "It's Sergeant Wallace."

"Sergeant, this isn't Fort Calgary. Or Fort Garry. This is Holt City. You're alone here. I don't know who killed Deek Penner, but whoever did won't want to get caught, is all I'm saying. There's a lot more going on here than you think. A little whiskey is just the half of it."

Durrant looked at the man a long moment and then turned and walked toward his brother.

NINE

TURNING THE SCREW

DURRANT WAS A MAN STEEPED in the legends of the North West Mounted Police. The Mounties had a reputation that they always got their man and they did it without having to resort to violence. Their motto was "maintain the right" which often translated to "keep the peace."

While most of the work that the NWMP did was accomplished peacefully, the myth was overstated by the Toronto media. Newspaper accounts of Mounties riding into distilling operations, being surrounded by rifle-totting moonshiners, and talking their way to an arrest often left out the seminal point: that the Mounties themselves had fashioned a reputation of sorts for the swift and effective use of force. While diplomacy was their carrot, the Enfield Mk II and Winchester repeating rifle were their sticks.

Durrant stood a moment on the road considering Ralph Mahoney.

"You been standing there watching me awhile . . ." Ralph said when Durrant stepped up to him. His voice was deeper than his younger brother's, his tone more self-assured. He drew on the cigarette after he spoke, the frail, dry paper crumbling a little between his fingers.

"I'm just trying to figure out which one of the two of you is more stupid," said Durrant.

"You got a big mouth, Mister . . ."

Durrant slapped the man across the face. Ralph Mahoney made as if to step into Durrant. Durrant grabbed him by the coat and pulled him towards him and looked the man in the eye. "You know the British Bulldog, Mr. Mahoney?"

Mahoney blinked. "I do. Snub-nosed little gun . . ."

"That's right. Same folks as make the Enfield that us Red Coats wear. I pack one in my coat pocket at all times. I lost my leg in a gunfight up on the Cypress Hills when I got caught reloading and it almost cost me my life. I don't aim for that ever to happen again."

Mahoney's face changed. "I was just . . ."

"I load mine with .442 Webley rounds. They're easier to come by out here, being made by the same folks that load the Enfield."

Mahoney broke Durrant's iron gaze. "I didn't mean no dis . . ."

Durrant interrupted him again. "My British Bulldog's aimed at your guts right now, Mr. Mahoney, and I'm not so steady on my feet. If I were to slip on this here road, I'd blow a hole in you big enough for a man to put his arm through." The two men stood in the fading light. So much for diplomacy, thought Durrant.

"Now, shall we answer a few questions instead of acting like a horse's ass?" Ralph Mahoney just nodded. Durrant let go of the man and stepped back from him. "I just got through with your little brother. He lied to me, Mr. Mahoney, and I don't like to be lied to, so I'm hoping it ain't a family trait."

"Pete must just be nervous; he ain't no liar."

Durrant, his voice icy, said, "He told me that during the card game on the night that Deek Penner was killed there was no toss-up between your boss and Deek, or with Devon Paine."

"It's been a long winter, Mister. Men get on each other's nerves."

"Men sometimes kill one another when they get on each other's nerves, Mr. Mahoney."

Ralph crushed out his cigarette with his fingers, the embers dying on his callused finger tips.

"So you admit that there was a row?"

"Tempers flared over a hand of cards is all. There was nothing to it."

"Sometime after the game ended, Deek Penner had his head crushed. The six of you were the last to see him alive, except maybe the killer himself."

"That's right, there was the killer who must have seen ol' Deek."

"He may have been one of the same men at the card game. Until I hear something that convinces me otherwise, that's the assumption I'm making."

"It weren't me, and it certainly weren't my little brother. Hell, we pulled Frank off of Paine."

"So it was Frank Dodds laid into Devon Paine. Man must be six inches smaller than Dodds. Not much of a fair fight."

"Mr. Dodds ain't known for being the fairest man at Holt City . . ."

"As I understand it, Deek Penner pulled all three of you off the man," said Durrant.

"Deek was a solid lad."

"Not solid enough. What did you think of him?" said Durrant, his tone softening.

Ralph Mahoney's eyes shifted through the woods. Durrant thought that he must be looking to see if he was being observed.

"He was a good man," Mahoney finally said. "Didn't deserve to die's for certain. But he was poking his nose into another man's business, and no good's ever going to come from that. He shouldn't have been nosing around. That's all."

"You think that got him killed?"

"That's not what I'm saying."

"What are you saying?"

"Nothing. I'm not saying nothing."

"You're afraid of Frank Dodds."

"No, sir."

"You're afraid of something, Ralph. I can see it."

Mahoney stood up straight. He was six foot three, and must have weighted two hundred and forty pounds, thought Durrant. But he suspected that under the layers of grey, ragged clothing he must be somewhat diminished after a winter in this hard, unforgiving country.

"Let's talk about Pete," said Durrant, looking around to where the younger brother sat waiting.

"He's a good lad, Petie," said his brother.

"So why did he lie?"

"Boy is just worried. He don't want to cross Frank. Frank's got a temper, everybody knows it. You seen it, didn't you? You saw Devon Paine's face."

"At least we've come clean about that part of the night."

"It ain't too hard to figure, is it?"

"No, Ralph, it isn't that hard. But Paine told me it was a horse."

Mahoney laughed. "What the hell would he be doing with his face down by a horse's foot!"

It was Durrant's turn to shrug.

"So of course Pete is scared. He don't want to lose his job, for one thing," said Mahoney.

"Wouldn't be too hard to find work come the spring."

"We got responsibilities. We send money home when we can."

"So you can't afford to lose your work for Dodds? Bob Pen would likely put you to work straight off if Dodds fired you."

"But that's come spring. That's still some time off, given the amount of snow we got this winter. They say there's still ten feet or more on the Kicking Horse Pass. It's going to be June before we start down the other side at this rate. What's the boy going to do till then? Walk back to Fort Calgary? He'd catch almighty hell . . ."

Durrant watched the man. "Who would he catch hell from?" Mahoney turned away from the Mountie a moment. "Look at me when I'm talking to you! Who would he catch hell from?" demanded Durrant.

"Nobody."

"From your old man, is that it?"

"They need the money. They can't keep up with the farm. It ain't nothing."

"Deek Penner was a patriarchal figure around this camp, wasn't he?"

"I don't know what that means."

"He was like a father to some. He sounded like a father to others." Mahoney looked down at his feet. Durrant continued, "Bet for some he sounded a little *too* much like their own pap for his own good."

"Deek weren't nothing like our old man," said Mahoney. "Got to being a little preachy sometimes, but not much like our old man, no."

Durrant nodded. "Maybe he sounded a lot more like your old man than you're letting on. I think that's why young Pete there didn't care too much for Deek Penner. Deek was onto the fact that you and your brother were in on Frank Dodds' moonshining and that's when

Deek got much too preachy. Maybe you couldn't raise a hand to your old man, but Deek Penner? That's another thing all together." Mahoney smiled a thin smile. He shook his head. "You don't think so, Ralph?"

"You got us all figured, don't you?" said Mahoney.

Now it was Durrant's turn to smile. "Losing his job ain't the only thing Pete is afraid of, though. Is it?"

"Maybe he's afraid of losing a few teeth if he speaks ill of ol' Dodds," said Mahoney.

"My guess is that you'd back him up."

"Against Dodds?"

"Against any man."

"Damn right."

"What's he got to hide?"

"Nothin'."

"I don't believe you."

"I don't give a damn!" said Mahoney, glaring at him, and the woods fell suddenly silent. From the corner of his eye Durrant could see Pete Mahoney stand up and in his mind played out the scenario of subduing both men. Mahoney must have read his face, and immediately looked down, submissively.

"Mr. Wallace . . ."

"Sergeant Wallace."

"Sergeant Wallace," Mahoney hissed, "You seem like a pretty bright fellow. You seem like you got a good head, as our Daddy used to say. You must know what goes on when five hundred men are holed up for the winter in a God-forsaken place like this. Sometimes men get on each other's nerves. Men is always looking for something to let off a little steam. A bit of fisticuffs, some poker, and a drink for the medicinal benefits from time to time."

"And a man is dead from this?"

"Deek Penner is dead, but I don't know why, Sergeant Wallace."

"Who's making the whiskey in this camp?" asked Wallace.

"I don't know," Mahoney said wearily.

"I think you do. I think your brother knows too. I think your brother is maybe very well acquainted with who is making whiskey here at Holt City."

"You had best leave my little brother alone, Sergeant Wallace." He didn't look at Durrant when he said it.

Durrant let his gaze slip in turn to the younger Mahoney. He could feel the tension radiating from the Mahoney next to him. He drew in a breath of the cool air and tasted the rich aroma of pine. He looked back at the man before him, his shoulders square to him, Durrant's face coming close to his in the dim evening light.

"Or what, Mr. Mahoney? Or what?" He let his left hand tighten around the slender handle of the Bulldog in his pocket, his thumb itching on the hammer.

"Or that piece of iron that you got there in your pocket is going to be all that stands between you and the devil himself, Sergeant. Between you and - the - devil - his - self." He drew out the words, each one punctuated with a jab of his finger towards the Mountie's chest.

For a moment Durrant imagined stepping back over the icy road and drawing the Bulldog on the man and pulling the trigger, the explosion of the powder in the compact cartridge cutting the silence of the woods like the bark of some angry cur. He drew in a breath and smiled, letting the image fade from his mind.

"You get in my way of finding out who killed Deek Penner, Mr. Mahoney, and it will be you who will be delivering a message to that self-same devil. I'll see to that myself."

IT TOOK DURRANT nearly an hour to navigate the ice road in the darkness. Several times he slipped, and once his crutch broke through the thin crust of ice and wood chips and he toppled forward, the crutch catching him in the chin, nearly knocking him senseless. The long walk gave him time to consider his interrogation of the Mahoney brothers. Durrant mused that while both men wore soiled and tattered overcoats that clearly hadn't been to the laundry all winter, neither of them had any evidence of blood on them.

Hungry as Durrant was, when he arrived back in camp he went directly to Dodds' cabin. The trail to the shack was well packed and a thick plume of smoke rose from the chimney. Even if he didn't relish the company, Durrant looked forward to being warm.

He knew that he could not intimidate the belligerent Dodds and would need to try a different tact. He stepped up to the cabin, and before allowing a second thought to enter his head, pounded on the door. A chair scraped against the floor and heavy, booted feet plodded across the crudely planed floorboards.

"What is it?" he heard Dodds bark.

"It's Sergeant Wallace, Mr. Dodds. I'll have a word with you."

"Blue Jesus, man, don't you ever rest?" The door was opened and Dodds stood before him in a grey undershirt and waistcoat. His hair was mussed and he looked as if he'd been sleeping. The odour of whiskey and oil hung heavy in the warm air that emanated from the cabin.

"I have some questions for you, please."

Dodds stood and regarded the Mountie a moment. Without a word, he stepped away from the door and walked back to the round table that filled much of the room.

"I hear you were putting it to a couple of my boys today," he said, taking his seat. Laid out on the table were an assortment of tools—peevies and axes, a few short-handled saws—along with a sharpening stone and a can of oil. Dodds took up one of the saws and began to carefully sharpen its serrated teeth with the rounded edge of a file.

Durrant stood by the door watching the man. The room was warm, the broad stove in the corner rattled a little, and the scent of body odour was infused with the oil and the tipple.

"That's what I want to talk with you about," he said. Dodds didn't look up. He made no response at all. "Pete Mahoney seems a good lad, but he's scared and I believe that he's covering for you." Dodds continued to file the saw. "He lied to me today, and if it wasn't about the killing of Deek Penner, then it was certainly to cover up your moonshine operation." Dodds picked up an oily cloth and rubbed it across the blade of the saw. "He might be a good lad, but he's a bad liar and if I have to break him to get to you, it won't keep me up at night."

Dodds grinned. "Just wondering what would keep a man like you up, is all?"

"Things you couldn't even imagine, Mr. Dodds."

"I bet I could," Dodds said, looking at Durrant for the first time since the man stepped foot in his cabin.

"Nevertheless, I aim to take *you* down, and if I have to take the Mahoney boys with me when I do, that will suit me just fine."

"You got this all figured out already, do you, Mr. Wallace? Pardon me, *Sergeant* Wallace." he corrected himself with a toothy grin, regarding the Mountie coolly. "Oh, I already heard you don't take too kindly to being referred to with the familiar. Sit if you like; I can't imagine it's pleasant to be on that thing all day long," said Dodds, nodding at Durrant's prosthetic. Durrant remained standing.

He continued, "So if you got it all figured out, why not throw the shackles on me now and put me on the next freight that heads for Fort Calgary? Why not haul me down to the station and send word to your man Steele that once again the Red Coats got their man?"

"Why not indeed?" asked Durrant.

"You can't and you won't. Cause you got no proof of anything. You got no proof of this notion that I'm behind Deek's murder, and you got no proof that I'm making whiskey in this camp. You got nothing."

"Oh, I've got a fair sight more than nothing."

Dodds grinned again and put down the saw, wiping his hands on the oily rag. He shook his head. "Maybe you do, but it ain't enough to convict anybody of anything, especially me."

"What did Paine say to you that night that made you lay into him so hard?"

"Paine and I didn't get mixed up."

"That's not what Ralph Mahoney tells me."

"Ralph?"

Durrant nodded.

Dodds snorted, and picked up a two-sided axe and began to file one of its broad blades. "Ralph, eh? It was just a harmless row, that's all. I don't see what it had to do with Deek Penner, no how."

"Deek got between you."

"Maybe he did, maybe he didn't. Deek got between lots of things here at Holt City, Sergeant."

"Did he get between you and the profit you hope to reap from making moonshine and selling it to the navvies come the spring?"

Dodds laughed. "You almost tripped me up there, Sergeant, with your clever talk. You came pretty close."

"Did he threaten you, Dodds? Is that it? Did he threaten to upend the applecart?"

Dodds shook his head. "You got a one-track mind, Sergeant Wallace."

Durrant's voice was low and flat, "Let me tell you something, Mr. Dodds . . ." But Dodds interrupted him.

"No, let me tell you something, Wallace," he said, his head snapping up, his grip tightening around the handle of the axe. "Let me tell *you* something. You don't know what the hell you're talking about. There might be moonshine in this camp, but it ain't moonshine that got Deek Penner killed, and that's for damned sure." It was Durrant's turn to shake his head. "Scoff if you like, Wallace, but it will be your fault when you get yourself banged on the head like our boy Deek Penner. At least as I hear it he saw it coming."

"You threatening me?"

"No, I ain't threatening you. Jesus Christ, man, you been here what, two days, and you already figure you can finger me for killing Deek, making whiskey, and wanting to ruin the whole goddamned CPR operation. Well, let me tell you, you don't know the half of it."

Durrant drew a deep breath. "Half of what?" he said.

Dodds laughed again. "You ain't going to hear it from me."

"As I see it, you got a choice to make, Mr. Dodds. You can keep your mouth shut and wait for me to finish my case against you, or you can tell me what you know and see if maybe I believe you."

"Why the hell should I help you?"

"'Cause right now, I got you figured for the death of Mr. Penner and for making whiskey, and their ain't no law in these parts but what I bring with me, so it will be my word against yours."

Dodds looked up at him. "We got courts in this country. Don't try to fool me that there's goin' to be some kind of rail-side justice served up."

"Nearest courthouse is in Regina. If you're lucky you'd get a magistrate in Fort Calgary. It would be awful if you tried to escape custody, is all I'm saying."

"Pretty tough talk for a one-legged man in a camp full of axes, dynamite, and pistols, Sergeant Wallace."

Durrant felt his left hand itch to hold the butt of this revolver; he feigned indifference to the threat instead. Dodds grinned and looked back down at this work.

"There's a spy here in this camp," he finally said.

"So you say. That rumour is all over camp."

"There's a spy. It ain't no rumour. We all knew it. All of us foremen and the contractors. We all knew it. Deek did too. We just didn't know who."

"Spy for who?"

"Grand Trunk Railway."

"What would they be spying for?"

"Get an edge on the CPR, maybe . . ."

"Edge on the CPR? The Grand Trunk is an eastern operation."

"They are trying to push their operation across the Great Plains. Hook up Toronto and Montreal with the Midwest and then maybe even the port of Seattle. Yup, they are buying up a bunch of the lines through the Missouri country. Rumour is that they want to piece together a line before CPR President George Stephen and his men could complete this one, and put them out of business."

Durrant was silent a moment. "So you think there's a spy here, but you don't know who he might be, or what he's up to?"

"Deek did."

"Deek Penner was onto this so-called spy?"

"Yes sir."

"And did he tell you or Wilcox what was going on?"

"No sir."

Wallace shook his head. "I think you're playing me, Dodds. I think you believe me to be a ten-karat fool."

Dodds didn't smile this time. "Sergeant, you can believe me or not. I don't give a damn. I'm telling you for certain: somewhere in this camp is a man who works for the rival railway. Some say that it was going beyond spying, that the Grand Trunk was planning on pulling something. What do you call it?"

"Sabotage?"

"That's it. Deek Penner was in charge of munitions. What do you think the best way would be to slow down the work of the CPR down the Big Hill, with all its blasting and tunnels? That's right. Deek Penner was onto this Grand Trunk spy alright. I think it might have gotten him killed."

IT WAS MIDNIGHT before Durrant found his way through the canyons of snow to his bunk. After he had left Dodds he had gone to find Thompson Griffin, Frank Dodds' number two man. He had been missing from the card game on the night that Penner was killed. Despite questioning the man's bunkmates in their crowded and reeking hovel, Durrant could not ascertain the man's whereabouts. According to the cluster of men he found there, Thompson Griffin was often absent until late in the evening, out making the rounds of the camp, looking for card games and entertainment.

Durrant then knocked on the door of the half dozen cabins that were clustered near where Deek had been killed. He questioned the occupants about any noise they might have heard, or if anybody had seen the man Christianson had reported running from the scene of the crime, but the men he spoke with were all insistent that they had heard nothing that evening.

Weary, Durrant turned towards the NWMP bunk. Durrant was deep in thought when he pushed open the door to the two-bunk cabin. He snapped from his reverie when he entered the room. In sharp contrast to the huts reeking of oil and sweat he had been in that evening, his was scented with pine smoke and fresh baking. He looked up to see Charlie sitting before him on his tick, deep furrows of concern cutting across the boy's forehead.

"You been waiting up on me, son?" said Durrant, closing the heavy door behind himself.

Charlie nodded, the worry still slicing across his face.

"You needn't have," Durrant said. "I can take care of myself." Durrant walked across the room, fatigue visible in his awkward gait and grey expression. He sat down heavily on the bed and pulled off his heavy coat.

Charlie stood up and went to the rumbling stove that occupied one corner of the hut. Then he stopped and turned and picked up the tablet from the desk next to the door and wrote something. He handed the tablet to Durrant.

Durrant breathed out heavily. "Yeah, I could use a little something," he conceded. The aroma of food began to make him feel light-headed.

Charlie went back to the stove and using a rag as an oven mitt took a plate from the top of the heating rack and put it on the desk. He then opened a tin on the rack and piled hot biscuits onto the plate. The boy found cutlery and set a place for Durrant to eat.

"You fixed me a plate at the mess?" The boy nodded. Durrant hefted himself from the bunk and hobbled, without his crutch, to the table and sat down. "My God, this smells good." He picked up the fork and began to shovel food into his mouth. "The camp cook make all this?" Charlie shrugged. "Cause these don't taste like the cow patties that he's been passing off as biscuits the last few days, is all. The only thing that cook's got going for him is that there's pie every night. It's not good pie, mind, but it's pie just the same. That's about the only thing keeping these men from a riot." Durrant finished his plate and sat back. "How did you make out today?"

Charlie took up the tablet and scribbled something. He handed it to Durrant. "Nothing yet, but you ain't done either." Durrant looked at the boy. "Okay, well, keep at it if you're able. I imagine it's not easy going, what with this snow turning soft as it has."

Durrant hopped back to his bed and sat down there again, blowing a long, low whistle through his teeth as he did. Charlie saw to the dishes as Durrant pulled at his prosthetic leg, releasing the suction valve and removing the limb. He rolled up his heavy wool pant leg to reveal the gnarled stump just below his knee. It was wrapped in a heavy bandage, which the Mountie removed and placed carefully on the stand next to his bed.

Durrant let his mind range over all the interrogations of the day. Amid all of the stories, he knew that there were fragments of truth. One thing was for sure: three different men had threatened his life that day, all of whom had something to hide, all of whom were among the half dozen to last see Penner alive. These three men were quickly becoming the focus of Durrant's inquiries at the end of steel.

TEN

200,000 POUNDS OF NITROGLYCERINE

WHEN DURRANT WOKE, HE FELT less confident than he had the night before. It was possible that he had Dodds exactly where he wanted him, but it was also possible that Dodds had *him* in the same place. That he woke feeling some doubt was a sign that Dodds' strategy to infuse uncertainty into the Mountie's mind was having its desired effect: to throw Durrant off his trail.

Still lying in bed, Durrant considered his conversations with the Mahoney brothers, and then with Dodds himself. He knew it was possible that the three men had conspired with one another around the theory that there was "more going on" at Holt City than met the eye. Ralph Mahoney seemed every bit capable of constructing a theory in coordination with his boss to lead Durrant astray. All Ralph would have to do was be obstreperous for the theory to bear fruit; Dodds could plant the seed and let it fester.

Durrant pulled himself from bed and discovered that he'd fallen asleep in yesterday's clothing. He decided to leave well enough alone and stayed in his smoky trousers and waistcoat. He attached his prosthetic leg, feeling it pinch on the raw nub of skin below his knee. There was some blood on the white bandage that he wrapped his leg with before he attached the prosthetic. He would have to relent and see Doc Armatage that day; if he didn't, he knew he risked infection.

Durrant strapped on his pistol. The day was perceptively warmer, so he pulled on his canvas coat and stuffed the British Bulldog in his left pocket and stepped to the door.

Charlie almost ran him over coming in. "Easy there, son," said Durrant. Charlie gave him a bashful smile as he pushed past him into the cabin. The lad turned and regarded him, one eye slightly cocked. "What is it?" Durrant asked. Charlie turned around to find the writing tablet and scratched out a line of text. Durrant took it and read it. "No, I do not want a bath!" he said. Charlie kept looking at him. "What are you, my goddamned mother?"

Durrant changed the subject and asked, "You find that club yet?" Charlie shook his head. Durrant noticed that he was quite wet. "You've already been out looking, haven't you?" Charlie nodded. "You should take my chaps, they'll keep you dry. They're in the trunk there. Don't fall through the ice. I got enough with one dead body in this camp," and then he stomped out into the day.

DURRANT MADE HIS way over the icy trails through the camp to the station. As he did, he could see just beyond the tracks, where Charlie had been methodically searching the banks of snow that extended out onto the frozen Bow River for the murder weapon. He knew that others in the camp could see the search grid too, and that whoever had killed Penner would certainly be paying attention to the lad's quest.

When he reached the platform he heard the sharp whistle of a train arriving from the east. Bob Pen was standing on the platform, his pipe clenched in his teeth. Durrant approached and the man nodded at the Mountie but kept his gaze eastward.

"Do you have a moment for a word?" Durrant asked.

Pipe bouncing, Pen nodded again and said, "Of course, Sergeant, but that's about all I've got. Two minutes out, at that bend, she is . . ."

Durrant heard the train whistle again. "You sometimes play cards with Frank Dodds and the Mahoney brothers?"

"I do at that," said Pen.

"But you didn't sit in the night Deek Penner was killed?"

"No sir."

"Why not?"

"Besides the fact that I can't stomach Frank Dodds?"

Durrant smiled. "Is there another reason?"

"None better, but indeed there is another. You see, I like to visit a number of different games. I'm an egalitarian. I like to take my winnings in as many different cabins as I can. That way, these fellas never grow tired of me and when I need them to haul in the morning, I can call them out and not have to watch my back, if you take my meaning."

Durrant was nodding. He could see the billowing smoke through the trees. Pen was still watching the tracks. "So you play at different games so that despite winning many hands, you don't have to worry that you'll not have men willing to work for you?" Pen nodded. "That makes sense. What game were you at on the eve Mr. Penner was killed?"

"I was with the Slovaks."

"How'd you do?"

Pen looked at the Sergeant." Marvellously, thank you." His pipe leaped up and down as he spoke.

"Your train's almost here," said Durrant. "I appreciate your time."

"Keep up your search, Sergeant. I can tell by the general state of agitation in the camp that you're making headway."

Durrant regarded him a moment and then turned his attention to the tracks. He watched through the trees as the tell tale plume of oily smoke emerged from the bend where the track bridged the Pipestone River. A moment later the locomotive arrived at the station and Pen greeted several dozen men who disembarked from the first boxcar. To Durrant they looked like hobos, but this was the first wave of navvies arriving from eastern locations, seeking work at the tail end of the winter camp.

Durrant watched the lads as Bob Pen brought order to their arrival at the end of steel. Pen pointed with his pipe to direct the men to the far end of the station platform where a buckboard sleigh hitched to a team of Devon Paine's draft horses was waiting.

Durrant leaned against the wall of the station and observed. Pen talked with the men, and before long his two assistants dropped from the seat of the sleigh and loaded baggage onto the sled. They drove the team back onto the icy Tote Road that followed the Bow River north and west. The men, dazzled by the brilliant light of the morning and the spectacular scenery all around them, blinked as they formed a rough line marching along the road too. Durrant guessed there would be no easy ride for these lads; they would walk along the ice road to the summit of the Pass where they would immediately be put to work.

Durrant watched them file past, his expression solemn and serious. Several of the men glanced at him, eyeing his crutch and his dour expression. Durrant let his coat fall open, the holster for the Enfield plainly resting on his left hip, so that they could see that the law did in fact reach all the way to Holt City. Some of the older men nodded to him; the young men simply cast their eyes down and marched on.

"First wave," Durrant heard a voice behind him. He started and turned. It was Hep Wilcox.

"Navvies," Durrant said.

"Two dozen down, twelve thousand to go."

Durrant shook his head. "Where are those men off to?"

"Kicking Horse Lake. We sent some men up there yesterday to start on the carpentry work for the camp. There are a few tents, a cook, a teamster, and a pile of lumber as tall as a building. Not much else. There's been a survey team there on and off for most of the winter. Fellow named Garnet Moberly, a limey, is leading it. He's been proving the survey down along the length of the Kicking Horse as far west as the Columbia River. Major Rogers is a great man, and a brilliant surveyor, but his line still needs to be established more clearly. That's now up to Moberly and his team."

Durrant nodded to the men marching along behind the sled on the ice road. "What will those men be doing?"

"We'll put them to work on the munitions plant, and building other camp structures. We have a foreman on site who will direct the construction."

Durrant watched the last of the men disappear into the woods on the icy Tote Road. The forest seemed to close in after them, enveloping them. Durrant turned and looked back at the munitions warehouse behind to the south, tucked close to the bridge that spanned the Pipestone River.

"I'd like to visit the Kicking Horse Pass in the next day or so. If Penner was to lead the blasting down Big Hill, then I need to see it."

Wilcox nodded. "I'm sure we can arrange passage for you. There are sleds heading out every few hours right now. Shouldn't be a problem."

Durrant said, "Tell me more about the munitions plant."

"The contract to build it was won by the Canada Explosives

Company of Mount Saint-Hilaire. Frankly, I don't know much about them. The contracts are won or lost in Ottawa. I don't pretend to know what gets into a Parliamentarian's head when it comes to this sort of thing."

"I would have imagined that the Canadian Pacific controlled contracts out of Montreal."

Wilcox laughed. "You have a lot to learn about John A. Macdonald's national dream, Sergeant Wallace. Parliament has been playing its hand in this all along, but with costs threatening to quadruple before we complete this railway, the Members of Parliament have taken a much more active interest in overseeing routine matters such as the letting of contracts. That interest is not just for egalitarian reasons."

"What do you mean by that?"

"I tend to speak out of turn on this sort of matter, but I find it very frustrating."

"Why's that?"

"While these men debate cutting costs from the comfort of their offices in Parliament, you can see we're not living in the lap of luxury here along the railway. Some of these men, while saying that we have to build more miles with less, are lining their own pockets. Surely this doesn't come as a surprise to you, Sergeant."

"It doesn't. Surely there must be some oversight?"

"Of course. There is a committee of members of both the governing Conservatives of John A. and the Liberals under Mr. Edward Blake. Supposedly, they keep tabs on the spending."

"Where do *you* fit in that spectrum?"

"I could honestly care less, so long as they keep paying their bills and sending me what I need to do my job."

Durrant pondered his next line of questioning. "The munitions contract is one of the biggest, as I understand it."

"It is that. It could be worth a million dollars or more just for the work between here and the Columbia River. The Parliamentary Committee that oversees the budget for the railway decided that this was a good place to trim costs and so they went with the cheapest bidder for the job. That's how the Canada Explosives Company got the work. There are others with a higher quality product, and with a better supply chain, in my opinion."

"So you're not happy with the contractor?"

"That remains to be seen, but they wouldn't have been *my* first choice . . ."

"Why is that?" asked Durrant.

"Problems with the product, mostly. It's unstable stuff to begin with. The Canada Explosives Company has had more than a few accidents with their nitro. Nothing that could be called gross negligence, but still, I have my concerns."

"Who would you have selected for the contract?"

"Well, that's irrelevant now, isn't it?"

"I'm just interested in who you think would have provided a better product?"

Wilcox thought a moment. "A better and *safer* product, Sergeant Wallace."

Durrant watched him, aware that he had dodged the answer. "Are you saying that Parliament, by interfering with this, is putting lives at risk?"

Wilcox shook his head. "You're putting words in my mouth, Sergeant. No, what I'm saying is that there are some places on this undertaking you can afford to cut corners. There are others you can't. Explosives is one of the places you can't."

"Don't you stand to profit with the Canada Explosives Company holding this contract?"

"Not under the Mount Saint-Hilaire company. Not direct. With Deek out of the picture, I've been asked to find a replacement, but I don't have any direct affiliation with that company."

Durrant thought about that a moment and said, "Tell me, sir, how much nitroglycerine are we talking about?

Wilcox grinned. "As much as we need. It's a lot, Sergeant. We won't know for certain till we get things underway, but the engineers tell us that there will be seven tunnels on the upper section of the Kicking Horse alone. It's more than two thousand linear feet! Plus more rock cuts and steep grades than you can number. We expect to move about thirty thousand cubic yards of rock and earth for every mile of track we lay. That's going to take upwards of two hundred thousand pounds of nitroglycerine."

Durrant let that number settle in. "You figure upwards of a million dollars is at stake?"

Wilcox looked down at his hands. "Well," he finally said, "that depends also on the final numbers and on the type of material blasted. The contractor gets more for the harder rock found up along the ridge of the Kicking Horse; less for the soft sediment in the valley bottom. And there's always the wild card . . ."

Durrant was beginning to feel like he was being played. He drew a deep breath and waited for Wilcox to dole out his information. "What is the wild card?"

"Whether or not the Canada Explosives Company keeps the contract. There's at least one other Canadian firm interested in completing the work, but it will cost more. Their bid was more expensive, but in my opinion they have a better product; safer, more stable."

"How much more would it cost?"

"Ten, twenty percent."

"What did Penner think?"

It was Wilcox's turn to consider the question. "I think Deek would have wanted the more reliable product. Remember, Deek was going to be there when the men were doing the blasting. If the nitroglycerine was substandard, then he was going to be standing next to the men who blew themselves up."

Durrant realized how serious a business this was. "The contract has already been won, hasn't it?"

"It has."

"So it's a done deal."

"Sergeant Wallace, you're going to find that in the business of the railroad, nothing is a done deal."

"Why would the CPR revoke a contract that was less expensive, even if the firm was questionable?"

Wilcox interrupted. "The answer is, they likely won't. Not unless there is some trouble with the munitions or if the plant can't produce what they promised."

"Nothing is a done deal."

Wilcox smiled. "Nothing is ever a done deal until the last spike is driven home. We're a long, long way from that day yet."

"LET'S TALK ABOUT this spy." Durrant leaned his left elbow on his good leg, taking the pressure off the stump that was already aching this early in the day.

Durrant and Wilcox now sat in the manager's office, the heat from the woodstove close, the window that faced the railway dense with moisture. They had just spent twenty minutes discussing the comings and goings in the camp. Durrant wanted assurance that a complete list of any man who had left camp since Penner had been killed would be furnished in short order.

"Who has been talking about this so-called spy?" he asked, stalling.

"It doesn't matter."

"Well, it does to me. It matters a great deal to me. This is one of the things that happens in a place like this, Sergeant Wallace," said Wilcox, looking around him and gesturing with his arms wide open. The action seemed contrived to Durrant given that they were in Wilcox's tiny office. "You shut a bunch of men up in a place like Holt City and they start to talk. It's like cards; it's entertainment. Nobody else in Holt City knows for certain that there is a spy here. As it is, I am doing everything I can to find this secret agent and drive him out."

"Or have him arrested," said Durrant.

"Yes, or that."

"Are you telling me that you are the only person in Holt City who knows for certain about this alleged Grand Trunk spy?"

Wilcox sat back and laced his fingers together across his trim stomach and let his head fall forward so his chin touched his chest. "I've been trying to keep this under wraps, as it were." He seemed to think better of saying anything more.

"Why?"

"For obvious reasons, Sergeant. What do you think would happen if word got out that somewhere among these five hundred souls there was a traitor?"

Wilcox pressed on. "You may not take this enterprise seriously, Sergeant, but many of these men do. They take it very seriously. Some signed on three years ago or more. Some of them started laying track above Lake Superior, and aim to see it through to Rogers Pass if they are able. If you ask why keep secret that there is a spy among them, let me tell you: so that they don't turn on one another. It's been hard enough keeping peace at the end of steel through this God-forsaken winter. Your presence here may well be a testament to my own failure. I'll be damned if I'm going to have these men at each other's throats accusing one another of being a spy." Wilcox looked at his fingers, his face flushed. He seemed to be contemplating what to say next. Finally he exhaled loudly and without looking up said, "I believe Deek Penner was onto the man.

"Shortly after we stopped work for the fall, around the 8th of December last year, Montreal sent word that the Grand Trunk was making noise that they were going to extend their operations west. They'd been making those sounds for the last two decades! But nothing ever came from it. That's why Macdonald had to do this himself, you see. If the Grand Trunk could have been relied upon to push their Ontario line west to British Columbia, Macdonald would have been able to fulfill his promise to the province without it costing the Dominion a hundred million dollars. But they couldn't. Now that we're actually within a year, maybe eighteen months of finishing this magnificent undertaking, the Grand Trunk is making sounds like they will push their lines west through the Americas and on to the Pacific at the Port of Seattle. That's just a hundred miles from Burrard Inlet where *our* terminus is. I didn't take it too seriously," Wilcox said, looking out the window. "Montreal did. They came to believe that the Grand Trunk had spies working in our camps."

"What makes them think that?"

Wilcox turned and looked at Durrant. "We have spies in theirs. It just makes sense, doesn't it?"

It was Durrant's turn to smile.

"Word come down straight from CPR General Manager Van Horne himself to be on the lookout."

"For what?" Durrant sat back in his chair and rubbed his leg.

"Suspicious behaviour. I didn't make too much of it, but early in the New Year, things started happening: we had a few accidents that couldn't be explained. Devon Paine lost some of his horses when someone left the stables open and they ran off. A whole siding of our sleepers caught fire. There was an incident with some nitro . . . Nobody was killed, but several men got burned badly.

"I asked Deek to look into it. He did, and the last I talked with him about it, just a few days before he was killed, he told me he had a man in mind and was going to deal with it directly. He wouldn't tell me who it was."

"Wouldn't tell you?"

"Said he didn't want to wrongly accuse the fellow."

Durrant looked down to hide his frustration. "Did Penner talk with anybody *else* about this?" Durrant was remembering the contents of Deek's pockets, and the coded correspondence with the man named Kauffman. Its importance seemed to take on new light.

"You mean direct with Montreal?" Wilcox shook his head. "I don't think so. No, he was reporting to me on this matter. I think he was going to confront the man." Wilcox was still looking at the window

The Mountie looked up. "Do you have any suspicions about who this might be?"

"I do not. I mean, there are a few men around that are more than a little odd, but nobody walking around advertising that they're on the Grand Trunk payroll or anything."

Durrant pushed himself up. He arranged his crutch and pulled on his coat. "Mr. Wilcox," he said, and Hep turned from the window to face him in the small space. "Thank you for the information."

Wilcox said, "Do you think that this spy might have known his cover was blown and that Deek was the one who had a finger on him? Do you think he might have done poor Deek in?"

Durrant regarded the man's face and noticed an eagerness there that hadn't been present before. "As you said yourself not an hour ago, Mr. Wilcox, nothing is a done deal as it pertains to this railway until the last spike is driven."

WHEN DURRANT LEFT Wilcox's office, he nearly knocked over Christianson. The man was standing near the door to Wilcox's office, a stack of wire correspondence in his slender hands.

"Good morning, Mr. Christianson," the Mountie said.

"Good morning, Sergeant Wallace. How are you faring with our sudden fine weather?" the small man asked, his eyes roving everywhere but on Durrant's face.

Durrant regarded the man. Hard to imagine him wintering in a place like this, but here he was.

"Tell me, John, what kind of records do you keep for the operation of this here wire?"

"Well, sir, any wire that gets sent is supposed to be entered in the journal there," said the man, pointing to his thick book of records next to the operator's station. "Any I send are entered there for certain. I imagine most others do the same."

"Who has authority to send a wire?"

Christianson put a finger to the side of his face and looked up, his face curling into thoughtful consideration. "Well, me of course," he said helpfully. "Mr. Wilcox. All the foremen can send and receive wires, but I don't expect most of them know how, to be honest."

"Deek did?"

"Oh yes, Mr. Penner certainly did."

"Who else?"

"Well, other than that, the wire's supposed to come and go through me. Some do take advantage of the situation. I can't be here every moment, and if someone comes in and decides to send a wire, then not much can be done to stop them."

"What about incoming?"

"Well, those that aren't collected right away end up over here," said Christianson. He showed Durrant the bottom of a crate that served as his inbox. "Every so often I walk them around to the men who are expecting them if they haven't been collected. Most fellas who are expecting a wire come right quick for it. It's better than getting the post in a place like Holt City."

"John, would there be any way for you to provide me a list of everybody who has sent or received wires?"

Christianson put his finger to his cheek again in exaggerated concentration. "You mean, besides them that I've got recorded in the log?"

"That's right."

"I don't believe so, Sergeant. Not unless the tape from the wire is left lying about, and that's not often."

Durrant looked around the spare room. "Alright then, I'll start with the log. I'll need to take it for several days."

"I can do without," said the clerk. "I've been meaning to petition Mr. Holt for a new one anyhow. Let me put some order to it, and then I'll give it over to you."

Durrant looked at the man. There was no guile in his voice. "Thank you," he finally said. "Now, I need to use your wire for police business, please," Durrant said, indicating that Christianson should return to his other duties.

Again Christianson agreed. He adjusted his spectacles, pulled on his coat, hat, and gloves, and took the journal. "You need anything else from me Sergeant?"

"I'll be just fine," said Durrant, taking a seat behind the counter where the telegraph machine rested.

When Christianson had left, he tapped in the code for the NWMP headquarters in Regina and signalled his intent to transmit. When the ready response came, he tapped out his message.

> To S. Steele.
> From Durrant Wallace.
> Update on progress at Holt City. Many suspects in murder of Deek Penner. Am narrowing search. Significant presence of whiskey production at end of track. Please advise.

Ask Winnipeg to question contract holders with CPR about relationship to Penner.

Check with other forces on known persons named Kauffman. Possibly with CPR or GTR.

Please advise on possible presence of GTR espionage and/or sabotage of CPR mainline.

He sat back. It seemed hard to believe that the entirety of his undertakings in Holt City could be summed up in five lines of coded text. As he sat waiting for a reply, he heard Wilcox's door open behind him and felt the man's eyes on the back of his neck, then heard the door close. Only after a long minute did Durrant turn around to see that the door was indeed shut.

A few more minutes passed before the telegraph machine buzzed with an incoming wire. Durrant put the headset on and tapped out the ready to receive message. The wire was from the NWMP:

To Wallace.
From NWMP.
Steele observing Métis near Fort Pitt. Will forward transmission.

That didn't bode well, thought Durrant. For Steele to be distracted from the railway work by the Métis meant trouble was brewing. Durrant bunched the piece of paper he had scribbled the message on, opened the lid to the stove, and threw the message into the flames. He stood, adjusted his coat, pulled on his hat and gloves, and stepped out into the afternoon light.

Durrant made his way to the mess tent where he ate his first meal of the day alone, and when he was done, stood at the door of the tent and looked up at the western mountains. There were too many loose ends. He had to start tying some of them off, or he'd never find the man who killed Deek Penner. In time he would have to brace all the men from the card game again, but it was too soon for that. He needed to give them all a day or two to reflect on the consequences of their falsehoods, and to develop a sense of security that maybe they had sidestepped his inquiry. Then, he could go back and see if he might catch them in their duplicity.

The first thing to do was to track down answers to several outstanding problems. Who is the mysterious man named Kauffman that Penner had been corresponding with before he was killed, and what does his coded message say? And next, who is the Grand Trunk spy, if even there is one, and what might have transpired between Penner and this rogue element in the camp?

As the afternoon began to wane, Durrant set off toward his bunk. By now Christianson would have delivered the log book of wires sent and received from the camp. He'd look through this to see if there was anything suspicious. It seemed unlikely that if the Grand Trunk had in fact dispatched a spy to Holt City, he would not be able to transmit his own wire correspondence.

As Durrant stumped his way back along the icy path to the NWMP cabin he drew near to the place where Penner had been killed, and he spotted Charlie far out on the frozen Bow River. The boy was trudging back and forth in the deep snow that had fallen over the ice, his head down, eyes scouring the drifts for the discarded murder weapon. Durrant watched his faithful companion plod through the snow, when suddenly the boy disappeared. His first reaction was to reach for his pistol, but inside of a split second, he knew this was futile.

"Charlie!" Durrant yelled towards the snow heaped river. There was no answer; no sign of the vanished boy. "Charlie!" he yelled again in futility.

Durrant looked around him. He was alone on the trail. The sounds of the camp surrounded him, but he stood apart from its goings-on. He started out toward the river, yelling as he plunged into the deep ice-encrusted snow. His crutch could offer him no support, and within two steps he had fallen on his side, the snow up around his ears.

"Sweet Jesus," he cursed, and then yelled again, "Charlie!"

Lying on his side, Durrant reached into his pocket and struggled with the pistol. The Bulldog came out, choked with snow, and he held it aloft, cocked the hammer with his left thumb, and fired, and then cocked and fired again. The retort of the pistol echoed off the face of the adjacent mountains. Durrant fired a third time, and then struggled through the snow toward the river.

Soon Durrant heard voices, and a moment later he looked up to see Grant McPherson plunging into the snow after him, followed by half a dozen other men.

"It's Charlie!" Durrant cried.

"Are you okay, Sergeant?" McPherson asked, trying to pull the Mountie up.

"It's Charlie, he's gone through!" Durrant cried in a panic-striken tone.

"Where?"

"There!" Durrant pointed from his prone position towards where Charlie had vanished into the frozen river.

"Cut some poles," McPherson called to the men who had gathered round. "Hurry now!"

McPherson let go of Durrant and high-stepped toward the river, his arms flailing to keep himself upright in the deep snow. A thick crust had formed on the surface, but beneath it the snow had the consistency of sifted sugar, and the man plunged up to his waist with every step. More men came from the camp, one bearing a length of rope.

"Careful, for Christ's sake!" one of the men yelled to McPherson, who was nearing the place where Charlie had vanished.

Durrant tried to crawl, but ended up face down in the snow again. Two of the men emerged from the woods with a sapling stripped of its branches and went to the aid of McPherson. Two more men helped the struggling Durrant to his feet, his left hand still tightly clutching his pistol.

McPherson turned to see the men holding out the sapling, while another man tossed him a rope. He quickly tied the rope around his waist, took the sapling, and advanced on the area in the middle of the river where Charlie had vanished. The three men took hold of the rope and held it fast as McPherson stepped to the very edge of the darkened spot. He slipped and the men holding the rope all strained at the hemp line.

McPherson disappeared up to his shoulders in the snow and seemed to dive into the unknown depths. The sun sank behind the ramparts to the west and as it did, the entire valley seemed to shudder with the coming darkness.

"He's got him!" a man called from the rope line. "Bring blankets!"

Durrant, wide-eyed, watched as the three men on the rope heaved and the form of McPherson slowly emerged from the depression in the snow, his right hand around the collar of young Charlie.

"He's got him," the man called again, as several others advanced on the site with heavy wool blankets. By this time, there were fifty or more men on the shore, watching the undertaking. The men on the rope gave a mighty heave, and then McPherson found his feet, stood up, hefting the boy up onto the snow. The men grabbed at him and swaddled him in blankets.

"He's okay! He's okay!" one of them called.

"Blue as the Major's tongue, but he's okay," the navvie cracked.

"Let's get him inside!" yelled another.

"Take him to my cabin," said Durrant, awash with emotion. "Call for Doc Armatage."

"Get the fire stoked," said another man.

"Go and do it," said Durrant. "We'll meet you there."

McPherson had swept Charlie up in his arms and carried him quickly through the snow. The man was soaked himself, and the snow clung to him so he looked like an apparition ploughing through the deep drifts along the river's bank.

"Help me, please," said Durrant to the men next to him.

"Mind putting the pistol away, Sergeant?" said one of the men from the munitions warehouse.

Durrant, with shaking hands, put the Bulldog in his coat pocket, and with the help of the two men, met McPherson on the trail. Charlie was indeed blue in the face, his eyes closed, and his teeth chattering. He held his body tightly with his own arms, his over-sized coat drawn around him, dripping with icy water.

"Let me get this lad inside," said McPherson. The procession made its way along the trail to the NWMP cabin, where the volunteer had run ahead to stoke the fire. "Blue Jesus," said McPherson halfway along the path. "This lad looks light but carries heavy."

"Put him there on his bunk," Durrant said when they entered the barracks, pointing. McPherson put the boy down and Durrant managed to squeeze past. Sitting heavily on his own bunk, he reached over to pull the blankets over the boy.

"He didn't go through the ice," said McPherson.

"What happened?" said Durrant, his face ashen.

"There was melt water under the snow, but above the river ice proper, two, maybe three feet of it. As cold as the river, mind you. Happens when it warms up in these parts, snow on the river melts from underneath first. Your boy here broke through the crust of snow and into that icy stew. He's a lucky one, that's for certain."

"We owe you a debt of thanks," said Durrant, turning from Charlie to look at McPherson.

There was a commotion at the door and Saul Armatage appeared in his shirtsleeves, his black bag in hand. He pushed past a couple of the men who were milling at the door and said, "Durrant, you okay?"

"I'm fine; it's Charlie. He went into the melt water atop the ice on the river."

Armatage entered the room and pushed the door closed in the face of the men clustered there. "Let's have a look." He went to the bedside and looked at Charlie, hunched and shivering in a ball. "Charlie, I'm Doctor Armatage. How are you?"

"Lad don't speak, Saul," stammered Durrant.

The doctor nodded. He put his fingers to Charlie's carotid artery and felt for his pulse.

McPherson stood in front of the stove, looking down at the boy. "I don't think a frail lad like this ought to be in the mountains, if you don't mind me saying, Sergeant."

"You're entitled to your opinion, and I've no mind to argue with you, given what you just done. This lad's been a big help to me, though. I don't know what I'd do without him," replied Durrant.

McPherson just nodded. "I best be changing into warm skivvies myself."

Durrant expended his left hand. "Thank you."

McPherson shook it awkwardly, as he wasn't accustomed to shaking southpaw. "Remember this the next time you come round with your inquisition."

"I'll broker no favours in my investigation, mind," said Durrant.

"I don't expect you will," laughed McPherson.

He stepped to the door, but stopped and turned to look at Durrant and at Armatage. Charlie seemed to have drifted off to sleep. The doctor was trying to strip the boy's jacket from him without any luck.

"Sergeant," McPherson said. "I might as well tell you, as I'm certain you'll find out anyway. Hep Wilcox asked me to take over Deek Penner's duties. I'll be running the blasting contract on the Tote Road and on the first tunnel come the spring. I just thought I should 'fess up, what with your . . . inquiries."

Durrant just nodded at him.

"Alright then, goodnight." McPherson closed the door behind himself.

Durrant and Charlie were alone in the cabin with Armatage. The stove rattled as it heated up. Durrant watched Charlie. "How is he?" Durrant asked the doctor.

Armatage smiled. "He'll be fine. But we've got to get him out of these wet things and under the blankets. He's knotted up pretty tight."

Charlie opened his eyes, a faint smile across his soft face.

"I've already lost one," said Durrant, his face white as ash, "I dare say I don't want to lose you."

Saul looked over his shoulder at Durrant. Durrant was shaken from his musing when Charlie coughed. "What is it?" Durrant asked the boy.

Charlie struggled to free himself from the blankets. With his left hand he pushed the doctor's hands away from his coat.

"Easy, son, easy now. You've got to keep warm. In fact, we ought to get you out of those frozen clothes."

Charlie shook his head. He pushed the blankets off with his shoulders. As Armatage tried to pull them back up, Charlie none too gently grabbed his left hand, forcing the doctor to stop.

"Charlie!" scolded Durrant, but Armatage stepped back from the boy.

Charlie shook his head. He took off his covers, exposing his sodden jacket and the Mountie's leather chaps, crisp with ice. A wide grin came over the boy's lips.

Charlie pulled back the coat with his left hand and with his right revealed a two-and-a-half-foot long iron star drill.

"HE'S FOOLHARDY," SAID Armatage in a hushed voice. The two men sat by the door of the cabin, Durrant with his prosthetic off. The doctor unwrapped the man's stump. The doctor finished removing the bandage and was now examining the raw end of Durrant's leg. He frowned.

"I don't like the look of this, Durrant. This prosthetic is never going to be like a *real* leg. You've got to take it easy on it. You can't go hiking up into the mountains as if it were real live flesh and bone. It's just not made for that. I know it's difficult," he said, still whispering. "I know how hard this is for you. I know. We marched west together, remember?"

"I can't forget."

"Good, then you know I understand. I saw what you could do as a man with two good legs. You were the best rider in your company. If you don't take care of this," the doctor said, patting the man's leg paternally, "you're not going to be able to walk *at all*. You and I both know what that will do to you."

Durrant looked down where the doctor's hand still rested on his bare skin. He could not feel the man's fingers there, just the burning of the wound that would never heal.

"Alright then," the doctor said. "Let's get this fixed up for you." Armatage reached into his black satchel and took out a glass jar of ointment. As soon as he opened it, the room was filled with a powerful medicinal smell that made Durrant wince. Armatage ignored him and applied the thick ointment to the Mountie's leg. As he did, he spoke. "You haven't been by to see Evelyn as yet. She's taken offence, you know."

"I don't mean any."

"Oh, I tried to explain that to her, but you know how women can be. She expects a visit at some point, Durrant."

Durrant stared blankly at his ruined leg.

"She doesn't know about your past, Durrant. Nothing before Regina, at least. She doesn't know about what happened in Toronto. She won't ask. It's just between you and me. I've never discussed it with her." Durrant showed no sign of acknowledgement. "And she can cook, Durrant. You should bring the lad Charlie by and let Evelyn cook you a meal. It's bound to be better than the mashed turnips and flat steak you get from the camp cook most nights."

The doctor had finished dressing the Mountie's leg. "If you can, leave the prosthetic off for the night and then put more of this on in the morning," he said, handing the glass jar to Durrant. "You'll have to take it easy on the leg. No more mountaineering adventures. Catch a ride if you need to go somewhere."

Durrant nodded. He knew from experience that agreeing was easier than arguing with Armatage.

"What about the boy?" Durrant asked. They both turned to look at the sleeping lad.

"He'll be fine . . . so long as he stops running fool's errands for the likes of you."

Durrant smiled thinly and nodded. Armatage stood and picked up his bag. He had arrived with no coat and didn't ask for one to see him home. Durrant was lost in thought.

"Durrant," the doctor said.

The Mountie turned and looked at him.

"Charlie isn't . . ."

Durrant held up his hand so quickly that Armatage stopped speaking. "Don't," he said. "I'll mind your advice for my leg, Saul, but enough with the sermons."

The doctor broke into a wide smile, his dark, narrow face a mass of lines. "Very well, Durrant. You shall keep your own counsel, as you always have. Good night." With that the man stepped into the darkness beyond the cabin's door leaving Durrant in the darkness contained by the four walls.

ELEVEN

THE HONORABLE MEMBER
FOR NORTHUMBERLAND

TWO MORNINGS AFTER CHARLIE WAS plucked from the frozen clutches of the Bow River, Durrant awoke to the whistle of a train approaching Holt City. The chinook that had blown for the last four days had come to an end, and the Bow Valley was once again gripped in winter's clutches.

Charlie was already up and out. He had heard the boy leave almost an hour before. The lad was a miracle to Durrant. That the boy had not frozen to death in the Bow River was one thing; that he had the presence of mind to grasp the object of his search as it was sliding into possible oblivion was another. Durrant had told him so. Charlie had seemed pleased. Now the boy was off having breakfast. Since being snatched from the waters by Grant McPherson, the speechless lad had become something of a celebrity around the camp, and Durrant could not have been more pleased.

Durrant had been out late the night before, talking with the men of the camp, verifying alibis and discussing Deek Penner's friends and enemies, and hadn't gotten in until well after midnight. Though most men in the camp regarded him with suspicion, some with outright hostility, he managed to find his way to more than a few card tables and conversations crowded around a leaking woodstove. He had even enjoyed a meal of Bryndzové Halušky, a traditional Slovakian meal of dumplings served with cheese and bacon. When Durrant had stepped into a crowded boxcar dormitory he had interrupted a card game and a meal cooked on the top of the potbellied stove. After the men had confirmed Bob Pen's alibi as rock solid for the night of Penner's death, they had dealt him into the game and fed him a helping of the hearty food. Next to Charlie's stovetop fare, it was the best meal he'd had in months.

Durrant heard the second whistle of the locomotive as it approached the platform of Holt City. He pulled on his prosthetic and dressed quickly, wanting to see who disembarked from the train, and who might stow away on it for the return trip to Fort Calgary. Dressed, he stepped out of the cabin into the morning.

He arrived at the same time as the train and joined half a dozen others on the platform. Most of these men were now familiar to Durrant. After a week in their midst he was coming to know them, and to know the camp's habits. At the last minute—the train squealing as it came to rest—Wilcox appeared on the platform from his office, pulling on his coat and gloves and donning a sharp bowler cap.

Durrant stood back and watched as the doors to the first two boxcars slid back and about a hundred men disembarked onto the platform. They milled about in a sort of orderly chaos as Pen, McPherson, Dodds, and several other foremen called to them, finding those who had been promised work and snatching up the most favorable among them that hadn't, but who looked as if they might fit their bill. As this happened, half a dozen other boxcars were being unloaded of their freight.

As the men filtered off, their baggage loaded onto sleds and their new employers extolling the virtues of work along the mainline of the CPR, a solitary figure stepped from the caboose of the train. This was a different sort of fellow for Holt City. The man was dressed in a full-length black coat, and as he paused on the snowy platform, he placed a beaver-felt top hat onto his neatly parted hair. He wore a long white beard thick through the chops, and his eyebrows shone above green eyes like icebergs. He adjusted his black leather gloves and took up a silver-handled cane to make his way down the platform. Durrant watched Wilcox move forward to greet the man, and the two of them shook hands and conversed on the platform amid the shuffle of freight and the sorting of labourers. The steam from the locomotive's brakes drifted like cotton threads across the sun-decked platform.

Durrant stood at the far end of the clearing, away from the tumult, and observed the goings on. Shortly, Wilcox turned in his direction and raised a hand, pointing directly at him. Durrant felt a hot wave wash up his body and colour his face. Wilcox leaned towards the man and Durrant could see that he spoke a few words into the man's ear before leading him Durrant's way.

This new top-hatted man was no man of hard labour. He looked familiar to Durrant, and as the stranger and Wilcox strode forward, Durrant searched his memory for how he might know the face.

"Sergeant Wallace," said Wilcox as the two stopped before him.

Durrant remained silent.

"Sergeant, this is Mr. Blake O'Brian . . ." Of course. Durrant's mind snapped to attention. "Mr. O'Brian is the Honorable Member for Northumberland and Vice-Chair of the House of Commons Select Standing Committee on Railways, Canals, and Telegraph Lines."

"It's a pleasure to meet you, sir," and Durrant extended his left hand.

The Member of Parliament reached out with his right and grasped it, unsurprised.

"It's a pleasure to meet you, Sergeant. Now, exactly what the hell is going on with our railroad here?" the man demanded.

THE TWO MEN sat crowded into Wilcox's tiny office. The Member of Parliament had placed his overcoat, gloves, and hat neatly on the desk. He sat upright in Wilcox's chair, his hand resting on his cane. Durrant noticed how smooth and soft the man's large fingers appeared.

Blake O'Brian was a man accustomed to speaking first. "Alright, Sergeant, I'll have a full report from you about the goings on here at the end of steel."

Durrant cleared his throat. "If you don't mind me saying so, sir, I report to Sam Steele, Superintendant for the North West Mounted Police."

"And he works for the Dominion Government, of which I am a senior Member."

"Of the Opposition, sir."

"I am an officer of the House of Commons, and as such, entitled to extract a report from you, Sergeant. Need I contact Steele himself?"

"The Superintendent is away on business, sir. The Métis."

O'Brian's face seemed to glass over a moment. "Yes, yes, a nasty business brewing there."

"Yes, sir."

"Sergeant," the MP said, his tone having levelled somewhat. "I am the ranking member of the Opposition on the Select Standing Committee on Railways. As such, I am here on behalf of Mr. Edward Blake himself, in his role as leader of Her Majesty's Loyal Opposition. I am here to ascertain the status of the progress of the mainline, and understand what barriers stand in the way of its completion, on time and on budget."

"Sir, your Mr. McKenzie was opposed to the rail line."

"What of it?"

"Only that I can't imagine you using anything I tell you to aid in its completion."

"Sergeant Wallace," the MP said testily, "I have only the best interests of the country in mind here. Certainly, while he was Prime Minister, Mr. McKenzie expressed some doubts about his predecessor's zeal for the Dominion railway. After all, it was so poorly handled by Sir John while he served his first term. I assure you, our new leader, Mr. Blake, wants to see the mainline completed as quickly as any other Member of Parliament in Ottawa. It is, after all, a matter of national pride, and a matter of unity, that this railway come into use, and soon!"

Durrant sat back in his chair. He regarded the man a moment. "Alright then," he finally said.

"You'll report then," said O'Brian.

"I'll tell you what I think relevant."

"I want it all, sir," said the MP.

"You'll have to settle for what I give you, sir. I am conducting a murder investigation, after all."

That seemed to take the wind out of the MP's sails, as he sat back and tapped his fingers on the fine handle of his cane. "Go ahead then, Sergeant."

Durrant told him about the circumstances surrounding the death of Deek Penner. The MP listened.

"So you think it might be related to the brewing of illegal whiskey?" the MP asked.

"It is possible. I know of at least one distillery in the vicinity, but I've not yet be able to locate it. I am reasonably certain I know which man is making and selling the whiskey—a federal offence, I might add—and that man was among the last to see Deek Penner before he was brutally murdered."

The MP was silent a moment. He pulled at the long tufts of white hair that grew like chops along the ridge of his cheeks. "Tell me, Sergeant, what authority are you acting under regarding the disruption of the whiskey trade?"

Durrant leaned back. "The Dominion temperance laws are clear, Mr. O'Brian."

"Of course they are, Sergeant," blustered the MP. "The selling of whiskey is illegal. *Possession* is not. I would imagine that if you were cooped up in this God-forsaken country for the long darkness of an interminable winter, you'd want a drink now and again too."

Durrant shook his head. "I would expect more from you, sir. I would expect a better understanding of the impact that whiskey can have on the construction of this railway."

"Do not lecture me," interrupted the MP. "I understand full well, sir, what its impact could be. What I want to know is why you are wasting your time on harassing this operation's foremen when you should be trying to find a killer."

"Did Mr. Wilcox tell you I was harassing someone in the camp?"

"No, he did not."

"Then who did?"

"All I will say is that the Dominion Government would do well to take this investigation more seriously. Why is it that they sent a single man, and one who obviously needs assistance here in the wilds, to undertake such an important investigation?"

Durrant was dumbfounded, and his face must have showed it.

"Don't get me wrong, Sergeant. I'm certain you're a capable Mountie. It's just that a murder investigation is such an important undertaking . . ."

"You would know because you've conducted so many, Mr. O'Brian?" The MP made as if to open his mouth, but Durrant stopped him. "I don't suppose to understand the parry and thrust of national politics, Mr. O'Brian. Do you come here to educate me on the undertaking of a murder investigation?"

O'Brian looked as if he'd been slapped. "Mr. Wallace . . ."

"It's *Sergeant* Wallace," said the Mountie, taking up his crutch and pushing himself to standing. "I am a veteran of the March West, sir, and have served Her Majesty for the last eleven years. My service has earned me the rank of non-commissioned officer and sergeant of the force. That service cost me my leg and the use of my right hand. I've suffered the jeers of drunkards and layabouts but I will suffer *no* such indignation from the likes of *you*. I report to Samuel Steele, Commanding, North West Mounted Police. I answer to no one else, and certainly not to you. You, of course, are free to contest that, but I should warn you: nobody in Holt City is above the law, and as yet, nobody is above investigation for this crime, and I should say that your appearance here so close on the heels of this grave wrongdoing is curious, to say the least."

The Member of Parliament rose shakily to his feet. "Sir," he stammered, "I demand . . ."

"You shall not have it," Durrant cut him off. "I will not apologize to you. Not if it was with my very last breath. Drunks and navvies might not, but you, sir, should know better. I dare say *you* do. Someone has been educating you as to my undertakings here, and I find that very curious indeed. Now, if you'll excuse me . . ." Durrant stepped past the Vice-Chair and out of the cramped office, and into the station's main room. He turned back and looked at the MP. "Welcome to the North West Territories," he said, and walked from the station.

DURRANT DID AS he had done for the last five days and counting. He unlocked the shed in which the frozen cadaver of Deek Penner lay and stepped inside. With his left hand, he trimmed and lit the wick of a tiny lantern. He bent to where the body was laid out on the cordwood that doubled as a morgue table. Durrant pulled back the oilcloth that covered the body, whose face was ringed in frost.

The day after the star drill had been recovered, Durrant had managed to shave the side and back of Penner's head in order to better match the suspected murder weapon with the dead man's wounds. They were a perfect fit. With the young Charlie acting as assistant, Durrant had laid the corpse on its side and fitted the eight-sided bit from the two-and-a-half-foot long length of drill steel neatly into place.

He held the drill and stepped back as far as he could and examined it. Penner was roughly six feet three inches tall. He was a big man. The drill angled down and to the right of Penner's skull. It was obvious that whoever murdered Penner was somewhat shorter. It was likely that the killer had struck from the left.

FROM THE SHACK that served as a morgue, Durrant headed along the pathway to the NWMP cabin, expecting to find Charlie waiting for him there when he arrived, but the room was empty. He stood a moment in the cabin wondering how to proceed when he saw the writing tablet propped on his own bunk. He stepped to the bed and picked it up with his left hand.

"Gone to have tea with Mrs. Armatage. Join us."

"Blue Jesus," muttered Durrant. He tossed the slate back onto the bed and made for the door.

Saul Armatage and his family had been afforded the most spacious accommodation in Holt City. Though temporary in nature, their cabin was well situated on the bank of the Pipestone River, set apart from the shacks of the men so that their carousing and tireless fiddle music wouldn't arouse the young family in the night. There was even a hand-carved shingle set on the wall next to the crudely fashioned door: SAUL ARMATAGE, MD.

Durrant paused a moment at the door. Through its thin frame he could hear the sound of a child crying inside, and the din of another banging on a tin pot. He could hear Evelyn Armatage's familiar laugh, a sound that spirited him away for a moment to the hospital in Regina where he had first met the light-hearted woman. He drew a breath and knocked. He heard Evelyn say something and in a moment the door open and his lad Charlie was standing before him, his face cracked with a broad smile, his blue eyes beaming.

"You had me worried a moment, lad," Durrant said sternly, and Charlie's grin faded perceptively. "You ought not to run off like that and leave me to think that our prey has struck again."

Charlie looked down a moment. From behind him he heard Evelyn Armatage call, "Come in, Durrant, you're letting the cold air at the place. And leave the boy alone. He's helping set out the tea!"

Charlie looked up and stepped to the side as Durrant entered the cabin. It was warm and smelled of fresh-baked bread. Durrant shouldered the door shut and turned to peruse the room. There was a table set in the middle of the square space, and along the far wall was a cook stove where two loaves of bread sat on the warming rack. The stove doubled as the source of heat for the room and filled the chamber with delicious warmth. Sitting on the floor by the stove was Oliver, now four years old, playing with a wooden train set. On a daybed on the adjacent wall, Evelyn sat holding the baby Ben to her breast. "Hello, Durrant," she said, beaming up at him. "Lovely to see you again!"

They sat at the table and took their tea. Armatage joined them from the adjacent room, which served as his clinic. It had been a light morning, he explained. One man badly bruised, but not broken, a hand caught when a log rolled on it at the mill site; another with a wound on his leg from an axe that ricocheted off a frozen stump and caught him in the shin.

Durrant sat stiffly at the table as Evelyn fed Oliver his tea, and Armatage held the baby, slowly bouncing the child on his knee. The doctor talked about the various maladies that might afflict a man while working in the mountains, prattling off a dizzying list of ailments that could strike a man down in his prime, seemingly overnight. Meanwhile, Charlie sat silently taking in the entire scene, a smile on his young face.

"This young man is quite the help," said Evelyn with a wink at Durrant. "I think he got the knack of baking bread on his first go."

Durrant looked at Charlie who only smiled back.

"If you're not careful, Durrant, I might steal him away from you to help here with the children." Evelyn was in her late twenties; she wore a long, heavy skirt and a sweater pulled tight around her slender frame.

"I'll have to keep a closer eye on the lad," Durrant said, forcing a smile.

Charlie moved the plate holding slices of the fresh bread and tinned meat towards Durrant, and when he awkwardly tried the cut the loaf with his left hand, Charlie deftly stood and took the knife from the Mountie and did it himself. He then poured tea for the family and for Durrant.

"Tell us, Durrant," said Evelyn, spooning porridge into Oliver's mouth as he fidgeted at the table, "how are you progressing with the capture of the killer?"

"Well," said Durrant awkwardly, "I suppose we've got several suspects at this time," looking at Charlie, in part to reclaim him.

"That awful brute Frank Dodds must be chief among them," said Evelyn.

"He is," said Durrant.

"And who else?"

"Evi, darling, Durrant might not wish to tip his hand. Recall," said the doctor with a sly smile, "that he's already inquired after *my* own whereabouts on the night of the murder."

"Well," said Evelyn with a wink, "if you must know, *I* was here in bed with my Oliver and little Ben. Though I'm not sure their word will stand up in a court of law as an alibi."

Durrant regarded the children. "No, I doubt it will, but if you're not careful, I'll have you all in leg irons before the day is out."

"That's the spirit," said Evelyn. "Now Charlie," she said, "be a good lad and see about that pie that we put in the oven." Charlie obediently rose to fetch the dessert.

"The truth is, Evelyn," said Durrant, looking down at his hands, the reddened right hand resting atop the left in his lap, "that I'm not certain which direction to take this investigation next. I have a long list of suspects, all of whom may have wanted Mr. Penner dead for one reason or another, and all of whom had access to the murder weapon. As yet, I haven't been able to determine who was most motivated to dispatch Mr. Penner. My list of suspects keeps growing longer and longer," he said, thinking of the arrival of the Honorable Member for Northumberland.

When they had finished their dessert, Charlie cleared the dishes and Durrant rose stiffly from his chair, leaning heavily on his crutch. "*We* must be off," he said, "as I have a fair number of men to question this afternoon. No doubt," he sighed wearily, "many of them will tell a familiar tale of virtuousness, but it must be done. Sooner or later I'm bound to find someone who will simply confess to this heinous crime in order to be rid of me and my maddening questions." Evelyn and Saul Armatage laughed and rose to their feet, the doctor shaking Durrant's left hand and Evelyn embracing Durrant and kissing his grizzled cheek.

"It's good to see you crack wise, Durrant," she said. "Don't be a stranger. Bring that lad of yours about for a proper meal sometime. He and I have so much we could chat about, if he only decided to speak."

DARKNESS HAD SETTLED over the broad girth of the Bow Valley. That evening Durrant sat in his cabin at the tiny desk, a candle burning in a cup set out next to a pad of writing paper. The woodstove crackled, warming him. The temperature outside had settled around ten degrees; the sky overhead was clear.

Deek Penner had been struck in the face by someone swinging a star drill from his left. That didn't mean, necessarily, that the assailant had been left-handed, Durrant mused. In fact, because the woods were denser on the eastern side of the track, it seemed reasonable to assume that this was where the killer had approached Penner. Durrant considered the angle of the weapon's mark on the murdered man's face and skull. That the blow appeared to come at a slightly oblique angle made him think that the killer was shorter than Penner, maybe somewhat less than six feet tall, and possibly a good deal shorter.

Next Durrant turned his thoughts to Penner's motivation that night: What mission was he on that could not wait until the morning, he wondered? His assailant must have known he would be coming and had lain in wait for his prey. Or maybe the meeting was pure chance. Maybe the killer simply seized an opportunity. But why would any man be out at night with a length of drill steel in his hands? No, mused Durrant, the murder had been clearly premeditated.

Durrant pressed his eyes shut. Two days before he'd been in the very snows where the murder took place. He opened his eyes with a start: step off the path and you might sink up to your knees, or waist, in the sugary snow there. The foot-wide pathways were packed hard, but the snow next to them was soft, and the attacker, unless he was a giant, would *have* to have swung from below. Unless he was on the path with Penner himself, in which case the attack could not have been made by surprise. Unless Penner was being accompanied by someone he had no fear of.

There were too many variables, thought Durrant, frustrated, and no way to verify any of them, unless the dead could speak. Durrant's rumination was interrupted as the door to his cabin flew open, a blast of cold air hitting him, a swirl of snow preceding a body wrapped in a heavy coat and a thick wool hat pulled close over the eyes. Durrant's hand leapt for the British Bulldog and in less than a heartbeat the hammer was cocked and the snub-nosed pistol levelled not a foot from the night visitor.

Durrant lowered his pistol. "You trying to get your face blown off, boy?" Durrant barked.

Charlie shook his head once and grabbed for the quill and paper on the desk. He scribbled something quickly. "Follow you. Quick?" Charlie nodded. "Why?"

"O'Brian," Charlie wrote. Durrant grabbed his bison coat and sealskin hat, and stuffed the Bulldog into his coat pocket. He snubbed out the candle with his fingers and followed Charlie into the darkening night.

IT TOOK THEM five minutes to reach the munitions warehouse through the inky blackness; Charlie practically dragged Durrant along the icy pathways. The trails were now frozen hard and slippery.

Many of the main pathways had been darkened with sawdust and the ash from the camps' stoves, making them easier to navigate, but the little-used path to the NWMP barracks had gone unimproved.

Durrant felt his leg aching by the time they reached the munitions warehouse, but when Charlie led him through the darkness to a place behind the building, out of sight of the broad front doors, Durrant forgot about his discomfort. He could see the boy's eyes were wide in the gloom. The lad took him by the hand as if he were a child, pulling him alongside the building as he cocked an ear towards the open boards that permitted daylight inside.

Durrant looked at Charlie and was about to speak when the boy held a finger to his lips and shook his head vigorously. They waited a moment like that in the darkness, the night around them cold and deep and still. Then Durrant heard a voice.

"Just what do you expect me to do?" the distant voice said.

Durrant closed his eyes to place the sound of the man's voice with a face. It was Wilcox.

"This business with the whiskey has become a problem, Mr. Wilcox."

Wilcox was talking with Blake O'Brian. "Since when did you take such a concern with temperance, Mr. O'Brian?"

"Since it brought the Mounties to Holt City, that's when," said O'Brian.

Durrant guessed that the two men were standing not twenty feet away on the other side of the wall. They spoke in low but not hushed voices.

"Durrant Wallace is onto Dodds. It won't be long before he shuts him down. I think he'll collar that fool for Deek's murder. Dodds has it coming. That Red Coat is a real bulldog."

"That's what worries me," said O'Brian.

"There's nothing to be worried about. Nothing at all."

"We'll see," said O'Brian.

"You're going to have to trust me, Mr. O'Brian."

Durrant could hear the two men shuffle in the warehouse.

"Okay. You've not let me down so far. But still, having the Mounties here in Holt City is not what we had planned for."

"The murder of Deek Penner will be solved shortly. I have every confidence. Wallace will be back to sorting the post and sending wires by the time the next chinook blows through. There's nothing to concern yourself with. Besides, he's obsessed with the whiskey trade; he isn't concerned about the contracts. He doesn't understand them."

The two men were silent a moment. Durrant pressed his eyes shut, straining to hear. When the two men spoke again, their tone was more hushed.

"Listen, Wilcox, I don't need to tell you how much is at stake here. This contract is probably the most lucrative expenditure for the whole of the CPR. It's got to be handled right."

"I know what's at stake, Mr. O'Brian."

"Parliament is tied up in knots over this. The expenditure is four, maybe five times what we thought it would be. The numbers are staggering."

"It costs a lot of money to put a railway where Fleming and Stephen and Rogers want it. The Kicking Horse Pass is a thousand-foot drop on the far side."

"What I'm telling you is that there's a lot of money to be made."

"I know exactly what you are telling me. Everything is proceeding as we discussed, Mr. Vice-Chair."

"What's it going to take for the Canada Explosives Company to forfeit the contract?"

There was a long moment of silence.

"Well? What will it take?"

"Something dramatic, I'm afraid," said Wilcox.

"That's what worries me, sir."

"It's a nasty piece of work, the Kicking Horse Pass, Mr. O'Brian. It's going to be a dangerous place for a navvy to find himself come the spring. I think we can assume that before the Tote Road is complete, more than a few of these fellows will be tucked in along side of the track. You'll have every right to raise questions of the safety of the explosives work when that happens."

Durrant opened his eyes wide.

"Alright," said Blake O'Brian. "I expect to be kept up to date on this matter. The Parliament of Canada will suffer no further abuse of the public purse."

"Of course, Mr. Vice-Chair," said Wilcox. "Now, let me show you the rest of the stores we've put up. And in the next couple of days, I shall show you to the Kicking Horse summit, where work has already begun on the short-lived munitions plant there."

Durrant heard both men laugh, the sound of their voices fading as they moved away. He turned to Charlie, who was wide-eyed, scanning around them. Charlie put a finger to his lips again. Durrant heard the large doors to the warehouse creak and watched as a light moved off towards the station.

Charlie tugged at Durrant's arm and the two of them made their way by another pathway back to their bunk. Durrant stopped them on the path. "Wait a minute, son," said Durrant.

Charlie looked around. The boy was obviously concerned about detection.

"Wait a minute," Durrant repeated. From where they stood they could not see the station. "I need to get word to Steele. I need him to look into this man O'Brian. I should have done it sooner." Charlie shook his head. "Yes, tonight," said Durrant. "Take me to the station."

Charlie looked around, getting his bearings. He tugged at Durrant's arm and the two men circled through the woods. When they reached the Bow, Durrant could see the station a few hundred yards up river. Charlie led him along the frosty path to the rail bed, and then along the tracks the last fifty yards to the empty platform. There was no light on in the station.

"Okay, boy, you go and see if you can eyeball O'Brian or Wilcox in that office of his. Be quiet, and be careful," said Durrant.

Charlie looked around him, then carefully picked his way across the tracks and up onto the station platform. Durrant watched him from his hiding place in the dark. He could just make out the lad creeping quietly up to the station along the wall. He knew he was asking a lot of the boy; he could not be certain that Wilcox or

O'Brian weren't dangerous. He did know that they were up to some malfeasance as it pertained to contracts.

Only Steele himself might be able to make the appropriate inquiries in Ottawa, Trenton, and elsewhere. Durrant knew that the police department in Trenton—O'Brian's home town—was rife with cronyism and political interference. It was possible that inquires into the Member of Parliament's affairs would at best be rebuffed, and worst, reported back to the MP immediately.

Charlie reached the door and headed for the window of Wilcox's office. The boy crouched down and crept along the platform on hands and knees. He was beginning to straighten up when suddenly a light came to life in the office, and Charlie ducked down below the window.

Durrant could clearly see the outline of a man through the frosted glass, a lantern held aloft, its pale yellow light puncturing the icy pane and trickling onto the station platform. Charlie lay prone on the bare boards beneath the window.

Durrant stood up. He felt for the pistol, but considered his next move. If Charlie faced detection, what good would his pistol do? If they found Charlie snooping around the platform, what more could they do than scold the boy and deliver him back to his bunk? If O'Brian and Wilcox were rigging contracts . . . Durrant considered his assessment of the danger they posed. Could a rigged contract be enough to motivate a man to murder? It certainly could if there was a million dollars at stake.

Durrant focused his attention on the light in the window. He saw Charlie look back over his shoulder toward Durrant. Hidden in the darkness, Durrant's hand signals to stay put were lost on the lad.

The light faded from the window, but soon the door to the station platform was pushed open, the frozen hinges protesting in the still night, and the two men stepped out onto the platform. The open door obscured Charlie from Durrant's view. The shaft of light fell across the platform, and Durrant could no longer observe where the boy was hiding.

Durrant held his breath as the silhouetted figures of O'Brian and Wilcox pushed the door shut behind them. In a second they would turn and the light of their lamp would fall across Charlie's prone form just ten feet from where they stood. The door was fastened shut and the lamp bearer—Durrant guessed it to be Wilcox—began to move.

Durrant slipped the Enfield—a better pistol for distance—from his holster beneath his coat. If either of these men laid a glove on Charlie, he would answer with force of his own. The Mountie held his breath.

The light of the lamp fell upon the platform beneath the office window—but Charlie was not there. Durrant exhaled a long stream of icy breath and felt his left hand relax on the hammer of the pistol. The two men walked from the station platform in silence. Durrant watched the lamp fade in the distance, and then disappear entirely.

Suddenly, Durrant felt a presence beside him, and he turned with a start. When he saw it was Charlie, he holstered the Enfield.

"Blue Jesus, boy, that was a close call." He looked at the lad, who was smiling. "You like sneaking around. Done that a lot, have you?" Charlie nodded. "Alright, lad," Durrant said, straightening. "Let's go and send this wire."

> From Durrant Wallace.
> To Sam Steele.
> Trouble at end of track. MP Blake O'Brian and Hep Wilcox overheard discussing explosives contracts and plan to rig transfer of demo contract from Canada Explosives Company to another party. Investigate O'Brian's business arrangements in Trenton. Inform of any involvement with TNT production. Concern that lives at risk in process. Send word soon.

It was past midnight when Durrant and Charlie once again made their way over the slick pathways to the NWMP cabin. Durrant's thoughts swirled with everything he had learned as they proceeded through the star-filled night.

The day's conflicts continued to play out in the Mountie's addled mind. Durrant knew little about the inquiry into such a crime as murder and he was beginning to feel in over his head. The North West Mounted Police had no investigation unit; their work on the Prairie didn't call for it. Most often serious crimes such as theft and murder didn't require an investigator so much as a fast horse. This was different. The culprit was likely hiding in plain view. Durrant knew that some of Canada's more advanced police forces, such as those in Toronto, Ottawa, and Montreal, were developing the ability to trace a man by his fingerprints, but such technology was not available to the North West Mounted Police. Even if it were, the murder weapon had been recovered from a pool of ice water. With no witnesses to the killing, and only Christianson's account of the discovery of the body, there was precious little evidence.

It seemed to Durrant that solving this crime would come down to the circumstances. It would be a matter of determining who had the most reason for wanting Penner dead, and then flushing that person from the cover of plain view. The list of reasons people might have wanted the man dead was growing. The threat that Penner might throw a spanner in Dodds' suspected moonshine operation was but one. The last few days had yielded two more: Penner's reported confrontation with the mysterious spy for the Grand Trunk Railway, and now this clandestine relationship between Hep Wilcox, the MP Blake O'Brian, and the munitions contracts for the Big Hill section of the CPR. The entire affair left Durrant at a loss.

TWELVE

MEANS, MOTIVE, OPPORTUNITY

MORNING FOUND DURRANT ON THE banks of the Bow River near its confluence with the Pipestone River. He was again lost in deliberation when he heard a noise behind him. Durrant's hand intuitively wrapped around the butt of his Bulldog.

"No need to draw your weapon, sir," came a lilting voice from just a few feet to Durrant's left. "I am unarmed, and a friend at that."

Durrant, surprised that someone had come so close to him without him hearing, began to pull the pistol from the pocket just the same. He turned on the man and saw a gentleman in a long tan coat standing but ten feet from him. He was clean shaven and dark in the face, his nose peeling with sunburn; only his eyes were ringed in white, as if he'd had them covered while out in the sun. On his feet were heavy leather riding boots, on his head, a thick beaverskin hat. The man clenched an unlit pipe tightly in his teeth.

As Durrant turned, the gentleman turned too and extended his left hand in greeting. "I am Garnet Moberly. I am the engineer in charge of, among other matters, the laying out of the Kicking Horse Tote Road, and for proving the survey of the Canadian Pacific mainline down the Lower Kicking Horse Canyon and on into the Columbia country." His accent was strong but clear. London, thought Durrant, but come to Canada by parts unknown.

Durrant let go of his pistol and stepped forward. Moberly moved two quick steps in and took Durrant's hand.

"Sergeant Durrant Wallace. North West Mounted Police."

"Indeed you are. It's a pleasure, sir."

"Pleasure is mine."

"I've just returned from the Columbia. Upon checking in with Mr. Wilcox I was informed of the untimely demise of Mr. Penner, and of your arrival at The Summit to ensure justice is done."

"The Summit?"

"Herbert Samuel and his brother Tom are fine lads, and no doubt the former is destined for great things, but I do not feel this cluster of shakes requires their name. This place has many a moniker: Laggan and Holt City among them, but it was called The Summit upon the arrival of the steel, and I shall call it that until our mainline is well and advanced from this glorious place and Her Majesty sees fit to bestow a proper name."

The two men contemplated one another for a moment It was Moberly who broke the silence. "Sergeant Wallace, would you fancy a cup of tea?"

Durrant looked at the man. He was trim and stood six feet tall, broad across the shoulders even under his heavy coat. For the first time Durrant noticed the white line of a scar across his left cheek that looked like an awkward crease that extended from his left eye all the way to the line of the man's jaw.

"That would be good," Durrant said.

"Very well, please follow me to my cabin. I'll have Mr. Jimmy bring us the service."

They passed Mr. Kim's laundry and the cut in the Bow River where the camp drew its water on the way to Moberly's cabin. Durrant noted it was of a much sturdier construction than the others in the camp, save the station and the general store. The boards had been roughly hewn, but they were fastened with butterfly joints rather than the crude construction of heavy nails. Where most of the other huts in the camp were chinked with mud or a slurry of turf and plaster, Moberly's walls were tightly constructed. There was no canvas roof; his abode sported a neat, if not practical, milled crown. His stovepipe was shining sheet metal, unlike the rusting and refurbished chimneys that adorned most other buildings.

Moberly opened the door to his cabin. "Please come in. I'll see that Mr. Jimmy brings us cakes as well as the tea service."

The interior was bright, and Durrant realized that the man had a functioning window in his domicile. A small bed was pressed against one wall, and on it a heavy pack, still bursting at the seams with winter gear, sat as though he really had only arrived back in Holt City that very hour. A small table was positioned against the wall on the opposite side of a warm, efficient looking woodstove. Where most of the cabins in Holt City had potbellied stoves or improvised ones made from upended barrels and jury-rigged tin cans as stovepipes, Moberly's seemed to be of the finest quality and perfect for keeping a small space warm in the worst conditions. Two small, folding camp chairs were set out by the stove. The room was cozy and smelled clean and fresh. Durrant would not have been surprised to see flowers on the windowsill.

"Sergeant Wallace, please, take a seat. Let me step next door to see to Mr. Jimmy, and make a swift return. I am anxious to hear your stories of adventure and learn what progress has been made in apprehending Mr. Penner's executioner."

With that, Moberly took his leave, and Durrant sat down in front of the stove. He opened his coat and let his numb right hand rest on his leg. He had a chance to look about the room. Next to the overstuffed pack rested a Martini-Henry breech-loading rifle, and beside that a pair of twin Webley revolvers. Durrant twisted in his chair to regard the rifle better. It appeared to have suffered heavy use; its barrel had several nicks and gashes, and along the shoulder stock was a long deep score. Mr. Moberly, it seemed, was a soldier.

Durrant let his eyes drift further. A stack of books rested by the bed on an antique table. Next to the books was an exotic figurine with the head of an elephant and the torso of a man. Most interesting to Durrant, however, were the spear, shield, and ball club that adorned the wall above the bed. Nearly five feet in length, the shield was tan, black, and white in colour. It appeared to be made from a hide, reinforced with a richly coloured wood. The spear was short with a broad tip and a thick shaft. The club was nearly as long as the spear, and looked both dense and deadly. Durrant thought about Penner's ruined face and head.

"I see you're admiring the spoils of war, Sergeant." Again, Moberly was there before Durrant had become aware of him. A cool gust of wind from the open door seemed to reach the Mountie after Moberly's words.

"You were in Africa?"

"And elsewhere."

"You fought in the Zulu war?"

"Not so much a war as a slaughter."

"For who?"

"Well spoken. The Empire had the last laugh, I dare say, but not before suffering serious losses." Durrant looked at the long scar across the man's face. "Indeed, Sergeant. We all carry our burden." Moberly then laughed and said, "I can't be certain if that spear is the assegai that took my eye and cleaved this line down my face, but it might well be."

"Eye?"

"Indeed, sir, this bobble," he said, pointing to the left eye, "is nothing more than a trinket, courtesy of Her Majesty."

Durrant made an effort not to regard Moberly for too long, conscious as he was of such an intrusion.

"And the club?"

"The Zulu call it a knob-kerrie. It simply completes the set, Sergeant." At that there was a knock at the door. "That would be our tea," said Moberly, turning smartly.

The gentleman opened the door and a dark-skinned man entered the room with a tea service that he placed between the two chairs before the fire. Durrant regarded the man Moberly called Mr. Jimmy: he had hair shorn very short and the almond-shaped eyes of the Orient, but his skin was darker than the Chinese that Durrant knew worked on the western section of the railway. Durrant guessed that the servant was East Indian. The man set the tea service: there was a pot of tea and cups, all of the finest china, along with a plate of cakes and biscuits. Milk and sugar were in matching bowls.

"Thank you, Mr. Jimmy." Wordlessly, the man left the room. "May I pour for you, Sergeant?"

"Go ahead," said Durrant, and immediately felt bad for assuming Moberly was asking because of his game hand. This might be the only cultured man in this corner of the North West Territories, thought Durrant.

Moberly poured the tea. "Milk or sugar?"

"Black is fine, thank you."

Moberly poured his and added a little milk from the service. "I'm afraid that the cakes may not be the freshest. Mr. Jimmy has been with me, of course, on the Columbia, and has had to dip into our stores. I think you'll find them favorable to the hash served in the mess tent."

Durrant took a small round cake in his left hand and bit into it. Indeed, it was very good. He nodded appreciatively.

"You're curious about Jimmy?"

Durrant sipped his tea and made eye contact with Moberly. "He's Indian?"

"Tibetan."

Durrant put the teacup down and regarded the man.

"I *was* in India for some time, Sergeant. This was more than thirty years ago now. I worked out of Calcutta on the rail lines running north towards Delhi and into the mountains. I left this employ after the rail reached Allahabad, and went north, with an interest in exploring the cultures and landscapes of the Himalaya. That is when I met Mr. Jimmy. He worked for me while I was employed by the High Commissioner in Rawlinpindi. We've been together now these twenty-five years . . ."

Moberly paused a moment. "They are little-known, Sergeant Wallace, the people of the Tibetan Plateau. They are among the last people on earth yet untouched by the clutches of progress. Mr. Jimmy is a Buddhist. They are a very peaceful people."

"But surely there are more interesting mysteries afoot, sir," Moberly added.

Durrant took a sip of his tea. It was simply the finest tea he had tasted since arriving in the west eleven years ago.

"First, Sergeant, I am anxious to learn something of the man himself. Tell me about yourself before we sink into the banalities of this prosaic crime."

"There is very little to tell," said Durrant, suddenly uncomfortable.

"I simply do not believe that."

"You may have to."

"No man would take an assignment at the end of steel in the deepest winter and arrive on one leg and with one hand and have only a mere lad in his employ, and a mute at that, and not have a story to tell."

"There may be a story, but it's not for the telling."

Moberly laughed. It was not the bark that Durrant had grown accustomed to in Fort Calgary or here at the end of steel; it was a cultured laugh, one that came in consort with the subject, not at the expense of him. It put Durrant at ease and he forgot for a moment that *he* was the investigator.

"Come now, you won't deny me the opportunity to hear of your travels across these great North West Territories, will you? I doubt very much that I shall have such an opportunity to hear first-hand of the March West and other adventures again."

"What leads you to believe I was on the March West?"

"Were you not?"

"I was."

"So tell me something of it."

"It's already been romanticized in the eastern press," Durrant found himself saying. "The reality, however, is somewhat different. How quickly we like to forget."

"I can only surmise," laughed Moberly.

Durrant found himself enjoying the sound of the man's voice. It was the first civilized tongue he'd heard in the year since leaving Regina, with the exception of his friend the doctor.

"Tell me, Sergeant, what made you join the force in the first place? You seem to me an educated man, one at least with a decent upbringing. Not a farm boy, for certain."

Durrant looked down at the teacup in his hand. "No, not a farm boy. My father was a merchant; he owned an import and export company and a warehouse complex on the Quay in Toronto. He was born in that city when it was still York Town. I was destined to take over that business, it seemed. I studied the law and was preparing for the bar, in fact. My father had raised me for that; I learned to read and write and do mathematics and to think: he sent me to school for several years at Upper Canada College and also the University of Toronto."

Moberly watched him. "A prestigious school, for certain, Upper Canada. The royal family has a stake there."

Durrant just nodded, his face suddenly pale. His left hand clutched the teacup tightly.

"But something happened," Moberly said after a moment's silence.

"I signed on with French in 1874 is what happened. I decided the city wasn't for me. It was many years ago now. A decade has passed," Durrant said, seeming to grasp the passage of those years for the first time.

"The secrets men keep," said Moberly his eye dark and piercing. Then he straightened and said, "So tell me, do you have a suspect for the murder of Mr. Penner?"

Durrant remained lost a moment, his own eyes not seeing the confines of the room around him but instead searching the far reaches of his memory for something now long gone—the motivation for the sudden about-face in his life. Then he said, "I have a number of suspects," without much conviction.

"Ah, indeed you must. Do each of these men have a motive, a means, and an opportunity?" Moberly inquired, leaning forward in his chair.

Durrant stiffened. He considered both the question and the man seated eagerly before him.

"Sergeant, I do hope my prying isn't considered inappropriate. You see, in addition to my time spent in Her Majesty's service over-seas, I have spent a fair amount of time in the service of Her Majesty Queen Victoria on the home front. I am, after all, Moberly, and as such have a long history in the service of the Royals. Some of that time, Sergeant, has brought me in close contact with New Scotland Yard. You may have heard of them?"

"Yes, in fact, several of our Mounted Police have spent time there."

"Not yourself, sir?"

"I'm afraid not. My posts have lacked such sophistication. I've been more aligned with the Cypress Hills than Cypress Way, London."

"Touché! Well, nevertheless, I will admit a fascination with the investigative procedure that New Scotland Yard and the Metropolitan Police Force have been, I dare say, *pioneering*."

Durrant became aware of the precarious position he found himself in. As of yet, the North West Mounted Police's role was to bring law and order to the Dominion Territories. They did not employ a dedicated squad of investigators as the police force in Toronto and Montreal did. The Mounties' role was to make peace and enforce treaties with the Indians and to disrupt the illegal trade in whiskey and rum. While they had a strong presence in places like Fort Calgary and Winnipeg, as yet the limit of their investigative process was to unhand an assailant from his smoking gun at the scene of a crime. In short, thought Durrant, he was in uncharted ground here at the end of steel, in more ways than one.

"Let me clear up a few matters, first, if you don't mind, Mr. Moberly."

"Of course, Sergeant."

"How long have you been away from Holt City?"

"It's been three weeks and a day that Mr. Jimmy and I, along with my survey team, have been down in the Columbia," he answered matter-of-factly.

"And there are those who would testify to that?"

"Yes, including our Mr. Wilcox."

"Very good. Now, about Mr. Penner. Did you know him?"

"I'd say better than most."

"When did you meet the man?"

"I arrived at The Summit on December 1 of last fall. I was asked by Mr. Van Horne to assist in the proving of the survey down through the Kicking Horse Canyon, where it meets with the Columbia; it's to be one of the most ambitious sections of the rail, you see, and very treacherous. Mr. Charles Aeneas Shaw, a proud Scot like you, Mr. Wallace, completed the trial line down this section in the summer. The lads back in Montreal sent him on a wild goose chase up to the Howse Pass in the fall. They were still hoping to find a line where the grade was more reasonable, and the cost per foot of steel wasn't so steep. The Howse provided them with an option, but the distance was much too far, and believe it or not, there is more snow in *that* country to the north than there is here on the Kicking Horse! The decision was made to stick with Roger's original route, as improved by Shaw.

My work has been to complete the location survey for the sections that Shaw didn't finish before being sent north.

"As Mr. Penner was the foreman for the contract handling all the explosives work both on the Big Hill and in the Lower Canyon, he and I made a trip all the way down the Kicking Horse shortly after work ended here on December 8. We spent two weeks together assessing the munitions requirements of various grades and routes. I found him to be a very knowledgeable professional, as well as a decent fellow and an affable travelling companion."

"That's saying a lot, I would imagine. What struck you about the man?"

Moberly took his teacup in his hands, and Durrant noticed for the first time that the man was missing the small finger on his left hand. Moberly sipped his tea thoughtfully and finally said, "His honesty."

"What do you mean?"

"Mr. Penner was as honest as the day was long. He was loyal to his employer, but never once did he suggest a course of action where the intent was to enrich his own self or those whose charge he carried. For example, there are many places on the Big Hill, and down through the lower Canyon, that even small changes to the survey of the line would mean hundreds or thousands of extra cubic yards of material being blasted and removed from the grade. The contractors get paid by the yard and by the type of material they are removing. Deek Penner would never entertain that as a consideration for a change in the location survey. If it meant compromising the safety for the men who would be doing the blasting, or an increase in the cost to the public purse, he would hear nothing of it."

"It was suggested?"

"Of course, but *not* by me; I have no need for such considerations. Sergeant Wallace, I have made a small fortune in my life, and my family is of considerable means. We've worked for kings and queens for many hundreds of years. I have no need for further material wealth, but there *are* those here that do. This railway will bleed your young Dominion dry, and there are a great many that will not rest until they have swindled the Canadian Pacific of its remittance."

"Did Mr. Penner have enemies?"

"I should say a few."

"Like who?"

"Anybody who might have fallen into the class of swindler, I would say."

"And that's a fair number of men, you believe."

"Who do *you* suspect, Sergeant?"

Durrant regarded the man. Durrant guessed him to be at least fifty, maybe fifty-five, but he appeared younger than himself.

"Sergeant," Moberly said as Durrant studied him. "You're wondering if you can trust me."

"I'm wondering if you are a suspect."

"I had no opportunity, as the Yard would put it. I was two hundred miles away. Nor did I have a motive. Deek and I have never quarrelled, except maybe to insist that the other have the last biscuit some cold morning down on the Columbia."

"You have means."

"Ah . . . yes, the knob-kerrie. Mr. Wilcox mentioned that Mr. Penner had his skull caved in with some form of bludgeon."

"The top of his skull, yes, but also his face.

"And you've not recovered the murder weapon?"

"We did, in fact."

Now it was Moberly's turn to look up in surprise. "Really?"

"Yes." Durrant quickly retold the tale.

Moberly studied him. "So you needn't examine it for evidence?" Moberly said, nodding toward the knob-kerrie. Durrant looked at the mace-like club on the man's wall. Moberly stood and took the shield from its nail and then removed the knob-kerrie. He handed it to Durrant, who remained sitting while he looked it over. "It has been used to kill men, Sergeant. Many, I would guess. Some of them my countrymen, I dare say, but it wasn't used to kill Mr. Penner, and certainly not by me."

"Your cabin is locked while you are away?"

"The finest Yale lock."

"And there was no sign of entry?"

"None whatsoever."

Durrant looked over the club, purely out of curiosity. He handed the weapon back to Moberly, who replaced it on the wall, followed by the shield.

"I'd say right now that Frank Dodds is my number one suspect," Durrant said when Moberly had sat back down.

The Englishman poured them both more tea. "Mr. Dodds is a crude and boorish man."

"I believe that he and Deek may have quarrelled over a game of cards the night that Mr. Penner was killed."

"I told Deek on several occasions that his weakness for cards would be his undoing," said Moberly, shaking his head.

"Well, it may have been his weakness for justice and honour that led to his untimely end," said Durrant. "I haven't any proof yet, but I believe that Deek Penner was onto Dodds' moonshine operation. I believe that he was going to fink on the man, and that Dodds may have killed him to keep him quiet."

Moberly was silent a moment while he contemplated this. He sipped his tea. "He had a clear motive, then," he finally said. "I have heard that Dodds was making moonshine and would be selling it to every bloody hand who stepped off a train from Fort Calgary come the start of work. He stood to profit a great deal from this."

"He also had the means," said Durrant. "He could have used the star drill to bash in Mr. Penner's skull. They are easy enough to come across. From what I understand from my inquiries, Penner left the card game after a row with Dodds. Stories vary, but I think that Dodds could have taken leave of his own cabin when the game wrapped up and sought out Penner to kill him."

"So why wasn't Penner found dead in *his* cabin? As I understand it, he was killed along the Bow River."

"I don't know. I don't know why Mr. Penner was out where he was, when he was, or how Dodds might have come across him where he was found by Mr. Christianson."

"John found the body?" asked Moberly.

"He did."

"That's interesting."

"How so?"

"Well, what was John doing out so late?"

"He was at the card game too."

"If the game broke up earlier, what cause would John to have to be on that track?"

"He claims he was delivering a wire to Deek himself."

"Did he produce this wire?"

"Not yet. I've asked him for it," said Durrant, feeling embarrassed that he hadn't followed up on this loose end. It also reminded him of the coded correspondence from the mysterious Kauffman. He decided that he would need to gauge Moberly more before he revealed all his evidence. Durrant started, "You think John . . . ?"

"I can't see John Christianson committing such a crime. I don't believe the man has the stomach for it; such a mousey little fellow. The fact that he found the body is interesting," said Moberly.

"And what about Dodds as a murderer?"

"That I *can* see. You have others, through, don't you?"

Durrant nodded. "The Mahoney brothers for the same reason as Dodds. Grant McPherson as he has now taken over Deek's position as foreman."

"I expect that there is much more to these explosive contracts than what we can see on the surface of things. There is a great deal at stake, in terms of money, and in terms of men's lives. Remember what I said, Sergeant, Deek Penner was a moral man, and a fine leader of men. He would not have condoned a course of action that would have put his men's lives in greater danger than was necessary from the nature of their already hazardous work."

"You think that Deek might have been mixed up in the explosives contracts?"

"Or that he knew of some nefarious undertaking that might cause alarm."

The two men were silent for a moment. Moberly sat forward, "What of physical evidence?"

"I was just considering that myself," said Durrant.

"I don't suppose the star drill had a name etched upon it?" Durrant shook his head. "I thought not . . ." said Moberly.

"What I do have," said Durrant, "is blood."

"Do tell!"

"Saul Armatage and I . . ."

"Ah yes, the good doctor; he's performed a post mortem, no doubt."

"Of sorts."

"I imagine more could be done if we were at Fort Calgary or Regina," said Moberly.

"Yes, but we do know that whoever killed Mr. Penner was likely covered with his blood. It would have been very difficult to commit such a crime without getting at least a little of the man's blood on you."

"Unless you wore something over your clothing and then disposed of it . . ."

Durrant looked up. He hadn't considered that possibility. He said so. "Like what?" he wondered aloud.

Moberly thought a moment, "Well, some sort of tarpaulin would be best, but that would be impractical."

"The next best thing," mused Durrant, "would be a cape. Like what us Red Coat's wear over our coats, even a greatcoat itself that could be burnt afterwards."

"Yes, that would do it."

"My lad Charlie found a buckle burned in a trash barrel, but nothing more," Durrant said, feeling suddenly impatient. He reached for his crutch.

"You aim to take your leave, Sergeant?"

"You've been a generous host," said Durrant. "The tea and cakes were very nice and the conversation useful."

"We've not discussed the spy as yet," said Moberly. "Hep Wilcox went out of his way just this morning to tell me of it. He suspects someone on Deek Penner's crew is spying for the Grand Trunk and aims to disrupt the spring work to cause delays and add costs to our undertaking. I certainly think there is a spy, just as the CPR has agents inside the Grand Trunk. This is the eighties, sir. We are in the age of information. My only question is the zeal with which Mr. Wilcox presents the intelligence, and why if he's so convinced of the wicked intent of this spy, he hasn't rousted him yet. It can't be that difficult."

"I was curious about that myself."

"I would let that curiosity carry the day, Sergeant."

Durrant pushed himself to standing. He pulled his coat closed and readied himself for the outside world. "I have one last question, if you don't mind, Mr. Moberly. It's of personal nature."

"I don't mind at all," said the gentleman, standing.

"Why are *you* here?"

Moberly laughed, and as he did, his face broke into its criss-cross of lines. "'For Queen and Country,' of course."

Garnet Moberly became suddenly more sober. "Sergeant Wallace," he said, "I think you might be the only other man besides me, here at the end of steel, who can appreciate what is happening. We are witnessing history unfolding. This country is too young yet to appreciate this, but in time it will. This railway will almost certainly be the defining moment in its inception. We are breaking the back of these mountains with this thin ribbon of steel, sir. It is indeed the most glorious time to be in the Dominion of Canada."

Durrant nodded. He extended his left hand, "Thank you for the tea."

Moberly took his hand. "You shall have to come again. I am bound once more for the Kicking Horse once we've resupplied, but when I return, I shall call on you to inquire after your progress."

"I hope to be long gone from this place by the time you return," said Durrant.

"I shall call on you at Fort Calgary then, or see you at the end of the line."

"You shall," said Durrant. "You most certainly shall."

THIRTEEN

THE BIG HILL

THE WIRE MESSAGE ARRIVED IN code from Fort Pitt, in the Saskatchewan Territory.

> To Durrant Wallace.
> From S. Steele.
> Proceed with caution. Extreme sensitivity in Parliament over cost overruns and pork barrel nature of contracts.
> Canada Company factory at Kicking Horse vital to mainline's budget and timetable.
> Will look into O'Brian's business dealings.
> Have found nothing on man named Kauffman within CPR and GTR. Will ask Ottawa Metropolitan Police to inquire further.
> Regarding whiskey production: CPR concerned. New orders: disrupt production within Temperance Zone.
> Noises coming from Dumont and others of resistance. Much activity within Cree Nation.

Durrant decoded the message as he ate breakfast at his desk. First, Durrant considered the overheard conversation between Wilcox and O'Brian. How might these two men's involvement in the explosives contract be tied to the death of Deek Penner?

Wilcox had said that it would take something dramatic to shake loose the contract from the Canada Explosives Company. Blake O'Brian had added that there was a great deal of money to be made. Could some disruption of the blasting of the Tote Road down the treacherous Kicking Horse Pass lead to a debate in Parliament? O'Brian would be there, calling for a re-examination of the munitions contract, one of the most lucrative in the construction of the entire

Canadian Pacific Railway. With Penner acting as foreman for the blasting operations on the Kicking Horse, there was an obvious tie-in to his murder.

Durrant considered his next steps. There was a pressing need to view for himself the Kicking Horse Pass and its precipitous descent so that he might fix in his mind what all this secrecy was truly about. Durrant was coming to understand that the land itself was a player in the mystery surrounding Deek Penner's death. He decided that it was time that he saw this place for himself. Durrant would also need to intensify his efforts to find the distillery he suspected Dodds operated somewhere. And he still had to expose the identity of the alleged Grand Trunk spy. For a moment Durrant wished that he had more men under his command so he could delegate some of the investigative matters. Just then there was a light knock at the door and Charlie stepped inside.

"Did he do it?" Durrant asked. The lad nodded. "Well, let's see." The boy held up the Mountie's crutch. "Well I'll be. Look at that!"

The peg of the crutch which had been so frustrating to Durrant since his arrival deep in the mountains had been altered by the camp's carpenter. It now bore a block of light-coloured wood four inches square; set in the bottom of this wood block were half a dozen small nails. Like the hobnailed boots that a mountaineer wore to provide purchase on snow and ice, Durrant now had a crutch custom-made for the frozen trails that criss-crossed Holt City.

Durrant stood and leaned on the crutch. The block made it taller, too, so he didn't have to bend so much. "This is splendid," he said, smiling at the boy. Charlie beamed back.

FOR THE THIRD day in a row the whistle of a freight approaching the end of steel pierced the silent mountains. Durrant and Charlie made their way towards the station, Durrant's stability on the trails greatly improved by the hobnailed crutch.

As the steam cleared and the men milled about, Durrant and Charlie approached a sleigh already half full of workers heading for

Kicking Horse Lake, the height of land between the Pacific and the Atlantic oceans. Bob Pen was sorting the men into teams.

"Can we catch a lift up to the Pass with you?" Durrant asked of Pen.

"No reason why not, Sergeant."

Pen introduced the pair to the teamster, who looked over his shoulder at the motley crew of navvies and labourers who had just disembarked from the westbound train. "Your boy will have to ride in back, but," he said, sliding over on the sleigh's seat, "you can ride up front here wit' me."

"Much obliged," said Durrant. "Charlie, son, lend me a hand here, would you?"

Charlie gave Durrant a leg up, and once he was settled on the sled's bench, Charlie passed up his crutch. Charlie hopped up with the others on the back of the sleigh and regarded the men. They were dirty from the long journey across the plains from Winnipeg; soot covered their faces and clothing. Most were not much older than Charlie. The journey from Holt City to the height of land began in silence, but soon the men began to exclaim as the mountains hove into view.

Within the hour the sleigh reached the steepest grade, and the teamster called for several of the men to dismount and push. Durrant noticed that young Charlie—by far the smallest of the lot—hopped off with the first of the men and lent a shoulder to the effort. The horses strained and farted and pulled the sleigh up the steep grade, and soon they were atop a broad, forested plateau at the height of land.

"This is it," said the teamster, looking over at Durrant.

"This is the pass?"

"There's a mile or so of level ground here." He pointed west. "Over there it drops off pretty steeply, down into the valley of the Kicking Horse River."

Durrant looked about. To the south rose sheer limestone walls, cirques, and ramparts, each one climbing higher than the next, until they crested with glacier-clad peaks that formed the implacable wall of the Continental Divide. He had heard men speak of a lake so blue that Tom Wilson had named it Emerald there on the eastern slopes of the Divide, just a few miles above Holt City. The men joked and referred to it as the Indians had: The Lake of Little Fishes. On the western side of those mountains was unknown country where the waters ran west into the Kicking Horse and on to the Columbia, and to the Pacific Ocean. The sleigh banked in a wide turn on the ice road and Durrant saw wood smoke rising up from the trees, a sure sign that progress had come to this desolate and lonesome region.

In a moment the sleigh pulled through a break in the trees and a small clearing provided them with spectacular views.

"This here is Kicking Horse Lake," said the driver. On the far western shore Durrant saw the source of the smoke—a fire burning slash on the bank of the tarn. Beyond it the woods had been cleared and a collection of tents could be seen, white against the dark forests behind them.

The Tote Road went straight across the lake, and in a few minutes the sleigh came to rest next to a snow-cleared area where more than a hundred men were at work constructing the munitions factory. After Charlie helped Durrant dismount, Durrant turned to the driver to inquire about a return journey.

"I'm back up with a load of supplies mid-afternoon. You can hitch a ride back down then if you like," said the teamster.

"That will suit us just fine."

"I'll look for you," said the man, and when his sleigh was free of its human cargo, snapped the reins and drove the two draft horses back across the lake at an easy gait.

Durrant looked around to get his bearings. "Mighty desolate place," he said, regarding the work going on about him. The snow and trees had been cleared back from a space a hundred feet in length and sixty wide, and that was where the bulk of the construction was being undertaken. Here on the summit of the pass more than fifteen feet of snow had accumulated. Durrant imagined that the task of keeping both the construction site and supply yard clear of snow throughout the winter was a Herculean task. The building had been framed and Durrant noticed a small steam-powered sawmill for cutting timbers for the building's siding and roof. A dozen men scrambled over the structure, while many more worked on the ground. More still could be heard at their saws and axes in the woods, preparing the right-of-way for the Tote Road.

Durrant and Charlie proceeded to the construction site, the smell of freshly milled pine conferring a freshness to the site that ran contrary to the hacked-out appearance of the place. Durrant found the site manager's tent and stuck his head inside. Three men sat at a table, a set of plans open before them. They looked up as he peered inside.

"Name's Wallace," he said.

"See Tom Bracket if you've not been assigned to a team," said the man on the far side of the table.

"Sergeant Wallace," he clarified, "North West Mounted Police."

"Of course," said the man. "What can I do for you?"

"I'm going to have a look around the camp, talk with a few of the men; just wanted to let you know."

"Much obliged, Sergeant. Let us know if you need anything."

"I will. Thank you. Don't suppose Garnet Moberly is around the camp, is he?"

"No sir," said a second man. "He's already headed down the Golden Stairs to the Kicking Horse, likely halfway to the Columbia by now."

Durrant nodded. "He doesn't waste time getting where he's going, does he?"

"Moberly comes and goes like an apparition around here. One minute he's here, the next he's vanished. His team can't keep up with him."

Durrant turned to Charlie who was waiting behind him. "Let's see if we can't follow the Tote to see what all the fuss is about," said Durrant. The two proceeded through the construction site and took up the Tote where it headed west through the dense pines growing along the summit.

Durrant moved more confidently, the hobnails on his crutch piercing the icy ruts. As they walked, Durrant's mind began to turn over the question of motive once again. Durrant communicated his thoughts to Charlie out loud, as if he was speaking to himself.

"Okay, we've got four possible motives, here. The first, and most obvious, is whiskey. It seems pretty likely from what we've heard that Deek Penner got his nose into Frank Dodds' business. That's not to say that there ain't others brewing the stuff down there at Holt City, but my guess is that Dodds is principally responsible. If Deek found out, maybe the two of them had some words that night at the card game; Ralph Mahoney as much as said so. If that's the case, maybe Dodds thought to eliminate the risk of our lad Penner ratting on him to Hep Wilcox. Certainly Dodd's a strong enough fellow to hoist a star drill to club Penner from behind . . ."

Charlie looked at him. "Right," said Durrant, taking Charlie's inference that he himself was slight but had held fast to that self-same drill rod. "But you're a strong lad," Durrant quickly said.

"So that's theory number one, whiskey as the motivation. Theory number two is the Grand Trunk spy. We're not a lick closer to discovering this man's identity or even if there is a spy. Wilcox insists there is one, and others seem to corroborate, though they are suspects themselves, aren't they? Wilcox insists that Penner was onto this spy, and I can't help but wonder if that's what the correspondence from this fellow Kauffman is all about. The trouble is the code; it's unintelligible, at least to me."

Again Charlie looked at him. "Just 'cause you can read, son, doesn't make you a code cracker." Charlie shrugged in a suit-yourself sort of way. "If you want to look at it, I don't see any harm. Ideally I'd like to get my hands on the code that the Grand Trunk uses for their wires. That's the way to do it. I just might see if John Christianson can come up with something for me there."

In the distance they could hear the shouts and calls of men at work, and felt the earth move beneath them as trees toppled to the ground. "That must be the cutting crew up ahead," Durrant said.

He stopped and turned to Charlie. "So that's theory two, the motivation for the killing being to avoid detection. If that is the case, mind, I would imagine that the killer would have skipped town on one of the near-daily freights that head back to Banff and onto Fort Calgary. According to Wilcox—a suspect himself, mind you—nobody has gone missing from the camp since Penner died. If they caught a freight, I could have Dewalt look for them in Fort Calgary. If they went for a walk in the woods, they would likely be long past prosecuting by now.

"The third motive is power. Grant McPherson has Penner's old job. With it comes more money, and more power." Charlie looked at him, his face twisted into a question. "Just because the man pulled you out of the drink doesn't mean he's not capable of killing a fella. He as much as admitted that himself. Plus, there's the matter of the blood.

"Devon Paine is the only man who's had a coat laundered. I know that don't make him a prime suspect as such, but it does make me ask questions. His face was certainly busted up, no doubt about it, and Dodds is the one that done it. Just the same, I haven't seen blood on another man's coat as yet, and nobody else has been down to the laundry. I just don't know what to make of that . . ."

Durrant's voice trailed off into the woods. They heard another tree fall.

"Then here is motivation number four. It's maybe the most obvious one: money. Penner was the foreman for the explosives work to be done on the Kicking Horse. Nitro. It's big money. You heard O'Brian the other night. It's damned near the biggest contract left on the Canadian Pacific mainline. The Canada Explosives people have the manufacturing contract, and now McPherson is going to run the show on the blasting side of things. "

Durrant continued. "It sounds to me like the Honourable Member for Northumberland and our own Mr. Wilcox have doubts about the Canada Explosives factory back there. Maybe they have cause to believe that the operation at Kicking Horse Lake will produce a substandard product. That *could* mean lives lost, and delays in construction, and one hell of a dust-up in Parliament. Mr. O'Brian would certainly benefit from that."

"Or . . ." he said, looking deep into the woods. They felt the earth shake as another tree fell. "Or ... I need to learn more about Mr. O'Brian and what his real motivation is for being at the end of steel at this time." Durrant smiled at the boy. "Come on, let's go have a look at this so-called Big Hill."

They made their way along the Tote Road to where it came to an end and a dozen men were working with Swede saws and double-bladed axes. Several of the men looked up as the one-legged Mountie and his boy walked into their midst.

"So lads, how far to the Big Hill?" Durrant asked. One of the men spit a stream of tobacco juice that coloured the snow a putrid brown.

"Just through that tangle of wood there," said another man, his axe set on his shoulder.

"Come have a look, Sergeant," one of the sawyers said and Durrant knew that his presence in Holt City was known to one and all.

The snow was deep, but there was a thick crust of ice on the summit of the pass, and several of the loggers walked with Durrant and Charlie, lending an arm where necessary. Durrant was suddenly struck that these men, working just five miles from Holt City, lived in a very different world from the one below in the valley of the Bow River. Their distance from the investigation of the murder of Deek Penner must make it seem so remote to them, working as they did at the very tip of man's progress into the wilderness, that they were beyond judgement.

It took a moment, but soon Durrant could hear the roar of mountain waters.

"There's open water," he said.

"That's Sherbrook Creek. It just opened up a couple of days ago. That warm spell that just passed melted a lot of snow."

"So this isn't the Kicking Horse River proper?"

"No sir, that there is just a tributary. The main stem comes in a few miles below. They say there is a waterfall up that valley to the north," the man pointed, "that comes down straight out of the clouds."

"I'll be damned," said Durrant.

They shouldered their way through the rough tangle of under-growth where the woods ended and found themselves on the verge of the raging torrent. The grade gave way below them, dropping steeply into the creek, its banks thick with bubbles and jagged shards of ice. The roaring waters dropped off suddenly where the gentle summit of the pass fell quickly toward the valley of the Kicking Horse River below. Trees grew along the rugged cliffs, but the descent was so steep that the top of one tree seemed to reach just where the roots of the tree below clung. All of this was cloaked in thick white mantle of snow.

Durrant and Charlie's eyes tripped from creek to tree to the vacuum of space beyond. It wasn't a wide open panorama, as Durrant had imagined it might be, but a close and narrow valley, filled with dark shadows and unseen depths. The mountains rose straight up from the valley floor, some eight miles distant, in perpendicular crags.

"So this water doesn't stop till it reaches the Pacific?" said Durrant.

"No, sir."

"Now these Golden Stairs, where are they at?"

One of the men pointed off to the left of the roaring creek. "The Tote heads off that way, right along that band of stone there. The Stairs is another half mile, where things get real tight, and the trail switchbacks. We'll keep going straight there, though it's going to take a powerful load of nitro to clear the path. It's a precarious track, for certain. There are places where two men have to turn sideways to pass one another. There's no room for a horse to turn around."

"What happens when one horse meets another on the trail?" asked Durrant.

The men looked at one another. "Well, we try not to let that happen. But let's just say there are a few poor beasts at the bottom of the drop off that didn't go of their free will."

Durrant looked around and saw that none of the men smiled; none were pleased with this prospect.

"You going to arrest Mr. Dodds, Sergeant?" asked the first logger, spitting another stream of tobacco juice.

"You fellas work for Dodds?" asked Durrant.

"No sir, we're under a different contract. We're following up on Mr. Moberly's team. They prove out the line and we come behind and cut it."

"Did Mr. Moberly pass this way this morning?"

"I think it was morning, in a technical sense," said the first logger. "Mr. Moberly and that Indian fella he travels with, Mr. Jimmy, don't seem to need any sleep. They came through around four this morning. The rest of Moberly's men followed him down after a proper breakfast. We're working to clear the route and catch up with 'em, though it'll be tough going on the Stairs with the snow and the avalanches."

Durrant returned his attention to the matter of Frank Dodds. "So," he said, "any of you fellas buying whiskey from Mr. Dodds? Or from anybody else, for that matter."

There was a moment's discomfort. Charlie looked from one man to the other. They were all a good foot taller than the lad, and had they wanted to, it would have been easy for the team of sawyers to overpower Durrant and the boy with their axes and nobody would have been the wiser.

"Sir, we all take a drink every now and again, but no, we ain't buying from Mr. Dodds, or anybody else for that matter."

Durrant thought better of pursuing it. "That's good, boys. You and me aren't going to have any trouble at all. Any of you got anything to tell me about the night Deek Penner was killed?"

"Most of these lads just got here, Sergeant," said the tobacco man. "I think Timmy and me is the only ones that have been here more than a week." The man named Timmy nodded. "We've both been here on the Big Hill all that time."

"Alright then," said Durrant. "What say Charlie and me let you get back to work, and we'll walk back to the Lake. I appreciate you showing us the sights."

The men nodded and began to make their way back to the survey line they were cutting. Charlie and Durrant began to follow, but not before casting one last glance over the breathless expanse of snow swept earth that was the Kicking Horse Valley. Durrant alone would see it again, though the circumstances would be much different when he did.

FOURTEEN

A SHADOW IN THE NIGHT

CHARLIE'S SCRAWLED NOTE ON THE writing tablet said, "Found the still, maybe . . ." They had arrived home at supper from the Big Hill and now Durrant was sitting at the desk in the NWMP cabin, a candle burning on its plate, puzzling through the question of motive. Durrant looked up at Charlie standing in the doorway, his face expectant. The boy looked down at Durrant, nodding.

"Where?"

"Up the Pipestone," he wrote. "Heard some men talking at dinner; one was Pete Mahoney. He goes there at night."

"I knew that lad was up to no good," said Durrant. "I read him like a book," he said, satisfied. Durrant started to pull his coat on. He holstered the Enfield and tucked the Bulldog into his coat pocket.

Charlie scribbled. Durrant read his question. "Now we track the rabbit back to his hole," said Durrant sounding energized despite the long day. He buttoned up his bison coat and leaning on his crutch, walked out the door. Charlie followed after him.

The man and the boy made their way through the camp to a set of cabins set along the main Tote Road where the Mahoney brothers lived. The night was very cold; the moon, now half full, wore a dense halo, portending an early spring storm.

Charlie pointed to indicate the Mahoney brothers' hovel. Durrant could see no lights, but a thick plume of smoke rose from the chimney. Together they sought the cover of a thick stand of trees just off the main road and waited.

"You think he's in there, Charlie?" Durrant whispered. Charlie nodded, not taking his eyes off the cabin. "You followed him back here, didn't you?" Again the nod. "You're getting to be pretty damn good at this, son."

Fifteen minutes passed. Durrant could feel the dull ache in his right leg turn to a searing pain. He rubbed the leg gently, drawing a look of concern from Charlie. Durrant raised a finger to his lips, as if the boy might choose that moment to learn the trick of speech.

"It's okay, lad," whispered Durrant.

Another fifteen minutes passed, and Durrant was considering giving up. The mercury hung just above zero, and he had lost much of the sensation in his right leg and his right hand. As he was preparing to say so, Charlie flinched and Durrant saw a lantern come to life in the Mahoney cabin. A moment later the flap of the canvas door was pulled back and a dark figure appeared, a lamp held before the spectral shape. The figure turned about, regarding the sleeping camp, and then made haste along the Tote Road.

Charlie and Durrant watched the man, the golden light casting a long, sinuous shadow across the snowy forest. He passed not thirty feet from where they were cloaked by darkness and carried on up towards the Pipestone. Wordlessly, both men rose from their crouch and began to follow at a safe distance. Durrant found the going very difficult; every step sent a spasm of sharp pain up his right leg, and he was having difficulty holding the crutch with his numb right hand. He pressed on, at times closing his eyes against the ache.

The lantern glow before them was like a will-o'-the-wisp drawing them across the Pipestone River and deep into the forest. Walking without a lamp, and without any sound beyond the crunch of snow beneath their feet, Durrant and Charlie found themselves in a tunnel of sensory deprivation. Along a network of circuitous paths that snaked through the camp, the ghostly form ahead of them led them eastward toward the mouth of the Pipestone canyon. Here the river was constricted by angular walls of limestone that in the summer would bunch the river up into small rapids. Now, with the first day of spring just past, ice and heavy snow still blanketed the ground. Above them the sky was reduced by half, the canopy of stars hemmed in by the dark shape of the canyon walls. The trail took to the river itself, weaving up over the ice-covered water.

Durrant became conscious of open water here and there. The snow and ice were beginning to melt, despite this evening's bitter temperatures. With only the feeble light of the stars to illuminate their path, the fear of plunging into the Pipestone River pulled at his mind.

But the cold water beneath them wasn't the only dread that plagued the Mountie. Durrant knew that if Pete Mahoney, or whomever it was they followed, suddenly turned around to return to the camp, there would be little place for the duo to hide. Here in the canyon they were without cover. Even as they passed the constriction and made their way back into the woods, hiding places were few and far between. Durrant and Charlie would simply have to throw themselves into the trees and hope the man was so distracted by his nocturnal journey that he would not see the tracks leading away from the trail.

What seemed like an eternity passed in this fashion; the sound of each other's breathing—and for Durrant, the searing pain of his leg—the only distraction from the suspense-filled trek. Despite these discomforts, Durrant grinned in the darkness. Fifteen minutes hard walking and Durrant saw the light slip from sight.

"That's got to be it," he said in a whisper. They had passed the constriction in the gorge and the canyon had opened a little. The sky was wide again, the trees rose in a swell that crested away from the river, and the veiled moon cast an eerie, ethereal light on the midnight snow. Durrant believed that just to the south was the area on the white-horned mountain where Frank Dodds' team was now logging.

"A little farther," said Durrant. "I want to get a good look at this place."

The men proceeded a few hundred more feet along the trail and then they hunkered down. In the pallid light Durrant could see a cabin. Twenty or more feet in length and half as many wide, it was well built of timber that had been planed straight and lightly sanded. A tin chimney rose from one end of the structure, a thin thread of smoke seeping from the stovepipe. Maybe Pete's job is to keep the midnight fires burning, Durrant thought. Keep the still churning away through the night; keep the prohibited perfumes from freezing up.

Through seams around the door they could see the lantern's light. Durrant wished he could see what secrets the shack concealed. If it was like most other moonshine operations he'd disrupted over his years as a policeman, the building housed a number of barrels where Dodds and his boys would ferment corn mash in water, adding scoops of raw sugar to the barrels to get it working. A couple of days into the operation, the fermented mash would be dumped into a large copper cauldron to boil. The fumes from the boiling mash then entered a long, twisted copper tube called a worm that was submerged in cold water. As the fumes condensed, the gas became liquid once more, and a thin drip would be caught in fruit jars, gallon jugs, or barrels, whatever Dodds could get his hands on. In the frigid temperatures the still had to be kept above freezing during the operation lest the cooling water crack the copper worm.

It was a simple procedure, and cheap. The corn and sugar could easily be obtained in Fort Calgary; maybe Dodds or Pete Mahoney was stealing it from the camp stores. Given the volume of food that the men at Holt City consumed, a few bushel bags of corn and sugar might not even be missed.

Durrant watched the cabin a while longer. "Alright," he finally said to Charlie, whom he felt shivering beside him, "I've seen enough."

The two stood and turned to leave, Durrant casting a last look over his shoulder to fix the place in his memory. They made their way down the narrow canyon of the Pipestone, doing their best not to step off into the sugary snow next to the narrow track. It occurred to Durrant that come the spring this path would be impassable. As the river rose, the narrow track along the banks of the Pipestone would disappear. Dodds likely had at least one other building on site where he was putting up his stores for summer distribution. Durrant would have to seek it out.

The men had walked another hundred yards to where the canyon was most confined when Durrant happened to look back along the path towards the cabin. What he saw horrified him: the ghostly light they had followed up the river to the still house was now behind them, and moving down the path toward Holt City.

"Charlie, we've got to get a move on!" Durrant said between gritted teeth, and the two picked up the pace. But the going was hard for the one-legged Mountie, and in a few minutes the lampbearer would certainly overtake them.

"Come here, boy!" Durrant hissed, and they quickly ducked off the trail and into the deep snow. The trees were closely set and concealed from the moon's glow by the rising cliffs and clouds. With luck, Pete Mahoney would be more concerned with turning into his bunk and would not notice their tracks, or maybe he would consider them the tracks of mule deer common to these woods.

They crouched behind the trees and waited. A moment passed, their bodies growing colder, the snow finding ways into the folds and tucks of their clothing. Then the light appeared around the bend in the canyon, and the trees on both banks of the Pipestone took on a celestial flush. Durrant held his breath. He rested his hand on the Bulldog. Charlie clutched Durrant's coat, crouching into the snow, his eyes wide.

The light grew closer. Not ten feet away the bulky silhouette of a man wrapped in a heavy blanket with a beaverskin cap pulled low over his ears and brow passed without stopping. Durrant believed the face to be that of Pete Mahoney, but he could not swear to it. The light faded into the distance. Durrant watched its progress. He waited another five minutes before he and Charlie clambered awkwardly out of the drift, the young boy helping Durrant to find his footing in the soft snow.

"Well, son," said Durrant, staring down the path. "I don't know about you, but I'm ready for bed."

THE DREAM WAS always the same. Durrant woke with a start from his nightmare, the Enfield pistol already in his hand. He lay silently in his bunk. There was no noise save that of the delicate breathing of the boy in the bed five feet from his own. Beyond that the world was devoid of sound. But something had woken him from the dream. Something out of the ordinary.

Durrant forced himself to listen beyond the soft sounds of

Charlie's breathing, past the squared-off logs and burlap of this crude cabin. Involuntarily his left hand slowly brought the pistol level with his searching eyes in the utter darkness of the night. Then he heard it, so faint that the sound might be mistaken for snow falling from a pine bough, but it was there just the same. Something or someone was on the other side of the thin, canvas-covered walls of the shack.

Durrant slowly pulled back the covers with his twisted right hand and gingerly swung his legs over the edge of the bunk. He would have to put the pistol down to affix his prosthetic; it was a risk he had to take. His ears reached into the night, alert to any sound beyond the walls of the small room. When his leg was in place, he took up the pistol again and pulled himself up, finding his crutch. The motion, or the faint sound of the nails from his crutch on the floor, woke Charlie. The boy sat up, his wool cap, which never left his head, pulled down over his ears, close to his eyes. Durrant put the barrel of the pistol to his lips as if to say hush, and then motioned for the lad to stay very still.

Charlie's eyes moved around the room, looking to see what had woken the Mountie. There was nothing to see in the dimness of the room. Durrant moved as easily as he could to the door of the cabin, and took up a place by the latch. Leaning on the wall, he pointed the pistol towards the door and with his crutch slowly opened it. Charlie crept from the bed, fully clothed, and found the Winchester in its place on the footlocker. Durrant looked at the boy and nodded.

The barrel of the Enfield preceding him, Durrant stepped into the doorway and swung the pistol back and forth. There were no signs of life outside the cabin door. He listened and heard, very faintly, the sound that an animal makes when it vanishes into the woods. A mule deer? He and Charlie had seen more than one since arriving at the end of steel. Durrant pressed forward, the Enfield extended before him, the moon high overhead reflecting off the blue-grey sheen of the weapon.

Durrant stepped around the cabin on the side where his bunk lay. His eyes scanned the silent woods. There was nothing; no one was there. Again, he inched his way forward, aware that Charlie was behind him now, the butt of the rifle held pressed into his shoulder. Silently the two reached the corner of the cabin and paused. Durrant drew a quiet breath, then pistol first, peered around the edge of the little house.

There was nobody there. The woods were dark and calm. He stepped forward. Charlie came around the corner too, his eyes searching the trees. The boy stepped up to Durrant and pointed at the snow. It had been recently disturbed, the deep tracks disappearing into the pines that bordered the railway and fringed the banks of the Bow River.

Charlie made to follow them, but Durrant reached out and barred his progress with his left hand, the pistol still clutched tightly in it. The boy stopped. They both looked down. Six inches from Charlie's foot sat a pail of dark, dense liquid. A long cord was tangled around the handle of the pail and extended into the snow. Charlie looked up at Durrant, his eyes filled with terror. Durrant cracked a grin.

"Guess we're onto something," he said, pulling the boy back from the bucket of nitroglycerine.

THEY CROUCHED IN the snow, Durrant instructing Charlie on how to dismantle the bomb that had been placed a few inches from their cabin. The boy gingerly unwound the fuse that had been wrapped around the handle of the bucket of highly volatile explosives. He then carefully removed the cord from the pail and placed it in the snow. He pointed and then held something up for Durrant to see—two matches that had refused to light. Durrant had once again been very lucky.

The Mountie turned and looked into the darkness. Unless a heavy snow came that night, he could follow the trail at sunup. His blood was boiling. He would not simply sit back while someone in this camp tried to take his life, and the life of this innocent young lad! Trying to kill a Mounted Police officer could land a man in the gallows. The act of placing the pail of explosives there was an offence punishable by hanging, but assailant would have to be caught first, and then guilt might be difficult to prove beyond a doubt.

"Come on, Charlie, we're going for a walk."

IT WAS NEARLY sunup when the two men arrived at the whiskey cabin for the second time in just a few hours. With Durrant walking out front, the Winchester held by the stock in his left hand, Charlie brought up the rear, toting the bucket of explosives. It was a delicate undertaking. The path, narrow and slippery when walking unencumbered, was made perilous by carrying pure nitroglycerine. What had taken them half an hour to traverse earlier in the evening—and would have taken Pete Mahoney just fifteen minutes to cover—took them nearly an hour. The lad dared not stop or ease the ache in his arms by resting the load in the snow, lest the jostle blow both men to pieces.

When they made the cabin, Durrant motioned for Charlie to wait back in the trees. He then walked straight up to the door and stepped to the side, then placed the muzzle of the Winchester on the heavy heart lock and fired. The lock, with a neat .44 calibre hole in it, held the door fast. The Mountie flipped the rifle forward, his left hand inside the finger lever, the weight of the weapon chambering the next round. Durrant fired again and the lock dropped from its clasp. He pushed the door open with its barrel and peered into the cabin. He hoped that he would find Dodds roused from sleep and grabbing for his own arms so Durrant would have the excuse to cut the man down. Instead, the cabin was devoid of life.

It was not *empty*, however. "Jee-sus," said the Mountie, stepping into the room. "Would you look at this?" He let the rifle fall to his side and looked around. Along one wall was the still, a cauldron perched on a low potbellied stove, the room thick with its heat. Beside it the worm descended into its cooling tank, a rain barrel. The water in it was cool but not frozen, packed with ice from the river. Next to it were sacks of corn and heavy bags of sugar.

Along all the walls, stacked three and four deep, were kegs of what Durrant assumed was corn whiskey. He stepped to the wall and put the muzzle of the Winchester against one barrel at breast height and fired. The cartridge blew a hole in the first barrel and the four barrels behind it, then embedded itself in the cabin wall. A coarse stream of brownish liquid spilled out onto the cabin. Durrant could smell the pungent aroma of the whiskey; he pulled the glove from his right hand and put a finger in the stream and tasted it. It was 75 per cent ethyl alcohol; pure corn mash. It was all the proof he needed.

"Charlie!" he called out the door. "Come on in here, and try not to blow us up as you do!" The boy appeared at the door, eyes wild, arms extended with the pail in front him. "Put that down here," said Durrant, motioning to one of the larger forty-gallon drums in the centre of the room. "That's it, so I have a clear view of it from out there by the woods. Good, now let's get out of here," said Durrant. The man and the boy beat a hasty retreat, leaving the cabin door wide open, as far into the woods as they could while still having a clear view of the pail of nitroglycerine resting atop the keg of moonshine.

"You want to do the honours?" Durrant looked at him. Charlie shook his head. "It's going to make a hell of a racket. Might want to get behind that big tree there," said Durrant. As the boy took cover Durrant bent down on one knee and using his crutch to stabilize his aim, levelled the rifle at the target. "Cover your ears, lad," said Durrant, and he pulled the trigger.

The cabin exploded. The concussion from the blast knocked Durrant backwards into the snow, the crutch hitting him in the face and the rifle flying from his hand. The boards and copper cauldron from the cabin rocketed into the woods, the angry projectiles striking trees and rocks with a deafening thunder. A wall of fire pressed out into the dawn and up toward the heavens and then a thick column of smoke arose from where the shack and its contraband had once stood. Far in the distance Durrant could hear an avalanche rumble down the frosted slopes of Dodds Peak.

When Charlie bent to help Durrant to his feet, the Mountie was laughing. "Well, that solves that, doesn't it!" he yelled. "Did you see that, son?" Charlie was grinning but looked worried. "Oh hell, I'm alright. Lord Almighty, I bet they heard that all the way clear to Fort Calgary!"

Charlie looked at the smoking embers of the cabin. The copper cauldron lay in several pieces twenty-five feet out on the snow-covered surface of the Pipestone River. Fragments of barrels and boards and the potbellied stove were scattered through the trees, having fallen just short of where Durrant and Charlie sat in the snow.

"Suppose we'll have a few folks from the camp coming to see what the trouble is. Who do you reckon will be the first?"

THERE WAS A faint light above the eastern mountains when the first men from the camp could be heard traversing the narrow gorge of the Pipestone River. Durrant and Charlie had started a small fire from pine limbs and boards and stood beside it warming their feet and hands. Durrant cradled the Winchester 73 his lap. He watched through the tangled smoke as the party advanced up the trail. He grinned when he saw who was in the lead.

"Dodds," he said. He shifted the rifle in his left hand and cradled it across his chest.

The group stopped when they saw Durrant and Charlie and the ruined cabin smoking behind them. There were half a dozen men standing with Dodds, including the Mahoney brothers, and Thompson Griffin, Dodds' right hand man at his cutting operation. Dodds' face was pulled into twisted question as he stood in the faint light of morning regarding the scene.

It was Ralph Mahoney who finally spoke. "What the hell happened here, Wallace?"

"I was hoping you might be able to tell me," said the Sergeant.

"Well, you're standing there warming your hands on the boards of that ruined cabin," said the elder Mahoney.

"It looks like someone's still blew up, Mr. Mahoney," Durrant mused.

"Jesus Murphy." Mahoney looked at Dodds.

"There are bits of whiskey keg scattered all through the brush here, and I think the kettle is out yonder on the river." Durrant gestured with a nod of his head.

"You did this," said the younger Mahoney brother, and he made a step towards Durrant. His older brother grabbed him by his shoulder.

"You seem troubled," said Durrant, looking the man in the eye through the wisps of smoke. His voice was low and flat.

Pete opened his mouth as if to say something, but no words would come out. Frank Dodds walked past Durrant to the ruins of the cabin. He kicked a few boards still hot with flames into the snow. He used the toe of his boot to move a piece of copper coil from the worm out of a pile of embers. Durrant watched him from the corner of his eye. The man's fists were balled up at his sides, his shoulders tight and pressed forward. Charlie too watched the man.

"Anybody care to file a grievance?" asked Durrant.

"Someone might have been killed!" barked Pete Mahoney.

"Someone indeed," said Durrant.

"*You* might have killed someone!" Pete barked again, incredulously, pointing an angry finger at the Mountie.

"*Who* is it that might have been killed?" Durrant asked.

"Shut your mouth," said Ralph to his younger brother. "Just shut up! Don't you see what he's trying to do?"

Durrant nodded. "Someone might have been killed this night," said Durrant, "but it wouldn't have been any of the lot of you. No, sir. The cabin was empty when we found it, wasn't it Charlie?" Charlie looked up and nodded.

"This here cabin was full of nothing but illegal whiskey, bound for sale to the men who are already arriving here by the trainload. Whiskey sold within ten miles of the CPR is illegal, and the only reason for having such a still is to sell whiskey. Unless someone here can make the claim that they was giving it away free for medicinal purposes."

Dodds walked around the smouldering still house.

"I didn't think so. Now, mind you, the pail of nitroglycerine that was the untimely end of these premises, that's a curious story if I've ever heard one," said Durrant. As he spoke those words he could hear more voices coming up the ice track that followed the Pipestone River.

"That'll be Hep Wilcox. There's going to be hell to pay," said Ralph Mahoney.

"Indeed, hell shall be paid," remarked Durrant.

Hep Wilcox came into view, accompanied by several other labourers from the camp, with Blake O'Brian drawing up the rear, his beaver felt hat perched atop his white hair, his long black coat and silver cane seeming comically out of place in such wild country. Saul Armatage followed the procession, his black bag in his hands.

"What in the name of God is going on!" demanded Hep Wilcox. He pushed the first cluster of men aside and strode straight for the ruined cabin. He saw Durrant and Charlie by their little fire.

"*You*," he said, drawing the word out in an ominous tone.

"Good morning, Mr. Wilcox," said Durrant, sounding almost chipper.

"I would like an explanation for this," said Wilcox.

"So would I. It seems that someone was brewing whiskey at Holt City, sir. Someone was brewing a great deal of whiskey. This of course is an offence against the Dominion of Canada, and it was occurring in *your* camp."

"I had no idea of these goings on."

"Is that correct, sir?"

"I had . . . Are you suggesting, Sergeant, that I was somehow aware of these illegal activities?"

"Sir, you were either aware of and failed to put a stop to them, or you were wilfully ignorant. Which will it be now?"

O'Brian pushed forward, pointing his cane at Durrant. "Now listen here, Sergeant. I don't think there is any cause for such accusations. That is simply out of line. Mr. Wilcox could not possibly know of the entire goings on in the wilds surrounding Holt City. Nor could he be expected, in the absence of any presence of the Red Coats, to enforce all the laws. It's simply not *his* job."

"The law has been in Fort Calgary throughout the winter, sir. A wire sent would have brought Dewalt and his men inside of a few days."

"What good would that have done?" demanded Wilcox. "Had I known of this trouble, and had I seen fit to call for reinforcements, what good would that have done? We have had a man murdered at the end of steel this fortnight, and what does Sam Steele do? Sends a man with one leg and a mere boy to discover the perpetrator and bring him to justice."

Durrant looked down at the fire. The men in the woods were suddenly quiet. Charlie looked from Durrant to Wilcox and then at all the cold faces looking at the Mountie.

"This still has been dealt with now," Durrant finally said. "I am certain there is another, and I aim to discover its location and deal with it accordingly. I also aim to uncover the identity of Deek Penner's killer, and that shall be done soon enough."

"Sir, your presence here at Holt City has done far more harm than good," said the MP for Northumberland. "Far more harm. This type of interruption into the work of these men is pure nuisance. I aim to tell Steele that and to report back to Parliament on my findings. If this is what the North West Mounted Police call an investigation, then I imagine this country's Parliament will have something to say about it."

Durrant laughed. "Sir, I am operating on direct orders from Steele himself. If you wish to see them I would be happy to oblige."

"Blowing up stills, putting men's lives at risk? Meanwhile the killer is likely halfway to Fort Benton by now."

"The killer is still in this camp."

"How do you know?" demanded O'Brian. Frost had formed on his wide beard.

"He left a message for young Charlie and me last night."

"What did it say?"

"There were no words," said Durrant, scanning the group of men.

"Speak plainly, man," said O'Brian.

"It was a message just the same. A bucket of nitro whose detonation I interrupted. It's a message I'll return in kind, in due course," said Durrant. "That time is coming upon us shortly."

Dodds kicked a board of the smouldering shack and it toppled down, sending a shower of sparks into the crisp morning air. He turned around, his gaze lingering on Durrant, before it moved to the crowd milling about in the woods. He spoke not a word, but walked past Durrant, his face hard and menacing, and proceeded down the path towards Holt City. The knot of men who had accompanied him followed suit, among them Wilcox and O'Brian. Only Armatage remained behind.

In a few moments Durrant, Charlie, and Armatage were alone in the dawn woods, the ruins of the shack still smouldering behind them, a difficult road laid out ahead. Armatage looked down at his friend, who remained sitting.

"Anybody injured?" the doctor finally asked.

"Hell, no," said Durrant.

"So you're okay?"

"Of course I'm okay. I haven't felt this good in years!"

Armatage shook his head and grinned. "That's what worries me, Durrant," he said. Both men were smiling.

FIFTEEN

CROSSED WIRES

AFTER EATING A QUICK BREAKFAST in his bunk, Durrant was determined to follow the tracks that led away from the site of the deadly bucket of nitro behind his cabin. Charlie insisted on helping and Durrant relented. It was mid-morning and the light was grey and flat so that the snow lost all definition, and the path where it wove through the trees could only be determined by close inspection. With Charlie acting as a crutch, the two men pushed their way through the low pines growing along the railway bed and close to the river bank of the Bow River. The path was winding and difficult, and Durrant wondered how the night-time intruder had managed to follow such a course without blowing himself to smithereens.

One word dawned on him: *practice*. The path they followed proceeded like this for more than two hundred yards, winding like a frozen snake through the pines, and finally terminating near the station itself. The two companions found themselves on the Tote Road, looking at the north side of the train platform. As the station was the centre of the tiny encampment, and pathways led to every other part of the settlement from this point, their tracking had led them nowhere. Durrant and Charlie looked at one another and then walked toward the station itself and the storage yards beyond.

"You stay here," Durrant said to Charlie, indicating the station. He then walked to the munitions warehouse, where loaded crates were being corralled, along with kegs of powder and sacks of material for manufacturing explosives.

"Grant McPherson about?" asked Durrant as he stopped one of the men carrying the heavy crates.

The man nodded to the back of the warehouse. There Durrant found McPherson talking with another man. Durrant stood quietly while they finished.

"A word, sir?" Durrant asked, and Grant nodded and motioned for the Mountie to step away from the men at their task.

"What can I do for you?" he asked.

"Been out on any moonlight strolls of late?"

"I'm afraid I don't know what you mean."

"Been out late in the evening wandering through the woods? Last night, perchance?"

"Last night I was in my bunk shortly after dinner. It's been busy days and it's getting busier. I've got near fifty men working under my charge, with supplies arriving daily to be shipped to Kicking Horse Lake."

"You got those who seen you in your bunk?"

"I've got three bunkmates who did. Mind, several of them were out till late playing cards and the fiddle."

"I'll want a word with them."

"You can have it. As usual, Sergeant, I don't know what you're getting on to."

"Last night someone left young Charlie and me a message: a pail of nitroglycerine and a fuse, tamped and ready for the match. It's only providence that I'm here to speak with you about it. I interrupted the man at his task of lighting the cord."

"Nitro, you say?"

"Pure stuff, I imagine. Powerful. Whoever set it carried it though the woods. I expect they were well practiced or we'd be finding bits of them scattered through the forest by the Bow this morning. That's why I come to you. Do I need to tell you that the attempted murder of a law officer is a hanging offence in this country?"

"I imagine it would be, Sergeant, but you're not going to hang me today. I was in my bunk, and there are those that can attest to that."

"Who else has access to nitro?"

"Anybody who has keys to this warehouse, I suppose," said McPherson. "A few more than I'd like. Deek Penner gave a few of the foremen access. The fellas who are working on the Tote Road and your friend Dodds."

"What does Dodds need explosives for?"

"Time to time he finds a Douglas fir that's suitable for bridge work, and uses a stick of dynamite to help bring it down. I haven't heard of him using nitro, through; much too strong for his purposes."

"What of Hep Wilcox?"

"Well, this is Wilcox's outfit. He's got the key to all the buildings in the camp."

"Hep know how to set a fuse?"

"I imagine he would. Before he come to Holt City and the railway work, he manufactured explosives back east."

The words hit Durrant as if a train had barrelled him over.

AFTER DURRANT LEFT the munitions storeroom, he went to the station, arriving just as another freight was steaming in from Fort Calgary. He sent Charlie back to their cabin, asking that he spend some time working on the coded wire transmission from the man named Kauffman. Durrant stayed at the station. He needed to update Sam Steele, and he wanted to dig further into Wilcox's past. As the freight exhaled a final blast from its brakes, another troop of young men looking to be a part of the excitement building at the end of track began to disembark. Bob Pen stood on a soapbox to address the men as they milled about.

"Alright, listen up, lads. The lot of you are for the Tote Road. Throw your bags on the sled there and those who can fit, hop aboard; those who can't, you'll be well and familiar with the Tote before you reach the Kicking Horse." With that, the men moved en mass for the sled that awaited them at the far end of the station. Pen watched them go and nodded at Durrant as he stumped past, making for the station.

The heat of the place felt good once he'd secured the door behind him. John Christianson was seated behind the counter, sorting the post. "Anything for me, Mr. Christianson?"

He looked up with a start. "No, sir, just a bunch for the fellas out at Kicking Horse, and for those around the camp."

"Nothing from my ol' Dad to get me through a cold mountain winter?"

Christianson shook his head. "No, sir."

"Lighten up, John. I'm only funning."

Christianson forced a smile. "Actually, Sergeant, I do have something for you."

"What's that?"

Christianson put down his bag of mail and went to the telegraph machine. He picked up the log book. "I managed to get this sorted out for you. I've got a record of everybody who's sent a wire over the last four months, pretty well since we've been holed up here. That is, them that have asked me to send it, or maybe Mr. Holt when I've been off."

"Anything interesting?"

"Nothing that stands out, Sergeant."

"Really, nothing strikes you as unusual?"

"Well . . . you'll want to look it over yourself, Sergeant Wallace."

"That I will, but what strikes *you*?"

The little man in front of him seemed to change momentarily. For a second, Christianson seemed to grow before Durrant's eyes. It wasn't that his physical stature changed, just his countenance shifted from diminutive to substantial and back in the blink of an eye. The change unnerved Durrant, and made him watch the man more closely.

"Most of Deek's correspondence was with his superiors back in Winnipeg, the men who own the contracts. He had some correspondence direct with the big bellies at Montreal and with the people at the Canada Explosives Company in Mount Saint-Hilaire. I don't think there is anything unusual there, Sergeant." Christianson showed Durrant the log book, his small finger scrolling down the list of signal stations that wires had been directed to. "See," he said. "I marked the initials of the sender and the receiver here for you . . ."

The Mountie stood beside and slightly behind Christianson, who sat on the stool next to the wire. From his position Durrant could look down and over the crown of John's head. He looked through the man's spectacles and wondered how Christianson could see through the accumulated grit on his lenses.

"What about Hep Wilcox?" Durrant asked, and Christianson turned to face him. Christianson thumbed through the log book, his face flushed and perspiration began to show on his brow. "Here you go, and this . . ." He flipped a page. "And this."

Durrant nodded. "Okay, I'll have a look at these. Tell me this, would you please?"

"Anything, Sergeant."

"The ones that are blank, where there are no initials, what does that mean?"

"I don't know who sent or received those wires," said Christianson.

"So why would someone mark the log?"

"I don't know." said John.

Durrant paused a long moment to study the man. Christianson was having a hard time keeping his eyes on Durrant. Durrant asked, "If this supposed Grand Trunk man wanted to send or receive a wire, he could do it without you knowing about it, correct?"

"He would if he knew how to operate a telegraph."

"Wouldn't be much of a spy if he didn't, would he now."

"I don't suppose he would."

"Any other way for us to learn if he's been sending wires?"

Christianson put a finger to the side of his face in thought. "Well," he said after some time. "You could always check on the other end."

Durrant stood up straight. "My God, man, you're absolutely right."

DURRANT SENT HIS wire to Steele, explaining the demolition of the still on the Pipestone River. Durrant was careful to make as little as possible of the incident with the pail of nitroglycerine outside their cabin, mentioning only that he awoke to find it there. He didn't want Steele dispatching reinforcements. Not yet, not before he had Deek Penner's killer in shackles. He also asked that Steele arrange a warrant for the procurement of the Grand Trunk Railway's wire logs so as to ascertain the identity of the inside man here at the end of track.

Satisfied with this undertaking, he set his mind to what he had learned about Hep Wilcox and Deek Penner's wire correspondence. While Christianson and others busied themselves around the station, Durrant studied the log book that Christianson had provided. He first read through all of the entries and familiarized himself with the codes of stations sending and receiving to and from Holt City. Most had the initials JC, HW, or DP next to them. Occasionally, Bob Pen had sent a wire, likely regarding his needs for skilled labourers, but most of the camp's recorded wire correspondence came from the other three men.

More interesting to Durrant were the wires that had been sent from Holt City that Christianson had *not* put a mark beside. These he studied with curiosity. He scrolled down these looking for patterns. It didn't take him long to find much more than he was expecting: an exact match. He looked up. Christianson was busy sorting the post.

Durrant set the wire transmission for send and keyed in the code that his finger rested on. He tapped in a quick message:

Station, please identify yourself.

He waited. A moment passed. Durrant could hear a clock tick somewhere in the room. He was aware of Christianson moving about the station. There was a buzz and Durrant set the wire to receive. As he tapped out the incoming code, Christianson looked up and started to move toward the telegraph table. Durrant stopped him. "It's for me," he said, without looking up. Christianson returned to his post. The message before him was in Morse:

House of Commons. West Block.

Durrant felt a flush of heat rush through him. Both Hep Wilcox and another person had been sending messages back and forth to the same station in the House of Commons. Durrant had a strong suspicion who it was that was sending and who might be on the receiving end of those telegrams.

Again, Durrant felt the pulse of impatience rush through him and he got to his feet, grabbing up the log book. He noted Christianson stop his activities as he strode from the wire station.

Durrant had a lot to think about as he went in search of the general manager. He hoped Wilcox might become more forthcoming if he provided an incentive for his honesty.

DURRANT FOUND WILCOX in his bunk. While he had taken great pains to search each of his other suspects' quarters, Durrant had not yet found the opportunity to search for a bloodied coat within Wilcox's personal space. That could wait no longer. Now, with the revelations made clear by the preponderance of wire correspondence between Holt City and Ottawa, he had more than one reason to further brace the general manager. Durrant tapped on the door of the caboose that sat on a siding not far from the station.

"What is it?" he heard Wilcox say from within.

"Mr. Wilcox, it's Sergeant Wallace." There was no reply. Durrant listened carefully, his hand resting on the hilt of the Enfield revolver. After a long silence the Mountie heard the bolt pulled back on the door. Hep Wilcox stood before him.

"Mr. Wilcox, I have a few questions for you." An expression of exasperation crossed the general manager's face. "May I step inside?"

Silently, Wilcox stepped from the door to allow Durrant inside, who found himself in a the small but ornate room. The caboose looked as if it had been decorated by a top designer from Chicago or New York City. A plush couch rested against one wall, bordered by small round tables that held the finest Tiffany lamps. A deep pile carpet lay on the floor in front of the couch, a low stool in the middle. Two equally well-appointed chairs sat at angles next to the couch. A gramophone was positioned against the opposite wall.

"You have a nicely made up accommodation, sir."

"It was a gift. A *loan*, in fact, for my use while here at the end of track for the winter."

"From whom?"

"From the CPR."

"Is that so?" Wilcox stood by the far wall, as if Durrant had backed him into a corner. Durrant shut the door behind him, but was careful not to throw the bolt. He looked around the room. Paintings of pastoral countrysides adorned the walls.

Wilcox did not ask him to sit, so the two men stood staring at one another. Durrant noted that door next to him was closed and imagined that it led to the man's bedchamber. "This doesn't look like a CPR-appointed carriage," said Durrant.

Wilcox stared at the man, his eyes dark. He said, "It's for use by the company brass while they are inspecting the line."

"I see," said Durrant. "Might I inspect your quarters?" he asked impulsively.

This caught Hep Wilcox off guard. "They are private, sir."

"This is a murder investigation, Mr. Wilcox. There *is* no privacy."

"You have *no* right."

"I have *every* right!"

Wilcox looked away and seemed to be considering his options. "I have nothing to hide. Go ahead if you will, Sergeant."

Durrant walked across the room, trying not to catch the nails of his crutch on the lavish, but borrowed, carpet. Wilcox stepped aside and Durrant opened the door to the bedchamber. It was a compact space, but adorned in similarly lavish fashion. A four-poster bed took up much of the room's space, and a heavy feather quilt was heaped on top. In the corner a small stove with brass trimming rumbled. A window looked out toward the banks of the Bow River. "I should like to look in your wardrobe, Mr. Wilcox."

"I really object to this treatment, Sergeant."

"I assure you, Mr. Wilcox, that each of my suspects likewise objected to such a search. You are no different than they are, sir."

Wilcox looked as if he had been slapped. Red-faced, he stepped into the room and opened the upright wardrobe that was crowded into one corner. Durrant looked through it, and finding several coats there, took them from their pegs and laid them out on the bed. He examined each of them in turn.

"Thank you, sir," he said, and stepped from the room. Wilcox said nothing. When he rejoined Durrant in the parlour, he found the Sergeant sitting in one of the chairs.

"I hope you don't mind me making myself comfortable," Durrant said.

Wilcox began, "Sergeant, I really must get back to work."

"This shouldn't take long. I have an offer to make you."

"Really?" said Wilcox. "What kind of an offer could you possibly make?"

"You tell me the truth about what happened the night Deek Penner died, and I will see that the Crown is lenient with you."

Wilcox laughed a harsh laugh. "I have nothing more to tell you about that night, Sergeant Wallace. I deeply regret Mr. Penner's death, as I have already attested over and over, but I had nothing to do with it."

"Oh, I don't think *you* killed Mr. Penner, but you are far from *innocent*." Durrant looked at the man.

The general manager still stood by his bedroom door. "What, exactly, are you accusing me of?" asked Wilcox.

"It's not so much an accusation, Mr. Wilcox; it's a question, and an honest one, at that. I know you've been sending wires to a station in Parliament. Who have you been corresponding with?"

Wilcox looked confused a moment. "Mr. O'Brian and I have shared correspondence, as he is Vice-Chair of the Select Standing Committee on the Railways."

"Your log books show dozens of wires sent."

"Did Christianson give you that information?"

"The log book is simple enough to interpret, Mr. Wilcox. My orders to people here are only being followed."

"Since when are you giving the orders in Holt City, Sergeant Wallace?"

"Since a man was killed here," said the Mountie. Durrant could see that he was going to get nothing more from Wilcox on this topic, so he changed direction in his questioning. "You used to make explosives, I gather."

Wilcox looked taken aback. He opened his mouth to speak, but no words came out.

"With whom were you employed?"

"I have . . . I should say I did, but that was . . . What has this got to do with your mandate here?"

"Mr. Wilcox," said Durrant, "how long ago did your association with an explosives manufacturer end?"

"Some time ago, Mr. Wilcox. Are you questioning my integrity? How is this relevant?"

"Everything is relevant, sir. Everything is relevant until *I* say it isn't."

Wilcox regarded the Mountie. He shook his head, "I worked for a time for an outfit that held the explosives contract for a spur line of the Burlington Vermont Railway. It was more than three years ago. It's why Deek and I got on so well, you see. I understood his work. He came to me for advice."

Durrant nodded, marvelling at the man's about-face. He pushed himself up and looked around the carriage one more time before stepping out onto the railway line, leaving a confounded Wilcox in his well-appointed sleeping car.

"THINGS JUST KEEP getting more and more convoluted," Durrant confessed to Charlie. They were sitting in their cabin; outside, snow had started to falling lightly. Durrant was sitting at his desk, and Charlie sat cross-legged on his bunk. He held the wire correspondence from Kauffman in one hand, and the writing tablet in the other. For most of the afternoon he'd been reading over the code, trying to find patterns that could be transcribed into English.

"Tomorrow, I'm going to track down all our suspects and see if I can't start putting the squeeze on people. It's going to heat up around here, I think," said Durrant, looking over his shoulder at Charlie. The boy looked up at him. "Okay, it's going to heat up even *more*. I think it best if you move about the camp as little as possible."

Charlie wrote a question mark on his tablet. "If someone has an axe to grind, I want it to be me they come to find. Not you." Charlie shrugged and returned his attention to his coded message.

Durrant looked down at the rudimentary list he was constructing on a piece of writing paper, using a nub of pencil he'd found in the desk. He'd written down the names of all the suspects he had amassed for the murder of Deek Penner, and then jotted down the words "means, motive and opportunity" and scribbled notes in each crude column. He was absorbed in this list when he heard the crunching of snow on the path to the cabin. Charlie heard it too, and put down the tablet. Durrant, seated next to the door, unholstered his Enfield and placed it on the table before him. The two men sat listening. The sound of the approaching footfalls seemed to echo in the dense, snowbound air. Despite their anticipation, the loud rasp at the door surprised them, and Durrant grabbed the handle of the pistol.

"Sergeant Wallace, it's Tom Holt."

Durrant breathed out.

"Come in, sir. The door is unlocked."

The door opened, and a swirl of snow entered the little cabin. The man who came in was wrapped in a heavy coat, and scarf and wearing a woollen cap like the one Dodds' sawyers wore. He closed the door behind him and brushed off a little of the snow onto the floorboards then unwrapped his face.

"Sergeant," he said, "I'm sorry not to have been around for your investigation; business has taken me to Padmore, to oversee the delivery of supplies. I just returned on the mid-day freight. There has been much to attend to."

"Well, thank you for stopping by. Would you care for tea? Charlie could brew up a pot."

"No, thank you both," the man said, waving Charlie to sit back down. "I can't stay long. I've got five cars of freight arriving for the stores tomorrow and I need to prepare the papers. I came to deliver something. Something I think you'll find very interesting."

"What is it?" Durrant asked.

Holt pulled a thick envelope from his jacket. He reached inside it and drew forth a sheet of paper. Charlie sat forward. "It's wire correspondence," said Tom, "intended for Deek Penner and sent a day before his death."

"Where was it? Why did he not receive it?"

"It was in Banff. Sometimes, if John doesn't receive a transmission, our man in Banff will pick it up; the signal for the two stations is practically the same. This has been sitting at the station there for two weeks. I was just made aware of it today." He handed it to Durrant.

Durrant turned to Charlie. The boy stood up and looked at the paper in Durrant's hands. "It's the same code, Charlie. Look here, it's signed Kauffman," said Durrant, pointing with his twisted right hand. "Can you decipher this code, Mr. Holt?"

"I don't recognize it. It's not one the CPR uses."

"It's a mystery to us as well, unfortunately."

"I'm sorry that Deek didn't receive it."

"So am I," said Durrant.

"Well, then, good night." Holt wrapped his scarf around his face and put his hat back on his head, opened the door, and stepped back into the swirling storm.

"Good night, sir."

Charlie indicated that he'd like the wire correspondence. Durrant handed it to him. The boy sat back down the bed and compared the two transmissions. Every so often he would jot a word or two down on his tablet, counting the letters, and then erase them. What struck Durrant about the lad was the intensity of his concentration. Half an hour passed and he didn't look up once.

Suddenly Charlie looked up, a broad smile on his face. He moved to where Durrant sat and pointed to a word on both pieces of correspondence, then to his tablet. He wrote "explosives." Durrant nodded. Charlie then pointed to more words and wrote "shipment," then "Northumberland Glycerol Company." Finally he circled a name that appeared halfway down the page on the second wire transmission: "O'Brian." Durrant looked at the boy. They both smiled widely.

SIXTEEN

WITNESS

THIS DAY BEGAN AS THE previous one had ended—with the arrival of wire telegrams. Before Durrant and Charlie had left their bunk to take breakfast in the mess tent, Christianson had knocked at their door. Pistol in hand, Durrant opened it to see that the snow was falling steadily in the woods around their bunk. The wind had abated and the temperature risen so that now, rather than blowing sideways, the flakes fell soft and thick on the ground. A foot of snow had settled around the cabin in the night.

"Do you want to come in?" asked Durrant.

"No sir, I've got to be getting back. Mr. Holt's got a huge shipment of supplies for the Kicking Horse today, and I've got to lend a hand. I thought you'd want this." He handed Durrant the coded message.

"Thank you, Mr. Christianson," Durrant said and took the message. "Hell of a snowfall," said Durrant to Charlie, pushing the door closed.

Charlie nodded as Durrant turned his attention to the wire. He took up the stub of a pencil and decoded it. "It's from Steele. He says we've gotten some assistance from the Montreal constabulary. They've seized the log book of the Grand Trunk: a man named Patrick Carriere is our spy." He looked up.

AFTER BREAKFAST DURRANT dispatched Charlie back to their cabin while he went to learn the whereabouts of Patrick Carriere. He first inquired with Bob Pen, and was directed to Grant McPherson. He found the new foreman in the munitions warehouse. They exchanged greetings and then Grant pointed out Patrick Carriere. "What do you want with him?" McPherson inquired.

"Friend of the family," quipped Durrant, turning his back on the man.

Carriere was of an average size, standing five foot ten, but thick through the chest. He wore a wool cap and a heavy wool sweater as he hefted sacks of kieselguhr, the thin powdery soil used to make nitroglycerine. He was loading them onto a handtruck for transport to the munitions factory—now under construction—at Kicking Horse Pass.

"Mr. Carriere?" Durrant asked.

"That's me," the man said, not looking up.

"I'm Sergeant Durrant Wallace. North West . . ."

"I know who you are, Sergeant. What do you need?" The man grunted as he hefted another load. "I've got to finish this before the next sled leaves for the Pass." Carriere stopped and looked at Durrant for the first time. The labourer was sweating. He wiped his forehead with the back of his hand.

"I want a minute of your time. Mr. McPherson won't mind."

Carrierre looked up at him. "You want to talk here?"

"Suits me fine. You know what this is about?"

"I haven't the foggiest idea, Sergeant."

"We've raided the Grand Trunk offices in Montreal. We know that you're working for them. We know that you've been sending them cables with information on the CPR's progress here at Holt City."

Carriere folded his arms across his chest. He was silent a moment. "You going to arrest me?"

"I imagine there will be some charges. At the very least you're going to have to leave Holt City. But I have more important business that I need to ask you about."

"Given my position, I'm not inclined to discuss much with you, Sergeant."

"We'll see. You worked for Deek Penner, didn't you?"

"I did, before Grant McPherson took over."

"Hep Wilcox tells me that he had asked Deek to try and learn the identity of a spy he suspected of infiltrating the camp."

Carriere broke into a broad smile. He laughed, "I see where this is going."

"Do you?"

"You think that I killed Deek Penner because he was onto me. Is that it?"

"Did you?"

Again the man laughed.

"You think murder is a laughing matter?"

"I think that you must be a little crazy is what I think."

Durrant stiffened.

"I mean no offence, Sergeant, but someone is selling you a line of bull. Deek Penner was a good man. He worked hard. He knew his business. He served the CPR faithfully. But *he* wasn't onto me. If Hep Wilcox told you that, he's a goddamned liar. Hep knew about my being in this camp as early as February, maybe the first week of March. He didn't ask Deek Penner to try and find me. Wilcox found me *himself*, or I suppose his man John Christianson did, as Hep isn't really all that bright. Come on, Sergeant, it's a tiny camp, and there ain't that many of us who can send cables. How long do you really think it would take to find a spy here?"

Durrant regarded the man. He fought back the feeling of foolishness that was washing over him.

"Walk with me, Mr. Carriere," said Durrant.

The man shrugged. Durrant started towards the door, where several large stacks of material were awaiting loading. Before they got to the door Durrant stopped, and with all his might grabbed Carriere by the collar and heaved him into the space between the sacks. Before the man could respond, Durrant drew his Enfield revolver and levelled it at the man's forehead. He pulled the hammer back, the firing pin hanging above a round in the cylinder.

"You're a liar," he said, his teeth gritted.

Carriere looked at him askance, "You're not going to shoot me."

"What makes you think that?"

"You're a lawman. It ain't the way the Red Coats do it!"

"It would be self-defence. I found out about you. You tried to flee custody. You attacked me in the effort to evade capture."

The two men stared at each other in the dim light, the muzzle of Durrant's pistol coming to rest on Carriere's forehead. A bead of sweat formed above his eye and dripped onto his cheek.

"You know, son, after being shot and left for dead, I'm not near as steady as I used to be, and these old Enfields, they have a reputation for a bit of a hairtrigger."

Doubt clouded Carriere's eyes. "What do you want?"

"The truth."

"I told you the truth."

"Did you kill Deek Penner?"

"No!"

"Who did?"

"How the hell should I know?"

"When did Hep Wilcox catch onto you?"

"End of February, maybe the first of March. Ask him!"

"Why wouldn't he turn you in if he knew?"

"I don't know. Maybe he didn't care!"

"I think you know."

"I swear I don't."

"What were you giving the Grand Trunk?"

"Just logistics; where the preparations were at for the Big Hill. Time tables, supply contract information, just that."

"Why would *they* care?"

"They're competitors! The Trunk is trying to buy up lines in the Midwest and out through Missouri country. They wanted to know where the CPR would run, and if it was going to meet its schedule. If it looks like it was going to fall behind schedule, or cost more, then the Trunk could maybe make a play for investments to complete its lines."

Durrant pressed the barrel of the pistol into the man's forehead. The skin around it turned white. "You were going to engineer an accident. Set construction back. Weren't you?"

"No! I was just passing information. The Grand Trunk has lots of spies. So does the CPR."

"Deek Penner found out, didn't he? He found out what you were going to do—kill some men while they were working on the Tote Road, or on the first tunnel down the Big Hill. He found out, and you killed him."

"I didn't kill Deek Penner," The man seemed to compose himself.

"I don't believe you," Durrant said as he lowered the pistol to the man's gut. "You're under arrest."

"What's the charge?"

"Espionage, for now. We'll see what comes of things."

"I want a solicitor."

"You'll get one, but first you're going to have to sit and stew up here a while."

DURRANT HAD TAKEN the spy Carriere to the station and presented him to Wilcox, curious as to what the man's expression would be. Wilcox remained implacable. Behind him, in the tiny office, Durrant could see the MP Blake O'Brian sitting with his hat in his hands, a look of concern on his pale face.

"I'll need a place to secure this prisoner," he said to Wilcox.

"You can put him in Deek Penner's bunk. We'll leave some wood and some food and you can lock the door."

"That will be fine. Nobody is to talk with him."

"So you've found your killer?" called the MP cheerfully over Wilcox's shoulder.

"Not yet, but I'm very close," said Durrant, taking his leave.

Durrant thought over the interrogation of his prisoner. He'd likely gone too far in the use of force, but he was running out of tools to get at the truth. He didn't think Carriere was lying, and that meant Wilcox *was*. Why would the man lie about his knowledge of the spy at Holt City? And why, if he knew about Carriere's presence at the end of track, would he tolerate it? He would need to make his rounds and question the key suspects once more before the trail went entirely cold, and before his suspects began to disperse with the coming spring construction schedule. The heavy snowfall had ground much of the camp's activity to a halt, so he thought it might work to his advantage. He decided to start with the hardest of the lot, Frank Dodds.

Durrant stood a moment at Dodds' cabin, the snow accumulating on his sealskin cap and his greatcoat, and contemplated the lack of tracks in the snow around the man's door. If Dodds had come and gone over the last twenty-four hours, he'd not left a single print as evidence of his passage.

Durrant hobbled up to the door, the snow a foot and a half deep. He knocked and stepped aside. He waited. Nothing. He knocked again. "Mr. Dodds?" he called. Nothing. He knocked and yelled a third time. He tried the door. There was a heavy Yale lock crudely affixed above the handle. He could get it off, but it would require more gunplay, and he imagined that he was pushing his luck in Holt City as it was.

It was plain that the man had not been to his cabin in the last day, maybe longer. If Dodds had somehow slipped out of Holt City, in which direction had he gone? If Dodds was now on the lam, that would put him at the very top of the suspect list once again.

Before he made those inquires, Durrant would pay a visit to Dodds' associates Ralph and Pete Mahoney. Durrant found his way through the shantytown of tents and cabins to where the brothers lived. He could hear fiddle music emanating from the tent. When he pulled back the flap the reek of sweat, cheap tobacco, and moonshine nearly knocked him down. Ice crackled on the canvas; as the snow fell on the tent it melted from the cabin's heat and then froze, forming a thick coating.

A dozen men sat on bunks or at the crude table in the middle of the room. A jug of moonshine rested on the table and several candles cast a rancid light on the half dozen lads playing cards. The fiddle music stopped; the fiddler sitting on the top bunk looked down at the silhouetted figure in the door.

"Ferme la porte," a man called from the back of the tent. Durrant stepped inside. His eyes adjusted to the light and he assessed the room for threats; there were so many he couldn't decide which ones to focus on. There were a number of rifles propped against the walls, and several double-sided axes hung from pegs or rested on the floor.

"Blue Jesus," said a man and Durrant recognized Thompson Griffin, Dodds' number two man on the cutting crew, at the card table.

"Afternoon, Mr. Griffin," said Durrant. He spotted the powerful Pete Mahoney sitting beside him.

"What do you want, Red Coat?" said Mahoney.

Durrant decided that having driven his fist into the hornets' nest, he might as well stir them up. "Thought I'd stop by for a hand of cards."

"Can you play cards with that gimp hand?" asked Griffin.

Durrant sized up the man. There was no doubt he was armed; most men had access to a shooting iron of some sort, and Durrant guessed this man would have a revolver tucked into his pockets somewhere. Durrant decided to defuse the situation rather than escalate it. He also thought to win some valuable information as he did.

"I can beat your sorry ass," he said.

"Let's see your money. This ain't no social event."

Durrant stepped forward, snow falling from his coat. He pulled a tight roll of script from his pockets and waved it in front of himself. "Find the Sergeant a chair," said Griffin. "Deal him in."

Durrant sat down, his back to the wall, and rested his crutch on the table.

He looked up at the fiddle man. "Can you play something by Bobbie Burns?" he asked.

The man looked down at Griffin. "Play him a song, Dean."

Griffin cut the cards. "We're playing penny ante, five-card draw."

Durrant reached into his pocket to find some coins and tossed a couple into the centre of the table.

The cards went around and they played a hand. Durrant lost on the final card to Griffin.

"Happy to take your money, Red Coat," said the man, grinning widely, showing bent and missing teeth.

"Let's play another hand."

"Ante up."

"I got a better idea. I'll play for money, you fellas play for answers."

Thompson cocked his head. The strains of the fiddle slowed. "What are you on about?"

"If I win, you give me answers for every two bits I bet."

"When you lose?"

"You keep my money."

Griffin grinned again. "Your deal."

Durrant dealt the cards, deftly flipping the face cards with his left thumb and forefinger. He looked around the room at the other players. Nobody had touched the bottle of shine at the centre of the table; nobody had said a word about it. With his left hand he picked up his cards. He frowned.

"Not much of a poker face, Red Coat," said Griffin.

"If you don't stop calling me that," said Durrant, not taking his eyes from his cards, "I'm going to shoot you in the head."

Griffin tensed. Durrant smiled.

"You're joshing me."

"Wanna find out?" There was a moment's silence, and then Durrant laughed. He threw four bits into the centre of the table.

"Who needs a card?" he asked. He dealt the next round of cards and placed his bet, another four bits.

"You're bluffing," said Griffin.

"It's going to cost you four answers to find out."

"How you going to know if I'm lying, anyway?"

"'Cause you'll still be breathing if you're telling the truth." Durrant looked at his cards.

Thompson Griffin grinned again. "You're just funning." The man fidgeted in his seat.

"Let's see everybody's hands."

The men laid their cards on the table. Griffin had a full house. He beamed.

"That's a pretty good hand," said Durrant. His right hand trembled a little as he thumbed his cards. He snapped his hand down on the plank table.

"Blue Jesus," said Griffin.

"I can't believe it," said Pete Mahoney.

"Why's that?" said Durrant, looking the man in the eyes.

"That's the same godamned hand that started this whole mess."

Durrant had produced a straight flush. He stared hard at Pete Mahoney. "First question is for you, Mr. Mahoney."

"I ain't gotta tell you a thing," he said, looking down.

"Tell me about this hand of cards."

"I'm not saying another word to you."

"You know what happens when a man cheats at cards in Fort Benton, Montana, Mr. Mahoney?" Pete looked up. The fiddle stopped. The room fell silent. They could hear the wind swirl outside as tiny pellets of ice drummed on the tent.

"Tell me about this hand of cards." Durrant could hear the ice on the canvas roof cracking.

"Aw, shit," said Pete. "Deek Penner beat the boss with a straight flush the night he was killed. I remember 'cause I was thinking what dumb luck it was for Deek to beat Frank at that moment. They'd been at each other all night."

"Did it come to blows?"

"Yeah, but not between Frank and Deek. It was Devon Paine that caught it from Mr. Dodds." The rest of the men were looking at him. Pete was still looking down. "He made a crack and Frank took it out on him. He knew better than to get into it with Deek. Deek pulled Frank off of him, but ol' Paine caught a hell of a beating." Several men laughed.

"Who was next to leave the card game?"

"That's three," said Griffin, smiling.

"I can count, sir. Who was next to leave?"

"Paine was. Had to go and put some snow on his face, then John, me, and Ralph."

"Thank you, Mr. Mahoney," said Durrant.

Pete looked up, his eyes filled with scorn.

"Final question, then, and it's for you, Mr. Griffin. Where are Frank Dodds and Ralph Mahoney right now? And you remember my rule," he said, his hand resting on the leather of his pistol's holster.

Griffin laughed. "That's an easy one to answer. I'm even goin' to tell you the truth. I don't know where they is. They ain't been seen since the day after you blew up that still on the Pipestone."

Durrant knew that Griffin was lying, but the lie told more than the truth at that moment.

DURRANT PUSHED HIS way through the heavy snow towards the station, where he expected to find both O'Brian and Wilcox, as he had before. When he entered the station he could hear both men in the tiny office; O'Brian was clearly angry with Wilcox. The shouting stopped when he knocked on the door.

"Sergeant," Wilcox said when he opened the door, exasperated.

"Mr. Wilcox, Mr. Vice-Chair, I'd like a word with each of you in turn, please."

"Sergeant, please, I understand the importance of what you are trying to do, but we are in the middle of something, and what with the late date, and the heavy snow, things are falling behind."

"I'm sorry if this murder investigation is an inconvenience, but I assure you, I'm close to making an arrest."

"Are you still of the belief that the Grand Trunk man isn't the killer?" called O'Brian.

"I don't believe so."

"Well then, who is?"

"Will you permit me a moment with Mr. O'Brian?" Durrant turned to Wilcox, who seemed to be barring the door. He stood aside to let Durrant past, who said, "Alone, please, sir."

Wilcox looked at O'Brian, who stared back, and then nodded. Durrant shut the door behind him.

"Is this to be another inquisition, Sergeant?"

Durrant leaned towards the Member of Parliament and spoke in a hushed tone. "I think a few more questions won't inconvenience you too greatly, Mr. O'Brian." The MP sat motionless. Durrant took Wilcox's seat and looked out the window. Turning back to the man, he asked in a voice barely louder than a whisper, "Why would Deek Penner have reason to be sending wire cables to the House of Commons, Mr. O'Brian?"

O'Brian looked stunned. "I haven't the faintest idea."

"And who within the House would be sending them back?"

"Again, I haven't the faintest."

"It wasn't you."

"I just said so, Sergeant. I find your line of questioning offensive . . ."

"Yes, yes, so you've said before. I find your lack of forthcoming equally offensive. I have several cables in my possession from the signal at the House of Commons to Mr. Penner. The log book shows several other signals sent in return. This wasn't from your office?"

"No sir."

"Do you know a man named Kauffman? William Kauffman?"

The MP's eyes were cast at the floor. "I do not."

"You've never heard this name around Parliament?"

"There are two hundred Members of Parliament, and each has his staff, and there are clerks and the Parliamentary Library . . ."

"So that is a no?"

"I have never heard that name."

"What sort of business is your family in, sir?"

"Pardon me?"

"Your business. What is your family business?"

"Sergeant Wallace, I am a Member of Parliament."

"Your business!" Durrant shouted.

"I don't have to answer these questions."

"Are you involved in the Northumberland Glycerol Company?"

"My name is not associated with that business."

"But you know it."

"Of course. It's a prominent business in my constituency."

"And it employs how many of your constituents."

"I can't say."

"Guess."

"I am not a guessing man, sir."

"One hundred?"

"Likely many more. It's quickly becoming one of the largest manufacturers of explosives in this country."

"The fact that the Canada Explosives Company of Mount Saint-Hilaire won the contract for the Big Hill—was a blow to your constituents?"

"What are you saying?"

"Only that losing that contract hurt your riding."

"We've won many others."

"We?"

"My constituents."

"You're not here trying to win back that contract?"

"I am here on Parliamentary business."

"Indeed."

"Sergeant Wallace, I am the Vice-Chair of the House of Commons Select Standing Committee on Railways, Canals, and Telegraph Lines. When the Liberals win office again, I will likely be elected Chair. In fact, I may be asked to sit as the Minister in charge of the railway for the government. I am well within my rights to inspect the work here at the end of steel."

"I am not contesting that, sir. I do find it odd that a man named William Kauffman has been sending cables from the House of Commons to the foreman who was to be leading the explosives work on the Big Hill just days before he died. And that you, sir, represent a riding where one of the largest employers is a rival explosives manufacturer to the one who won the contract for the Big Hill. Tell me, sir, is the Northumberland Glycerol Company a contributor to your campaign war chest?"

O'Brian stood up. "I will not take this any longer, Sergeant. Steele will hear from me, and so will the Minister! This is an outrage!" His face was as red as blazing ember, his massive sideburns wild.

Durrant pushed himself up. His voice was stern and even as he said, "You are *not* here by coincidence, Mr. O'Brian. I can tell you that much. You *are* lying to me. I will find out the truth about why you are here. I can assure you that the law does not require that the killer be present at the murder of a man to find him guilty of conspiracy to commit the crime. Am I clear?"

O'Brian put his hat on his head and left the office.

"Mr. Wilcox?" Durrant called his voice raspy. Durrant stepped from the room, but no one was there.

BEFORE HE LEFT the station, Durrant went to the telegraph machine and sent a wire to Fort Calgary to ask that Lieutenant Dewalt keep watch for both Frank Dodds and Hep Wilcox. He gave Dewalt a description of both, and requested a constable meet each train coming from the west until the matter had been cleared. Dewalt would not like the implication of the request—that Durrant could requisition troops—but he had to be thorough. Did he believe that either man had left Holt City? No, he did not. It was, however, possible that they might try, and he needed to ensure his prime suspects didn't disappear eastward before he could brace them one last time.

When Durrant returned to his cabin, Charlie was waiting for him. It was late in the afternoon, and the heavy snow had brought down the darkness early to the deep valley. Charlie stood by the door, the Winchester rifle in his hands when Durrant entered. The boy lowered the rifle when Durrant stepped inside.

"What is it?" Durrant demanded. Charlie put the rifle down and picked up a scrap of paper from the desk and handed it to Durrant. Durrant read it aloud.

"I seen Deek Penner's merder. Meet me in the stables after dark." Durrant put the note down and looked at Charlie. "There something else?"

Charlie nodded. He picked up the writing tablet. "Someone was in the woods?" asked Durrant. Charlie nodded. "When?" Charlie scribbled. "Alright. We're going to the stables together. Get your coat. We're going to put an end to this."

THE SNOW SWIRLED before them on the path like something out of the wildest vision of Hades. As night fell the wind picked up, driving the snow against the men as if it were buckshot. Though not as cold as it had been, the wind was bitter and tore at their coats and found its way down their necks, so that by the time they reached the barn and stables, both were shivering.

"Alright, son," said Durrant, standing before the blackness of the stables. "I'm going to head in and talk with whoever saw Mr. Penner killed. I need you to stay here and cover me. You understand?" Charlie nodded. Durrant handed him the Winchester. "If anybody else comes in through these doors, I want you to fire a warning shot up in the air. If they turn on you, you cut them down. I know this ain't what you signed onto, but we're in this together, and frankly, son, I need your help. I won't ever let you down, and I know you won't let me down, either. Can I count on you?" Charlie nodded.

"Alright, get yourself out of sight and stay as warm as you can, maybe hunker there out of the wind," Durrant pointed to a snow-covered buckboard wagon. "I'll make this as brief as I can."

Charlie stepped towards the wagon and crouched down, disappearing up to his waist in the snow. He held the rifle before him awkwardly, but his attention was rapt. Durrant considered how much had changed in his life, that a mere lad was covering his back while he braced a witness.

Many things had changed, though. Two weeks back on the job—the real job—had returned purposefulness to Durrant. Maybe that was why he hadn't asked Steele to send him reinforcements after the incident with the nitroglycerine. Maybe that was why he was relieved now that heavy snow had effectively isolated him and Charlie at the end of track. As he closed in on a possible witness, maybe that was why he was able to stand upright and walk with more ease than he had in three years. He was alive again. Alive, and doing the work that he had signed on to do in order to keep the opaque darkness at bay.

The door to the barn was latched when he reached it. He glanced back over his shoulder at Charlie's shape through the falling snow. The boy still held the rifle before him. It felt good to have someone at his back again.

Durrant reached up and unhooked the latch to the barn. Gravity pulled the door towards him, but then the wind pushed it closed, so that he had to pull hard to open it wide enough to step inside. The scent of hay and horses wafted over him as the wind propelled him into the space. Over the gale he could hear the animals breathing and shuffling. He propped the door ajar by wedging it hard into the snow, then quickly stepped to one side of the room. As he did, he slipped the Enfield from its holster. The British Bulldog was in his outside coat pocket. With the pistol pointed at the dark space in front of him, he walked forward.

The building held twenty horses in two rows of stalls. Durrant moved from one stall to the next making his way towards the back of the barn. He could hear nothing else in the dark over the breathing of horses and the wind howling outside. Halfway to the tack room at the far corner of the barn, Durrant risked a look back over his shoulder. The door was still ajar; snow was swirling in as the wind pushed at the boards.

Durrant looked back down the centre of the barn. He stepped out and moved down two more stalls, the horses shuffling, their heavy flanks pressing against him while he tried to find cover next to their rumps. He heard the wind howl louder and shake the door, and then it slammed shut.

He turned and brought the pistol up before him with a start. The room was dark as the inside of a mine. He didn't move. A muffled sound came from the far end of the barn. He remained perfectly still. The horse next to him jostled his body and he held onto his crutch to keep it from clattering to the floor. There was someone in the barn. He heard a floorboard squeak and then go quiet. He could hear a man breathing. He slowly raised the pistol and felt his finger brush against the trigger. His thumb itched to pull back the hammer, but he feared even that sound would give away his presence. He heard a man draw another breath. He sensed movement in the middle of the barn and levelled the pistol.

The sound of a voice almost caused him to pull the trigger. The voice said, "Sergeant Wallace . . ." It was a small voice, that of a man fearing for his very soul.

"I'm here," he said, pistol still before him.

"I can see you. Don't shoot me."

"Who is it?"

"It's Devon Paine."

"Mr. Paine, I've got the drop on you. Why don't you shed some light on this situation?"

"Yes, sir," said Paine, and he moved again. Durrant saw a shape pass him in the dark and in a moment, a candle was lit in the tack room and Paine stepped out again. He was holding the candle on a tin plate in one hand and a double-barrelled shotgun in the other.

Durrant drew a long breath. He eased the hammer back, no longer concerned about the noise it would make, his adversary squarely in front of him. Across the forward sight of the Enfield, Durrant watched as Paine seemed to calculate his next move.

"Put down the gun," said Durrant. Paine did as he was told. "Step over there, well away from it." Again, Paine moved.

"You write that note?"

"Yes, sir. I did. I saw Deek Penner get killed."

"I SUPPOSE I know the answer to this, but I feel I should ask anyway. Why the hell didn't you tell me this when I first questioned you?" Durrant sat on a wooden tomato crate, his prosthetic extended before him. The tack room smelled of freshly oiled metal and the rich tang of leather. Charlie stood at the tack room door, the Winchester at port, watching the entrance to the barn. He still had his scarf pulled up over his face. Paine sat on another crate with his back to the harnesses on the wall.

Paine looked down. "You don't know these people," he said. "I was afraid of what might happen."

"I don't blame you. It would have made things easier if you'd come forward and told me, though."

"Easier for who?"

"For me, I guess. Did you see the man who killed Penner?"

"Not his face, just the shape. It was dark and I was far away."

"Tell me what happened."

"Well, some of it you already know. That bastard Dodds came at me and laid into me pretty good. You understand, Sergeant, I'm not a big man, but in a fair fight I can hold my own. I'm not so bad with my hands, you see. Put a sawed-off shotgun in my possession and I can take care of myself. I used to ride with the stagecoaches down in Wyoming and Colorado. I told you that, didn't I? I think I might even have killed a man once . . ." His voice trailed off. "It was a fair fight. The Marshall told me so. I shot the man right off his horse when he was coming for the strongbox. *That* there's the gun that did it!"

Durrant regarded the sawed off shotgun. It was a Remington Whitmore 78, one of the most popular and effective guns of the day.

"Anyways, I'm not bragging on it. I'm just saying I can hold my own. Dodds is a big man and he really come at me. He busted my nose and knocked out two teeth!" Paine pointed at the gap in his dental work.

"Them Mahoney brothers tried to pull him off, but I don't think they was trying too hard. That's when ol' Deek just moved all three of them off me. He was a big lad, that one. He just pushed 'em all off me. I don't think even Frank or Pete would pick a fight with him. Not face to face I mean."

"What happened next?"

"Deek and Frank got into it about moonshine. Deek said he was going to report Frank to Hep Wilcox and that would be the end of things. Hep knew all about what Frank was doing. Everybody did, but Hep knew that if Deek ratted Frank out, he'd *have* to do *something*, or lose his contract as general manager here at Holt City. Frank knew it too."

"You think it was Dodds that killed him?"

"Well, I just don't know. I left next after Deek. I didn't want to hang around lest maybe Pete and Ralph and Frank all lay into me and then it would be just John and Grant there, and they ain't much for fighting. I think Grant could hold his own, but John is just a little mouse of a man.

"I went off to put some snow on my face, and I got to thinking I should go and tell Deek what I knew. I drove the team that dropped that milled lumber off for Frank's still up the Pipestone. I didn't know what he was building, I really didn't. I just did what he told me; I mostly work for him, see. That was in January after the Pipestone froze good and hard. Anyway, I thought I'd tell Deek what I knew so I went and knocked on his door, but he was gone. I guessed that he was going to the station to wake up Hep, or maybe to send a wire. Maybe he wanted to get the drop on Frank, right?"

"I think you guessed right."

"So I followed along the path to the station, and that's when I saw it."

"What did you see?"

"I was just where the path goes alongside the tracks when I saw Deek up in the distance, heading back into the trees. I was maybe a hundred yards back. It was pretty dark, but I could tell by the size of him and the way he walked—kinda like a big ol' draft horse—that it was Deek Penner. I was just going to call to him when someone came at him from behind. Just jumped out from behind one of them little pines. Deek turned around, but I don't think he saw the blow coming. I think he turned just a second before he got hit. I saw the man swing at him with something and knock him down, and then he stood over Deek and hit him again and again."

Paine had an absent, ghostly look on his face. From the door Charlie looked toward the man and Durrant could see that the man's pain had registered with the boy. Durrant motioned for Charlie to keep his eyes on the barn door.

"I couldn't do nothing. It all happened so fast."

"What happened next?"

"Well, I was going to run, you know? Just run. But I couldn't move a muscle. I just stood there. Whoever it was that hit Deek then grabbed him by the legs and began to pull him into the snow, toward the river."

"The river was frozen over."

"Oh yeah, and lots and lots of snow. Even more than now. I guess they was going to leave the body there and come the spring it would just melt through. I don't know, but the going was real tough. The snow was deep and the murderer was having a hard time. That's when I think he saw me."

"Really? What makes you think that?"

"They just stopped pulling. He sort of looked up in my direction."

"What did you do?"

"I ran off." Paine looked down at his hands. The candle flickered on its plate, the dark shadows playing across the faces of the men and the tack that hung around them.

"Back the way you'd come?"

"It was the only way. The snow was too deep otherwise, and the way to the station was blocked. I circled around a few times, afraid whoever it was might be hunting me. I waited an hour before coming back to my bunk here." Paine was silent a moment, then he added, "I'm real sorry about not talking with you before."

Durrant looked him over. "It's alright. I have a few questions. How big was the man that you saw hit Mr. Penner?"

"It was so hard to tell. He had a heavy coat on. He was shorter than Deek, but most are. He came at him from the deep snow so he seemed a lot shorter, like he was sinking up to his knees."

"That matches what I have seen of the wounds on Deek's head, Mr. Paine." Durrant considered his next question. "Would you say the man was as heavy as Deek?"

"No, sir. He wasn't as big in the shoulders. I could see that much."

"Bigger than you, though?"

"I can't say. The coats, you know . . ."

"I understand. Everybody looks the same when they've got four layers of wool on," said Durrant. Paine nodded.

"What was the man wearing on his head?"

"A beaverskin hat."

"You didn't see the man's face?"

"No, sir."

Durrant drew a deep breath. "Before you ran away, did you see John Christianson come along?"

"No, sir. There was nobody else there. You don't think John could have . . ."

"At this point, Mr. Paine, I think it's best that I keep my convictions to myself. I urge you to do the same." Paine nodded. "I'm going to take my leave now," Durrant said.

"What do you want me to do?" asked Paine, standing up.

"Should this case ever come to a trial, you will be an important witness for the Crown, Mr. Paine. I urge you to keep quiet about what you have seen, at least until I can clear this matter up."

"When will that be?"

"I have nearly all the pieces in place now. There is way more to this than meets the eye. I'm going to go at once to the stationhouse and wire my superiors what I know about the various nefarious undertakings here at the end of track. Come the morning, I will begin to make my arrests, with or without reinforcements. Too many of the principal players are already beginning to fly."

Paine nodded again, looking bewildered.

"You had best stay out of sight, Mr. Paine."

"I got a place that's safe," he said.

"Good, then," said Durrant.

"I figure I'm not just hiding from one man, am I?"

"No, sir, you are not."

SEVENTEEN
EVIDENCE OF CULPABILITY

DURRANT AND CHARLIE STEPPED FROM the barn into the thick of the spring storm. The wind pushed at the door as they squeezed through. Durrant shouldered the door aside before he scanned the howling darkness for any foe. He spoke close to Charlie's ear. "I'm going to walk you back to the cabin, and then I need to get to the station to wire what we've learned to Steele," he said. "We'd best get a move on. This snow is going to slow me down some."

They proceeded along the Tote Road at a snail's pace, Charlie breaking trail and Durrant doing his best to push through the accumulating snow, walking with the Winchester at his side. They reached the NWMP cabin without incident and Durrant gave Charlie instructions: Close the door behind him, keep the Winchester close at hand, and if anybody but himself should come to the door, don't let them in. If they try to force the door, shoot.

Charlie's face was ashen at the handing down of these directives. Durrant smiled again and said, "You'll be alright son," and with that he disappeared into the dark.

Durrant did all he could to make haste to the station. It was already midnight, and he felt a pressing urge to report his conclusions to Steele. He felt he was reasonably certain as to who the killer was, but was less confident that this man had acted on his own behalf. Given what he suspected, he didn't think that he could win a conviction from a magistrate without actual physical evidence. While his principal suspect had a clear opportunity to kill Deek Penner, and had sufficient access to a means, his motive was complicated at best. He simply had no obvious reason to kill Deek Penner. Durrant concluded that the murderer almost certainly had collaborators, one of whom held sufficient sway over his actions to convince him to undertake the crime in the first place. For Durrant, this left one significant problem: he didn't know who that conspirator was, at least not with any certainty.

By the time the Mountie reached the station, he had begun to devise a strategy to entrap the conspirator for the egregious crime and put an end to the investigation once and for all. What he saw there changed that completely and gave him the final piece of physical evidence that he needed to win a conviction.

He stepped onto the snow-covered platform in front of the station and made his way to the doors of the building. At first all appeared quiet, but he took pains to proceed with caution, knowing that at least two of the men he suspected as conspirators were unaccounted for at present. When he reached the doors, he put a hand on the handle and was about to pull when, through the frosted glass, he saw a light flicker. There was someone in the station. Durrant paused and looked around in the darkness to ensure he was alone. The wind and the heavy snow deadened any other noises, and Durrant feared being approached unbidden as Deek Penner had been. Confident that he was alone in the gloom, he pressed closer to the door to try and see who was burning the midnight oil.

His own breath and the snow obscured his vision through the bevelled window, but in a moment he could see who it was that haunted the station so late at night. John Christianson himself was at the wire station, his head down, unaware of Durrant's surreptitious undertakings. "What are you up to?" Durrant whispered under his breath. He watched for five minutes, the faint light in the room just enough to make out Christianson's concentrated effort to send and then receive a wire in return. Durrant could make out his arm moving, obviously tapping out a code, and then transcribing the return message.

Durrant watched for signs of Christianson's other persona, the one that he so rarely displayed to the outside world, but that at least one man in this camp had come to know and use to his advantage. He didn't have to wait long, and then, even the trail-hardened, "moccasin-footed" Mountie was shocked by what he saw.

His face pressed close to the window, Durrant watched as Christianson finished transcribing a short message. He took the headset from his capped head and placed it carefully on the orderly desk and then removed his spectacles and pressed his fists into his eyes, as if exasperated by the news he had just received. He sat that way for a full minute, and Durrant was about to relieve the pressure on his own aching leg when suddenly Christianson jumped to his feet, and grabbing the Phelps Model 1880 from its place on the desk, ripped it from its adjoining wires and hurled it across the room. The machine collided with the opposite wall and Durrant saw a flash of light as the telegraph machine exploded into a thousand pieces. The shrapnel careened across the station and clattered across the floor.

Durrant stepped back from the window but continued to watch the scene through the frosted glass. Christianson pounded his fists against the table; the entire desk and cabinet of pigeonholes shuddered as he hammered at them again and again. He sat down and, fists balled once more, pressed them into his face. That was when Durrant's crutch slipped on the icy snow and sliding from under his game right hand, rapped against the door. With a quick breath the Mountie stepped back from the window, and as deftly as he was able hid from view, pressing up against the wall next to the door. He drew a breath and held it, tasting as he did the adrenaline that suddenly surged through his system.

Christianson's face appeared in the glass of the door a moment later. His visage was dark, his eyes shadowed in the dimness of the night. In his peripheral vision Durrant could see the man scan to and fro, his face twisted with rage. If the man opened the door at that moment, Durrant would have no choice than to bear down on him with his pistol in hand.

The snow swirled and the door creaked and rattled in the wind. Durrant could *feel* Christianson's presence just feet from where he stood with his gloved left hand awkwardly on the hilt of the Enfield. Then, Christianson was gone. Durrant carefully stepped back and moved towards the door. Once more Christianson was at the table that had once held the telegraph machine, but now was largely bare. He had his fists balled once more and sat hunched over in agonized thought.

In that moment Durrant determined to change tack. As the events of the next twenty-four hours would unfold, the Mountie would later consider over and over again if this adjustment in his own direction might have set events in motion that slowly spiralled beyond his control.

Durrant decided something drastic had to be done to discover what Christianson had just learned and to find out who he was in cahoots with, so he stepped into the station.

Christianson looked up.

"John," Durrant said. "I'm sorry, I didn't know you were here."

Christianson didn't have his glasses on and he appeared to look around for them, then peer in Durrant's direction.

"Oh, it's you, Sergeant," he said, fumbling around. His eyes were darting back and forth across the room.

"Are you alright, Mr. Christianson?"

"I am not," said the man. "Something terrible has happened." As quick as a flash, Durrant watched Christianson concoct his story. "It's simply terrible."

"What is it?" asked Durrant, crossing the room to the counter. He stood behind it, his unseen hand on the pistol.

"Someone has destroyed the telegraph machine!"

Durrant feigned to see the ruined machine for the first time. "Blue Jesus," he exclaimed.

"I was woken by the sound, you see," Christianson stammered. "As you know, sir, my bunk adjoins this wall here. I heard a terrible crash, and when I came just now to see what had happened, I found the Phelps ruined! Smashed to pieces!" He pressed his fists into his eyes again and shook his head.

"Who, man?"

"I don't know. I didn't see him."

"Do you have your suspicions?"

Christianson looked at Durrant, his face shifting back and forth between rage and fear. "I can't say for certain. My guess is that the murderer has come to destroy our only way of communicating with Fort Calgary. What with the storm, we're cut off!"

Indeed, thought Durrant. He stayed silent.

"I had best report this to Mr. Wilcox, if I can find him, sir. He'll need to know."

"Do you know where he is?"

Christianson was silent a moment. "I don't. I'll have to undertake a search."

Durrant considered this. Finally, he said, "Do that, sir, and report back to me at once. Avoid Frank Dodds and his men at all cost, Mr. Christianson." Durrant paused and watched the man begin to stand. "Where are your spectacles, Mr. Christianson? I can't imagine you'll get far without them."

John looked around him on the desk. "They were here just a minute ago. I must have dropped them."

Durrant stepped around the counter. The fragments of the wire machine were everywhere. Christianson was scanning the floor for his specs. The Mountie joined the search and abruptly stooped and picked up the wire-rim glasses from amid the rubbish.

Christianson looked up at him at the same moment. Durrant leaned his crutch on the counter. Christianson straightened up in his chair. Durrant could see the man calculating, but he needed to see something for himself before he returned the eyeglasses to their owner.

"Let me tidy these up for you, Mr. Christianson," said Durrant. "I have a clean handkerchief right here in my pocket." Durrant reached inside his great coat, remnants of snow falling from the cape, and pulled a cloth from the breast pocket of his waist coat. He held the glasses up to the lantern light to examine them, as he had seen his father do a thousand times.

"My goodness, John," he said, "I don't know how you could see with these things on." Christianson's face was blank as he watched the Mountie examine the spectacles. Durrant looked through them. And as he did, he found the final piece of the puzzle that he could use to convict John Christianson of Deek Penner's murder. There, amid the fingerprints and smudges on the lenses of the spectacles, was a fine spray of now brown droplets, clustered around the edges of the specs where the man's careless fingers hadn't cleaned them away. The mist of blood spatter was hard and dried and had faded from bright red to nearly black, but it was unmistakable.

In that instant Durrant made another choice: instead of arresting the man on the spot, he would allow Christianson to lead him to his conspirators. He pretended to clean the man's glasses with his cloth and then tucked it back in his pocket. He could see the man watching him as he fumbled a moment and then extended his game right hand, the spectacles gripped loosely. Christianson stammered out his thanks.

"Now, sir," Durrant said. "I am for bed. I'm sorry that I cannot send my wire as I intended. I shall have to wait for the next eastbound train to send news to Fort Calgary. In the meantime, sir, I suggest that you get yourself indoors as well. If this killer shattered our only means of communications with the outside world, then who knows what he might be willing to do next?"

Christianson was watching Durrant very carefully. For a moment their eyes locked and Durrant saw the man as he really was. He felt a wave of revulsion pass through him, and then that too ebbed and the hex was broken.

"I will make one effort first to find Mr. Wilcox, and then I will be for bed myself."

"Lock your door, John," Durrant cautioned the man.

"I will, Sergeant. I will."

DURRANT WAITED FOR John Christianson for half an hour. He stood near the corner of the munitions warehouse, where he could see the station through the snow, and watched. He was cold and his leg and hand were searing with pain, but he had to try and see if Christianson would lead him to Wilcox. The man could not have left the camp, and he had not returned to his posh quarters in the well-appointed caboose.

When Christianson finally did leave the station after nearly an hour, he circled around behind Holt's store and went immediately to his bunk. Puzzled, Durrant watched for another ten minutes, the snow biting his face, catching in his eyes, and accumulating on his beard. He could not wait all night. He stood for another ten minutes and when finally he saw that the light was out in John Christianson's room behind the station, he too made his way slowly home.

If Durrant had known that he could probably have saved not just one life but two by waiting just a few minutes more, he would have suffered all the frozen fury of hell to do so. He could not have known what fate held in store that night, nor that he could have changed the course of events with timely intervention.

EIGHTEEN
FLIGHT

DURRANT AWOKE WISHING THAT GARNET Moberly had remained in Holt City—The Summit, as he called the lonely place at the end of steel—rather than vanishing down to the Columbia River Valley. What Durrant needed most right now was a partner, someone to help puzzle through what he had learned the pervious evening. Young Charlie was bright and had been helpful in all manner of ways since signing on for Holt City, but what Durrant needed was a conversation with someone who was smarter than he was. Someone to help him sort through some of the myriad of mysteries that remained surrounding the death of Penner.

What Durrant did know for certain was that Christianson had killed Penner. The blood spatter on his glasses clearly testified to that. But why? Who had conspired with him? Durrant was certain that some combination of Hep Wilcox, the general manager for winter operations at Holt City, Blake O'Brian, the Member of Parliament for Northumberland, and Frank Dodds, the foreman in charge of the logging, were entangled in this affair. Today he would have to find out which of these men were involved and how, and what their connection was to Christianson.

It was possible that Christianson was part of the ring of men who were involved with the brewing of illegal whiskey led by Dodds. Dodds could use a man like Christianson as a way of procuring supplies and evading detection by the CPR brass. Christianson could be cut in on the profits from the sale of the perfumes. Durrant didn't think that Dodds was sophisticated enough, though, to have a man like Christianson on his crew, regardless of how helpful it might be. No, Durrant believed that Wilcox or O'Brian or both were entangled with Christianson somehow. All he needed to do was complete his theory about the triad's motivation and he could arrest all three.

There also was the matter of Devon Paine. When he had left Paine the night before the man was clearly frightened. He'd locked himself in the barn, his Remington double-barrelled shotgun near at hand. He wasn't going to run from a fight; he just wanted to see it coming. Durrant had left a clear message with the man: do not tell another soul of his suspicions. There were too many unanswered questions yet to make an arrest, and talking about it would only flush the suspects from their holes and possibly beyond the reach of the law.

When Durrant woke, Charlie had prepared breakfast on the small stove in their cabin. As he ate and dressed, he made his plans for the day. He would first go to the station and try to question Christianson one last time, in an effort to force him to reveal who his co-conspirators were, and what role they had played in Penner's death. Right now, the thin mountain air was filled with lies, and he wanted to see if he could trip up the duplicitous Christianson with one last inquest. He would try to locate the errant Wilcox. And finally, he would check to see if Dodds had resurfaced. If he had, he and the moonshiner would have a heart-to-heart about his undertakings at Holt City. If Durrant played his cards right, he could return to Fort Calgary with three if not four men in his custody to await the magistrate.

Durrant strapped on his pistol, pulled on his greatcoat and told Charlie his plans. "Stay put today, alright lad?" Charlie nodded. "This thing's going to come to a head today one way or another. Keep the Winchester. If anybody comes through that door other than me, you let them have it." The boy's expression was pallid. "You might want to wait and see that it's *not* me before you unload . . ." Durrant winked at the lad. He was having fun, and this day would mark what he hoped to be a triumphant return to his role as an officer of the law.

Durrant checked the action on the Winchester and made certain that the rifle was loaded. Then he checked his own armament, pulled on his gauntlets and sealskin hat, and headed for the door.

The morning was still grey and oppressive but the snow of the last twenty-four hours had come to a temporary halt. Nearly two feet had fallen, thick and heavy like a quilt across the frozen earth. It made the going tough for most people around the camp, but at least the routines of the operation were returning to normal after the blizzard. The crews that worked the slopes below the white-horned mountain would be icing the haul road used to skid the sleepers down to the railway. Durrant knew that Dodds and young Mahoney wouldn't be on the job site that day. He was also pretty sure that Hep Wilcox, whose job it was to oversee such matters as when a foreman had skipped out on his contract, would not be looking in on Dodds that day.

As he pushed his way through the snow, Durrant considered how he would handle Christianson's key role in this whole affair. Though Durrant believed that Christianson was to be the least of his troubles that day, he had to approach the man carefully. If Moberly were here at that moment, he might remind Durrant that there was more than just a man's immortal soul at stake. A country was at stake as well.

By the time Durrant had pushed his way through the snow to the station, he had worked out a plan to get Christianson to tell him exactly what he needed to know.

He found the station as busy as ever. Men were clearing the fresh snow from the rickety platform. Later that day, if the tracks could be cleared around Castle Mountain—the halfway point between Banff Station and Holt City, where even heavier snows had fallen—another freight loaded with supplies for Holt's store would arrive and would need sorting before being sent on to the Kicking Horse camp. A dozen men milled about there, using push shovels and brooms to clear the way. Bob Pen nodded at Durrant as he walked past. Inside the station the postal clerk was sorting the outgoing mail.

"Is John Christianson about?" Durrant asked the man. He noticed that the remnants of the Phelps 1880 had been cleared from the floor.

Pen looked up from his task, his face quizzical. "I ain't seen John all morning," the man said.

Durrant looked around the room. He felt his face begin to flush. He had to find Christianson. He walked the length of the station and left through the wide doors, strode across the platform, and found his way around the back of the station to where Christianson had a tiny room. When he arrived he found the door locked from the outside, as if Christianson had left and secured his quarters.

Durrant knocked on the door and pressed his ear to the planks. He could hear no sound. He knocked again and still heard nothing. He looked down at the snow at his feet. The new snow had been disturbed sometime in the night. He looked around him and then knelt awkwardly, putting his left hand against the cabin for support. The top-most layer of the remaining snow was almost as fine as baking flour; he leaned forward and carefully blew on the powdery snow. It swirled up in his face and settled down away from the door. He blew again, gently. More snow swirled up. He studied the impressions there; he could see only one set of tracks going in and then coming out of the cabin, but he could not tell if they belonged to the deceptive Christianson or another man. He blew one more time; now much of the top layer of snow had dissipated. Durrant studied the ground, his face just a foot from the snow's crust. There Durrant found what he was searching for—tiny dark red droplets. Blood.

The Mountie pushed himself to standing and drew the Enfield from its holster. Standing back, he took careful aim at the Yale lock on the door and fired. The shot rang out across the tent city. The lock shattered. Durrant pulled it off its clasp and pushed the door open with his shoulder.

The room was dark and cold. A narrow band of watery light from the open door fell across the bare wood floor. Durrant stepped inside, his pistol up. Christianson lay face down on his bunk, a blanket covering his shoulders and head. His left arm, stiff with cold and rigor mortis, was extended at an awkward angle. His right arm, likewise taut, seemed to be clutching at the rough-hewn log wall where the cabin abutted the main station. Across that wall was a wide swatch of blood.

Before taking another step Durrant looked at the floor. There were a few droplets of dried—or possibly frozen—blood there, leading out the door and into the snow.

Durrant heard voices behind him. He turned to see several men there, drawn by the sound of the pistol shot. The postal clerk was among them.

"You men," he demanded, "stay far back. This is a crime scene." The men pushed forward to get a better look and Durrant turned on them, his pistol still smoking from the discharge of the cartridge. "Don't make me tell you again," he waved the pistol across the door to indicate the demarcation.

The men stepped back. "You," he said, the pistol pointing at a man bundled in a heavy woollen sweater that was flecked with ash and sawdust. The man looked at the barrel of his pistol. "Run and fetch Saul Armatage." The man was still staring at the smoking barrel of the gun. "Be quick!" Durrant yelled, and the man snapped out of his trance and bolted toward the doctor's quarters.

Drawing a deep breath, Durrant turned back to the small room. He advanced on the body knotted there, taking note that the air in the cabin was chilled. He stopped and checked the tiny stove: it too was stone cold. He took two more steps, careful not to disturb the blood on the floor, and reached down and took hold of the blanket. He pulled it back. The face and skull once belonging to Christianson was all but gone. In its stead, a pulpy mass of bone fragments and brain and congealed blood remained. The bunk and blankets were heavy with blood, and Durrant could see that many of the blows had been delivered while the man was lying face down on the tick. A broad spatter of blood, bone, and brains had painted the wall. Whoever had killed Christianson had also likely been coated in the mess.

Just then there was a loud knock at the door. Durrant wheeled, his balance awkward, and brought the Enfield up towards the portal.

"It's me, for Christ's sake!" said Armatage. He had his black satchel in his right hand. Durrant didn't say a word, but turned back to the gore. "Blue Jesus, would you look at this . . ." said Armatage.

"He's certainly beyond worldly cares," muttered Durrant. He looked around the darkened room. Faces peered at him from the open doorway.

"Give me a moment, Saul," said Durrant. He let his eyes further adjust to the dimness, scanning the room's shadowed corners. He soon found what he was looking for. On the wall opposite the bed, behind the door, another cord of blood decorated the wall. He drew an imaginary line in the air between the blood on the wall and the mutilated body on the bed.

Armatage saw it too. "He was first attacked there," he said, pointing to the spatter of blood behind the door. "And then he stumbled back onto the bed?" asked Saul.

"Or was pushed," said Durrant. "Can you tell if he was still alive then?"

"Let me have a look." Armatage stepped into the close room.

"Close the door, Saul. Shut out the goddamned gawkers." Armatage did as he was asked. The room was dark, the only light from the thinly transparent window, now crowded with the faces of several men trying to see the carnage. "Watch the blood," said Durrant, pointing his pistol at the floor.

Armatage carefully stepped around it. He bent to examine the body. "He was likely alive," he said.

"How do you know?"

"Well, his heart was still beating when he was hit here. You can see this spray of blood here," he said, tracing a line that ran halfway up the wall. "A lot of force involved. The heart was still pumping out blood when he was hit there. *That* blow likely killed him."

"How long ago?" asked Durrant.

"Need to take his temperature to tell you for sure. In this cold it wouldn't tell us much anyway."

"Can you guess?"

Armatage pulled a glove off and touched the man's face with the tip of his finger. The blood was cold and tacky to the touch.

"I've no way to tell," said the doctor. "He could have been here for hours."

"Blue Jesus," grumbled Durrant. It had been just past midnight when he had seen Christianson return to his bunk. Now he wondered if the assailant had been waiting for John in the room, or if he had come shortly after he himself had returned to his bed.

Durrant scanned the room, and his eyes fell upon the stove. He thought to check it to determine if a fire had been lit that night. He opened it and waved his hand inside, then stooped to sniff for the scent of a fresh fire. There was nothing to indicate the stove had been lit the night before, a few grey coals but no heat whatsoever.

Durrant put his pistol on top of the stove and picked up the crooked iron poker resting on the wall beside it. He pushed the ashes around in the hob, peering into its tiny darkened opening, then pulled out a few soot-coated pieces of wood and a balled-up piece of paper. It was the kind that Durrant had seen Christianson using to jot down telegraph messages the night before. He held it up to the faint light from the doorway.

It was a transcription of a telegram. It read:

The deal is off.

There was nothing to indicate who had sent it, or for whom it was intended, but Durrant didn't need that to be written down to understand the message's meaning. This was what had caused Christianson to fly into his rage the night before. This was, in all likelihood, what got him killed just minutes, or hours, thereafter.

Armatage was examining the body. "He's been hit half a dozen times. The assailant used something akin to a pry bar, Durrant. Maybe one of those used to open crates, you know. Like what Tom Holt has for uncrating supplies. You can see here," —Armatage was pointing to the destroyed face of Christianson— "where there is a reasonably neat incision that perforates the skull and goes clear on through into the brain cavity. When the killer struck John here," he concluded, his finger indicating the spot, "and then drew back for another blow, he pulled out some of this mess," said Saul, indicating the bone and grey matter on the wall.

Durrant stood up and handed Armatage the note.

"I don't understand." said the doctor.

"I don't have all the pieces, but here's what I think," he said, turning towards the door. "Mr. Christianson here," said Durrant, nodding towards the bed . . .

"What's *left* of him," said Armatage without humour.

"Mr. Christianson," continued the Mountie, "received that wire correspondence sometime late last evening. There was likely more to it, of course. That's just the transcription. I think it may have been from the Northumberland Glycerol Company and sent to either Mr. O'Brian or the general manager, Hep Wilcox. I think that the Glycerol company was still hoping to win the contract for some of the lower Kicking Horse work, and that O'Brian, Wilcox, and our man Christianson had promised them that they would deliver that contract. For a price. Christianson here was the bearer of bad news to the others. My bet would be that the Northumberland company got cold feet. The news of Deek Penner's murder has likely reached their ears and they have cut their losses.

"I saw this man around the time the wire came in, Saul. He was in the station when I went to alert Sam Steele of my conviction that John here killed Deek Penner. I saw him through the window in the door, and watched him destroy the wire machine in his fury. I later went into the room and he had returned to his belittled state of being. It was then that I noticed that his glasses had blood upon them. It was old and dry, but to my mind there is no doubt that it was Deek Penner's. This man, after all, claims to have discovered the body. It stands to reason, doesn't it?

"I left him then, hoping that he might lead me to Hep Wilcox. Instead, he just milled about at the station, and then came back here without searching for his boss. It is possible that I missed something, because somehow he got word to Wilcox, or possibly Mr. O'Brian."

Armatage continued to ponder the corpse of John Christianson.

Durrant continued. "Somehow John delivered the news, and reported to his colleagues that I was on to him. My guess is that Mr. Wilcox didn't take that news too well. I guess that he sent John back to these very quarters and then followed him here, taking him by surprise when he answered the door. When he left, he took his dripping murder weapon with him, likely for safe disposal elsewhere. The blood on the door stoop had been left just before the snow had stopped, before first light this morning."

Saul listened to the Mountie's explanation, nodding. "You said, on to *him*. Don't you believe Hep Wilcox killed Deek Penner too?"

"No. I'm certain that John Christianson did. The blood on his spectacles is the proof."

"How? He's just a runt of a man, and Penner was a strapping lad."

"True, Deek Penner was a big man, and strong, but surprise is a powerful weapon and John wouldn't have aroused any suspicion. He's a diminutive man, but he's stronger than he looks. I had him lift something for me the other day that I deliberately underestimated for him and he proved himself able-bodied enough."

"That's not evidence of his culpability, Durrant."

"Of course it isn't, Saul," said Durrant. "The killer's fist blow to Deek Penner's face came at such an angle as to suggest a man of lesser height. How much lesser, we'll never be able to say for certain, but at least four inches, and likely more. Some of that could be accounted for by the deep snow next to the trail where he was killed. Some would also likely be explained by the killer being a fair bit shorter than the victim. John here is four inches shorter than Deek Penner."

"But still, Durrant ..."

"There is the blood spatter. The blood is simply an infallible piece of evidence, Saul. You'll recall that when you and I first examined Deek Penner's corpse, we discussed how the killer must have gotten some blood on himself. In all my efforts to ascertain the killer's identity I'd not been able to find a single piece of clothing that had blood spattered on it. I checked with the laundry and the men that work there assure me that none of my suspects had been in with clothing requiring the laundering of blood. I've even gone so far as to search the rubbish piles and fire pits."

"I believe that was a job you assigned your lad Charlie ..."

"Yes, Charlie did the physical search, but I stood by ..."

"Not the same when you're rummaging through a pile of stinking trash, is it?"

"All he found was a belt buckle. There was no way to tell if it was from a greatcoat," Durrant continued. "Last night we got a message from a man who claims to have seen the murder."

"Good lord, man, why didn't you say so?"

"As you have said yourself, you're a doctor, not an investigator." Armatage looked wounded by the remark. "The boy and I handled it. We went to see this witness and gained useful, though not incriminating, evidence from him. He's frightened, and rightly so. I already had my suspicions. I don't know if there is a theory about this sort of thing, but if there is not yet, I shall have to propose one: the man who finds the body should be the prime suspect."

"John."

"Yes, *John*. Had he burned his own coat, he could easily have requisitioned one from Mr. Holt's stores without arousing suspicions. I went to the station last night to follow up on my notion. I meant to check his spectacles. It was just a hunch, and it proved correct." Armatage watched him. "Have you ever noticed that when John thought he wasn't being observed, he was much more ..." Durrant searched for the right word, "... steady? When you were watching him at the wire, or talking with him, he'd seem as if he was always a little nervous. Dropping papers, stammering, that sort of thing, but catch him unawares, and he was a different man altogether. Well, I saw both men last night."

"I've heard of such men, Durrant," said the doctor. "It's a new field of study, and I really don't follow it as closely as I should. Some are calling this sort of fellow 'insane without delirium.' These men can be a normal part of our social order and hide a tendency for violence, even homicidal violence, in plain view of the entire world.

"I don't particularly care for any such classification," snorted Durrant. "But I know a madman when I see one."

"Mind you, the spectacles won't be much good to you now." Armatage said, and looked at the glasses lying on the floor where Durrant had found them. They were shattered and covered in fresh blood.

"Unless you've got a way to tell one man's blood from another?" asked Durrant.

"There is no way to do that, Durrant," said the doctor. "I'm afraid the eyeglasses won't help you make your case against John with his own blood on them now."

Durrant was shaking his head. "If I'd simply apprehended him right then and there, the man would likely be alive right now and I could bring him to trial."

Armatage was shook his head. "You think that Hep Wilcox would have let you come between him and a man who could drag him down?"

"I *would* have come between them."

Saul looked down and nodded his head. "Yes, I believe you would have."

"I had to let John lead me to Hep, and anybody else who was involved. John might have been mad, or at the very least, greedy, but he wasn't in this alone. I didn't believe that. So I needed him to run to Wilcox and O'Brian and anybody else who was involved. That cost him his life."

"I wouldn't spend too much time mourning the death of this man," said Armatage. "He was a killer and he would have hanged." He was silent again, and then asked, "So, now what?"

"Now I have to find Hep Wilcox."

"Durrant, if John told him that you were on to him, won't he have tried to run?"

"He may have. I've got Dewalt watching the station in Fort Calgary, and there really is only one more direction to go."

"The Kicking Horse."

"That's right."

Armatage watched Durrant considering the remains of John Christianson. "You're taking responsibility for this man's death, Durrant. I can see it on your face. I know you too well for you to hide it from me."

"I don't know what you're talking about."

"You're thinking that you keep making mistakes and they cost people their lives."

"Saul, I don't want to get into that now," growled Durrant, his face down, his eyes suddenly boring into Armatage. "You can put your head games on the shelf, doctor."

Armatage recognized the look. He drew a quiet breath and asked, "What do you need me to do?"

"I need to watch over Patrick Carriere. He's my prisoner, but I can't keep an eye on him and apprehend Wilcox. Can you do that?"

"Of course, Durrant."

"I need you to send word to Steele of what's transpired and ask him to send me a couple of men to help with the transport of these prisoners. Please ask Bob Pen if there was another wire machine here at Holt City. They may have one from a boxcar station from last summer's construction season. Failing that, the next train that comes in must be dispatched forthwith to Fort Calgary with my request."

"Prisoners? Plural?" asked Armatage.

"Yes, I'm going to find Hep Wilcox. He's to face justice for this murder, and his part in Deek Penner's demise."

DURRANT BURST FROM John Christianson's tiny room and turned on the men that crowded the door. "You sir," he said, pointing with the Enfield at the postal clerk. "You will get me a lock to secure this room!" The man disappeared towards Holt's store. "The rest of you lot," he said, waving the weapon back and forth before the amazed group of men, "Get back to your work. Now!" he commanded. The men started grumbling and cursing, and then began to disperse. The postal clerk returned with a brand new heart lock and handed it to Durrant. There were two keys. "Anybody else got a key for this?"

"No, sir."

"If someone gets into this room, I'm holding you responsible."

"Yes, sir."

Armatage had pulled the bloody blanket back over Christianson's head and left the room. Durrant affixed the new lock to the door.

Durrant suddenly felt that there was a lot to do and very little time to do it. His first responsibility was to his prisoner, Patrick Carriere. He went as quickly as the heavy snow and his game leg would allow to Deek Penner's cabin. He made note that there were no tracks in or out in the heavy snow. He unlocked the man's door and Carriere stood up.

Durrant said, "You're still alive, I see."

"What's the shooting all about?"

"There's been another murder."

"Shot?"

"Bludgeoned."

"Who?"

"John Christianson."

"Well, I've been here all night."

"You're not a suspect."

"Who is?"

"None of your concern," said Durrant. "Saul Armatage will be looking in on you, making sure you've got food and enough wood to keep warm. If you do anything to try and escape I will hunt you down. Is that understood?" Carriere nodded. Durrant closed the door and locked it.

Next he had to locate the man he suspected of killing John Christianson. Durrant made his way back to the station. Several men were trying to peer into Christianson's tiny room through the oily glass window.

"Get the hell away from there," he bellowed as he limped past, and the men dispersed again. Durrant entered the station like a cyclone and went to Wilcox's door. The postal clerk and several other men watched him with concern. Durrant pounded on Wilcox's office door.

"He ain't in there," said the clerk.

"You have a key?"

"No, sir."

"You," said Durrant, pointing at a strapping young man who was hefting a load from behind the counter.

"Yes, sir?"

"Come here, lad." The boy hesitated. "I ain't going to bite."

"That ain't what I'm afraid of, sir."

"Come here!" Durrant bellowed and the boy did as he was told. He was six feet tall and broad in the shoulders and legs. Durrant sized him up. "Kick in this door!"

"Sir?"

"Kick it in. Now!"

"Yes, sir!" The boy stepped back and then kicked in the door. A single effort was all that was needed and the flimsy door shattered, the door frame splintered into a dozen pieces.

"Obliged," said Durrant, walking past the lad and into the cramped office. The boy smiled and stepped back.

The room was empty. Durrant ransacked the desk, uncertain of what he was searching for. It seemed as though nothing in the cramped room could explain the man's whereabouts or how Wilcox or O'Brian might be involved. Durrant leaned on the general manager's desk a moment and looked out the window. At first he focused on the world beyond the glass: the mainline and the sidings, all running parallel to one another, and beyond them, the river and the forested hills rising up to the mountains. Durrant stood there a long time and eventually his eyes began to blur. As he tried to refocus on the outside world again, he caught a strange reflection in the bevelled glass.

He concentrated on it and realized that he was seeing a sheath of papers reflected in the window, but they were not *on* the desk. Durrant pulled the small table toward him and the papers fell to the floor. They had been lodged between the desk and the wall. At some point Wilcox had toppled some of his own materials and forgotten to tidy them up. Durrant bent to collect them.

Most were waybills and correspondence concerning rudimentary operations at the tiny station at the end of track. Durrant quickly scanned through them. He felt a rush of warmth as he recognized the fine paper that John Christianson used for transcribing wire correspondence. The transcription contained two paragraphs: the top paragraph was in the same code that Durrant and Charlie had been cracking. This was a piece of correspondence from the mysterious William Kauffman! Durrant felt his heart beat faster as he scrolled down the page quickly. The second paragraph was also in John's hand, but this was written out in plain English. Durrant quickly read it:

> To Deek Penner. Confidential.
> From William Kauffman. Office of Vice-Chair,
> Transportation Committee, House of Commons.
> MP O'Brian meeting with Northumberland Glycerol
> Company once more. On good authority O'Brian
> and Mr. Wilcox taking drastic measures to interrupt
> contract owned by Canada Explosives Company.
> Northumberland Company's majority shareholder

Douglas Klein, O'Brian's father-in-law! Advise you forward your information to NWMP. O'Brian to arrive within week at end of line.

The final piece of the puzzle seemed to click into place for Durrant. Bill Kauffman was the MP O'Brian's assistant in Ottawa! He and Deek Penner had been working together to discover the MP's and Wilcox's undertakings. Before Deek could report his findings to the North West Mounted Police, he had been killed. Christianson had intercepted the wire, cracked the code, and delivered the message to Wilcox. Wilcox had instructed Christianson to seize the first opportunity to kill Penner. Christianson had chosen a moment when all of the suspicions would be focused on Frank Dodds and his moonshining operations. As a fallback, Hep Wilcox had allowed the spy for the Grand Trunk railway to continue to operate at the end of steel, so that when he and O'Brian did engineer an accident on the Tote Road, or while teams of men were hauling explosives up the line to the Kicking Horse Pass, the rogue would take the blame.

Durrant shook his head and put the wire correspondence into his breast pocket. He looked up from his distraction to see Bob Pen looking in the window. Durrant wheeled and limped back out of the room, through the main doors and onto the platform. "Mr. Pen," he said, "I wonder if you would tell me where Mr. Wilcox has gone off to this morning?"

Pen looked him over. "I made him out this morning. He was in an odd way. I noted that he was headed up to Kicking Horse Pass. Left before first light. He's taken a buckboard up the Tote Road with a load of dynamite. Him and Mr. O'Brian. I believe they've gone out to test the potency of the latest shipment."

"Was anybody else with them?"

"I don't believe so."

"You've been a big help, sir."

Durrant would now have to return to the Kicking Horse Pass. Another man's life was at stake.

NINETEEN

PARTNERS

THERE WAS LITTLE TIME TO think. Durrant made his way across the tent city toward the barn and stables where he had been less than twelve hours ago. He drew his pistol as he came near. He cracked the gate on the Enfield's awkward self-extracting system and ejected the spent cartridge. Reaching into his pocket, he slipped a live round into the cylinder. He latched the gate and pulled back the hammer on the revolver before stepping into the barn.

"Mr. Paine?" he called. The barn was quiet. There were just four horses in their stables, and they looked up at him when he called. "Mr. Paine," he called again, "it's Durrant Wallace." Nothing.

Then he heard, "Step forward, Sergeant."

He looked up and could see Devon Paine's face looking down at him through a trap door in the ceiling. "If you've got that shotgun up there with you, you had best keep your hands off it, Mr. Paine."

"I got it, but it's not in my hands," Paine said.

"Come down here," Durrant demanded.

"Is Hep Wilcox about?"

"No. Come down."

Paine disappeared from the window and Durrant raised the Enfield for action. A long rope ladder dropped from the hole and hit the floor of the barn. Several of the horses started. Durrant saw Paine's riding boots emerge from the trap door. He lowered the pistol. In a moment Paine was before him.

"Was Wilcox here?"

"Yes, sir, he was. With that MP, O'Brian."

"When was this?"

"Almost two hours ago now."

"Christ Almighty," said Durrant, looking around in disgust. "You speak with him?"

"No, sir."

"What about last night? After we talked? Did you go to him and tell him about what we discussed?"

"No, sir."

Durrant told Paine what had transpired in the night.

"Wilcox and O'Brian came in just about sunup and called for me. After your visit last night, I didn't say a word. I didn't let on I was here. I don't think Hep knows about my spot up top. I just sat tight. He took two horses for the buckboard and went out."

Durrant said, "They went up Kicking Horse Pass way. Loaded with dynamite."

"What the hell for?"

"I don't know," said Durrant, but he had his suspicions.

"Is there another buckboard you could set up for me to take to the Pass?"

"Sure, of course."

"Could I catch them on their way?"

"Not with two hours' lead time. They'd be beyond the heavy grade by the Kicking Horse Lake by now."

Durrant looked at the horses in the stables.

"Saddle two horses, Mr. Paine. I need to chase down my lad Charlie and fetch something from my cabin, and when I return I want those horses ready to go."

WHEN DURRANT REACHED his cabin and opened the door he was surprised that Charlie wasn't there. Blue Jesus, he thought, when I need the lad the most he's gone off on me. The Winchester was gone, meaning at least the lad wasn't unarmed. In a sort of blind frenzy, Durrant quickly took an extra box of cartridges for the Enfield and his heavy mittens from the trunk and stuffed them in his right pocket. He feared his right hand freezing again and losing the ability to manage the crutch. There was no time to wait for the lad. Durrant was on his own now. He locked the trunk and left the cabin. He made haste back to the barn through the overcast morning.

"YOU CAN RIDE with your leg like that?" asked Paine. Less than ten minutes had passed and they were standing next to a pair of saddle horses.

"I don't know," said Durrant, regarding the beast next to him.

"Have you?"

"No."

Paine looked concerned. "Do you need a hand up?"

Durrant shot him a look, then he relented. "It would help."

Paine came over and laced his fingers together and Durrant allowed himself to be hoisted into the saddle.

The feeling was dizzying. It had been nearly four years since he'd sat a horse. He felt the animal move beneath him and instinctively pressed his legs into the animal's flanks. He slipped his left foot easily into the broad winter stirrup, but he couldn't control his right foot and it flailed against the horses flank, causing it to whinny and step to the left. Durrant closed his eyes and concentrated on moving the prosthetic into place. He missed again and the toe of his boot connected with the horse's ribs, causing it to tremble.

"I'll give you a hand," said Paine. Durrant spat and cursed. "Look, Sergeant," said Paine. "This will take you some time, but I've seen it done. Down south, lots of fellas ride with one leg, one arm. Hell, I've seen it all. It will take time, though."

"We ain't got time right now."

"Which is why you should shut up and let me help," said Paine, not too gently.

The remark struck Durrant like a cold hand. He looked down and nodded. Paine guided the prosthetic into his stirrup.

"Where's your lad Charlie?" Paine asked.

"Don't know. I don't have time to chase him down."

"You're not going up to the Pass alone are you?"

"You see any likely reinforcements?"

"Me."

Durrant regarded the man. Paine stood at the ready, his shotgun resting on his shoulder.

"You sure you're up to this? Last I saw, you was hiding out in your attic."

Paine smiled. "I don't mind a stand-up fight," he said. "I just don't want nobody sneaking up on me."

"Saddle up," said Durrant.

Paine tucked his shotgun into the saddle scabbard and stepped up onto his own mount. He looked at Durrant and grinned. "That there's Princess. She's *real* gentle," he winked and kicked his horse into motion.

Durrant spat again and did the same.

The Tote Road ran west out of the camp. The heavy snow made the going hard. It also made it clear that a single buckboard had passed that way, its twin runners gliding over the icy ruts of the road, ploughing through the deep snow that covered them. It will slow them down, thought Durrant, guiding the horse into the ruts. The beasts were shod with heavy winter shoes that had spikes in them like the hobnailed bottom of Durrant's own crutch. It gave the animals purchase on the icy road.

For the first few moments of the ride Durrant kept the horse at a canter. The sensation of not being able to press the horse's flanks with his right foot felt disquieting. Soon the discomfort was overtaken by another emotion: elation.

Durrant had learned to ride on his family's farm on the outskirts of the burgeoning city of Toronto and had been sitting a horse since he was four years old. While others in his company had complained of saddle sores, he had risen to the rank of Sergeant based on his leadership from behind the pommel. Steele had seen to that, promoting the man to lead his detachment in part because of the way the young Durrant handled horses. Two of Durrant's mounts had died from starvation while on the now famous March West, but that was far fewer than what most men lost, and Durrant had treated those two as if they were fallen comrades.

Now back in the saddle, riding wracked—tight to the saddle and with full-length stirrups- —Durrant knew that this was the final piece of what had been missing in his life since he had been zipped, sidelined to casual duty while awaiting a medical discharge. Durrant had been a Mountie, a pony soldier, and that had been taken from him that afternoon in the Cypress Hills.

Durrant felt as he had not for many years; a man complete, a man who was competent to carry out the task the world had asked of him. He snapped the reins and his horse stepped up the pace, her heavy shoes cutting into the ice beneath the deep snow, each stride sounding like the clack of a small-calibre pistol in the crisp morning air. Durrant caught up to Paine's horse and the two men rode hard and fast over the ice road, the parallel tracks of Hep Wilcox's sleigh converging at a point in the far distance.

"So," called Paine, as their horses fell into a rhythm beside one another, "care to tell me what we're getting into here?"

Durrant thought about it. "I'm not entirely sure myself," he finally called back, breathing hard.

"Wilcox killed Deek Penner?"

"No."

"Who?"

"John Christianson."

"Why?"

"Fealty," said Durrant.

"Speak plain, man."

"He was what we Red Coats would call vapid. He killed Deek Penner because Hep Wilcox told him to. Wilcox could see John's mania, and took advantage of it to suit his own needs. John was no pawn. He could think for his own self, but he also was beholden to Wilcox for his position, and Wilcox played the man like a fiddle.

"I think Hep Wilcox and Blake O'Brian are in cahoots with each other. I found out this morning that O'Brian's father-in-law is majority owner of The Northumberland Glycerol Company. O'Brian represents the constituency where the company employs hundreds of men. The Northumberland company lost the contract to the Canada Explosives Company. Wilcox and O'Brian figured that if the Mount Saint-Hilaire explosives were proven unreliable, then the CPR would have to award the contract to the number two bidder."

"O'Brian's father-in-law," said Paine.

"That's right."

"How?"

"I think they were going to engineer an accident. Something big."

"Like blowing up the plant at Kicking Horse?"

"Christ, I hadn't even thought something that big. I imagined an accident while blasting on the Tote Road, or the first tunnel."

"That sort of accident happens all the time. It might kill some men, but it would be business as usual. It would have to be way bigger, like a train blowing up, or worse."

Durrant shook his head. It was a dark business.

"Deek found out. How?"

"O'Brian has an assistant in Ottawa. A man named William Kauffman. He must have uncovered things on his end. It wouldn't be too hard if he was paying attention."

"He wired Penner," said Paine.

"John intercepted a wire," said Durrant. "He as much as admitted it. Told me he was delivering a wire to Deek and that's why he was out looking for him that night. He could never produce it. Truth wasn't far off; it's just that the wire would never get to Deek at all. John was onto Deek and this Kauffman from the start. He was informing Wilcox and O'Brian instead. John knew the code that is used by Parliament, and instead of bringing Deek the missing wire, he gave it to Wilcox and Wilcox instructed John to kill the man. He and Wilcox must have decided the time was right, what with your row with Dodds and all."

"But I saw. I was a witness."

"That's right," said Durrant.

"They didn't really count on you showing up here at the end of the line. They figured it's too far from Fort Calgary. The Mounties won't care. Men get killed along the line all the time."

"That's right. Hep Wilcox could have wired that he had the man responsible in custody."

"Who?" asked Paine.

"At first I figured that they were aiming to pin this on Frank

Dodds. But I think maybe they were aiming to hang the accident with the explosives on Patrick Carriere."

"Who the hell is that?"

"Worked for Deek. Turns out he was spying for the Grand Trunk. Hep knew about it, but didn't turn him in."

"Then you show up."

"Well, I give credit to Sam Steele. He saw the importance of solving this, though I think he'll be as surprised as everyone that this ain't just about whiskey or espionage."

"Dodds is innocent?"

Durrant laughed. "No goddamned way. He just didn't kill Deek Penner. He's up to something, though."

Paine looked at him, his face red from the wind, and said, "So it ain't over yet."

"No, it ain't. Let's ride," said Durrant, and he urged his horse into a light gallop over the snowy road.

WITHIN AN HOUR they reached Kicking Horse Lake. Smoke rose from the recently completed sawmill there and from the cook shack that was likely serving the mid-day meal. Even at noontime the summit of the pass was much busier than it had been just a week before. Already there were three or four hundred men amassed on the shore of the lake, working on the munitions factory, labouring in the sawmill, or working to clear the Tote Road and rail line right-of-way. As they rode into the camp Paine swung from his horse and threw the reins over a hitching post in front of the camp's general office.

"Let me see if Wilcox has passed this way," he said, not waiting for an answer from Durrant.

Durrant turned his horse and scanned the camp for any sign of his quarry. He asked the foreman supervising the work on the adjacent munitions plant if he'd seen Wilcox.

"Yeah, I seen him," the man said. "Not but thirty minutes ago he and some fella in a top hat rode through. Said he had a shipment of dynamite for the Big Hill. I told him I hadn't heard of such a thing, and he just went on down the Tote Road like he owned it."

Durrant looked towards the snow-covered Tote Road. "Down towards the Big Hill?"

"That's right," said the foreman, spitting a stream of tobacco juice into the snow at his feet.

Durrant thought a moment. "You seen Garnet Moberly up here?"

"Yeah, he came through this morning, just before Mr. Wilcox."

"How much before?"

The man thought. "Maybe an hour."

"Could he get down the Big Hill in snow like this?"

"Well, I know I sure as hell wouldn't try, but that Moberly has some pluck to 'im. I'd say he'd be down on the Kicking Horse by now."

Durrant nodded his thanks. He stepped his horse close to the tent and yelled to Paine, "Let's go, I've got a line on him!"

Paine emerged and swung into his saddle. "Fella said there's a storehouse about five hundred yards up the Tote."

"I know the place. It's where Hep is heading."

"What's he aiming to do there? I thought he was going to engineer some kind of accident with the munitions plant."

"I think his plans have changed." Durrant told him about the scrap of paper found in Christianson's stove. "I think he's just trying to erase any remaining evidence."

"You mean O'Brian?"

"That's right."

"And you."

"That too," said Durrant, but he grinned widely when he said it.

"Alright, let's go," said Paine.

They rode on at a trot, both men scanning the woods for the explosives-laden buckboard. The tracks continued between the trees. In places the Tote Road became soft, as the day had warmed, and the horses punched through. Now that he was in the saddle Durrant was reluctant to get out again, but after a couple hundred yards the horses could go no further.

"They haven't iced the road this morning," said Paine. He stepped off his horse and patted her withers. She trembled a little, her front legs up to her forelocks in the deep snow. "It's okay, girl, you're okay."

He gently pulled on her reins and the horse stepped out of the snow onto the path, knees close together. "This is as far as we can ride, Sergeant Wallace. Wilcox drove the buckboard out this way this morning, but I'd say by now he's mired in the soft snow too."

Durrant looked down at the road. The sled had gone through with its heavy load of explosives, pulled by two stout horses, but that was hours ago, when the snow was still frozen hard. Now that thick crust was melting and even their single horses were punching through. Durrant pulled his game right leg from the stirrup, being careful not to snag it and fall face down from the top of his mount. He got his left leg over the rump of the horse and dropped to the ground. It was only then that he realized that he hadn't brought his crutch. He stood there a moment, the horse breathing hard beside him, its heat rising in sheets of steam in the cool mid-day air. Durrant pressed his ruined right hand against Princess for support.

"You okay?" asked Paine, looping the reins of his horse over the branch of a spruce tree. He pulled the Remington side-by-side shotgun from its scabbard.

"Yeah, fine," said Durrant.

"Let me catch up your horse there," said Paine and he came and took Durrant's horse by the reins. Durrant slowly pulled back his hand as Paine led the horse to the tree and threw the reins next to his own mount's.

Durrant waivered a moment and then stood up straight.

"You ready?" said Paine, not noticing Durrant's hesitation.

"Let's go," he said.

The first five or six steps felt just like the first five or six strides on the back of Princess. He didn't fall. The snow was deep and he pushed forward carefully, focusing on each step, looking up to scan the woods every few feet. Paine looked over at him and may have realized, too late, the challenge facing Durrant. If he did, he had the good sense not to say anything.

"Another hundred yards," whispered Paine.

Durrant drew the Enfield from its holster and held it carefully in front of him.

The woods were dense along the trail toward the tiny clearing where he and Charlie had stood and marvelled at the magnificence of the Big Hill and Kicking Horse Valley. Clad in dense snow, the forest obscured their view beyond the immediate surroundings. There were no sounds from the thick woods save the occasional thump of snow falling from an overburdened pine to land in a heap at its base.

As Durrant stepped through the heavy snow, he scanned the woods, swinging the Enfield from one side of the trail to the next. Paine walked a few feet behind and to the side of the Mountie, his shotgun aimed straight ahead. They proceeded slowly. A whiskey jack flew in an arc across the path and both men stopped, startled. Paine muttered, "Goddamned bird . . ."

Another twenty yards and the Tote Road entered the small clearing. Durrant could see the buckboard wagon, outfitted with skis, and its hitch of two horses at rest. The buckboard appeared to still be loaded; its skis sunk deep in the snow. Nobody had reported an explosion while they made their inquiries at the camp. Maybe they had arrived in time. Durrant could hear the ruckus of the creek plunging out of the mountains to the north and raging down the steep drop towards the Kicking Horse Valley a thousand feet below. The sound grew louder as they reached the edge of the clearing.

Durrant held up his hand and Paine stopped. He pointed to the far side of the clearing. Paine nodded. Crossing behind Durrant, he made his way low and slow along the edge of the trees. Durrant surveyed the clearing. In the distance, he could see the soaring space that opened beyond the cluster of trees at the steep banks of the creek. He looked hard for any sign of movement. There was none. Had Wilcox led O'Brian away on foot from this point? If so, to what fate?

Durrant looked over at Paine, who was hunched at the edge of the trees like a hunter stalking his prey. He was glad to have Paine with him.

Paine motioned to the Mountie, pointing to something behind the buckboard.

Durrant, pistol held in front of him, made his way stiff-legged through the deep snow of the clearing, taking a wide circle around the wagon. He stopped when he saw what Paine was pointing to. Tied to a spindly aspen was Blake O'Brian. His silver-handled cane and his smart black top hat were at his feet in the snow. He was gagged, and had a heavy hemp rope wrapped around him at least a dozen times. His hair was wild and fluttering in the light breeze, and there was a heavy gash on the side of his face. His head lolled forward as though he were unconscious. Durrant looked back toward Paine, but the wagon had come between them. He stepped toward O'Brian. O'Brian moved his head but didn't look up. Durrant tried to see Paine but he still could not. He took one more step.

At that moment Durrant was struck from behind with such force that he blacked out momentarily, falling face forward into the snow, his arms sprawling, the Enfield flying from his grip. The snow was supple and he regained consciousness when he hit the ground, but with his game hand and leg, and his eyes filled with stars, he couldn't get any purchase on his surroundings to right himself.

As he flailed, the snow and dizziness clouding his eyes, he heard Paine shout and then Durrant heard the deep roar of a double-barrelled shotgun blast. Durrant managed to roll over so he was facing the sky as this happened, only to see Hep Wilcox bending down toward him.

"Drop the shotgun, Paine," Wilcox said, gritting his teeth. He grabbed Durrant by the collar with his left hand. In his right he held a heavy dark object. "Drop it or I'll turn his head to pulp," Wilcox hissed.

From his position Durrant could make out the shadowy outline of the forest's edge and see the shape of Paine there, the shotgun smoking and levelled at Wilcox. "Shoot him," he managed to whisper, but Wilcox shook him violently and raised the heavy object to strike.

Paine threw the shotgun down in the snow. Wilcox grinned. "Good riddance, Durrant Wallace," he said, and the world went dark.

TWENTY

KICKING HORSE

THE DREAM HAD ALWAYS BEEN the same: the earth frozen, the snow falling, the horse dead on the ground at his side. He had been left to die. But he had *not*. For more than a day and a night he lay on the stony back of the Cypress Hills. He had lived. Many a night thereafter he wished he had not. Now the dream was different. Now he *wanted* to live. He climbed through the darkness back to the daylight. Hand over ruined hand, he pulled himself back from the dream into world of the living.

Durrant came around. He blinked into the white earth and the world wheeled into focus. The first thing he saw was Wilcox cracking the breech on the double-barrelled shotgun and loading another shell in the firing chamber. He then flipped the breech shut and turned, smiling at Durrant.

The Mountie was sitting in the snow next to the buckboard wagon, leaning against one of its runners. His prosthetic leg was missing. His hands were roughly bound in his lap with some bailing twine. A trickle of blood worried his left eye. Durrant looked around him. O'Brian was conscious and staring glassy-eyed at him. His face was as pale as the snow; his hair fell in tattered strands into his eyes. He hung against the heavy ropes that secured him to the tree. Lying in the snow at the far side of the clearing was the body of Devon Paine.

"What have you done?" Durrant said to Wilcox. Wilcox said nothing but turned his attention to O'Brian.

"What have you done?" Durrant roared.

"Please, Mr. Wallace, I'm working here," said Wilcox, the shotgun held lightly in his right hand. He stepped towards the MP and pulled the man's chin up so he could look into his face.

"Nobody," he hissed, "backs out of a deal with me." He spat into the MP's face. The man closed his eyes and shook his head.

"Nothing to say for yourself, O'Brian?"

"Not to the likes of you."

Wilcox puckered his lips and nodded. "Very well then." He strode back to the wagon and pulled back the tarp. "Have you ever primed a cartridge of dynamite, Mr. Wallace? Oh, pardon me, *Sergeant* Wallace?"

"You're going to pay for what you've done here, Wilcox."

"It's rather a simple operation, really. The whole thing, however, is very volatile. Not so much as nitroglycerine, mind you. But then, you've already discovered that, haven't you?" The man laughed, "That's why Mr. Nobel patented this less temperamental form of explosive."

Durrant now realized it had been Wilcox and not Dodds who had set the explosives next to his and Charlie's cabin.

"Ah, the penny drops," said Wilcox, smiled as he removed three sticks of dynamite from a box on the back of the wagon. "How perfect that you should have had that boy of yours carry that pail of explosives so far into the woods and destroy Dodds' whiskey operation. How perfect!"

He hunched down by Durrant. The Mountie looked him in the eye. The man seemed to have completely lost control of his faculties. His eyes seemed both vacant and wild at the same time.

"So here's how this works. First, we secure the charges together like this," he said, wrapping the explosives with a thick adhesive paper. "Next, we set the fuse. You need to use a tool that won't create a spark when you do this, or you'll blow yourself to Kingdom Come. It happens. Not as much as with the liquid form, but it happens." He removed a long, narrow tool from his pocket and pressed it carefully into the centre of one of the sticks of dynamite.

"There," he said, putting the tool back into his pocket. "Next, the fuse itself." He inserted a long black piece of cable into the opening of the cartridge of dynamite. "Now, we're all set." He said, smiling and standing up.

Durrant pulled at his hands as Wilcox walked to O'Brian's side. The MP watched him the whole way.

"Mr. O'Brian," said Wilcox. "It was such a good plan, wasn't it? Engineer a catastrophe here at Kicking Horse Pass. The first train to pull into the siding here would be loaded with raw materials for the munitions factory. There would be a terrible accident. The Canada Company's plant would be destroyed and its defective explosives would be to blame. The Northumberland company would then get its due. So much money at stake," said Wilcox, turning to Durrant, who had stopped pulling at his hands. "So much money, maybe as much as a million and a half dollars' worth of work. Do you have any idea how much money that is, Sergeant?"

Durrant sat motionless, his hands crossed.

"It's more than you or I could ever dream of. Mr. O'Brian here got careless. His aide in Ottawa intercepted a wire, one not sent in code. This fool here ruined everything," said Wilcox, suddenly surging with anger. He pointed the shotgun into O'Brian's face. He pressed the barrel into the man's eye; Durrant watched the MP wince in pain.

"So now . . . now we've got to clean up the mess here," he said, lowering the shot gun. He tucked the weapon under his arm and then pulled at the ropes that bound O'Brian. He tucked the three sticks of dynamite into the ropes and let the long fuse trail down the man's chest. He reached into his pocket and pulled out a box of safety matches.

"How long would you say this fuse is, O'Brian?" O'Brian looked down. "Not long enough?" Wilcox said.

He struck a match on his thumb and lit the fuse. It sparked to life and immediately the tail of long black cord began to burn away.

"Two feet," Wilcox said. "I'd say . . ." and he stopped and looked pensive, "about a minute."

Wilcox turned away from O'Brian, the shotgun tucked under his arm, and began to walk across the clearing to where Paine's body lay face down. Durrant detected motion out of his peripheral vision. He turned and through the blood in his left eye could make out a dark shadow in the trees. Though the scene was nearly black and white, the motion seemed to blaze with color. It was a man, moving fast and low through the trees, a long wool coat trailing out behind him. Durrant struggled with the twine of his wrists.

Wilcox detected the motion too, and wheeled, the shotgun dropping from under his arms into his waiting hands. His right finger found the trigger guard and slid into place.

The man in the trees suddenly had two pistols in his hands. He seemed to float across the top of the heavy snow.

The fuse burned down.

The shotgun exploded and a heavy round of buckshot burst into the trees where the man dodged through the woods. Snow fell to the ground and the green spruce boughs were shredded by a thousand razor-like ball bearings.

Durrant wrestled awkwardly with the twine, pulling with all his might.

Wilcox stepped back and as he did his finger found the second trigger and the shotgun blazed again. The man in the trees raised both pistols, and still running in the deep snow, fired both at the same time. Durrant looked to see the shoulder of Wilcox's coat suddenly dance with frayed fabric. The general manager, his face awash in panic, stopped and dropped to one knee. The man in the trees fired again, and Wilcox's hat flew off his head. His face registered terror. The breech of the shotgun snapped open; Durrant watched as the man in the trees ran into the clearing, both pistols still held straight out in front of him.

The fuse burned down. Less than a foot remained.

It was Garnet Moberly who had appeared from the darkness of the woods. His coat flew out behind him like a cape; his face bore a look of resolute determination. He closed the distance to O'Brian and fired both pistols again, the shots missing their mark but forcing Wilcox to stumble back in the deep snow.

Wilcox chambered two rounds and snapped the shotgun closed. With Wilcox only forty feet away, the shotgun reloaded and pointed at him, Moberly *stopped* shooting. He looked away from Wilcox, took both pistols in his left hand, and grabbed the clutch of dynamite from O'Brian's chest. Durrant's left hand, now free, found the British Bulldog. Durrant and Wilcox raised their weapons at the same time, but Durrant fired first—two rounds as quickly as his thumb could work the double-action hammer—and the left shoulder and arm of Wilcox's coat bloomed with bright red blood. At the same time, Moberly freed the dynamite from its ropes around O'Brian's body.

Wilcox staggered back, the shotgun still in his hands, and Durrant fired a third time, hitting the man in the right shoulder. The third shot took him off his feet and he landed, eyes open, in the snow.

Moberly threw the dynamite as hard as he could; the charge exploded fifty feet from him still high in the air, out over the raging Sherbrook Creek. The concussion from the explosion knocked the man to the ground. He shook his head, took the pistol from his left hand, and with both revolvers now held before him advanced on Wilcox. For the first time Durrant could see that the man wore babiche sticks on his feet—the webbed snowshoes so widely used by the Cree and other northern Indians.

"This one's still alive, Sergeant," he said, looking down on Wilcox, his three bullet wounds coloring the snow beneath him. Moberly raised both pistols and took aim at Hep Wilcox's head.

"That's how he'll stay, Mr. Moberly. This is Dominion country."

Moberly holstered his twin Webley revolvers under his long coat and picked up the shotgun and checked the action. He then went to Paine and knelt beside him.

Durrant reached up to the sled and hoisted himself upright. "Is he alive?"

Garnet looked back and shook his head.

BY THE TIME Durrant had affixed his prosthetic, a dozen or more men had arrived from the operation at Kicking Horse Lake. Moberly had untied O'Brian and propped him up against the sled where he sat with his head in his hands. Moberly then rounded up a crew and had them unload the dynamite and pile it inside the shed that stood back in the trees. While that operation was underway, he turned to Wilcox, who lay on his back bleeding into the snow, and dressed his wounds using burlap from the load of dynamite.

Durrant, meanwhile, went to Paine and looked down at the man. His leg would not allow him to kneel. Paine's chest had a rent in it a foot wide where he had been shot at point-blank range. He had given up his gun and been shot with it. Durrant stashed that in his memory bank as a lesson.

GARNET MOBERLY DROVE the buckboard, and O'Brian sat beside him in the middle of the seat. Durrant, his Enfield in his left hand, sat on the outside. It was getting dark when they set off for Holt City. The two horses from Devon Paine's stables trailed behind on long lead ropes. Wilcox was wrapped in a blanket on the bed of the wagon, and he drifted in and out of consciousness. Paine's body was wrapped in a tarpaulin next to him.

The sunset was gaudy: a broad smear of purples and crimson across the western sky beyond the valley of the Kicking Horse River.

Durrant finally had a moment to collect his thoughts. "I thought you'd gone down the Kicking Horse."

"I was going to give it a day to settle down. There's a nasty piece of business down a ways called the Golden Stairs that's near impossible to negotiate in deep snow, in particular with a heavy load.

"I was at the company office when your man Paine came in," continued Moberly. "I don't think he recognized me. He was just asking about Hep there, and this fellow . . ." he nodded at O'Brian. "I came out and saw two riders heading toward the pass and I knew there was trouble. I was halfway to the clearing when I heard the shotgun blast. I couldn't even be certain it was you, not till I got to the clearing and saw you on the ground."

"You saved us all."

"Maybe . . . you *might* have got that little Bulldog out in time. As it turns out you, saved me."

Durrant smiled, "Maybe. I would never have gotten to O'Brian here. Not with one leg."

"So what's going to happen to these lads?" Moberly asked.

"Well, as soon as a freight comes in from Fort Calgary, there will be a couple of constables on board that can take them back to the barracks there. If Mr. Wilcox lives, that is."

"It could have been fixed that he didn't," said Moberly. "Still could."

"I'm pretty tempted by what he did to Mr. Paine, but no, we need him alive. At least, if at all possible, he needs to stand trial."

"The Queen's laws shall reach to every corner of the Empire," said Moberly, his voice taking on an exaggerated accent.

"Something like that," said Durrant.

"And what about this rascal?" said Moberly, nodding at O'Brian again.

"He'll be up on conspiracy charges, in all likelihood."

O'Brian opened his mouth to speak.

"You've got something you want to say?" said Moberly.

The MP made a sound in his throat. "My family has the best lawyers in the Dominion at their service," he said. "We'll see about those charges."

"We could always dispose of them both," said Moberly with a smile.

The MP made the sound in his throat again.

Durrant just nodded solemnly.

"And what of you, Sergeant Wallace?" asked Moberly.

"Back to Fort Calgary, after a day or so wrapping things up at Holt City . . . at The Summit. I'll find that truant lad Charlie and head home."

"Home?"

Durrant felt his body deflate a little at the word. He had never once felt at home at Fort Calgary, and wondered if he ever would. He had proven he could ride now, but it seemed unlikely that Dewalt would take him on as a regular in his constabulatory. With the mystery of Deek Penner's death all but wrapped up, he felt a sudden wave of fear come over him. He could not go back to sorting the mail or sending and receiving wire correspondence. He had been zinged and zipped, but not zeroed, as the Mounties would say. Wounded and sidelined, but still alive. He was still capable and able to defend the right of the Dominion.

"You should sign on with the CPR."

"What would I do?" Durrant asked.

"Anything you want."

"I want to be a Mounted Police officer."

"Then that is what you must do," said Moberly.

TWENTY-ONE

THE LAKE OF LITTLE FISHES

IT WAS AN HOUR PAST dark when Durrant, Moberly and their buckboard arrived back in Holt City. The sky was clear and a new moon balanced on the top of the white-horned mountain and stars beyond counting filled the horizon. They drove the wagon first to the station where they found a cadre of men to attend to Hep Wilcox. Durrant dispatched one of the men to find Doc Armatage, and when he returned Durrant instructed him to do what he could to keep Wilcox alive. Durrant put Bob Pen in charge of the man's security while he attended to his two prisoners and to Devon Paine's remains.

They drove the wagon to the stables and unhitched the horses. Durrant led them and the two trailing animals to the barn where he gave them a bucket of oats and a bucket of water each. Moberly roused some of the men from a nearby cabin to help him carry Paines' body to the tack shed, where they laid him in his tarp on the floorboards. It seemed a fitting mortuary for the man. Durrant vowed that he would get a proper burial at Fort Calgary when they finally got back that way, and when the frost left the ground.

Before leaving the stables, Durrant found his crutch where he'd discarded it in front of the barn and propped himself up on it once more.

Moberly said that he would head back to his own quarters for the night and then return to the Kicking Horse in the morning to meet up with Mr. Jimmy and the rest of his survey crew. Durrant shook his hand.

"This isn't the last you'll see of me," said Moberly with a grin.

"I hope not."

"I'll call in on you in the morning."

Durrant nodded his agreement and then slowly made his way across the camp to his bunk. He was dog tired and famished and he hoped to hell for his own sake that Charlie was there and had a hot supper waiting for him on the stove. He reached the cabin and with the last of his energy hefted the door wide. The cabin was dark, stone cold and empty. Durrant let his eyes adjust to the dim room, his hand on the hilt of his pistol. When he could see well enough he found the lamp on the table, trimmed the wick, and lit it with a safety match he struck on his thumbnail. The lamp cast a hollow orange glow over the frigid room.

The space appeared exactly as it had when he had left for the Kicking Horse Pass so many hours before. Durrant scanned for some sign that might indicate that Charlie had come and gone, but there was nothing. His small table with his book and the stub of a candle, his locket, the trunk at the foot of his bed, Charlie's coat on his tick, the small desk, the writing tablet, and the piece of oily chalk that Charlie used to scrawl messages. The hair on the back of Durrant's neck stood on end. He picked up the tablet. He had ignored it that morning.

It read:

Wallace:
We have Charlie. Leave Holt City. When you have reached Fort Calgary, send word and the boy will be released.
Dodds.

He threw the tablet down on the desk and it broke into a dozen pieces. The exhaustion that he had felt moments before evaporated in a hot rush of anger. He slammed his fist into the table. Like hell, he through. Like hell he would leave Holt City. Like hell he would leave Charlie in the hands of Frank Dodds. He turned and stepped back out into the night.

MOBERLY RESPONDED TO the furious pounding at his cabin door with a Webley pistol drawn. "Good lord man, it's not been twenty minutes!" he said, opening the door wide. "I haven't even gotten my boots . . ."

Durrant cut him off. "They have Charlie!" His face was as white as the winter that lay on the ground. His eyes were wide, a deep line cut across his face tracking his concern.

"Who does?"

"Dodds."

"How do you know?"

"They left me a note."

"*Dodds* can't write."

"Charlie can. It was in his hand."

Moberly was already pulling on his coat and strapping his pistols around his waist. "What did they say?"

Durrant recited the note.

Moberly stepped back inside.

"Where do you think they might be hiding the boy?" asked Durrant.

Moberly closed his eyes a moment. "I don't know, but I know who we can ask."

"Ask?"

Moberly grabbed Paine's double-barrelled shotgun off the bunk where he had put it twenty minutes earlier. "*Ask.*"

THEY STOOD A moment outside the tarpaulin cabin. Just a few days ago Durrant had won two hands of poker and procured valuable information as his winnings in this hovel. Now a life was at stake; there would be no five-card draw this night.

A thin stream of smoke rose from the rickety chimney; the sound of a fiddle being played and men's laughter leaked from the canvas walls.

"They aren't going to give up their companions easily," said Moberly to Durrant. "How far are you willing to go?"

"An innocent's life is at stake. I put him in this peril, so I'd say pretty far."

Moberly nodded. He kicked in the door and burst into the room, the double-barrelled shotgun pressed to his shoulder. Durrant stepped in behind him, the Enfield pistol cocked and held straight out. He levelled it on one startled face and then the next.

"Evening, gents," Durrant said. There were a dozen men in the cabin. Neither of the Mahoney brothers, nor Griffin was among the dark faces that stared back. Two jugs of moonshine sat out on the table and several of the men held tin cups. Durrant picked a clean target and fired the Enfield; the tin cup in the man's hand jumped from his grasp, moonshine spraying across him. The bullet missed a man's leg by an inch and then feathers burst into the air from a tick on a low bunk behind him.

One of the men at the table began to rise quickly. Moberly bore down on him, swinging the butt of the shotgun into his face, mashing his nose, a spray of blood decorating the canvas wall of the shack. The man fell to the floor, clutching his face.

Durrant drew the hammer on the Enfield back. He searched for another target, but all of the tin cups had been hastily placed on the table.

"Alright," he said, "I've got a question. Every time I have to ask it after the first, I'm going to send one of you boys to hell. We clear?"

Nods around the table. Moberly scanned the room with his shotgun.

"Where is Frank Dodds holding my lad Charlie?" asked Durrant.

Several of the men looked at each other. Durrant watched their faces, the way their eyes met one another. He stepped towards the table, the Enfield seeking a mark. The room was dead quiet, the air thick with the reek of bodies and booze and tobacco. Nobody spoke.

"Alright then, I'm going to ask it again in three seconds," he said, and he took another step toward the table at the centre of the room.

"Two seconds . . ." The hot barrel of the Enfield found what it was looking for. Durrant pressed it against a man's forehead. He was a big man, bearded and dark, his eyes ringed with blue, and his fingers still touching the cup on the table. The man's eyes snapped up to Durrant's.

"One . . ."

"Jesus Christ," the man said. "He's at the Lake of Little Fishes." Durrant pressed the barrel into the man's forehead. He winced. "He's at the lake. There's a shack there. They took your boy there this morning. You're supposed to leave Holt City. If you don't they'll kill him."

"The Lake of Little Fishes?" said Durrant.

"Yeah, that's what the Indians call it."

"Tom Wilson's lake," said Moberly. "Emerald Lake, he named it when he saw it a couple of years ago. Edwin Hunter took him there; said the Indians called it the Lake of Little Fishes."

"Garnet, you know where this place is?"

"I've been there. I *know* the cabin."

Durrant eased the barrel back from the man's forehead. There was an angry round mark where the hot barrel had singed his brow. He reached up and rubbed it, keeping his eyes fixed on Durrant.

"If I so much as smell one of you navvies following me, I'll shoot you in the face. If I get to this Lake of Little Fishes and find Charlie isn't there, or that they've hurt him, I'm going to come back here and kill every single one of you. Is that understood?"

The men nodded.

"This is your last chance to get the story straight," said Durrant.

Nobody spoke. Moberly looked at Durrant. Durrant nodded and slowly backed out the door, Moberly following. When they were outside, Moberly reached into his pocket and took out a heart lock and slipped it on the door's latch. He fastened it shut and smiled at Durrant.

"Be like one of these idiots to get up and go for a piss right now," said Moberly. "Wouldn't want you to have to shoot him because of it," he smiled.

"Let's go," said Durrant.

THE GOING WAS extremely difficult, but not as hard as it might have been had several men not trodden the same arduous route up the side of the valley in the last few days. The tracks of those who went before them were obvious. Durrant was certain that *someone* was in the cabin on the shores of Tom Wilson's lake and that Charlie was likely there with them. The two men stood on the western bank of the Bow River where the tracks plunged into the darkened woods.

"From here we start up the side of the valley," said Moberly. "It's about three miles, if memory serves, and we'll have to climb about five hundred feet or more to reach the lake. The going will be steep in places . . ."

Durrant's face was set with determination. "Let's get a move on," he said, looking at the stars. "We want to be on their doorstep before first light."

"All things considered, I figure two or three hours," said Moberly.

Durrant nodded and Garnet turned into the woods. He wore his babiche sticks and took the lead, their broad webbing packing the trail down for Durrant to follow. They paralleled a winding creek most of the way, though they would only see its icy waters once or twice; it was under six or more feet of accumulated snow. Even with Moberly's trail breaking, the going was arduous. The day's adventure had opened up the wound on Durrant's right leg so that it bled now. He could feel the warm liquid seeping down his trouser and onto his prosthetic.

In the shadow of the woods neither man could see much. After an hour of walking Durrant's senses had attuned themselves to listen to the steady sound of Moberly's snowshoes against the crusted snow and the rhythmic cadence of his breathing. By now, thought Durrant, Charlie might have lost hope. He could not know that instead of turning tail and slinking back to Fort Calgary, Durrant had instead been waylaid from his rescue mission and had been drawn to the crest of the Kicking Horse Pass to face Hep Wilcox.

He had drawn this boy from the mundane world of Fort Calgary into a dangerous and reckless adventure, and for what? Durrant had to admit that his purpose had been selfish: his own redemption. As he listening to Moberly trudging up the slope before him, Durrant had to also ruefully admit that the March West, and all that came after it, had been his own final effort to escape the intolerable suffering he had endured in Toronto.

"MR. WALLACE, THE baby is coming!" It was his father's errand boy standing in the door of his crowded office. The boy's face was flushed and he was breathing hard.

Durrant looked up from his ledger. "What are you talking about, Vincent?"

"It's Mrs. Wallace, sir. She said to come and get you. The baby is coming!"

Durrant sat staring at the boy. A thin thread of light pressed through the soot-smeared windows high up on the red-brick wall. The light struck the crates that lined Durrant's office, stacked seven and eight high, each leaning precariously into the room. The baby wasn't due for more than a month. Six weeks, if the doctors could be believed.

"She said to come quickly, sir."

Durrant stood up, the ledger slapping shut. He reached for his derby and put it on over his closely cropped hair. He was a young man, built for action, and he bolted from behind his desk, running past the boy and out of his office.

The outer room was crowded with the men who toiled for his father: shippers, receivers, packers, and inspectors, all milling around a confluence of desks, each piled high with papers and ledgers. Durrant ran past them, not seeing them, the men looking up from their work as the prodigal son, his coattails streaming out behind him, dashed past. He nearly bowled over his father coming through the door from the warehouse. Though Durrant was a solid man at twenty-one, he paled next to the broad shoulders and powerful physique of his father.

"Durrant, where are you going in such a hurry?" The older man still had the Scottish lilt despite twenty-five years in Upper Canada. He pushed his glasses up on his red nose.

"It's Mary, Father. The baby is coming!" Durrant's face registered fear and joy.

"Go, son!" his father said, stepping aside and slapping him on the back. "Go! Catch up to Peters before he unhitches the buggy."

Durrant ran past him and sprinted through the warehouse. Wallace and Son import-export business had never been busier, but this morning Durrant saw little of it. The baby was coming and it was early. He wondered if someone would have alerted the doctor, and hoped that he wasn't too late to be at home when the child was born.

He found Peters in the drive shed next to the warehouse. There were a dozen rigs outfitted for delivery, but they were slow and cumbersome affairs. What he wanted was his father's personal carriage, with the two solid black stallions hitched to make haste across the city.

"Hold up there, Mr. Peters!" Durrant called as he raced across the garage.

"Mr. Wallace, sir!" said Peters. Durrant took the reins from him and led the horses and their hitch back out into the morning sun.

"The baby is coming!" Durrant yelled to Peters by way of explanation, and the teamster helped him re-hitch the horses to the carriage. Durrant jumped onto the bench seat and snapped the reins. Peters watched as the horses stepped up and the buggy sprang forward, its wheels catching on the rocks and cobble stones outside the sprawling warehouse.

Durrant snapped the reins again and the horses jumped to a hard canter, the cart lurching around the corner of the warehouse and out onto Front Street. Durrant half stood in front of the buggy's bench seat, pulling the reins to steer the horses around traffic on the busy thoroughfare. He heard the yells of men he sidelined in his haste, and the whinny of horse teams that were pulled up fast as he careened through traffic. The red-brick warehouses of the Quay gave way to the grey marble facades of the city's financial district, and Durrant pressed the horses, yelling at them to pick it up, and calling to people on the streets to stand to and make way. Pedestrians yelled at him and called him a reckless fool, but he pressed on, the horses at a gallop now, the wheels of the buggy going clackaty-clack on the city's cobblestone drives.

It took him less than ten minutes to reach his modest home on the western side of the city's financial district. The horses were sweating and foaming at the mouth when he pulled them up fast in front of the abode. Durrant had lost his hat and his eyes were wild with anticipation and fear. He took the steps three at a time and when he reached the front door he burst inside.

The house was quiet. He stood in the foyer and looked around. "Mary?" he called.

Ms. Agatha appeared at the top of the steps. "Mr. Wallace, please, come quickly," she said. Durrant could not tell if the old woman's normally stern face was more ardent at that moment.

He took the stairs at a run and when he reached the top paused. "Is Mary well?"

"The doctor is with her. She's been asking for you."

Durrant tried to press past the housekeeper but she grabbed his arm. The strength in her hand surprised Durrant and he looked at her sternly.

"The baby is too early, Mr. Wallace. Too early . . ."

"Let me pass, Agatha." She released her grip and he knocked on the double doors at the end of the hall and stepped inside.

The room appeared bright but felt full of shadow. The doctor was at the bed, his nurse wringing blood from a towel.

"Mr. Wallace, you're here," said the doctor.

"I came as quick as I was able. Is she alright?" Durrant asked, looking at the shape of his wife in their bed.

"The baby is coming now," said the doctor.

"Durrant?" Mary's soft voice seemed distant and haunted.

"Mary, I'm here," he said, stepping to the foot of the bed. There was a pale ghost between the sheets, a broad stain of blood on the covers.

"Durrant, I'm very cold . . ."

Durrant looked at the doctor. The man was focused on his business beneath the reddened sheets. Durrant could smell iron in the room. He stepped to the side of the bed and stood there awkwardly. His wife looked at him, her face white as ash. She reached a hand to him and he took it as if it were made of porcelain.

"I'm cold, Durrant." She was sweating.

He sat and gathered the blankets around her, the doctor focused on his work. Then she screamed, and Durrant, startled, squeezed her hand. But Mary didn't feel his strength. Her eyes were closed and she had bitten her lip, a thin lattice of blood forming there. He pressed his face to hers and he could hear her breathing, a staccato sound that seemed utterly unnatural.

"Durrant . . ."

"I'm here, Mary."

"Durrant . . . I'm so sorry." The sound of her breathing stopped.

Startled, he looked at her, and then he turned to the doctor, his face so twisted and corded that he looked not twenty-one but much older.

The doctor fumbled a moment and held up a bloody body that seemed much too small to be that of a human child. The nurse quickly took it from him and swaddled it in a linen blanket, wiping the smear of blood and mucus from it. The child did not cry. The doctor quickly stepped to Mary's side and put his ear to her chest. He felt for a pulse. Then he simply stood up, his hands red with the blood of his patient, the room suddenly very cold, and very empty.

IT TOOK A week for his father to find him. He'd left the home that he and Mary had shared for just over a year just before sunrise the next morning. He had sat with the bodies throughout the night. He named the little boy Donald after his grandfather. The nurse had cleaned the child and wrapped him in fresh linen, and then, upon Durrant's insistence, had left the house and Durrant in their brooding silence. Durrant had bidden Agatha to leave and locked the front door when she did. He ignored the periodic knocking.

Durrant placed the boy next to his mother on the bed, and he sat in a chair by the window and watched them throughout the starless night. What thoughts rove through the young man's mind that evening: the cruelty of God and the desperation of humanity; the farce that fate made of a man's plans for this world. All of his study, all of his planning, and the planning of his own father, so his life would tack on a predetermined course: law school, passing the bar, becoming a lawyer, inheriting the family business; a wife and children and a stately home. In a moment of unexplainable malice all of that could be capsized and washed away in a sea of tears.

He shed no tears. When the first birds began to sing outside his window, Durrant simply stood up, unlocked the doors and left the house. He passed a bewildered Agatha on the way out and said, "Call on the mortician today . . ." and closed the door behind himself before she could protest.

It was a week before his father found him. Durrant had navigated his way through the city like a walking corpse, seeking out the dark locales where he didn't have to see his own wretched pain and disillusionment, and where he could hide from any familiarities from his past life. When his father found him, Durrant had already made up his mind.

"I'm leaving in two weeks," the young man said. He was wearing the clothing of a labourer, with no hat upon his head and his face covered in a week's growth of patchy beard.

"For the West?" His father asked, his eyes soft on his son, his hands resting on the table between them where Durrant was drinking beer.

"For Winnipeg. Fort Garry."

His father was silent a moment. "If you wish to travel, son, I can arrange it. Wallace and Son are respected in ports of call around the globe. It wouldn't be difficult to make the appointments."

Durrant finished his beer and looked around for the barman to refill it. He nodded solemnly at his father sitting upright across the table from him. "I don't want to travel under the family name, father."

"You could sign on as a hand, you wouldn't have to represent me or . . ."

"It's not that," Durrant interrupted him with an upturned hand, his eyes dark and cold against the familiar kindness of his father. "It's not the name; it's what it's associated with. I simply want to leave *everything* behind, at least for now. I just can't have anything to do with this life. Not for now."

His father nodded. "So you'll take a train to St. Paul and then sign on to a wagon bound for Winnipeg?"

Durrant nodded. "And then the March West. Colonel French is assembling a force of some three hundred and fifty men. They are to be called the North West Mounted Police. It's to be a grand adventure," Durrant said without enthusiasm. His father noticed that his son clutched a golden locket in his hand. He knew without asking which likeness it possessed. The old man put his hand on his son's and held it tightly.

It was the last time Durrant saw his father, but not the last Durrant would see of that great metropolis spreading out into the inland sea.

IN THE DARKNESS Durrant could make out the sound of running water off to their left. "Creek's opened up," said Moberly. He had stopped up ahead of Durrant. The Mountie laboured up the steep incline behind him, each step bringing a searing pain into the stub of his leg, each movement encouraging the pulse of blood that had now seeped into his boots.

"Is that going to hamper our efforts?" asked Durrant.

Moberly shook his head, then said, "It shouldn't."

Durrant said, "Let's keep going."

Moberly looked at the man, taking the measure of his stamina, and then continued on up the pathway through the forest.

The March West was now history, thought Durrant: his own, and his young nation's. In those lean, desperate days along the Canadian prairie, without enough food, and with their horses falling dead beneath them, the expeditionary force of the North West Mounted Police had forged what was bound to become one of the great stories of the Dominion. For Durrant, it was only the beginning of his own private hell. No matter how far he rode each day, what extra duties he took on around camp each night, how hard he worked himself and what physical discomfort he bore, each night when he wrapped himself in a too-thin blanket, the bodies of his wife and son were there on their bed with him. He could not outride them; only time and the swift passage of days into years could soften his suffering and replace it with a sort of callused fortification born of endless labour and devoted attention to his service to the Dominion of Canada.

Justice became his armour.

When he had been shot and left for dead eight years after the March West, the bullet that took his leg and the frostbite that mangled his hand had pierced that armour and left him more than a cripple. For the last two weeks at Holt City he had found some semblance of the peace that being a purveyor of justice had brought him those eight years he sat in the saddle and wore the scarlet serge. For the last two weeks he had remembered the purpose that came with serving your queen and your country. He was a North West Mounted Police officer; he wasn't a postal clerk. He would either be reinstated as such, or he would leave the service for good.

Durrant thought about Charlie. What would become of young Charlie should Durrant leave the NWMP? Even if he survived Frank Dodds' wrath, young Charlie was now forever tainted by his affiliation with Durrant. He would take Charlie with him. Whatever happened next, the boy would be encouraged to accompany him. Durrant needed the boy and now the boy needed him. He might somehow become like the son Durrant had lost.

They walked for two hours, Durrant ignoring the burning pain in his leg. He could feel the nub of skin and bone bleeding freely where the prosthetic's suction socket affixed to his ruined leg. By the time the track began to level out and the forest opened to reveal a star-filled sky, he could feel the blood staining his trousers and growing tacky in the heel of his boot.

In a moment Moberly stopped in the path and hunkered down. Durrant came up beside him.

"The lake is just beyond that clearing. There's a large, frozen swamp on its shore. The cabin sits to our left of it, on the southern edge of the clearing."

"You think they might have a sentry posted?"

"I would."

"Can we get off this trail and steal through the forest?"

Moberly looked back at Durrant. "Sergeant, this snow is five feet deep. I might make it, sir, but you will not."

Durrant nodded.

"This is going to have to be a frontal assault or nothing, I fear." Moberly looked back toward the lake. "Let me be so bold as to suggest a plan. As fate would have it, I have been to this cabin before and am familiar with its . . . peculiarities. That, sir, gives us a *considerable* advantage." Moberly was smiling in the starlight.

BY THE CONSTELLATIONS, it was four in the morning when the two men advanced from the cover of the woods and into the clearing that marked the swamp on the shore of the Lake of Little Fishes. Durrant could plainly see the spectacle of wonder that surrounded them. The lake itself was more than a mile long and half a mile wide, ringed on three sides by implacable mountains. At its far end a valley climbed up towards the star-swept heavens. By the light of those stars and the waxing moon they could see snowfields and glaciers mounting a peak that seemed to jut perpendicularly from the earth. That sheer wall of ice and stone marked the Continental Divide.

They made their way along the snowy trail that skirted the swamp on the left and stopped when they saw the shoreline in full. Moberly pointed out what they had been looking for—the orange glow of a fire on the shoreline a hundred yards or more from where Moberly said the cabin would be. Durrant nodded and the men advanced. They proceeded another furlong and then Moberly spirited off into the deep snow to the right of the trail. Durrant waited, watching, trying to discern the shadowy figure as Moberly crossed the frozen swamp.

The firelight flickered on the lake's shore, and Durrant could see the outline of a man there. He waited, counting to one hundred, and then to one thousand, breathing slowly to stay calm. He checked the action on his pistols and pulled his gloves on tight. He ignored the searing pain in his right hand and the freezing blood that coated his leg and iced up in his boot.

When he got to one thousand Durrant walked slowly forward along the path until he was fifty yards from the fire. He stopped. He could see the outline of the sentry. The man cradled an old single-shot Sharps 74 across his knees. He seemed not to be able to see Durrant.

Durrant stepped forward a few more feet and then cleared his throat. The sentry snapped to attention. He stood, the rifle being held at port as he tried to see beyond his own fire to the source of the sound. Moberly stepped in behind him and brought the butt of the shotgun down into the man's skull. The sentry fell over, his body narrowly missing the fire. Durrant closed the distance and arrived as Moberly was throwing the Sharps far out into the snow of the swamp. He reached into the man's coat and came out with a Colt Navy revolver. He checked the load on the weapon and then tucked it into his belt. They then moved the man back onto his log and propped him up with a piece of heavy wood, hoping that from a distance his posture might appear natural.

Durrant watched the cabin. It was nestled between the shore of the lake and the heavy dark forest of spruce and pine terracing up the soaring cliffs above. A light seeped from around the main door of the shack. Durrant knew from his discussion with Moberly that there were no windows on this side of the cabin.

"Alright," said Moberly. "Let's go."

They moved together along the shore of the lake, Moberly with the shotgun pointed ahead, Durrant with his Enfield held at the ready. There was no sound, and neither Durrant nor Moberly could detect any motion along the shore, or from the cabin itself.

"Right then," said Moberly. "For Queen and Country," and again, he slipped back into the woods that ringed the shore of the approach.

Durrant stopped and looked back where they had come from. It seemed that no man had followed, and the sentry was still propped against his log. Unarmed as he was, if he woke he would as likely flee as re-enter the fray.

Durrant counted again. Reaching one hundred, he scanned the dark woods for Moberly but could detect no sign of him. He continued along the path. When he reached the front of the shack, he stopped and listened. He pulled a deep breath into his lungs and then stepped to the side of the front door and knocked. He waited and knocked again, loudly.

"Blue Jesus, Tanner, is that you? You're supposed to be on lookout. Pete, get the goddamned door," he heard Dodds bellow from within.

He waited and in a moment the door to the cabin swung open. A long yellow swath of light fell across the snow, interrupted by Pete

Mahoney's massive bulk. Durrant waited for Pete to step outside.

"There ain't nobody here," he said as he turned. He was armed with Durrant's Winchester 73.

Durrant stepped away from the shadow of the building and levelled the pistol at the man.

"Jesus," Pete said, and began to bring the Winchester up to fire.

"I'll blow you to hell, Pete," said Durrant as he jammed the gun into the man's face. "Throw down that rifle." Pete hesitated and Durrant thumbed back the hammer. The young Mahoney boy tossed the rifle into the snow.

"Now step back inside."

Mahoney did as he was told and Durrant stepped inside after him. The room was close and hot. He quickly took in the surroundings, counting four men in the tiny room. Behind Pete, Durrant could make out the man's brother Ralph and Thompson Griffin standing next to him. Durrant thought he could make out the diminutive form of Charlie in a chair behind Griffin. Dodds was sitting on a cot next to a woodstove. On the stove was a copper pot with a coiled copper worm attached that descended into a cold bath of melted snow. Three or four dozen empty bottles lined the far wall. A giant woodbox was built into that wall, adjacent to the stove.

Durrant could see that Griffin held a pistol over Charlie. He still could not see the boy's face around the men standing between him and the lad.

Dodds leapt to his feet. Durrant levelled his pistol at the man, but continued to watch Pete. "Don't reach for it, Dodds." Dodds stood his ground.

"Well, if the law hasn't arrived. You should have taken our advice and left Holt City, Red Coat. This is no place for a cripple."

"I'm not going anywhere, not without Charlie, and you're not either," said Durrant. Dodds laughed. Durrant thumbed the hammer on his pistol.

Dodds stepped forward. "You shoot me and your friend here gets it right between the eyes," he said, nodding toward Charlie who was covered by Griffin's pistol.

"Let the boy go and we'll walk out of here. You might get off easy with the magistrate," said Durrant.

Again, Dodds laughed. It sounded more like a bark. "Boy? Boy? Step aside, lads, and let Sergeant Wallace see his *boy*."

The three men fanned out in a row, all now facing Durrant in the closed space. Durrant focused on Charlie. Something was terribly wrong. The lad was tied to a chair, his legs bound around the ankles to the chair's legs, his arms knotted behind his back, and his head slumped forward. Where Durrant expected to see Charlie's now trademark wool hat, a tangle of brown hair stood on end.

"There's your boy," said Dodds.

"Charlie?" Durrant asked, his pistol still pointed at Dodds. "Charlie, look at me."

Charlie looked up. The dishevelled hair framed the familiar face with its soft complexion. The eyes were the same, but without the hat to conceal the fine features of the forehead, they were clearly the eyes of a young woman.

"Charlie?" Durrant said again.

The woman nodded.

"Got yourself fooled pretty good, didn't you?" said Dodds. "Imagine our surprise when we get him up here and found out it was a little lady. I'll tell you, it's been a long winter at Holt City. I don't mind telling you we were pretty pleased."

Durrant looked at the young woman. Her left eye was black and she had a cut on her lip. A crust of blood had formed around her nose. "They hurt you, Charlie?" Durrant asked. The eyes bored back into him.

Durrant pulled his attention off Charlie and looked at Dodds. He drew a deep breath. "You're under arrest for kidnapping," he said. "You *all* are."

As he spoke, the lid on the woodbox burst open. A cold gust of air swept into the room. The men turned toward the movement, three of them scrambling for their guns. Durrant quickly shifted his aim from Dodds to Griffin and squeezed the trigger of his Enfield twice, the bullets catching Griffin in the chest. The man's body twisted and fell.

Garnet Moberly took them by surprise as he rose from the wood-box, the double-barrelled shotgun held at the ready. He fired at the nearest man. The force of the blast lifted Ralph Mahoney off his feet and flung him into the wall next to Durrant. Moberly fired a second time and Ralph's body hit the floor.

Pete Mahoney turned back into the room to fire from the hip at the Mountie. Pete's shot missed, but Durrant's quick shot didn't. The Mountie dropped his crutch and moved fast toward Charlie's exposed position amid the swirl of bullets. He fired the remaining four rounds, one bullet twisting Pete sideways, then Durrant collided with Charlie's chair and the two of them hit the ground together.

Dodds raised his weapon and fired at Moberly, hitting him in the left arm. He then spun to face Durrant, his face set with rage, and fired at the moving target, his bullets striking the wall just above Durrant's shoulder. Moberly, stumbling from the woodbox and dropping the shotgun as his injured arm gave way, pulled out his twin Webley revolvers. With one, he sent a wild shot at Dodds, and with the other he shot Pete again, spinning him into a heap on the floor.

Dodds now turned and returned fire on Moberly, the two men less than fifteen feet apart. In the spray of bullets Moberly was thrown against the back wall of the cabin, bottles of moonshine exploding from the force of his body. Durrant dropped the spent Enfield where he lay, Charlie beneath him, and reached for his second pistol. The weapon came quickly to hand. As Dodds fired at Moberly, Durrant raised the short-barrelled Bulldog and shot Dodds in one swift motion.

The din of gunfire ceased. The room was blue with the smoke from the volley of rounds. Durrant pushed himself up and went to Moberly, his pistol still aimed at Dodds, who lay prone on the bunk.

"Garnet," he said, hunching down as best he could to see if the man was still alive.

The gentleman looked up at him. "How'd we do?" he asked.

Durrant smiled. "Looks like very well. Charlie," he said as he walked over to untie her. "You okay?"

Durrant wasn't certain which surprised him more, that Charlie was a woman or that she answered. "I'm fine, Durrant."

Durrant retrieved the Winchester and handed it to her. "Cover them," he ordered. "If any of them make a move, shoot them."

"Gladly," she said.

"Just a couple of holes in the shoulder and arm here," said Moberly. "Nothing serious."

Durrant returned to Moberly and tore up a rag to tie off the two wounds. He checked on Dodds, who had been shot in the leg and stomach and was glaring at Durrant. Ralph Mahoney was alive, but conscious. Pete Mahoney and Griffin were dead.

"So," said Durrant. "Can the two of you make it down the mountain and see about getting some help for this lot?"

Moberly looked at Charlie. "I don't see why not," he said. He extended a hand to the young woman. "Garnet Moberly."

She smiled. "Charlene," she said. "Charlene Louise Mason."

TWENTY-TWO

REVELATIONS

HE HAD FALLEN ASLEEP SITTING in a chair in the corner of the cabin as he waited.

"You're going to be alright, Durrant," a voice said. The snow fell gently down, landing on his eyelashes as he blinked up into the swirling grey sky, into the face that looked down at his. "You're going to be alright."

He blinked again and the faces came into focus. Patrick O'Connor and Tommy Provost from Fort Walsh.

"We've got a tourniquet on your leg, Wallace," said Provost. "We need to get you to the Doc."

"My horse . . ." said Durrant. He tried to lift his right hand to point. It was still clutching the Enfield. He could no longer feel his fingers.

"Mack is dead, Durrant. I'm sorry."

"From the woods. It was an ambush."

"You were close, Durrant. Very close. We know who they are. Salinger and Merry are following their tracks."

"They knew who *I* was. They used my name."

"Like I said, you were in close. We'll get them."

"My hand."

"It's pretty badly frostbitten. We need to get you to the Doc. Let's see if we can't get him up into the saddle," said Patrick O'Connor.

"I can't ride," said Durrant.

"You'll be okay."

"My leg. I can't ride." Durrant felt hot tears rolling down his face.

"It's okay. You're alive. It's going to be okay."

Durrant closed his eyes and felt the snow tickle his face, catch in the day's growth of beard that had speckled his chin while he lay there on the frozen earth. He felt the men lift him and he pressed his eyes closed, felt his leg go limp and his hand lose its grip on the Enfield, felt it slip from his grasp and fall to the earth.

"DURRANT," SAID A voice he didn't recognize. He opened his eyes and the pistol came up and pointed at Dodds and Pete Mahoney lying on the bunk. His eyes focused and he could see that they were as he had left them; bandaged, bleeding, and unconscious.

"Durrant," the voice said again. He slowly took in the rest of the room. The walls were pocked with bullet holes. Broken glass from the tiny window and from the jugs of fractured moonshine was scattered across the floor; the room reeked of corn mash whiskey. He looked around and a woman he didn't know was kneeling close to him.

"Are you okay?" she asked.

Charlie. Charlene. "I'm okay."

She turned and nodded to a silhouette at the door. Moberly came in. His arm was in a sling. Saul Armatage followed, his eyes immediately on Durrant. Moberly turned and looked at the two injured men on the bed and the dead on the floor. "Constable, you can come and collect these men now," he called.

Durrant stood up. He felt very old, and very tired. His leg pulsed; the left trouser leg was soaked through with blood.

"Durrant, you're still bleeding," said Charlie.

"It's fine," he said through gritted teeth.

"It's not fine."

The first constable entered the room. He wore the greatcoat and sealskin hat, but Durrant could see the red serge beneath the coat and the black riding boots that clicked on the floor. The man turned to Durrant. Durrant didn't recognize him.

"Corporal Deuer, sir," he said, saluting Durrant. "What are your orders, sir?"

Durrant was momentarily dizzy. "These men need medical attention. They are to be transported back to Holt City, stabilized, and brought to Fort Calgary as soon as you are able to make arrangements on the eastbound freight. Can you look at their wounds, Saul?"

Armatage turned and saw the two men bleeding on the bed for the first time. He hesitated. "They need attention more than I," Durrant said. Armatage went to them.

"We've commandeered half a dozen men from the camp, sir. Mr. Pen said they are all good men," said Corporal Deuer.

"Pen's a good man, too. Very well, get a move on, Corporal," said Durrant.

The Mountie nodded and yelled for his colleagues to join him. Before the room became crowded with activity, Durrant pushed past Charlie and Moberly and stepped out into the morning. Dawn had broken. He walked a few paces along the path, with Moberly and Charlie behind him, and then stopped on the shore to regard the new day.

The peaks of the Great Divide were set on fire with a ragged light. The face of the farthest peak beyond the Lake of Little Fishes stood in sharp relief; its glacier clad summit bore a rosy glow. All around it, peaks jutted into the azure sky of dawn. Durrant drew a deep breath and marvelled that all of this splendour sat on the edge of the broad valley where the steel road would soon pass, bearing with it commerce and men and woman and children, all bound for places yet unknown, altogether comprising the pulse of a brand new nation. He sighed deeply.

"What is it?" asked Charlie. He looked at her. He did not know this person.

"Nothing. Nothing at all," he said.

She nodded.

"I'm sorry," she said.

"For what?"

"For deceiving you."

He nodded. "I almost got *you* killed," he said.

She shrugged. It made Durrant smile to see this stranger take on the characteristics of the boy he thought he knew.

"This is beautiful," Charlene said.

"The Canadian Pacific brass built that little cabin back there so that big bellies on the railroad could come up here and appreciate the grandeur," said Moberly. "I visited it once last fall, and was relegated to stocking the woodbin for some section manager. Glad I did. That's how I knew that the woodbox had two hatches."

"Took you long enough to show your face," smiled Durrant.

Moberly looked at him askance, but his frown soon faded to a broad grin. "Well, I had to get all the damned wood out before I could make my entrance!"

"We made a bit of a mess of the CPR's little cabin," said Durrant.

"I expect they will rebuild."

Durrant nodded. "If they're going to make a tourist attraction out of this place, they're going to need a better name. Lake of Little Fishes doesn't do it justice."

"Don't forget, young Tom Wilson called it Emerald Lake."

Durrant nodded. "Think that will stick?"

"I don't know."

"I was thinking Lake Charlene," Durrant finally said.

The girl smiled.

"Lake Charlene Louise . . ."

WITH A BILLOW of black coal smoke and a great frayed balloon of steam the eastbound train slowly pulled from the station. Two days had passed since the rescue on the shores of the lake. Durrant sat on a padded bench next to a window in the caboose of the freight. He stared out the porthole at the snowy forest that rose up in swells toward the peaks above.

The three men he and Moberly had captured alive—including the sentry who had simply stumbled back to Holt City with an aching head—had been taken by freight to Fort Calgary. According to a wire from Sub-Inspector Dewalt, received on a replacement telegraph machine found in the stores at Holt City, the men were all still alive. Frank Dodds was nearest to death, his body riddled with bullets. Even the Fort's doctor was astonished that he had survived. The bodies of Devon Paine, Deek Penner, Pete Mahoney, and John Christianson had also been dispatched to the Fort for burial in the spring. Durrant vowed to attend the interment of Paine and Penner.

The MP Blake O'Brian and the spy Patrick Carriere had been dispatched to Regina. They would appear before a magistrate and be charged with various crimes, but not before Durrant had questioned them.

Hep Wilcox had also been dispatched to Regina to await arraignment on charges of murder, attempted murder, and conspiracy. In all, six men had been taken alive at the end of the line. Four more were transported enclosed in rough-hewn pine boxes, constructed from wood fittingly cut on the slopes of Dodds Peak, for burial at Fort Calgary.

Durrant watched as the valley of the Bow River slipped past. The train began to pick up speed on its way to Donald Siding and then Castle Mountain.

"A penny for your thoughts?"

Durrant snapped out of his reverie and looked at Charlie sitting across from him. Her hair had been washed and brushed and no longer stuck straight up like a wire brush. Instead it lay soft and flat around the curve of her face. She wore a heavy skirt borrowed from Evelyn Armatage. Durrant regarded her a minute. He could see, with her hair always under the heavy wool cap, and without recourse to hearing her soft feminine voice, how he could have been fooled. Some investigator, he thought, smiling.

"I was thinking about something that O'Brian told me before we sent him away in shackles."

"What was that?"

"How easy it had been to come within a hair of engineering such a catastrophic accident."

"But they didn't. You stopped them."

"We," he said. "We stopped them. You and Mr. Moberly get as much credit for that as any." Charlie blushed and looked down at her hands folded on her skirt. "He said that if it wasn't for Bill Kauffman tipping off Deek Penner, they would have pulled it off. An explosion at the plant might have killed dozens of men, maybe more. That would have set off a firestorm of debate in Parliament. I think O'Brian would have ended up being the hero. He could have stepped up with a solution—the Northumberland company takes over the explosives contract—and history would have been changed. The Kicking Horse would be known not for the extraordinary effort of men forging a path through the most rugged wilderness in this new land, but for a terrible tragedy."

"You're starting to sound like Mr. Moberly. Have you heard how his surgery went?" Charlie asked.

Durrant nodded. "I got a wire this morning. Two slugs dug out of his arm and shoulder. Said he would add them to his collection."

"That *does* sound like Mr. Moberly."

They sat quietly awhile.

"You know what bothers me the most about all of this?" he asked after a spell. "That Deek Penner had to die. I think that he was the kind of man that I would have respected and liked very much. Honest, hard working. A good man. And that John Christianson got so entangled in this."

"He was a killer."

"Yes, he was. He was also a victim. He paid the ultimate price for allowing himself to become trapped by greed and by the passions of men who had long ago learned to manipulate others to their will. He had a mania to him, but so do many men. He simply could not control his, but instead allowed others to control it for their own will."

"I wouldn't spend too much time grieving for John Christianson," Charlie said.

"Maybe you're right," said Durrant.

"Of course I am." She smiled and looked out the window.

The train slipped down the wintery valley. They passed Castle Mountain and then made the long turn in the transect that brought Mount Rundle into view. The train began to slow for Banff Station.

"Did you hear that they have discovered hot springs here?" Charlie said as the train ground to a halt at the tiny station.

"Is that right?"

"Three men, two of them brothers, up in the woods there, just above the river, in a cave."

"I suppose you'll be wanting a bath then," he said.

She smiled. "Oh, to dream," Charlene said.

The train started again and followed the river towards the station and roundhouse at the newly renamed siding of Canmore. They slipped the bonds of the mountains and were steaming towards Fort Calgary. Durrant felt the change in him, and in Charlie. In Charlene.

"What are you going to do?" he asked.

She sat motionless a while, watching the peaks slip away behind the train through the greasy soot stained window. Finally she said, "I don't know."

"You won't go back. Not to the ranch. Not to him. I won't allow it."

"Of course I won't. I don't need *you* not to allow it. I left because if I stayed there, in that bleak place, with that monster of a man, I would likely be dead by now. I ran away, changed everything about my life, so I would not have to endure the horror of life with him. He tried to kill me once. If I was to return, I know he would try again. No, I won't go back to that place, or to that man."

Durrant felt a hot ember kindle deep in his heart. God have mercy on the soul of that man should Durrant ever meet him. "I just don't think that I can go back to work in the stables now," continued Charlene.

"I doubt they'd have me. There really isn't much work for a young woman to do in Fort Calgary now. Not that's proper, at least."

"What are *you* going to do?" she asked after a time. They had crossed near the Morley Ranch and were steaming past the confluence of the Bow with the Ghost River.

He didn't answer. "Durrant?"

He shook his head. "I guess that's going to be up to Steele."

"Have you heard word?"

"Nothing yet, but I know this: I can't go back to sorting the post. I can't sit at the Fort and send and receive cables. I can't take the census. I'm a North West Mounted Police officer. I may not be able to ride like I used to, but I can police. I think I've damn well proven myself."

"You've changed, you know."

He looked at her. "How so?"

She was silent a moment. Her eyes were so very kind. "When I first met you, there in the stables, and on the train up to Holt City, and in the first few days in that place, you seemed so very sad and angry. In time, it was as if . . . Have you ever watched a snake shed its skin?"

He shook his head.

"It's the same snake," she said. She held out the fingers of her left and with her right hand illustrated how the snake wiggled and twisted its body to lose its old casing. "It just grows out of its skin. It leaves the old skin behind. It doesn't need it anymore. It's the same snake, but it's completely new. *You* became new," she said.

"I became who I was before," he said.

There was a long pause. "There's something else," she said.

He wouldn't look at her. He stared at the foothills as they rose and fell on the horizon.

"Durrant, I saw the locket. The woman, the baby. I saw it on your nightstand."

"I'm not going to talk about it . . ." His voice was sharp.

"It's okay. You don't have to. I just want you to know that *I* know. And I understand. We've all suffered loss that we can't confer."

He said quickly, "It was just that you . . . you could have been *that* boy. I joined the March West to escape that loss, and now I feel like I've lost *that* again." He couldn't meet her eyes.

A long moment passed and they heard the train whistle. He knew that they were approaching Fort Calgary and the outskirts of the town.

"Durrant," she said.

He kept his gaze down. She reached across and put her soft fingers on his game right hand. He looked up at her. She was looking straight into his eyes. Her eyes were so very blue, and so very kind. "Durrant, I don't think you've lost anything."

CRAIGELLACHIE

THE NO. 28 LOCOMOTIVE BEGAN to slow for the first switch. Two blasts of its horn let the switchman know that all was well.

Durrant watched from the window of the coach. The panorama of peaks and forests sped past. He held his breath a beat too long and found himself gasping for air. He had heard that the very first train to descend the Big Hill had derailed, and many others afterward had too, even though safety switches and runaway lanes were in place to keep trains from plunging over the side into the valley of the Kicking Horse. Talk now was that when the CPR and the Dominion recovered from the initial cost of the mainline, they would attempt some marvel of engineering by constructing a series of spiral tunnels through the sides of the mountains to lessen the grade of the descent on the Big Hill.

A lot of good that did Durrant on November 4, 1885. Durrant pressed his face to the window and peered back in the direction they had travelled, toward the receding summit of the Pass. He thought of the day a year and a half earlier when an innocent life had been lost on that crest; when Devon Paine had been gunned down in his naive attempt to save Durrant's own life. He thought, too, of the moment on the shore of the Lake of Little Fishes, or as it was now called, Lake Louise, when he came to see Charlene for who she really was.

Tom Wilson, the old rascal, had renamed that sapphire blue lake after his most recent sweetheart. Tom had told Durrant in Fort Calgary recently that while guiding a party from the Association of the British Advancement of Science, he had shown the now famous lake to Sir Richard Temple and his daughter, Louise. Louise had demonstrated a preference for the sparkling lake, and Wilson for Louise, and so it was that Tom renamed it right then and there. If the monarchists wanted to believe the gem of water was named for Princess Louise Caroline Alberta, let them.

So much had happened. He stretched out his right leg. After the debacle at Holt City, Durrant had returned to Regina and received medical treatment for his game leg. Armatage had bandaged him up but there was little more that could be done at the end of steel, and the only prosthetics specialist in the North West Territories was at the fort in Regina. Despite all that had happened in the ensuing eighteen months since he left Holt City, it felt as good as a prosthetic could: so good that except for the harshest conditions of winter, he no longer felt the need for the crutch. He tapped the silver-handled cane on the ground. It had been a gift, albeit indirectly, from another man whose life the Kicking Horse had almost stolen.

"I've no bloody need for a cane," Moberly had told him after the Honorable Member for Northumberland had given him the relic for saving his hide there in the snowy woods. "You might take note of the handle, old chap," said Moberly with a wink, when they had met in the barracks in Fort Calgary early in April. Indeed, the cane's secret had come in handy in a tight spot recently.

Durrant tapped it on the floor of the coach again. They had passed the final switch and were levelling out towards the siding of Field.

The Canadian Pacific Railway had at last earned the support of Parliament, but it wasn't because of its merits as a unifier of the fledging nation. The rail held strategic importance for transporting troops and military cargo in combatting what everybody now called the North West Rebellion, or simply the Métis War, but what Durrant had learned to think of as the Riel Resistance.

Durrant closed his eyes. He had come close to losing his life on the frozen earth of the Cypress Hills, and again on the summit of Kicking Horse Pass. At Batoshe, in the aftermath of that bloody battle at the end of May in that very year, Durrant had almost lost his soul. He closed his eyes and pushed that shadow from his memory. He would not dwell on that now. That was a story for another time.

The coach Durrant travelled in was at the back of a six-car train that had left Calgary that morning, and had been steaming west from Montreal for nearly a week. Along the way it had picked up a number of prominent passengers.

Durrant became aware that a man was standing before him. He cleared his throat and looked up.

"Sergeant Wallace?"

"That's me."

"Sir, Superintendant Steele would like a moment of your time, please."

"Of course." Durrant pushed himself up with the help of the fine silver-handled cane.

"Follow me, sir."

Durrant put his bowler hat upon his head and straightened his wool dresscoat. He followed the man to the end of the coach, through the crowded smoke filled dining lounge, and then into the car named "Metapedia," an exclusive coach reserved for the CPR brass. Durrant had never been inside.

It was plush and warm and had low lights affixed to the wall with ornate brass fixtures. Chairs were arranged as if in a parlor and men sat about in expensive suits, drinking glasses of brandy and smoking cigars. Durrant ignored the violation of the temperance laws. He wasn't a Mountie today, he was a guest of the CPR, though several men took note as he passed, eyeing the holster that supported his Enfield hanging below his coat. Several of the men nodded to him and one said his name and he nodded in return and tipped his hat.

"This way, sir," the man said, and led Durrant to the far end of the car. The man slid a door marked Private and ushered Durrant inside.

There was no one in the room. Four chairs were arranged next to a stately desk. Windows on both sides of the private office gave spectacular views of the passing scenery.

"Please have a seat. Superintendent Steele will be in shortly. Do you require anything, sir?"

Durrant shook his head and sat down in one of the leather chairs. He drew a deep breath and exhaled slowly. He had spent the better part of his convalescence since the North West Rebellion in Saskatchewan. He had even made a return trip to Fort Walsh and the Cypress Hills. He had intended to resume an old inquiry there, one that had never been solved: one that involved the shooting of a NWMP officer. He had new leads and Durrant had learned a thing or two about tracking down those who hid in plain sight.

The door that connected the private room to the adjacent car slid open and Steele stood before him. Durrant rose and removed his hat. Steele stepped in. He was a broad man, straight in the spine and upright in every way. Steele reached out his left hand and Durrant shook it.

"It's good to see you again, Sergeant."

"And you, sir."

"Please sit a moment so we can talk in private."

"Of course, sir."

Each man took a seat in one of the armchairs.

"I'm glad to have you along on this sojourn, Wallace."

"I was glad for the invitation."

"I'm sorry we could not extend it to others in your party." Durrant shrugged. "Believe it or not, resources for the CPR are tight." They sat in silence a moment, Steele regarding the Sergeant.

"You'll recall, Sergeant, that after Batoshe I put in a request to Parliament to create an investigations unit within the North West Mounted Police." Durrant nodded. "They have turned me down. There will be no such unit. There's no money for it, and the politicians claim that there's no need."

"I understand, sir. It was a good idea, but I understand."

"You're more indulgent than I am, Wallace," said Steele, his face red. "Nevertheless, Sergeant, I am of the conviction that there *is* a need. Kicking Horse and Batoshe have proven that and the need is growing. Policing is changing in the North West Territories. With the railway all but complete, and towns and settlement taking their place here in the West, the need for the sort of skills you have developed will increase."

Durrant sat quietly while his superior regarded him. After a moment, Durrant asked, "What do you propose, sir?"

"I'm going to continue to call upon you to serve under my

command, Wallace. It can't be official, you understand, but you're going to head a unit for special investigations. You'll report directly to me. It's going to have to be done quietly, Sergeant. I understand that might go against the grain of your natural disposition . . ." Steele regarded the man a moment, and then smiled. "Can you do that, Durrant?"

"Yes, sir. I believe I can."

"Good, then," said Steele. He stood. Durrant pushed himself to standing.

"Congratulations then, *Inspector* Wallace." Steele saluted the man, and Durrant did the same.

"Thank you, sir."

"Now then, Inspector, there is someone I'd like you to meet."

"Yes, sir."

Steele moved to the door that separated the cars and drew it open. He said a few words and stepped aside. A broad, powerfully built man entered next. He wore a heavy beard and his eyes burned with an intense fire that Durrant had rarely seen. He was smoking a fragrant cigar. The man manoeuvred his bulk into the room and reached out his left hand.

"I'm William Cornelius Van Horne," the man said.

"Durrant Wallace, sir."

"I know who you are. Superintendant Steele has told me all about you."

Durrant looked at Steele who motioned for Durrant to sit.

"How can I be of service to you, sir?" Durrant asked when they were all seated.

"You know what I do for the railway, son?"

"Yes, sir. You're the general superintendant of the CPR."

"That's correct."

"You built this railway."

Van Horne laughed. "Me and twelve thousand others."

Durrant smiled. "Yes sir."

"I need a favour from you, Inspector Wallace."

"What can I do for you?"

Van Horne puffed on his cigar, filling the room with blue smoke. "It's more what I don't want you to do."

"And what's that, sir?"

"Tell your story."

Durrant watched the man. Van Horne regarded him as he drew on his cigar. Durrant could see Steele look from himself to Van Horne and back.

"I want you to keep quiet about what happened at Lake Louise and up on the Kicking Horse Pass and at Batoshe."

Durrant regarded the man thoughtfully.

"We're going to build a hotel on the shore of Tom's Lake Louise. And we're going to make a National Park around the hot springs at Banff. It's going to help us recoup the coffers of the treasury. The CPR has been a tremendous expense. We'd like, for the time being, the focus of the tourists to be on the scenery, on the mountains, on the glaciers, and such. We're fearful of what the eastern press might do to the tourist trade if they got hold of your tale. Inspector, you did one hell of a job for us at Kicking Horse Pass and up at Lake Louise. One hell of a job . . . but it's not the story that we want tourists and the damned Ontario press getting hold of right now."

Durrant nodded. He cleared his throat. After a long uncomfortable moment, he said, "Of course," and watched as Van Horne breathed out, his shouldered relaxing. Durrant continued, "Superintendant Steele has already spoken with me about Batoshe. It was a most . . . unfortunate turn of events. No need to sully both the CPR and the North West Mounted Police. If you feel that the story of the Kicking Horse and Lake Louise is best untold, then I will respect that."

"For the time being," said Van Horne. "Who knows, in time, these stories might only increase the demand to see the sights, but now, with things so fragile, and Macdonald facing an election and all, well . . ." Van Horne's voice trailed off and he puffed on his cigar.

"Will there be anything else, sir?" Durrant turned to Steele.

"Thank you, Inspector Wallace, that's all for now."

"We're glad that you could make it to Craigellachie with us, Inspector," said Van Horne, rising. Durrant pushed himself up on his cane. "It's going to be a great day. You'll be in the tin-type we make of that event, mark my words. There might not have been a railway if it wasn't for what you did on the Kicking Horse Pass. This will be a great event! The last spike! The end of the line!"

"Yes, sir," said Durrant, propping his bowler on top of his head, and shaking hands with Van Horne and then Steele. "The end of the line, at last."

WITH GRATITUDE

Writing a novel is all encompassing. The novelist is often distant, distracted, sneaking away to pen a bit of dialogue or prose when he should be attending to the dishes. For her undying support I offer my deepest gratitude to Jenn, my wife, without whom none of this would be possible.

I am not a historian, so I turned to those with expertise for help: E.J. (Ted) Hart and Lena Goon from the Whyte Museum of the Canadian Rockies, Dianne Precosky from Fort Calgary, and Jo-Anne Colby of the Canadian Pacific Achieves were all generous and helpful. Graeme Pole, author of *The Spiral Tunnels and The Big Hill*, answered many of my questions about the history of the CPR at the Kicking Horse Pass.

During several stages of the research and writing of this book, it was necessary to take up residence in the Canadian Rockies. Friends Wendy Frances of Banff and Joel Hagen and Nadine Fletcher opened their homes to Jenn and me for that purpose.

The original notion for this series of novels came in 2006 when I was working with my friend and business coach Dan Spinner. I am grateful for his encouragement at that delicate time.

Ruth Linka, of TouchWood Editions, is a fabulous publisher to work with. I'm indebted to her for her support and enthusiasm. I can't wait to continue our partnership

Frances Thorsen, who edits the Durrant Wallace series for TouchWood, and who from behind the counter at Chronicles of Crime books in Victoria, BC, dispenses unparalleled advice on the world of crime and mystery writing, deserves much of the credit for any success *The End of the Line* enjoys. Working with her on the publication of this novel has been one of the best editorial experiences I've had in my twenty years of writing.

And to all the booksellers who help their customers and readers find *The End of the Line*, I extend my appreciation and gratitude.

THE THIRD RIEL CONSPIRACY

DURRANT WALLACE WILL RETURN IN 2013 in *The Third Riel Conspiracy*. It is the spring of 1885 and rebellion has broken out in Canada's North West Territories. Amid the chaos and strife of the Battle of Batoche, Reuben Wake is recuperating in the Zereba—a defensive structure built near the battlefield—after suffering a gunshot wound the previous day. As the final day of the conflict reaches its crescendo, Wake is murdered: shot at point-blank range. Hours later, Terrance Le Biche, a Métis man, is arrested for the crime: Wake's own pistol is found in his coat. Le Biche protests his innocence but he admits he had every *intention* of killing Wake, except someone beat him to the foul deed.

Durrant Wallace, of the North West Mounted Police, is requested by Superintendant Sam Steele to travel with haste into the fray to assist with peacemaking. Arriving at Batoche, Durrant is perplexed by the strange circumstances surrounding Reuben Wake's demise. When the Mountie begins his own investigation into what motive Le Biche might have had for the assignation, he learns that there are *many* who wanted Wake dead, and had the opportunity to commit the crime during the chaos of Batoche. Their grievances with Wake mirror the varied causes of the North West Rebellion itself.

What Durrant Wallace uncovers during his two-month odyssey into the origins of the discontent in the Canadian West is a series of covert conspiracies surrounding the life and death of Métis leader and prophet Louis Riel himself. Was Reuben Wake's death related to his involvement in one of these conspiracies? Or did his trickery and evil temperament simply catch up with him on the banks of the Saskatchewan River?

Durrant Wallace and his colleagues Garnet Moberly and Dr. Saul Armatage must reconstruct the four days of the Battle of Batoche, and delve deeply into the motivations of the suspects, the Métis, and their followers, among them the tribes of the Cree and Sioux Indians, in order to evaluate who among them actually killed Reuben Wake.

Visit www.DurrantWallace.com for updates, maps, and interactive features!

STEPHEN LEGAULT is an author, consultant, conservationist, and photographer who lives in Canmore, Alberta. Stephen is the author of three other books, including the environmentally themed Cole Blackwater Mystery series, which includes the titles *The Cardinal Divide* and *The Darkening Archipelago*. Please visit Stephen online at stephenlegault.com or follow him on Twitter at @stephenlegault.

Other books by Stephen Legault

Carry Tiger to Mountain:
The Tao of Activism and Leadership (2006)

THE COLE BLACKWATER SERIES
The Cardinal Divide (2008)
The Darkening Archipelago (2010)

For information on new books in
the Cole Blackwater series,
the Durrant Wallace series,
or other books by Stephen Legault,
visit stephenlegault.com/writing